WILD CARDS XI

DEALER'S CHOICE

D0872494

DISCARD

The Wild Cards Universe

The Original Triad
Wild Cards
Aces High
Jokers Wild

The Puppetman Quartet
Aces Abroad
Down and Dirty
Ace in the Hole
Dead Man's Hand

The Rox Triad
One-Eyed Jacks
Jokertown Shuffle
Dealer's Choice

Solo Novels
Double Solitaire
Turn of the Cards
Death Draws Five

The Card Sharks Triad
Card Sharks
Marked Cards
Black Trump

Stand-Alones
Knaves Over Queens
Deuces Down

The Committee Triad
Inside Straight
Busted Flush
Suicide Kings

The Fort Freak Triad
Fort Freak
Lowball
High Stakes

The American Triad
Mississippi Roll
Low Chicago
Texas Hold'em

WILD CARDS XI

DEALER'S CHOICE

Edited by
George R. R. Martin

Assistant Editor
Melinda M. Snodgrass

And written by

Stephen Leigh

Edward W. Bryant

John Jos. Miller

Walter Jon Williams

George R. R. Martin

TOR

A TOM DOHERTY ASSOCIATES BOOK

New York

This is a work of fiction. All of the characters, organizations, and events
portrayed in this novel are either products of the authors' imaginations or
are used fictitiously.

WILD CARDS XI: DEALER'S CHOICE

Copyright © 1992 by George R. R. Martin and the Wild Cards Trust

All rights reserved.

A Tor Book
Published by Tom Doherty Associates
120 Broadway
New York, NY 10271

www.tor-forge.com

Tor® is a registered trademark of Macmillan Publishing Group, LLC.

The Library of Congress Cataloging-in-Publication Data is
available upon request.

ISBN 978-1-250-16815-3 (trade paperback)
ISBN 978-1-250-16814-6 (ebook)

Our books may be purchased in bulk for promotional, educational, or
business use. Please contact your local bookseller or the Macmillan Corporate
and Premium Sales Department at 1-800-221-7945, extension 5442, or by
email at MacmillanSpecialMarkets@macmillan.com.

First Edition: September 2020

Printed in the United States of America

0 9 8 7 6 5 4 3 2 1

to mom
with love

FRIDAY MORNING

September 21, 1990

FRONTIER AIRLINES FLIGHT 8, Los Angeles to Newark, raced to beat the morning, to meet the sun. It would lose, but only slightly. At 39,000 feet, the sky was spangled with other suns. They twinkled significantly less than they would if seen from the ground.

The man in 14A pressed his broad forehead against the cold window. He could pick out no familiar constellation. He hadn't expected to. Still, he missed the southern cross, as the Europeans called it. To him it was the great mirragen, the hunting cat with claws spread, leaping upon its prey.

Hunting . . . He wondered if his weapons were still intact in his checked bag, deep in the belly of the 747. It wasn't as though he were smuggling a MAC-10 or an Ingram. If there were any questions, it would be easy to declare his weapons as art. He smiled. If a hollow-point slug split your heart or a nullanulla smashed your skull, you were just as dead. Art could be fatal.

He smiled grimly, fingering the rough-cut opal that hung from the leather thong circling his neck.

A patch of lights far below slowly moved past the craft and disappeared behind. The man wondered which city that had been. This was such a vast land, but then he was accustomed to vast lands. Still, two continents and a major sea in two days were a bit too much travel to absorb easily. He knew he would be joyous in the extreme when he was back on solid earth, land that didn't vibrate to the marrow of his bones with the buzz of jet engines.

While the occasional distant lights beneath him clearly moved, relatively speaking, the stars above remained constant. He was glad for that.

Then the voice told him to sleep. He didn't wish to, but the seductive whisper curled through the avenues of his skull and wrapped his brain in soothing warmth. He fought it. But he drifted, the voice gently reproaching him and reminding him of who he was . . . "You who returns to the stars, you are summoned."

And Wyungare slept.

He descended toward the lower world, the place where he would meet and speak with the warreen, his animal guide. This time, he clambered along rocky ledges before finding the broken places where he could use handholds to lower himself to another tier of stone. This painful process went on for a long time, though the angle of sun to his right did not seem to change.

Finally he was among trees and the slope was gentler. The grass beneath his feet soothed his skin and began to heal the ragged places where the rough stone had abraded his soles. He heard a cry from overhead. Looking up, he saw the graceful ga-ra-gah. The blue crane rode the wind with indifferent ease.

"Welcome, Wyungare."

The man looked down and saw the warreen. The lower half of the creature's bulky body was wet with mud. It seemed recently to have visited the edge of a water hole or river.

"Hello, cousin," said Wyungare. "I hope you are well."

"As well as can be expected, all these evil things of late considered. Thank you for visiting."

"There is little to do on the airplane. This is no sacrifice at all."

"Hmph," said the warreen. "You wouldn't catch me up in a thing like that. Those wings are so little blessed with grace, it would appear to fly with no more ease than cousin dinewan."

"Consider that a 747 is constructed to fly, and that cousin dinewan chose to fly no more."

"So?" The warreen snorted. "Our cousin could soar again if he so wished."

"Not for a long, long time. I fear his physical form has evolved to reflect his long-ago choice."

The warreen shook himself. Drying mud flew. "I still say he could change his mind, emu or no."

The two of them walked farther into Googoorewon, the place of trees. The sunlight was hot, and the dappled shadows cooling Wyungare's skin felt good.

"The times are no better outside the dreamtime?"

Wyungare shook his head. "They are not."

"Nor are they *within* the dreamtime," said the warreen. "That maira, that paddy-melon of a fat boy, his vision keeps floating before me."

"And that's who I seek. If I find him in the land of Tya-America, I will speak with him."

"And if that does nothing?" The warreen's tone was edged. "You must kill him."

"I would prefer not to."

"I am aware of that desire," said the warreen. "You are a healer, but a warrior too. If it demands a warrior's task, then you must perform it."

Wyungare nodded. "If it is necessary, then I shall. But if I can, I will make sure the task will not be necessary."

"Good fortune," the warreen said politely. Then he tipped his head back, muzzle indicating the sky. "I fear we are about to receive an object lesson in thinking to heal demons."

The shadows gathered together on Wyungare's skin. Clouds roiled, jostling for position, and masked the sun. A cold wind began to bend the trees.

The blue crane still soared far above. Her cry echoed across the Googoorewon.

The sky convulsed and lightning speared valleyward. A mallee exploded into a fountain of crackling sparks. Wyungare took a step backward. The burning scrub eucalyptus was only a score of paces distant. The wind curled and whipped dark smoke into his face and eyes.

More lightning pierced the earth. More trees became torches. The acrid scent filled Wyungare's nostrils.

One bolt never reached the ground. Cousin ga-ra-rah shimmered with a nimbus of vibrating light. Then she exploded. Feathers of blue crane drifted down around Wyungare and the warreen like leaves before the winter season.

"And what will happen to her children?" the warreen asked somberly. "In Tya-America, where you go to visit, who will guard such as the millin-nulu-nubba?"

"They are called passenger pigeons," said Wyungare. "I fear it is already too late in the waking world for them. I had no idea that this was the cause of the loss of their patron and guide." He shrugged. "The evil can, of course, travel through waking time."

A final feather landed desultorily at his feet. Both Wyungare and the warreen cried for their cousin. When they had grieved, the sky was bright again with sun.

"I'm going to go back up," said the man. "I do not know when I'll be back."

"Sooner than you now suspect," said the warreen. "The fat boy will make sure of that."

"You make a prophecy?"

"No," said the warreen sourly. "I need only look about me."

Wyungare saw the flickering overlay on the Googoorewon: an island lapped with waves, a walled castle like the ones he'd seen in European movies, monsters.

"All right." Wyungare shrugged. "I'll be back." The man lifted his palm in farewell and started up the mountainside.

"I think this will be difficult," called the warreen after him. "All your cousins will be concerned. I will do what I can."

"I know," said the warreen, raising his voice to cover the widening distance. "I will show my appreciation when I can."

"Just stop the depletion of the dreamtime," said the warreen, voice fading out.

Just like the ozone layer, Wyungare said silently. Not humorous. Accurate. Damn the fat boy! Europeans seemed *never* to have the slightest cognizance of what they truly did to the world. Everything was *now*. Everything was *me*.

As he climbed higher on the rocky mountainside, ever closer to the newly mottled sky, Wyungare thought: Whether it comes from the muzzle of a gun or at the tip of a pointed bone, change will come. This is the single irrevocable law.

Billy Ray stood alone in the prow of the Coast Guard cutter, his face turned into the biting wind. He blinked involuntary tears from his eyes as the cutter sliced through the choppy waters of the Narrows, just south of New York Bay. The predawn wind was cold, but it felt good upon his face. It felt damn good to feel anything.

Ray hadn't seen any real action since the fiasco at the Democratic National Convention when that ugly hunchbacked bastard with the buzz-saw hands had gutted him like a fish. It had taken long months of rehabilitation for his fingers and jaw to grow back and the flesh, muscle, sinew, and bone that Mackie Messer had cut apart to knit together again. During his time in the hospital he'd played the battle over and over again in his mind, still losing every time.

Ray heard soft footsteps on the deck behind him, and put up the hood on his black fighting suit before turning to face the Coast Guard captain who commanded the cutter. The fight with Messer had done even less good to Ray's face than it had to his psyche. Messer had cut off half of Ray's lower jaw. It had grown back unevenly, giving him a lopsided look that would've been comical if it weren't so damn ugly.

"We've spotted the freighter, sir," the captain said with more disdain than respect. Ray, after all, was only a civilian who had special orders that made him part of this operation. He was an ace, which gave him a certain cachet, but he was an ace who had gotten his ass kicked on national television.

Ray nodded. "Is the boarding squad ready?"

"Yes, sir," the captain said. He sketched an unenthusiastic salute.

Ray looked back over the Narrows. He didn't know who had

dropped him into the middle of this smuggler interception, but he was grateful for the opportunity. Ray needed action as badly as an addict needed rapture. He could feel his heart already starting to race, the adrenaline coursing through his system as he spotted the target ship in the predawn darkness.

It was a tramp freighter illuminated only by lines of multicolored running lights. Flying the flag of some third-world country whose waters it had never even seen, it lumbered through the choppy waters south of the Narrows like a pregnant fat lady, leaving a spreading slick of waste oil in its wake. It had to be the ship their informant in the Twisted Fists had told them about.

The Twisted Fists were radical joker terrorists whose main targets were antijoker groups and governments in the Middle East. They were a studly bunch that Ray grudgingly admired. They took no shit from anyone, which was fine with Ray as long as they kept their asses out of America. Running guns to the rebellious jokers holed up on Ellis Island, however, was a definite breach of good sense.

Ray and the boarding crew climbed into the cutter's launch and silently slipped away. They'd almost reached the freighter when, according to plan, the cutter put on its full display of lights and Klaxons. The captain hailed the freighter, ordering it to heave to just as they reached its bow.

"Up hooks," Ray said quietly as the launch bobbed up and down next to the freighter. Two men in the bow stood on wide-braced legs and tossed grappling hooks over the ship's rail thirty feet above their heads. Both caught on the first try, and Ray went up one of the trailing ropes like a starving monkey up a banana tree. He didn't wait for the rest of the squad. He couldn't hold himself back anymore.

Fighting was all that Ray lived for. He didn't formulate policy or make decisions. He was a weapon, always primed and ready to explode. When pointed in the direction of a foe he'd erupt like a heat-seeking missile aimed at the sun and nothing could deter him from his course.

He hadn't seen any real action since Messer had cut him so badly. He'd taken part in a raid the Secret Service had conducted on Long Island, but that hadn't amounted to anything. Supposedly on the trail of hot computer criminals, they'd targeted a small outfit called Jack Stevenson Games that published kids' role-playing games. Ray was among the agents who'd busted in with guns drawn and warrants flapping to find themselves in a room full of goofballs who had nothing more lethal than twenty-sided dice. The Secret Service had still hauled everything away, computers, files, dice, and all, and then Ray had spent more than a month wading through piles of game manuals filled with crap about dungeons and hit points and saving rolls only to discover that you committed computer crime in these games by rolling dice real well.

But this was the real thing, the first step on the road to redemption. Ray slipped silently over the rail and crouched on the deck in shadow. It was quiet, but huge pallets laden with tarp-covered bundles of freight blocked Ray's vision in all directions. There could be an army of Fists lying in ambush among the twelve-foot-high freight bundles, though the only immediately visible men were aft, in the lighted bridgehouse.

So far the timing had been perfect. The Coast Guard had given the warning required by law and the assault team had gained the freighter's deck without opposition. Now to see if the tub was carrying guns like their undercover man claimed, or just a shitload of cheap South Korean VCRs.

Ray gestured silently to the men who had clambered up the ropes after him. They dispersed, some heading aft to take control of the bridge, others following Ray among the freight toward the hatches leading down into the hold.

The central hatch swung open before they could reach it and a squat figure climbed out onto the deck and peered around in the darkness. A spotlight from the cutter speared him and he shrank back and threw up two pairs of arms to shield his eye.

It was a joker, Ray thought, and a damn ugly one, with half a dozen pairs of arms spouting from his rib cage and a huge central eye right smack over the bridge of his nose. But the fact that the freighter had a joker crewman meant nothing. It wasn't illegal to be a joker. Not yet, anyway.

The joker squinted in the glare and screamed in a high-pitched whine that seemed inappropriate for his powerful-looking body. His lowest pair of arms brought up an assault rifle that had been dangling on a shoulder strap and he triggered a burst in the general direction of the Coast Guard cutter.

Ray's uneven features split wide in a crazy grin. "Put down your weapon!" he shouted. "You're under arrest!"

The joker whirled, his huge eye blinking blindly as he stared into the darkness where Ray stood. He fired at the sound of Ray's voice, but Ray had already moved. The joker's fusillade whined harmlessly over the freighter's rail, and then the solitary gunman was cut down by a barrage of return fire that blew him out of the spotlight's unmerciful glare.

"Told you to put the gun down," Ray said. He glanced right and left at the others. "Let's try to take the next alive, okay?"

The guardsmen were too disciplined to grumble, but Ray could almost feel their sarcastic glances. These men knew Ray's reputation as a brutal brawler, and here he was chewing them out for taking out an armed and dangerous smuggler. They thought, maybe, that he'd gone soft. That Mackie Messer's vibrating hands had cut something out of him. That the long, painful months in the hospital had leeched out his fire.

But they were wrong. Ray hadn't gone soft. He just wanted all of the gun-running bastards for himself.

All the freighter's lights and alarms were blaring by now, though there was still plenty of shadow left on the deck. The tub's captain wasn't following the orders to heave to and kill all engines. He was trying to make a run for it.

That was insane, Ray told himself as he skulked in shadow, making his way silently toward the bridge. They couldn't expect to hide or receive sanctuary even if by some miracle they eluded the Coast Guard and reached Ellis Island.

Ray heard a whisper of movement in the shadows to his right, and his conscious mind clicked off. He moved without thinking, pivoting on his right foot and ducking low. Something big, flat, and pancake-shaped swooped down from a tarp-covered pile of freight behind him. If it had been the size of a normal human being it would have missed Ray. But it wasn't, and it didn't.

It slammed Ray to his knees, smothering him in a cloak of rubbery skin. Ray pistoned backward with both elbows, but they sank
into yielding flesh without doing any apparent damage. For a moment
he panicked. He imagined buzz-saw hands coming from out of the
smothering darkness and carving off bits of his body. He fought to his
feet with a wild surge of strength, still enveloped in the clinging folds
of resilient flesh. He struck out blindly and felt his hand connect with
something solid. There was the satisfying crack of snapping bone and
his attacker pulled away.

He looked at the joker and laughed. "It's Flying Squirrel Man," Ray
said as another jolt of adrenaline pushed through a nervous system
already juiced to the max. He grinned without realizing it, a mad light
dancing in his eyes.

The joker did look a little like a flying squirrel—if flying squirrels
were seven feet tall with more muscles than the average linebacker.
The smuggler was holding one arm pressed to his rib cage where Ray's
last blow had broken a rib or two.

"Where's the moose, squirrel?" Ray asked.

The joker charged him with an angry growl, raising his arms above
his head and spreading the mantle of skin that hung from his wrists
to his ankles. He was big, strong, and pissed. Just the way Ray liked
them.

Ray straightened out of his crouch and hammered the joker hard
in the solar plexus. The smuggler went down and this time showed no
inclination to get up.

"Come on," Ray spit through clenched teeth, "come on you pussy
bastard."

The joker curled into a fetal ball, arms wrapped around his stomach. Ray snarled wordlessly. Some small part of his mind told him
to slow down, but most of his consciousness was submerged in the
powerful need to find another foe. This one had been too easy. Much
too easy.

He reined in his savage disappointment and went down on one
knee next to the joker. He rolled the Fist onto his face and pulled
his thickly muscled arms away from his still-heaving stomach. The
smuggler tried to resist and Ray put his knee in the small of his back

and leaned down, hard. The joker went limp and Ray slipped a set of plastic cuffs on him. He started to get up, stopped, and added another pair. He patted the joker on the fanny. "Have a nice day," he said, and left him bound on the deck.

The rest of the team had also met with opposition. Ray could hear gunfire popping around the bridgehouse like it was the first day of duck season. He moved toward the sound. The team seemed to be containing the smugglers. He passed one of the men guarding a handful of nat sailors who looked as if they wanted no part of the fight. Apparently simple hired hands, they didn't have an ideological ax to grind like the Twisted Fists, and had decided to hang it up before someone got hurt.

The core of Fist resistance was centered around a group of shrouded pallets stacked in front of the bridgehouse. Ray found a member of the assault team huddled under cover provided by a freight gantry.

"There's about half a dozen of 'em hiding around those bales," the guardsman told Ray. "We can't get at 'em without crossing open deck. And they don't look like they're about to come out. Hey—"

He was going to add "come back," but Ray was already gone.

Ray covered the open space before most of the smugglers even knew he was there, but one managed to swing his machine pistol around and let loose a burst in Ray's general direction. A slug clipped his upper thigh and another notched his rib cage, but the shallow wounds had already healed by the time Ray reached the startled joker.

He yanked the weapon from the joker's hand and threw it back over his shoulder. There was no time for niceties of judgment. For Ray there rarely was. He hit the man hard, once, and moved on before the joker hit the deck.

There were three pallets of freight stacked nearly twelve feet high in front of the bridgehouse at the freighter's stern. Behind each of the pallets were two other identical columns. The intersecting walkways between them formed a maze within which Fists were hiding like cornered rats.

The Fists shouted to each other. Two thought that someone had penetrated their cover. Two thought the others were nuts, that they'd seen shifting shadows. Another voice shouted that someone had tried to charge them but Fred had gotten him. At least he thought Fred had gotten him.

That voice was the closest, one stack to the right. When Ray reached him he was still calling out questioningly to the already unconscious Fred.

"Here I am," Ray said quietly from behind. The smuggler whirled, finger tightening on the trigger of his Uzi.

But Ray had already closed the distance between them. He grabbed the smuggler's gun wrist and twisted. The Uzi belched harmlessly at the sky. There was a sharp crack and the joker screamed in agony as Ray snapped his wrist. The smuggler dropped his weapon and Ray dropped him with an open-handed blow to the jaw, then moved on deeper into the maze.

Two jokers called out, the two who were convinced that someone was among them. They dropped their weapons and walked into the open, hands held over their heads.

The two left decided to play it cagey. They moved deeper into the maze, side by side, weapons out and covering opposite directions. There was only one way they weren't looking.

Ray climbed one of the freight bundles. He waited patiently, watching the smugglers below him edging away—they thought—from the action, and dropped down on them like a sack of cement, smashing them to the deck. One hit facefirst and was instantly out of it. The other lasted long enough to throw a futile punch and take one of Ray's that split his cheek halfway to his earhole. He bounced off the freight bundle and slumped over his comrade on the deck.

"I got 'em all," Ray called. But he was wrong.

A shadow fell over him, and he jerked around in time to see an astonishing sight. It was the moose he'd joked about earlier. Or an elk. Or some damn thing. Except it walked upright like a man. It was a man, a damn big man, maybe eight feet tall, with a rack of antlers that would do any buck proud. A lot of his height was in his hairy, satyrlike legs, but he also had a deep chest, broad shoulders, and well-muscled arms. A horn of some kind was slung around his neck, resting against his massive chest. The guy was not only big, he was smart. He'd kept his mouth shut when Ray had penetrated the Fists' defenses.

As Ray watched, the joker plucked a huge bundle of freight from the nearest stack and threw it at him. Ray dived backward, tumbling into a group of onrushing guardsmen.

"What is it?" one of them asked as the bundle hit the deck, bounced, and skidded to a halt against the rail.

Ray shook his head. "One of the damnedest jokers I ever saw."

"Let's get—" one of the guardsmen started to say, then fell silent as they heard the eerie sound of a horn blowing, an ancient, shivery sound that seemed to belong to an earlier age when wild huntsmen roved forest and fen with packs of hounds slavering at their heels. It unnerved everyone, even Ray, and for a moment no one wanted to go back among the stacks of freight. And then it was too late.

The horned joker burst from cover upon the back of a magnificent black horse whose eyes glowed like green fire. Its sharp hooves kicked out and one of the guardsmen was catapulted backward, spraying blood all over his comrades.

The horse took three magnificent bounds and leapt over the rail.

"We've got him!" Ray shouted. There was no way a horse, no matter how big, beautiful, or mysterious, could outswim a Coast Guard cutter. They had the horny bastard.

But when Ray rushed to the side of the freighter and looked over the rail he didn't see a floundering horse swimming in the bay. He saw a horse, as dark and majestic as an iron statue at midnight, running serenely across the tops of the waves, its hooves barely dipping into their crests. And on its back, turning to stare at them, waving a fist as a promise of retribution, was its antlered rider, his eyes glowing green with the fire of a demon.

The Outcast stood at the end of the cavern. Ahead, there was darkness and a cool wind that brushed back his long hair. The Outcast raised his staff above his head; the blazing amethyst at the knobby summit of the stick erupted with light.

The actinic light from the staff just touched the far side of a canyon, revealing that he stood on the brink of a dizzying precipice.

Directly across from the Outcast, a large platform jutted out over emptiness. Leaning out, the Outcast could see nothing else—neither above, below, nor to the sides. The staff's light faded away in all directions into blackness.

The Outcast grinned.

"You could use some light in this place, fat boy." The voice came from behind him. The Outcast whirled, his cape flowing. A penguin in a funnel hat grinned at him. It wore ice skates on its pudgy feet, gliding toward him as if the broken, rocky floor of the corridor was glare ice.

"I was just about to add some of that," the Outcast replied. He turned back toward the black canyon. *"Now!"* he said loudly.

A rumbling came from the emptiness below them, a roaring of torn, fractured rock rising in volume until the Outcast clapped his hands over his ears. Peering down, he saw glowing red cracks appear. Fountains of molten rock spewed from widening crevices on the distant floor, thick lava flowing out. The chill of the cavern vanished in a gust of coiling heat. Tornadoes of frantic air spun around the canyon walls.

The Outcast laughed, clenching his fist in triumph. "Yes!" he crowed. "Look!" he shouted to the penguin over the din. "Look what I can do!"

The penguin skated to the opening, spun once gracefully, and peeked gingerly over the edge.

Far, far below, molten rock collided and heaved in a sluggish, thick river. The fiery glow of lava washed the canyon cliffs with the hues of hell and brushed the distant roof of the cavern with crimson. The rift in the floor of the cave was a hundred feet across and twice that in depth, ripping through the earth like a raw knife wound. A narrow, crumbling ledge edged this side of it, following the lava-etched stone walls in either direction. The fissure angled away into deep perspective on either side, continuing into the unseen distances as it curved in a slow arc.

"You really need a railing," the penguin observed. "You're gonna get sued if some tourist falls." The creature cackled, the funnel hat on its head nearly falling off with amusement. The Outcast, dressed in somber dark clothes with thigh-high leather boots and a wide, black leather hat, gave a brief chuckle.

"It *is* impressive, isn't it?" he said. "Bloat's Moat, they're going to call it." The heat had chased away all the coolness. The skin of his face tingled as he gazed down.

"It's not my climate of choice, Your Bloatness Sir," the penguin remarked. "But yes, very impressive. Why, you could probably build something half-decent if you really tried."

Bloat—or rather, the dream-image of Bloat: the handsome raven-haired hero he thought of as the Outcast—scowled. "Damn it, why are you always criticizing me? Nothing I do is ever good enough."

The penguin grinned up at him, though the glittering black eyes were expressionless. As with all his dream creatures, he was deaf to their thoughts. After a moment the Outcast sighed. He raised his staff once more. The amethyst flared again and rock flowed like pulled taffy from the end of the corridor, arching over the deep canyon in a thin bridge, the far end touching down on the platform across from them. Another cave entrance led out from the platform in the direction of Jersey City.

"There," the Outcast said. "My little lava moat goes all around the Rox just behind and below the Wall. The passage over there"— he pointed across the bridge—"leads to another corridor circling just inside and well below the Wall. There are passages out from it and up into the Wall itself. I'll send someone down to guide the jokers through the caverns; any intruders can simply get lost—and I've set some interesting hurdles for them."

The satisfaction on the handsome face was open. He was almost smug. "I dreamed it all. I built every piece of it myself and the power grows stronger every day. Each day I can do more with it, and each day the fucking nats are getting more and more scared of me. I *am* the governor. The Rox is *mine*."

"Not yours, bubba. Not entirely, anyway," the penguin retorted. The creature was sweating; beads of moisture darkened the fur. "Man, some of the things I've seen down here don't come from *your* mind, Your Overstuffedness. There's a great big hairy spider, and a dog-faced griffin, and that Polynesian thing Tangaroa that ate three jokers yesterday . . . You want me to go on?"

The Outcast was scowling. "They come from my *other* dreams, the ones where I'm walking in someone else's world. You know that. I've seen the spider there, and that Tangaroa thing. They leaked in. I'm sorry, okay? Quit complaining."

"Everything's connected, fat boy. When you realize that, I'll quit complaining. You *really* think the nats are done with you? You really think that they're just going to let the Rox keep growing and growing? Hell, they're already howling about what you did to the goddamn Statue of Liberty, which by the way shows an abysmal lack of taste and sensitivity on your part; it looks like something you'd see in *Penthouse*. You think they're just gonna keep doing *nothing* when the Wall hits Battery Park?" The penguin hawked and spat a gob of ugly green stuff on the floor. "You spend too much time dreaming and not enough thinking."

"I'm powerful enough to stop them now. The jumpers are still here and since Blaise left and Molly took over, they're more under my control than ever. The Rox is bigger than ever. We have hundred of jokers here and more come every day. I have more traps and barriers set up."

"And the nats are more pissed than ever too."

"I can handle them," the Outcast said sullenly.

"Yeah. You and your fucking dreamstuff."

"*You're* part of my dreamstuff, penguin."

The creature made a rude noise. "That's my burden and I have to bear it as best I can. If you *really* knew how to use your power, you'd set up shop somewhere else."

"Sure. Like maybe Hawaii, huh?" The Outcast snorted. Below them, lava waves thrashed and broke against canyon walls. "The trouble with you is—"

The Outcast stopped, cocking his head as if listening to something only he could hear. "Whassa matter?" the penguin asked.

"Something going on out in the bay. Chickenhawk . . . the tower watch on the east side is all in an uproar . . . something about someone riding a horse out in the bay . . . C'mon."

The Outcast rapped his staff against the rocky floor of the cavern. The amethyst blazed and they were suddenly no longer in the caverns but in Bloat's Castle—the old Administration Building, now transformed into something from the land of Faerie. The Outcast could see the body of Bloat—*his* body—almost filling the huge lobby. High up on that vast mountain of pasty white flesh, stick-thin arms and shoulders sprouted along with a pimply, fat-cheeked boy's sleeping head. PVC pipes jabbed into that mountain of flesh; stinking black mounds of waste lay along its flanks; the sides were streaked and stained with the tracks of the excrement. Yet despite the foulness of the body, the setting itself was splendid. The lobby sparkled like the interior of a lavish diamond. The columns supporting the distant roof were cut crystal, the walls were glass, the girders and supports silver and gold, the floor an intricate pattern of azure and ruby tole.

Dreamstuff, most of it, though the huge torch that sat just behind Bloat's head and dominated the setting was real—having once graced the hand of Liberty. The Outcast surveyed his home with pleasure, not wanting to relinquish the dream and wake up once more as Bloat and knowing that he must.

As he hesitated, they heard a dull rattling like a stack of plates being jostled, and Kafka entered the lobby. The roach-like joker scuttled toward the sleeping Bloat.

"Governor! Wake up! Chickenhawk is claiming that one of your creatures is coming in over the bay. The Twisted Fists had a skirmish with the Coast Gu—" Kafka stopped, swiveling his stiff body to look at the archway where the penguin and the Outcast stood. The Outcast's and Kafka's gazes met. In his head, Kafka's mindvoice was wondering who was with the penguin.

"You can *see* me? You really *can*?" the Outcast started to say, incredulous, and in that moment, his orientation shifted and he was suddenly Bloat, staring down at Kafka from atop the grotesque heights of his body. The penguin, alone now, waved at him from the archway and waddled away. Kafka's thoughts were confused, wondering if he had actually seen anyone with the penguin at all, and then he dismissed the incident entirely.

Too damn many strange things around here . . .

"Did you hear me, Governor?"

"I heard you," Bloat said, and his voice was no longer the Outcast's mellifluous baritone but his own adolescent squeak. "Be quiet and let me listen a moment." Bloat let the flood of voices in his head wash over him, picking out the mind of Chickenhawk in his high tower in the castle.

Strangest damn thing . . . a monster horse with glowing eyes and the guy with the antlers . . . riding on top of the damn waves . . .

"It's not mine," Bloat told Kafka. "Not outside the Wall. But it's heading this way."

"I'll alert Molly and get a reception committee together."

"Good. We'll see what happens when it hits the Wall."

Bloat closed his eyes again, waiting, listening to the eternal commentary inside. Closer, closer, and then he felt the mental push at the edges of his awareness. *Prod, prod:* the Wall pushed back against the will of the intruder. "It's *not* mine," Bloat said aloud to Kafka. "And there's only one intelligence; the horse is an extension of his mind, somehow; they're linked. Calls himself Herne the Huntsman . . . Ahh, there—he's through. A strong desire to be here. Forget Molly, Kafka—you and Shroud go out with a party to meet him. Herne has some information for us."

Bloat opened his eyes as Kafka nodded and relayed the instructions from a walkie-talkie around his neck.

Bloat twisted his atrophied shoulders so that he could look out from the glass-walled castle to the darkness of the Wall. "This should be interesting," Bloat said. "Very interesting."

The bodysnatcher woke up pissed.

She rolled off the futon onto the cold flagstone floor, and got to her feet, groggy and disoriented. It made her mad. This meat was as hard to start as an old car on a cold morning. She shook her head to clear the cobwebs away, and stumbled to the window. She made a fist, slammed it hard against the rough stone wall. Blood dripped from her knuckles. Somehow the red wash of pain made her feel stronger.

From the courtyard below, she heard the shouts of joker guards, the clatter of weaponry, the metallic clang of the portcullis as it fell. Her lancet window overlooked the battlements of the inner keep and the narrow stone causeway that connected the fortress to the outer wall, a good mile south across the vast salt expanse of the moat.

A man on horseback was thundering down the causeway.

The bodysnatcher watched him come. The causeway was barely wide enough for two men to walk abreast, a stone ribbon stretched over the deep black waters of the bay, but the rider came on at a hard gallop. His horse was gigantic, black as a starless night, its hooves striking sparks off the stone as it charged. The rider looked almost as huge.

A door banged open behind her. "What's going on?" asked Blueboy. He came up beside her, a slender black kid no more than sixteen, naked under a torn policeman's shirt that he wore unbuttoned like a cape. Blueboy liked to jump cops and appropriate their uniforms and badges. "Jesus," he said as he stared out the window. "What the fuck is that?"

"A joker," the bodysnatcher told him. Jokers disgusted her, but this one was magnificent. The rider's eyes were glowing green, and his legs were the hindquarters of a stag. A huge rack of golden antlers grew from his forehead.

The rider drew up his horse before the gate. "Open," he said. It wasn't a request. His voice was a bass rumble. He was naked and golden, legs and chest covered with coarse red hair. A red-fawn mane grew halfway down his back. *"Open!"* he roared again.

There was no answer from inside the walls. The rider pulled on the horse's braided mane. The stallion reared back, snorting, and brought its front hooves down hard on the portcullis. Wrought iron rang and bent. The jokers on the battlements flinched, and brought their guns to bear.

"Let him in," the bodysnatcher called down to them.

"You gone *crazy*, Zelda?" Blueboy asked.

"Don't call me Zelda," she snapped. She'd killed Zelda herself, stuffing a sock in her mouth and pinching her nostrils shut until she suffocated, after she'd been left blind and crippled. Since then the bodysnatcher had stolen a half-dozen bodies, but even the ones that looked good from outside felt wrong on her. She never kept them long; they didn't fit.

There was the sound of running footsteps in the courtyard below. A squad of armed jokers spread out across the cobblestones. Kafka was with them, rustling faintly as he ran. The little brown cockroach-man carried a walkie-talkie instead of a gun. "Governor says, open the gate," he announced.

"That's what I've been telling them," she called down.

The portcullis got halfway up and stuck, bent hopelessly out of shape by the blow it had taken. The rider dismounted and left his horse outside as he entered the castle. He had to duck low to get his antlers under the portcullis.

Inside, surrounded by jokers clutching automatic weapons, he straightened to his full height, towering over all of them. With his antlers, he stood well over ten feet. Across his chest was slung a magnificent golden horn, carved in the shape of a dragon. Cloven hooves clattered on the cobblestones as he moved, and his genitalia swung heavily between his legs. There was no doubt that he was male. The bodysnatcher looked from the stag-man to Blueboy's more modest equipment, and laughed. The other jumper flushed.

"Take me to your governor," the rider commanded.

Kafka nodded. "Shroud, Mustelina, escort him to the throne room. Elmo, see to his horse."

"What horse?" he asked. He threw back his head and laughed. His laughter was loud and deep as thunder.

The bodysnatcher glanced back beyond the gate. The huge black stallion had vanished as silently as smoke. There was nothing out there but night.

"Jesus," Blueboy said, beside her. He shivered and wrapped the policeman's shirt a little more tightly around his skinny chest. "What's going on?"

"Go get Molly," the bodysnatcher told him. "Tell her to meet me in the throne room."

The rider had to duck again to pass through the archway. He was the most beautiful thing she had seen since her own body had been taken from her. She wanted him.

Kafka had lingered behind the rest, walkie-talkie crackling in his chitinous grasp. *"Zelda!"* he called up. "His name is Herne. He's an ally. The governor says if you jump him, you die."

Herne the Huntsman—who was sometimes Dylan Hardesty—was like every last joker who had ever come before him, the first thought Bloat caught from the man was pity laced with scorn.

Whoot a bloody ugly t'ing it be . . .

"A bloody ugly thing indeed, but jokers should be the last to worry about someone else's appearance."

Herne reacted very little. Maybe the frown deepened. "A person cannot stop his thoughts," he said. The joker's voice was as low as anything human could get, festooned with a cultured British accent quite unlike the one in his mind—*something northern and low-class?* Bloat wondered. "The Twisted Fists told me you could read minds."

Bloat followed the elusive thought-threads and saw a shipment of guns; a battle on the water, death. None of it was very clear, but Bloat knew from long practice how to focus a person's mind. "You were bringing guns," he said, "and a warning." As he'd known it would do, the words sent Herne back to the attack of minutes ago.

. . . the nats had Carnifex with them, Hartmann's old goon . . . hate the feeling of running from the ass but the information is more important than the guns . . .

"How many jokers did you lose when the Coast Guard hit you?" Bloat asked. "How many did Carnifex kill?"

Herne's huge eyes blinked. He seemed to appraise Bloat once more. The memory that Bloat could see was a raw, oozing wound, and the anger Herne radiated could almost be touched. "There were six of us, all of them my friends, and I will pay back Carnifex for what he did. As you said, we were bringing weapons to the Rox. We—I—also had more. They are going to hit the Rox, Governor. They are going to hit it hard."

"Who told you this?"

"I can't tell you that." And in his mind: *. . . Matt Wilhelm. Furs . . .*

"You already have." Bloat giggled, and Herne frowned at the

screeching titter. Kafka sighed and rolled his eyes at Bloat, impatient as always.

"This isn't a joke, Governor. I don't care about your parlor tricks. Read my mind, that's fine—go ahead. It saves me my breath. They *are* planning to strike. Hartmann's been placed in charge. There are aces involved, as well as the military. This is entirely serious. What are you going to do about it?"

"Very little that I'm not already doing." Most of Bloat wanted to deny everything that Hardesty was saying. That part of him was confident, almost arrogant. The nats had broken on the shore of the Rox twice now; the third time would be no different. Bloat was fairly certain that they wouldn't even try. "Hartmann and some others are coming over today—a peace conference. We've already set it up. They've lost too many lives already. They won't want to lose any more. This talk of an attack is a bluff, an empty threat."

He listened as Hardesty mulled that over and heard the answer even before the man spoke the words. "Governor, maybe they think that if they *don't* take the Rox, all those lives were wasted."

"No," Bloat said, but inside, the old frightened kid, the one who'd cowered before the neighborhood bullies, who'd been taunted and picked on and abused—that Teddy, *he* was scared. He remembered.

". . . if they'd just leave Teddy alone . . . Yes . . . Well, thank you . . ."

His father hung up the phone. He shook his head at the overweight child hugging his knees to his belly on the sofa, the bloodstains from his nose dark on a torn T-shirt. "I just talked with Roger's mother," his dad said. "She said that she'd talk to the boy."

The combined relief and anger in his father's voice told Ted how nervous and timid his father had been making the call. Now he stood in front of Ted, still shaking his head. "Really, Teddy, I don't know why you can't simply avoid these children. It's your fault, really. They can't pick on you if you're not there."

Ted tried to argue—he told his dad how they'd corner him in the lunchroom or the playground, how they'd wait for him on the walk home from school, how anytime he stepped outside the brownstone stoop they'd BE there. The arguments didn't do any good. They never did.

The next day, Roger and his friends waited for Ted after the last bell.

"You got me in trouble," Roger said. "You're gonna pay, asshole." Ted limped home with a torn jacket and pants, another bloodied nose, a black eye, and a chipped tooth.

Ted understood revenge. Oh, yes. He understood it very well.

"No," Bloat said again. "There's no reason for us to get panicked about the situation."

In his mind, he heard the myriad voices of the Rox awakening, many wondering about the arrival of Herne. Molly Bolt was already heading for the castle from the jumpers' tower on the other side of the island. "But I suppose we need to let people know," he continued reluctantly. "You certainly don't make it easy to keep things quiet. Kafka—if you'd arrange things. You know who we'll need."

The junkers were stacked eight high along the Jersey shore: a wall of rust, broken glass, twisted metal. The car on top was a DeLorean. The morning sun still glittered off the brushed stainless-steel finish, but the frame had been twisted so badly that the gull-wing doors would never close again. It looked like a silver bird trying to take flight.

Up on the hood, high atop his junkyard battlement, Tom Tudbury stared through a pair of binoculars. The Rox was a good five miles northeast across the bay, but even at this distance, its towers were plainly visible, etched against the pink glow of the dawn. Its southern wall had engulfed the Statue of Liberty, her green copper flesh fusing seamlessly with the stone. Only the familiar crowned head remained the same. Below the neck, Liberty was nude and voluptuous. She had a huge oak-and-iron gate between her legs.

Something about it suggested the witch's castle from *The Wizard of Oz*. There were shapes wheeling about some of the towers that reminded Tom uncomfortably of the flying monkeys that had terrified him when he was six.

It was the last place in the world he ever wanted to visit. He had been there once; that was enough. But in a few hours, he was going back. "Damn Hartmann," he muttered aloud.

Tom lowered the binoculars and clambered down, careful to watch his footing as he stepped from car to car, the metal shifting ever so slightly beneath his sneakers. He walked back through the junkyard with his hands shoved deep in his pockets. The place hadn't changed much since he was a kid, coming here to visit his friend Joey DiAngelis.

It was hard to believe Joey was gone now. He'd moved his family clear down to North Carolina two weeks ago. Tom couldn't blame him. Not after last month. Corpses were still washing up on the Jersey shore, features bloated beyond all recognition, faces half-eaten by eels, with only their dog tags to say who'd they been. Joey had Gina and the kids to think about, and Bayonne was just too damn close to the Rox.

On the news the other night, they said two million people had moved out of the New York metropolitan area since the last census. Most of them in the last four years. Manhattan real estate was selling like waterfront lots along the Love Canal.

The dogs started barking as he neared the house. Tom had gotten them from the pound after he and Joey and Dr. Tachyon had faked his death a few years back. It was lonely being dead, and the dogs gave him plenty of warning whenever a stranger approached the junkyard.

He paused on the steps to scratch Jetboy under the chin, then went inside. The shack looked run-down and abandoned from the outside, the porch sagging, the windows boarded up. But Tom had spent a lot of time and money fixing up the interior.

A big-screen television dominated one wall. Tom had left it on when he went outside. CNN was rerunning its interview with Gregg Hartmann again. Tom fixed himself a mug of coffee and sat down to watch the broadcast once more.

This was a national emergency, Hartmann told Wolf Blitzer. He quoted John Kennedy and Tom Paine. Many of his ace friends had come forward already; he hoped others would volunteer to help out in this crisis. "With great power comes great responsibility," he said. They wanted Starshine, Modular Man, Jumpin' Jack Flash, Water Lily, Chimera . . .

They already had the Great and Powerful Turtle.

Tom sipped at his coffee. It was too hot. He blew on it to cool it down.

"This afternoon's meeting will be our last best hope for a peaceful solution," Hartmann told Blitzer. He asked everyone listening to pray for their success.

It was smart of them to use Hartmann. Tom didn't trust politicians, least of all George Bush and his right-wing friends. But Gregg Hartmann was different. Tom had *believed* in Gregg Hartmann. When the senator had his nervous breakdown in Atlanta in 1988, and lost his hard-won presidential nomination, it had almost broken his heart.

Tom had witnessed the carnage last month, when the military tried to take the Rox. Hartmann was right; they *had* to make Bloat and his followers listen to reason. If not . . .

He didn't want to think about it. Hartmann would negotiate a settlement, he told himself. He *had* to.

Joey had a spare room down in North Carolina. He had urged Tom to move down with them, before the shithammer came down. "This is where I belong," Tom said simply.

He turned off the television. In the silence of the morning, he felt utterly alone. Joey and Gina moved down to Charlotte. Tachyon gone to the stars, back to his homeworld Takis, no telling if he'd ever be back. That was most of the people who knew he was alive right there. Dead men don't make a whole lot of friends.

But it was only Tom Tudbury who was dead. The Turtle still had miles to go before he slept.

He finished his coffee, and went to get his shell.

Travnicek was facing south again. He had been doing that a lot lately, just standing there in the still light of dawn, motionless on his terrace above the park. His organ cluster, which looked like a lei made from H. R. Giger flowers, had blossomed around the featureless blue dome of his head. Petals, tentacles, sensors—whatever they were—had come erect and were tracking south like some kind of organic radar.

Modular Man did not think this was a good sign. Travnicek's obsessions were rarely healthy.

"Sir," he said, "do you still want me to join the government aces at Ebbets Field?"

He spoke from the shelter of the penthouse door; where neighbors in the surrounding buildings couldn't see him. Normally he flew in and out only at night, but he'd been delayed by the necessity of sorting the 65,000-odd dollars he had stolen, on Travnicek's orders, from a Brink's truck while its drivers were drinking coffee in a Roy Rogers.

Travnicek had an uncanny ability to detect money—not that it required much skill in the case of a Brink's truck. And Modular Man was very good with locks, particularly the electronic kind.

Modular Man was wired to obey his creator and to protect him. He didn't have any choice in the matter.

"Sir?" he prompted. "Ebbets Field? Senator Hartmann's request to help him in the battle against the Rox?"

If he was lucky, he thought, Travnicek would order him to steal something else.

"The Rox?" Maxim Travnicek didn't have to turn around to address his creation—the mitteleuropean accent came out of a trumpet-shaped blossom on the back of Travnicek's lei. "So go," he said. "I want to see recordings of that place. It's . . . *interesting*."

If he were human, the android thought, he would have shuddered at the tone of that *interesting*. "Sir?" he ventured. "There is probably going to be a fight. I might get injured."

"I built you *twice*, toaster," Travnicek said. "If you get blown up again, I'll build another one."

There was no point, the android knew, in pointing out that since Travnicek had become a joker he'd lost his ability to construct much of anything. Travnicek would just deny it, then order him to do something humiliating.

"If you're sure, sir," Modular Man said. "If you've got enough money to—"

"*Go!*" The blue-skinned joker waved an arm. "And fuck you!"

"May I take my guns first?"

"Take whatever you want. Just stop bothering me."

Modular Man took the microwave laser and the .30-caliber Browning.

It looked like it was shaping up to be that kind of day.

The potpourri of thoughts around Bloat were amusing in their diversity.

Kafka was radiating his usual sour paranoia and annoyance with the "juvenile behavior" of his compatriots; Zelda (who these days insisted on being called Bodysnatcher) was wondering whether she'd done a hundred bench presses this morning or just ninety. That was just mind-static: she'd been trying different strategies to keep him from reading her thoughts for the last few weeks. Shroud was gazing at his hand and wondering whether it was a little more translucent today than yesterday; Video was replaying the arrival of Herne a few hours ago; Molly was staring at Herne and speculating graphically about what she'd like to do with him (and whether it would be physically possible—evidently she'd seen some of the porno films in which he'd starred). Herne had become more his daytime personality of Dylan Hardesty; Hardesty was guiltily remembering an earlier Hunt and how good it had felt to kill the victim . . .

And the penguin, as usual, was mind-silent—like all of Bloat's creations. The penguin was staring at him, but he could sense no thoughts at all behind the blank gaze.

None of them were particularly thinking about the subject at hand. Bloat blinked and cleared his throat.

"Look, people, you've all heard Hardesty's information from the Twisted Fists," Bloat said loudly. Thoughts shattered and refocused on the sound; Bloat grinned in quick amusement. "So who here thinks we got something to worry about?"

Molly sniffed. The bodysnatcher crossed her arms across the middle-aged woman's body she was wearing and scowled. Video silently, emptily recorded. Shroud grumbled inwardly. Hardesty looked at the others expectantly.

"I do, Governor," Kafka said. His carapace rattled like a child's toy as he shifted position. "I've been telling you this since the last time, sir; they aren't just going to leave us alone. They never do." Dark images of the aces' raid on the Cloisters ran unbidden in his head. Kafka rattled his carapace gloomily. "Bush is a hardass when it comes to confrontations—he's shown that abroad and he's shown it with anti-joker legislation."

"We have a conference with Hartmann today," Bloat reminded him. "A *peace* conference."

"The Japanese were negotiating with Washington when they attacked Pearl Harbor too," Kafka said. "This time they'll use the aces to help. Pulse, Mistral, the Turtle . . . The fact that Hartmann's involved cinches it—they want him because he knows the government aces best, through SCARE. *This* time they'll use the aces to help."

"Aces can be jumped," Bloat answered, taking the words that Molly was about to speak and smiling at the annoyance on the young woman's face. "If they're jumped, they're *ours.* Aces will also hit the Wall and not be able to get through, just like nats. My dream creatures will eat them, just like with the nats. The jokers here are well armed."

"Governor, that's all true, I suppose, but—"

"We're *fine* here," Bloat interrupted. "I don't see what we got to be worried about. Hey, you should see what I've done with the caverns."

"Shit." The bodysnatcher stretched like a tawny lioness. "Dreams ain't gonna keep the fuckers out." Then, a moment too late: "Governor."

Bloat managed to smile at the woman. The image of her mind was Bloat-As-Weenie, impaled on a stick and roasting over a fire. He was making tiny little squealing sounds as the fat hissed and the skin bubbled.

"Governor," Hardesty interjected, driving away the vision. "You want to believe that they won't hit you. It's not realistic. I say you can't afford to be complacent, and it's not enough just to strengthen your defenses here. Hit them first. Hit them before they're ready. I, for one, will help—I've a score to settle with Carnifex." With the last statement, Bloat could feel a fountaining of heat in Hardesty's mind and, behind it, the raging power of the Wild Hunt.

"Listen, we have enough firepower of our own," Bloat insisted. "There are—what, Molly—almost a hundred jumpers here? Each one of them can give us an ace. We have my Wall to send back at least part of any invading force; I can also summon the demons from my dreams, and they turned the last attack into a rout—those abilities seem to be growing every day. We have a few aces of our own, like Croyd."

"Who's asleep in the east tower, who we can't wake up, and who knows what abilities he might have when he does." The penguin grinned wide-mouthed up at Bloat. "Hey, just being fair, your Prodigiousness," it said. "I still think you should just walk away from the whole thing." It cackled.

Bloat tried to shrug and failed, his emaciated shoulders drooping. What was left of his human body in the gargantuan bulk of Bloat was slowly deteriorating. He shook his head instead, and flakes of dandruff in the wispy hair fell like snow. "Croyd will wake up or we'll find a way to get him awake if we need him. We also have people like Shroud, who can hide and attack unseen. The Twisted Fists have given us modern weapons—we're better armed now than a month ago. We have the caverns underneath in which to hide, food stores to last for a few weeks, and since the Wall has reached the Jersey shore, we've better supply lines. The nats'll settle this politically. Through negotiation, not fighting."

"Great, Bloat." Molly Bolt scowled. The young girl leaned against one of the crystalline pillars, her arms folded over her leather jacket. "You make it sound so damn easy. But what if you're wrong? What happens to the caves if *you* get taken out, huh? What happens to the Wall or your demons? I think Mr. Well Hung here's got the right idea. Let's take the offensive."

"*No.*" Bloat's voice broke with the word. It came out half-strangled and more bleat than shout.

"Why ever not?" demanded Hardesty. "I should think you'd stand a better chance picking your own time and place to fight."

"Don't you see?" Bloat asked. He realized his voice sounded almost desperate and tried to slow down, to lower the pitch. . . . *if only I could call up the Outcast. They'd listen to the Outcast . . .* "It's one thing to defend yourself. It's another to attack first. If we make the first move, we're not any better than they are. Especially when we haven't even *talked* to them yet."

Zelda guffawed loudly; Molly frowned. "Look at us," Molly said. "Look around you. They *are* better than us. I say kick their butts first, before they gear up to do the same. Nothing's gonna change the way they feel about us—they hate our fucking guts."

"Molly, I've shored up the defenses," Bloat insisted. "Go down in the caverns and look. We have the bay as a moat, we now have a lava moat in the lower sections. We're *safe* here. I'm getting more powerful; hey, *we're* more powerful. Don't you see," he continued, as loudly as he could. "Don't *any* of you see? They *want* us to attack. They want an excuse to come in with everything and take us out. I say that we shouldn't provide them the reason."

"You want us to stand here and wait to be hit," Bodysnatcher said.

"I say we should *leave*," the penguin muttered. Bloat ignored it.

"That's exactly what I'm saying, Zelda," he answered. "I'm the governor here."

"I knew that was coming," the penguin said. It skated away to the back of the crowd. Hardesty watched it, a puzzled look on his face.

The bodysnatcher snorted. "So much for democracy in action. Why'd you even bother to call us here, *Governor*? You already knew what you were going to do."

"I needed to tell you how important all of this is," Bloat told her. "Hey, I'm the one who can read minds, after all. I knew what you were thinking. I needed you to hear it so that none of you go off and do anything stupid."

From Zelda, there was a sudden, desperate counting in her mind, masking whatever her thoughts might have been. A grudging acceptance radiated from Hardesty and Molly, though Bloat knew they remained unconvinced. Shroud and Kafka also had their doubts, but Bloat knew that they'd follow, whatever he ordered.

"For the time being," Bloat said, "I'll have jokers manning the Wall towers to keep a lookout. I'll continue to build the defenses around the Rox. We'll wait until we hear what Hartmann has to say. In the meantime, Shroud can go over to J-town with Charon and contact the Twisted Fists—you can tell them what's happened and get any new information they have. And the rest of you can *wait*."

Bloat glanced at each of them in turn. Only Zelda held his eyes, and in her mind there was the flak of surface thoughts. . . . *hate you* . . . The phrase leaked out from underneath, contemptuous and sinister.

"This is the Rox," he told them. His hand waved awkwardly at the Statue of Liberty's torch on the wall behind him. "Our land and our country. I won't let them take it away from us. I promise that."

Bloat wished he were as confident as he tried to sound.

Ebbets Field had been sealed off and surrounded by troops. The curb was lined with jeeps, supply trucks, and staff cars. A tank squatted right in front of the ballpark.

The shell left a long shadow on the pavement as it floated silently up the street, past the police barricades. Snug in its claustrophobic interior, Tom swiveled slowly, scanning each of the television screens that lined the curving walls. The soldiers on the street below were pointing and gesticulating. One of them produced a camera and took a few snapshots. Tom figured he must be from out-of-town.

He pushed up. The shell rose another fifty feet into the air, moved slowly over the ballpark. Sentries had been posted on the scoreboard. The dugouts were full of sandbags and machine guns. Uniformed men were bustling all over the outfield.

A miniature Rox had risen on the infield.

The castle sat on top of the pitcher's mound. The curtain wall bisected home plate and circled the bases. Everything had been duplicated in astonishing detail. Teams of enlisted men were putting the finishing touches on the huge tactical model, under the supervision of junior officers.

Near the Dodger dugout, a man in a blue-and-white costume was arguing with General Zappa and a couple of his aides. Even from this height Tom recognized Cyclone. His jumpsuit was shiny sky-blue Kevlar, accented by an oversize snow-white cape that fastened at wrist, ankle, and throat and drooped down behind him. Tom zoomed in. Exterior mikes tracked, locked.

". . . making this much more complicated than it needs to be, General," Cyclone was saying. "These amateurs are just going to compromise the operation."

The general was taller than the ace, dark and saturnine, with a black mustache. "As far as I'm concerned, Mr. Carlysle, all of you civilians are amateurs."

"I don't consider myself a civilian," Cyclone said. "I had a special Air Force commission during Nam. General Westmoreland—"

"General Westmoreland isn't running this operation, I am," Zappa interrupted. He was wearing an Arab headdress, for some reason.

Tom smiled. Zappa was all right. For a general, anyway. He turned on his microphones. The voice of the Turtle, amplified and distorted by his speakers, boomed down over the infield. "NICE MODEL, GENERAL."

Vidkunssen, the big blond major in mirrorshades and Air Force blue, glanced up and said, "Soviet satellite reconnaissance. Got to give it to the Russkis, they didn't miss a thing."

That was swell, Tom thought, but he had the uneasy feeling that Bloat could change the physical layout of the Rox anytime the big boy put his mind to it. In which case, your Soviet satellite reconnaissance and a dime still wouldn't get you a cup of borscht.

He floated to hover above the field. "WHERE'S HARTMANN?"

"On his way," Zappa said. "With another volunteer."

"Another unnecessary volunteer," Cyclone said. His real name, Tom knew, was Vernon Henry Carlysle. He was about fifty, just a shade under six feet, with the same coloring as his daughter Mistral—fair skin, hazel eyes, light brown hair that moved easily in the wind. The hair had started to recede, but his flier's body was still taut and well muscled. "My daughter and I can handle this situation alone, I tell you. They're only a bunch of jokers. There's no need to put anyone else at risk."

"NO NEED TO PUT *ANYONE* AT RISK," the Turtle announced. "WE'RE GOING TO WORK OUT A PEACEFUL SOLUTION."

"We all hope you're right," General Zappa said. Cyclone did not look convinced.

"Of course, we do need to plan for contingencies, in case Senator Hartmann's mission should fail," a new voice put in. A plump civilian stepped from the dugout tunnel. He smiled at everyone and gestured up with the pipe he was smoking. "You must be the Great and Powerful Turtle."

No shit, Sherlock, Tom thought, but he said, "GUILTY. THEY TOLD ME IT WAS BAT DAY. I GUESS I WAS MISINFORMED."

The civilian smiled. "Nonetheless, we're pleased to have you with us. I am Phillip Baron von Herzenhagen of the Special Executive Task Force."

Tom didn't have the vaguest notion what the fuck the Special Executive Task Force was supposed to be. And right now, he didn't especially care. A girl had emerged from the dugout shadows to stand beside von Hergenbergen or whatever his name was.

She looked all of eighteen, her blond hair knotted in a ponytail, a black-and-orange Minnesota Giants baseball cap shading bright blue eyes. *Great,* Tom thought, *the army brought cheerleaders.* Only this cheerleader was wearing a Kevlar-armored vest and cradling an M-16 instead of a baton.

"This lovely young thing," von Hagendaas began, "is—"

The girl stepped out onto the field. "Danielle Shepherd."

"Legion," von Harglebargle finished.

"Danny," she insisted. She pushed back the Giants cap and flashed an engaging, lopsided smile at his cameras.

"Miss Shepherd is an ace as well," von Handydandy added.

Tom looked at her again. She was very cute, but even with the bulletproof vest and the M-16 she looked like she'd be more at home in a girls' softball championship than in combat.

"GREAT. TERRIFIC." Tom didn't know what else to say. Forty-six years old, and he still got awkward around pretty girls.

Von Herglebergle smiled. "And if you'd care to turn around . . ." Tom caught a flicker of motion in the corner of his eye, off one of the screens behind him. He spun his chair around 180 degrees.

In deep center field, beside a weathered advertisement that promised

Abe Stark would give a free suit to any batter hitting this sign, a wide double gate opened slowly. Sunlight shimmered blindingly off polished chrome armor as a massive metallic shape lumbered onto the field. It looked like a tank on legs.

"Detroit Steel," von Herzenberzen pronounced.

Detroit Steel was seven feet tall and four across. He must have weighed as much as the Turtle's shell; with each step, his feet sank a good ten inches into the soft outfield turf, leaving elephant-sized potholes to drive the Dodger groundskeepers crazy. He looked like he was moving in stop-motion animation.

Danny Shepherd might be a new one on Tom, but he knew all about Detroit Steel from *Aces* magazine. It wasn't a robot. There was a man inside that armor, an unemployed Detroit autoworker who had tinkered together the suit in his spare time to become Motown's foremost public ace. His exoskeleton gave him strength to rival Golden Boy's. Supposedly he'd built the whole thing out of scrap metal and old auto parts.

Detroit Steel came to a stop beneath him. The reflection off the chrome was blinding. A single cyclopean headlight was mounted in the helmet above the tinted eye slit, and a whole bank of them across the massive chest. Vintage Caddy tailfins decorated shoulders and helmet. A radio antenna telescoped out from behind one ear. All it needed was a set of fuzzy dice.

"*Yo, Turtle,*" Detroit Steel said, his voice boisterous, hearty, and full of static. "*Good to be working with you. My kid's a big fan.*"

"THANKS," Tom said, uncertainly. The feds were bringing in aces from all over the country. Cyclone operated out of San Francisco. Detroit Steel was from Michigan. He didn't know about Danny Shepherd, but the Minnesota Giants cap might be a clue. The local heavyweights had already been lined up: Mistral, Pulse, Modular Man, Elephant Girl.

"This will be the most powerful ace strike team ever assembled," von Hergenbergen promised. "One of my aides is in Japan right now, talking with Fortunato. We're also following up leads on Chimera, Manta Ray, and Starshine. We've offered pardons to the Sleeper and Jumpin' Jack Flash."

Fat chance, Tom thought. Starshine and J.J. Flash were both "friends" of Cap'n Trips, currently off in space somewhere with Dr. Tachyon and the private detective Jay Ackroyd. The last time Tom saw the captain, he'd been climbing into a spaceship, waving like it was the *Queen Margaret* and he was off to cruise the Virgin Islands.

"*Going to kick some serious ass,*" Detroit Steel said. Tom wished he were as sure.

Ebbets Field seemed empty even though there were a lot of people present—the absence of crowds in the old wooden grandstand, and the lack of anything so interesting as a ball game to attract attention, made the huge field seem like a vast, obscure memorial to a cause long forgotten. A few soldiers ran about the bright green infield stringing wire, putting up antennae, testing a sound system. . . . Someone was noodling around on the club organ, trying to hunt-and-peck his way through "Take Me Out to the Ball Game." There was a huge model of the Rox built on and around the pitcher's mound. Armed sentries were posted at intervals around the park's perimeter, and both dugouts had been turned into sandbagged machine-gun posts.

Modular Man had been here twice before. He recognized Cyclone standing by the Dodger dugout. Near him were a number of people in uniform and a huge robot seemingly assembled out of junkyard spare parts. The Turtle floated enigmatically overhead.

The android landed nearby, beside a lean man in uniform who wore an Arab headdress.

"General Zappa?" Modular Man said.

"Call me Frank." The mildly southern voice issued from beneath a clipped military mustache. Zappa nodded toward the other man, who wore an Air Force uniform blouse unbuttoned over a Judas Priest T-shirt. "This is Major Vidkunssen. Big Swede."

Modular Man shook hands with the major. Words flashed across the electronic scoreboard. U.S. SIGNAL CORPS KICKS ASS.

The robot—or was it a suit of armor?—gave a brief hiss of hydraulics.

Oiled pistons slid in their sleeves, and little servomotors whined as it extended one paw.

"Detroit Steel," he said. "Made in America."

Modular Man gazed upward at the behemoth's metal face and shook his head. He noticed that Detroit Steel had old auto fins on his shoulders and that the headlight on his helmet seemed to have come from a 1957 Chevrolet. There was a Lincoln hood ornament screwed to the top of his head.

"Perhaps you're long-lost cousins," suggested Cyclone, "if not twins, separated at birth."

For the robot's sake, Modular Man hoped not.

Cyclone introduced Modular Man to a young blond woman named Danny Shepherd, who seemed rather small and fragile to be wearing a uniform and carrying a gun.

"Could I speak to you privately?" Zappa asked Modular Man. He led the android out to the pitcher's mound, where a ghetto blaster on top of a miniature battlement was blaring Middle Eastern music. Vidkunssen followed them.

"What I'd like to ask you to do," Zappa said, "is take a flight over Ellis Island, drop some leaflets, and scope out the defenses at the same time. Think you could do that?"

"I suppose."

"There's supposed to be this kind of mental field around the castle so that people don't want to get inside. But you're a robot, right?"

"An android."

"Android. Sorry. Anyway, the mental field shouldn't be a problem. Will it?"

"I don't know. I'll try."

AIR FARCE ARE WIMPS, said the scoreboard.

"And you seem to have enough firepower to keep the demons away." Zappa's eyes narrowed. "Where'd you get that machine gun, exactly?"

Modular Man had stolen it, actually, from a National Guard warehouse. "I'd rather not say," he said.

Zappa and Vidkunssen exchanged looks. Someone on the organ was trying to play "96 Tears."

"You fought with the army during the Swarm invasion," Zappa said. "You have an idea of the kind of information we'd be interested in, right?"

"I suppose."

Zappa looked down at the huge model. "The problem is that our military reconnaissance satellites aren't set up to cover the East Coast. NASA has been trying to get a Delta launch ready, but there are storms over Cape Canaveral right now and they've scrubbed the mission till Monday at the earliest. We've been buying intelligence data from the Russians, and we can overfly the Rox with a reconnaissance plane, but in each case it takes time to get the pictures to my office.

"We'd also like to know where Governor Bloat is. Where he is physically."

"If we can neutralize him," Vidkunssen said, "most of our problems vanish."

"The others might surrender without him," Zappa said. "That would be a good thing."

Vidkunssen looked up. "Limo coming, Frank."

"The draft evader or his emissary. Better change the channel."

Vidkunssen grinned. "Makes you want to shoot quail, don't it?"

He pressed a button on the boom box and the Arab music was replaced by the sounds of John Philip Sousa. He buttoned up his blouse over the Judas Priest T-shirt, then tossed an army cap to Zappa, who put it on in place of his Arab headdress.

Modular Man turned to see a black limousine driving slowly from a gate off in left field. Plainclothes security men hung on it or trotted alongside.

A plump, red-faced civilian was walking toward the limo from the Dodgers dugout.

"Hey, it's the man himself!" Zappa had altered his voice to sound like an overeager deejay. "Here with his backup band, it's the King of the Links, the Sultan of Suave, the Man a Heartbeat Away from the Oval Office Itself—here they are—*Danny and the Dynamos!*"

The car came to a halt and one of the security men opened the rear door. The vice president stepped out and smiled. Zappa and

Vidkunssen drew themselves up and saluted. Dan Quayle returned the salute and smiled again.

"Stars and stripes forever," he said.

"Yes, sir," said Zappa. "I agree with your sentiments, actually, but I think it's 'American Eagle March.'"

ITS' THE VEEP, said the scoreboard. The letters, including the misplaced apostrophe, flashed brightly. There was scattered cheering from the bleachers.

Quayle turned to Modular Man and offered his hand. "Glad you're with us," he said.

Modular Man wasn't quite certain how to respond to this. "Good," seemed appropriate enough.

The plump, pink-faced civilian arrived.

"Mr. von Herzenhagen," Vidkunssen said. "Special Executive Task Unit."

Modular Man shook hands. Von Herzenhagen addressed Quayle. "I've just been on the SCARE hotline. Senator Hartmann's coming out with a new recruit."

WHERE'S GEORGE??? said the scoreboard. Zappa turned to Vidkunssen. "Gunnar," he said, "would you go up to whoever's running the scoreboard and tell him I'm going to rip his arms off if he doesn't knock it off?"

"No problem," said Vidkunssen. He trotted away.

Zappa looked at von Herzenhagen, then at the Rox model. "I was just going to ask Modular Man to take a flight over the Ro—over Ellis Island, and drop some leaflets."

Von Herzenhagen gave the android a fatherly look. "Good," he said. "Anything we can do to convince those people to give themselves up."

A small military helicopter arrived over the stadium and drowned out any further conversation. It circled the stadium twice and then flared and came to a landing near second base.

Modular Man noticed that when the aircraft came near, some men appeared from the dugouts with shoulder-fired rockets. Just in case, he assumed, the craft turned hostile.

You never knew with jumpers.

The rotors began to slow. Gregg Hartmann got out, followed by a lean man in civilian clothes. Afterward, moving slowly on account of arm and leg shackles, was a strikingly handsome dark-haired man in plain civilian dress.

Snotman.

Cold dismay rolled through the android's circuitry.

Snotman, weighed down by the shackles, shuffled toward the pitcher's mound under the guidance of the civilian. Gregg Hartmann came ahead and shook hands with the group.

"General Zappa?" The thin man held up an ID case with a badge. "I'm Gregory, U.S. Marshal. I'm to release this man into your parole. Sign here."

Snotman looked up at Modular Man. The look was not friendly.

Zappa signed the forms that Gregory held out, then undid the arm and leg shackles. Zappa offered to shake his hand, but Snotman chose instead to rub his chafed wrists.

"I'm General Zappa. This is Mr. von Herzenhagen, Vice President Quayle, and Modular Man."

Snotman's cold blue eyes stared at the android. "We've met," he said.

Gregory got into the helicopter, and it lifted off into the sky.

"I'm glad you're on our team," said Quayle. Snotman didn't answer. Von Herzenhagen whispered into Quayle's ear. Quayle seemed surprised.

"You're ah—" he said.

"The Reflector. Call me Reflector."

Quayle grinned in relief. "I suspected something—frankly—far more disgusting. I thought you were a joker that dripped, uh, mucus and—"

Quayle's speech faded beneath Snotman's frigid glare. Quayle swallowed, then said, "We're glad you've chosen this means to redeem your debt to society."

Snotman's answer was simple. "I'll kill any freak you like if it gets me out of Leavenworth. Not that Leavenworth is that *bad*, mind you, for someone like me." He gave a thin smile. "I sort of run the place, actually. And the food's better than what I'm used to."

Quayle paused. "Well," he said, "I think it's particularly good of you, considering you're a joker."

"I'm not a joker." The voice was sharp. "I *used* to be a joker. Croyd changed me, and now I'm the Reflector."

Von Herzenhagen stepped closer. His look seemed quite sincere. "We're glad you're with us, Reflector."

"I hate jokers," Snotman continued. "I've got a lot of scores to settle with jokers. They gave me a lot more shit than the nats ever did."

"Whatever the reason," von Herzenhagen said.

Zappa looked from one to the next. "One big happy family," he said.

Tom had heard enough. He was getting queasy feelings about the company he was keeping. Von Hagendaas was bad enough, but now that Dan Fucking *Quayle* had showed up, he had to say something.

"YOU GUYS SOUND LIKE YOU JUST CAN'T WAIT TO GET IN THERE AND START A WAR," Tom said. "DAMN IT, SENATOR HART-MANN IS TRYING TO SETTLE THIS *PEACEFULLY*, REMEMBER?"

"Of course we do," Vice President Quayle offered. "But if his mission should fail, we have to be prepared to—"

Tom was out of patience. "TO *WHAT*?" he interrupted. "TO START KILLING JOKERS? WHY? ELLIS FUCKING ISLAND IS A GODDAMN RUIN BUILT ON TOP OF SHIP BALLAST. NOBODY GAVE TWO SHITS ABOUT IT UNTIL THE JOKERS MADE IT THEIR OWN."

"Turtle has a point," Danny Shepherd said quietly.

"Ellis Island is a national monument," Quayle said. "It belongs to the people of the United States, not a gang of joker terrorists. Uh, and the Statue of Liberty too. Even more so."

"Let me remind you that Bloat and his people have formally seceded from the United States," von Hegenberg said stiffly. "That constitutes treason."

"No one has more sympathy for the jokers than I do," Cyclone said, "but that doesn't excuse terrorism."

Snotman glared up at the Turtle with open hostility. "Five will get you ten he's a joker himself inside that tin can."

"*Hey,*" Detroit Steel put in. "*Jokers, blacks, aliens, it don't make no difference to me. This is America. But the law's the law, right? And they been killing people, right?*"

"We lost almost six hundred men last month," General Zappa said softly. "Good men. Brave soldiers."

"I SAW THE BODIES," Tom said. "I SAW PLENTY OF DEAD JOKERS TOO. LET'S NOT FORGET WHO INVADED WHO. YOU GUYS HAVE HIT THE ROX TWICE, WITH NOTHING TO SHOW FOR IT BUT CASUALTY LISTS. NOW YOU WANT US TO DO YOUR DIRTY WORK FOR YOU. ACES AGAINST JOKERS. MORE BLOOD, MORE KILLING. WELL, FUCK THAT SHIT."

Tom realized that most of the enlisted men in the ballpark had stopped whatever they were doing. Everyone was watching the little drama down on the infield.

"Turtle," Gregg Hartmann said quietly, "you're right, the jokers out there are victims. I know what they've suffered. But this isn't the way. You know it, I know it, Bloat probably knows it too. He can't win. Bush will never back down now. He's too afraid he'd be perceived as a wimp."

Dan Quayle gave Hartmann a startled look. "You can't—"

Hartmann ignored him. "Those are political realities, whether we like them or not," he continued. "The country is *afraid*. The jumpers terrify them, and intelligence claims there are more than a hundred jumpers out on the Rox. And Bloat . . . that castle, of his . . . the Wall . . . armies of demons out of Hieronymus Bosch . . . all of a sudden, no one seems to know the limits of Bloat's powers, or what he might do next."

Inside his shell, Tom shifted uncomfortably in his seat. "You can't argue with that kind of fear," Hartmann was saying. "The Rox is going to fall. Bush will use everything he has to bring it down, up to and including nuclear weapons. That's why this afternoon is so important. We *must* convince Bloat that he cannot win. And for that, I need your help."

"I'M ALL FOR TALKING WITH BLOAT," Tom said. "BUT WHAT IF HE WON'T LISTEN?"

Hartmann sighed. "Then each of us will have to search his own conscience, and do what we must. But I tell you this—the Rox is a wild card problem. Wild cards should clean it up. There's too much fear and hatred in this country already. The nation needs to see that not all wild cards are terrorists and killers. They need to be reminded that some of you are heroes."

Hartmann's familiar eloquence hadn't left him when his political career came crashing down in Atlanta. He was as persuasive as ever. "ALL RIGHT," Tom said. "I'M IN."

Von Hagendaas smiled. "Of course you are," he said. "I never doubted it. We're offering them amnesty, you know. You can't get more fair than that."

"They don't deserve amnesty," Snotman said angrily. "*I* deserve amnesty. They deserve punishment. Humiliation. Pain. Everything they gave me. Doubled."

"That kind of attitude won't do anybody any good," Danny Shepherd told him sharply.

"I think . . ." Modular Man began.

Snotman turned on him. "You're a machine. Nobody gives a damn what you think. We might as well ask the jeep its opinion."

The android gave him an apprehensive look, and fell quiet.

General Zappa said, "I saw the body bags at Fort Dix after last month's try for the Rox. If there's one chance in the million that talking will save that from happening to my command, I'm taking that chance." He turned to Gregg Hartmann. "You've got the ball, Senator. Just put it right over the plate."

Building things was one of the Outcast's favorite pleasures. Adding to the maze of caverns underneath the Rox was bliss. The Outcast grinned as he worked. Anymore, he could actually *feel* the energy coursing through him. The channel in which the power ran was almost visible, leading from his mind to the sleeping vastness of his Bloat-body—the engine driving the fantasy of the Rox. The governor's body was a deep well and the Outcast drank deeply from his other self.

Every day his surging will was stronger. Every day he could do more, as Bloat gorged himself on the waste products of the Rox. Every day he could spend more time dreaming himself as the Outcast, no longer trapped in Bloat.

Ahh, my dear Kelly/Tachyon. I wish you were here. I wish you could be with me now. I could love you the way you deserved to be loved, you and little Illyana . . .

That was the only sadness in him at all. The Outcast hummed tunelessly as he worked, and he smiled.

Tendrils of purple-blue light splashed from his fingertips and from the stone set in the knob of his staff, leaping out into the darkness of the cavern far under New York Bay. He wove the light like a fabric, fashioning it.

"Let me guess: a dragon."

"Right," the Outcast said, not looking at the penguin. The voice was enough to tell him who it was. "Every good dungeon needs a dragon."

"Y'know, fat boy, for someone with a half-decent imagination, sometimes you ain't as creative as you could be. I mean, c'mon, a dragon's such a *cliché*. A standard, overused icon like a unicorn. You read too much Tolkien as a kid, y'know that? I think—hey! Whassa matter?"

The lines of force composing the Outcast's blossoming dragon form snarled and twisted, the solidity of the contours fading. "I don't know . . ." he said. He raised his staff higher, straining to pull more energy from Bloat's reserves. Something drained the energy from him, pulling it away. As the Outcast struggled to retain control, a huge, glowing white sword materialized. Swinging through the darkness with an audible *whuff*, the weapon sliced the birthing dragon in half and then shattered into a hundred streaming meteors. The penguin made a sound like a strangling cat. Pumping furiously with its tiny legs, it skated away over the rocky ground, its funnel hat askew. The Outcast reverted to Teddy behavior at the magical assault, burying his head in his hands as streamers of burning phosphorus hissed past him.

"This isn't the way," a voice said. Teddy (*No,* he told himself, *I am the Outcast. Not Bloat, and especially not Teddy . . .*) peeked through his fingers. An ancient, olive-skinned man in a brightly colored serape was staring back at him. The old one's face was leathery and almost flat. It had an Indian look to it, alloyed perhaps with Spanish blood, like pictures Teddy/Bloat/Outcast had seen of native South Americans.

"You have interfered too many times. You ignore all the signs, and you're utterly ignorant of what you're doing," the old man said. "I can no longer tolerate this. You make the Old Ones angry. They curse me." Muscles wobbled in an empty bag of skin as the old one flung his arm out. "I brought you here to deal with you."

For the first time, the Outcast noticed his surroundings. He was no longer in the Rox's caverns but on a lonely peak in the midst of a tall range of mountains. A cold mountain wind scoured his face. To breathe the frozen, rich air was both painful and exhilarating all at once.

"Hey, man, I don't have no quarrel with you," the Outcast said. He tapped his staff on the ice-glazed rocks so that the amethyst glowed warningly. "Just leave me alone."

Bloat had two types of dreams. Lately, he was most often wandering the Rox as it truly was, usually as the Outcast and often in the company of the penguin. But the initial dreams, the ones that had first hinted at the power, in *those* dreams he walked in a surreal world, one littered with symbols and images and strange landscapes, a world that shifted under his feet and where things of myth and legend and tales lived all jumbled together. That strange place had always seemed real too. Still, he'd never had both dreams together. It had always been one or the other. This was the first time one had blended into the other.

He willed himself to wake up, to be Bloat again, sitting in his fantasy castle in his fantasyland.

He remained where he was.

"You are Bloat," the old man said. "Teddy."

"I'm the Outcast, not Bloat. And Teddy died years ago."

The leathery face cracked and folded under the freight of a brief smile, yet the lips were the only part that moved. The eyes—dark and brown like plowed earth—had no amusement in them at all. Instead, they were sad, gathering with tears. "A name means nothing and everything." Then the smile vanished, as if it had never been there. There was only the quiet sadness and behind it, like a thundercloud, a lurking violence.

"Yeah. So who the fuck are you? Are you someone else I dreamed up?"

The Outcast knew that his defiance stemmed at least partly from the ignominy of having cowered like poor Teddy during those first few seconds of contact. He stiffened his full lips, let his muscular chest widen and fill. He could see the sinews rippling in his forearm as he gripped his staff. He looked fierce and wise. He looked *good*.

The old man barked laughter. "I'm nothing of *yours*," he answered softly. "Do you really have such an inflated sense of your own worth that you think you can rule *this* place?" The man spat; the globule hit the rocks and froze instantly. "You may call me Viracocha."

"Great. Viracocha. You dragged me to this damn mountaintop?"

Viracocha nodded. He spread his hands wide as if in benediction; at the same moment the sun broke through the cloud cover. Great columns of dusty yellow shot down from the sky, touching the blue spines of the mountain range. "This is my land, a vast place, but only a small part of the greater vista beyond."

"Very pretty. You probably do a great business with picture post-cards."

"You mock me."

"You were first in your class, weren't you?"

Viracocha hissed, a sound like that of a thousand writhing vipers. The sibilance echoed from the stone cliffs surrounding them. "You are an abomination, Teddy," Viracocha shouted. "You steal from all of us. You send your creatures to walk here where they don't belong. I listen to the whispers in the winds; I'm not alone in my anger. They all talk of you, those who may walk here, and they spit when they say your name. I tell you, Outcast or Bloat or Teddy—you don't know with what you play."

"I play with my own power."

"No." The infinite sadness in the old, rheumy eyes hardened. "You have no conception of what it is you do or how you do it or why."

"Tell it to the fucking nats," the Outcast shot back. "I handled them. I built a whole place all my own. I'm the *governor.* I'm the Outcast. I'm the one who built caverns, who gave life to dream creatures, who built a wall and palaces and gardens on a barren island. *I* did that, man. I got too many real things to worry about than dreams like you."

The Outcast could feel his power returning and settling in his bones. He could sense the link to the sleeping Bloat-body, stretched across some intangible mind-barrier he'd never felt before. He could move his will back along the lines of power to that division and push; he could open a rift in the dream and find his way back. The realization calmed him. His breathing slowed.

"Look at you," Viracocha said. "You've become so full of yourself. The others—they said that you'd learn, that you just needed help like any fledgling. 'We should be patient,' they said. They dismissed my warnings, saying that you'd lose your ability to interfere with us or that your own kind would take care of you finally. But none of that has happened. You've grown from an irritating scratch to a gaping wound in our land. I say it is time to stop the bleeding and close that wound."

"Right," the Outcast said. "I get it now. You're from my subconscious, aren't you?—like all those things that Kelly"—he stopped himself—"Tachyon said. You're all the fears I've had of the Rox failing."

"You still do not see it, Teddy." Viracocha had on his sad gaze again; no, he was actually *weeping,* the old fart. The white-haired head shook dolefully. "Look!" he cried aloud, lifting his hands to the sky again, his gaze there now, not at the Outcast. "You see! It is as I told you—he does not comprehend. He is hopeless."

The ground rumbled underneath the Outcast's feet. Stones slithered from the heights and crashed nearby. The grating dull thuds echoed through the misty landscape as if in answer to Viracocha's words.

The old man's gaze fell upon the Outcast like a bludgeon. The eyes were dry now, and malevolent. His stare burned the Outcast like the heat from a fire. "You must die," the old man whispered. "All heroes die." Each word was like a knife thrust, and the Outcast's body staggered with the impact of them as if they were physical blows. "Die now, Teddy," Viracocha said again. The Outcast had gone to his knees, breathless, his heart pounding against the cage of his ribs. The world spun softly around him at Viracocha's invocation. He thought he heard laughter.

The Outcast's breath was leaving him. Through the swirling dark, Teddy heard the taunting voice of Roger, his old neighborhood tormentor, he heard his parents, who had abandoned the child tainted by the wild card virus.

"*Damn* you!" Teddy growled deep in his throat. The anger lent him the strength to rise to his feet again, taking on the Outcast aspect once more. He could feel the knobby wood of the staff in his hand, and its purple brilliance caressed his face. He pulled himself up the length of the wood.

"*Damn* you!" he said to Viracocha, whose stare was now touched by fear. The Outcast rapped the bottom of his staff on the cold stones of the peak. He felt the power surging, moving from Bloat to himself, filling him. He pointed his staff at Viracocha like a weapon. The old man lifted his chin, and his gaze went hard and unreadable. "That's right, you old fucker. I can roast you right where you stand and there ain't a goddamn thing you can do about it."

"But you will not," Viracocha declared. "I know you, Teddy."

"Damn it, I told you that I'm the fucking *Outcast*!" His staff trembled in his hands. The power spat and crackled, leaping from the end of the staff. He could barely hold it back.

"I could have killed you," Viracocha said. "I will yet, if I can. But you . . ." Viracocha sighed. "Go home, Teddy," he said. "Use your precious power and leave me."

The Outcast didn't know how to answer. The dream-energy of Bloat hissed like static in his ears and he couldn't think. He exhaled, harshly, wordlessly, then spun around. He released the surging power and it screamed from his staff like a banshee, a whirlwind dervish that enveloped him, swept him up and dizzily away.

When it set him down again, he was back in Bloat's body. Bloat-black was rippling and sliding down his sides.

The man called Gary Wanatanabise cleared customs easily, the one complication coming when the uniformed officer stumbled over the name on the forged passport. "Listen, how the hell *do* you say this, sir?"

"Wah-na-tah-na-vee-say." What he didn't say was that the "Gary" was from his true name; the other was effectively a joke stolen from a television commercial created by the imperalist AT&T. Wyungare had seen it on a bootleg tape of *Twin Peaks* smuggled into Western Australia.

"So what's it mean?" said the customs man a bit imperiously.

"Sweet land of boundless opportunity."

"Oh, yeah?" The officer even smiled. "That's real nice."

Wyungare picked up his unopened bag off the carpeted table.

The officer looked away toward the next haggard traveler. "Have a nice day."

A little ragged from lack of sleep, Wyungare wanted to say, *Thanks, but I've got other plans.* He restrained the impulse. It would most likely be a very long day. He didn't want to spend a large portion of it in a steel cage.

He took the bus into the city and wondered at the skyline growing larger before his eyes. Then the road dipped into the Holland Tunnel and Wyungare felt the pressure of the river running overhead. It was not a comfortable feeling. He sensed a certain amount of filth in the water.

After disembarking at the Port Authority Terminal, he checked a map posted under graffiti-defaced plastic and ventured into the gray morning outside. The moment he cleared the door, he was rushed by a half-dozen beings he took to be Manhattan jokers.

"You wanna cab?" said a man with his face cracked like the bottom of a river in high-summer drought.

"Hey! I getcha one with the lowest fare you can imagine. Where you goin'?" It was a woman with a bright pink face and her lips turned vertical rather than horizontal.

"Uptown, sir? I can get you a good one. Real fast!"

"Me! Pick me!"

"No, don't listen. I get you something special."

"Thank you all, but no thank you." Wyungare pushed his way through without actually touching any of them. "Sorry, friends." Nor did they touch each other. It was a complex choreography of desperation. All the jokers were physically large, whether male or female. The Aborigine supposed they would have to be, if they were to earn a living acting as gladiators for incoming travelers in need of a cab.

He found a subway stairs and descended from the imminent sunrise. Wyungare had been provided with transit tokens as well as cash. Though he'd never been in a subway station before, he'd seen them in plenty of films. With confidence, he dropped a token into the turnstile slot and pushed through. One gate over, a small gang of four Asian teenagers hopped fluidly over the turnstile as if they were a closely spaced line of English jumpers. They ignored an outraged yell from the change booth.

Wyungare glanced up to make sure he was on the downtown side of the tracks. At the same time, he felt the ghost wind that he guessed meant that a train was approaching from up the tunnel. He turned and saw the wavering light.

The train rattled and hissed into the station. Wyungare, keeping tight hold of his bag, boarded a middle car.

He got off at 14th Street and walked across town. It didn't take all that long, and it was good to stretch his legs. They had been cramped on the airplane.

The city was starting to come to life. Not that New York City ever truly slept—Wyungare remembered Cordelia's opining that. This morning, the atmosphere seemed shot through with tension. The Aborigine could pick that up without any need of special powers. Something was indeed in the air. Or maybe it was simply the daily index of paranoid urban tension building up.

When he encountered the water, he turned south. Eventually he reached South Street, and the aging waterfront building bearing the sign Wyungare sought: the Blythe van Renssaeler Memorial Clinic. He knew he was in Jokertown; the people passing him on the street proved that. This was the Jokertown Clinic.

He didn't hesitate. Right through the front door and past the reception desk. He was travelworn but presentable enough especially for Jokertown. As long as he appeared to know what he was about, Wyungare didn't anticipate being challenged.

There was no percentage, though, in pushing his luck. He found the door to the stairs and went up to the second floor. Wyungare stepped briskly down the dingy corridor. He glanced curiously to either side. Some of the doors were open. It was like walking through a huge Advent calendar of misery.

A scream issued from the doorway to his right. Wyungare saw what appeared to be a nat—a man, with the exception of his face. His head cradled on an oversize pillow, he stared at the Aborigine and screamed again. His features looked as though they were formed of melting wax; they appeared to be slowly running down the side of his head. Only his bright blue eyes were still in their proper locations.

Wyungare looked through other open doors. He remembered the ancient print he'd seen of *Horrors of the Wax Museum*. He approached the end of the corridor. Around the corner, he thought. He'd been counting room numbers. Two doors down.

The fluorescent illumination seemed dimmer here. There were no outside windows in this section of the hallway. Doorways loomed like dark gaps in a jaw full of diseased teeth.

The door to room 228 was closed.

Wyungare slipped it open, moved inside, stared around the room. One dim lamp illuminated some sort of bed; actually more of a padded, contoured table. The alligator was cradled in that bed. Wyungare detected movement. A set of rollers moved beneath the fabric under the alligator's belly. The mechanism that activated them hummed, clicked, and then the rollers recycled, starting their massaging movement again.

"Magic fingers," Wyungare muttered. The perfect alligator tranquilizer. He heard a questioning *miaow*. He looked down and saw a large black cat looking up at him. They stared at each other for a few seconds. Then Wyungare slowly hunkered down and ran his fingers firmly across the feline head and down its neck. The cat purred, the sound something like that of a bus idling.

"Cousin mirragen, I know you, even though I've not seen you before. Cordelia told me of you and your mate. You are a friend of the one called Bagabond, true?"

The cat continued to purr. He was about twenty-five pounds and solid black, though his fur was beginning to grizzle. He pushed himself against Wyungare's lower leg. The man looked at the feline's coat and guessed him to be at least twenty years old. The cat was still solidly muscled. He was missing a small notch from his right ear.

Wyungare stood and turned to the recumbent alligator. Twelve or fourteen feet long, the reptile breathed regularly, but otherwise displayed no signs of life. "And this is your friend?" he said to the cat. "Jack Robicheaux? Cordelia's uncle." He nodded with satisfaction. "He sleeps. Perhaps he dreams. We'll find out." The black cat yowled. "Yes, cousin, your friend actually lies far from here. Let me find out *how* far."

The Aborigine again hunkered and unzipped the cheap, floral-print suitcase. He took out a candle and firestone, a small drum with the stick slipped into the lacing, and an abbreviated loincloth. With a sigh of relieved comfort, he slipped off the European clothes and donned the cloth. He used the firestone to light the candle, then dripped enough warm wax on the end of the table by the alligator's snout to serve as a candleholder. Then he turned off the lamp.

The cat watched interestedly as Wyungare settled himself on the floor and set the drum between his knees. The man picked out a basic rhythm, the beat of the river, let it repeat, worked a variation, settled into the sound.

He was still aware of being in the hospital room; but he was simultaneously aware of walking through a thick pine forest. The humidity was high and his skin felt sticky. It was hard to see the sun. He looked up and saw intermittent flashes of hazy light.

The man entered a clearing and passed a decrepit frame house. Time had not spared the boards; they possessed a soft gray shine. Before he rounded the front corner, Wyungare heard a small sound. A whimper. He stopped and looked carefully beyond the juncture, the side of his face pressed comfortably against the gray clapboard.

He saw a humped shape pinned beneath the rectangular shroud of a screen door. Wyungare carefully approached. He found the body of a young boy lying on his belly, the screen door over him. Someone had staked the door to the earth with long, rusted spikes. The boy's body filled out the pliable screening as though it had been molded there. The wire over the boy's buttocks was wet, rusty with blood. He whimpered. His fingers twitched at the rough mesh.

The young Jack? Wyungare thought. He knew that Jack Robicheaux had been reared in a rural southern Louisiana parish back in the time of Earl Long. His niece Cordelia Chaisson had told Wyungare that. When he contracted the wild card virus, Jack had imprinted on the pervasive bayou image of the alligator. That reptile had become the alter ego of his shape-changing ability. Now doubly cursed and dying of AIDS, Jack Robicheaux's human avatar apparently lay very far indeed from the waking world.

Who did this? Wyungare wondered to himself. *Which monster?* He was afraid he knew. "Do you wish release?" he asked aloud. He thought he already knew the answer.

The boy turned his head slightly to the side and looked into Wyungare's eyes. The boy's eyes were dark and liquid, echoing the black, tangled hair.

"I should not interfere," the man said, "but I think there's not enough time for you to solve your own lesson." He touched one of the steel spikes and tried to wiggle it back and forth. It was solidly driven into the ground.

He heard the sound.

Wyungare started to turn, to look over his shoulder. In the other world, the waking place, he was aware that someone had opened the door to Jack's room, had paused in the halo of outside light, was looking around, reacting—

He felt the force slam into his head and start to shut down all his autonomic systems. His heart, his lungs—He could see the shadowed eyes of the intruder and knew he was being killed by a woman.

Something dark and heavy streaked through the black room and slammed into the woman's back. She tumbled forward onto her face on the cool tile floor, the breath going out of her with a *whoof.* Her chin led and her teeth clicked together. The woman lay still for a moment, seemingly stunned.

The killing pressure left his mind.

With apologies, Wyungare abandoned the imprisoned child and returned to the waking world. He shook his head and blinked a few times.

The black cat was purring and licking the woman's cheek with his rough wet tongue. She groaned and tried to raise her head. The cat nuzzled her face and she recoiled. "Stop it!"

Wyungare walked over to her and bent down. The woman's long, curly hair was soft and just as black as had been the boy's in the other world. "You okay?"

The woman pushed the cat firmly away and tilted her face toward his. Her eyes matched the color of her hair. "*You?*" she said, sounding shocked.

"It ain't Mel Gibson, young missy," Wyungare said. "It is memorable to see you, Cordelia." He reached to help her up.

Cordelia sat up without any aid. She grabbed Wyungare's proffered hands and pulled the man down beside her. "You son of a bitch," she said. "You self-centered political asshole."

Wyungare said, "Cordie—"

"Don't 'Cordie' me," Cordelia snapped. "It's been four years since you saved my life in the Outback. Four years since we were lovers and we fought the spider-woman and—" She shook her head violently. "Not a letter, not a call, not even a damned card at Christmas, love."

"I—"

Cordelia ignored his attempt to say something. "I know, Wyungare. You were busy being a revolutionary and I was just a kid." She punched him in the shoulder with the heel of her hand. "Dickhead! Just *like* a guy."

"Cordelia," he said, "I'm sorry."

And she laughed. "You're lucky I've lived in New York for a while. I can take this shit." Cordelia wrapped her arms around him. "It *is* you. I can't believe it. What are you *doing* here?"

"I called your apartment. Your roommate said you were running peculiar early errands and planned to visit your uncle before you went to your job. When I rang up the clinic, they said Jack Robicheaux could have no visitors, but I was able to get his room number when I told them I wished to leave you a message when you arrived. I thought I would find you here."

"That's not exactly what I meant," said Cordelia. She traced a fingertip across his face as though recapturing a route on a forgotten map. "I mean, why are you here in New York instead of eating grubs in the middle of Australia?"

"I heard Manhattan had many good restaurants."

"Smartass," she said.

"I couldn't exactly telephone ahead."

"Tell me all about it later."

"What are you doing?" It occurred to him that there was some mild shock in his voice. Her hand traced his body lower. The waist-cloth was little protection. He was hard now, very erect indeed.

"Excuse me," said Cordelia. She stood and Wyungare heard the sounds of whispering fabric. Then she was back down where he was, straddling him, gently moving so that he slid up into her. He moved easily.

"Cordelia—"

"Ssh. Later we'll talk, *mi chér* . . ."

But later wasn't *much* later. The door swung open with a crash. Wyungare looked up and saw a hybrid of man and horse filling the doorway with arms folded. He wore a brilliant white coat that matched the albedo of his lush mane and had a stethoscope around his neck.

The joker doctor squinted and said to someone Wyungare couldn't see, "Well, Troll, it looks as if we'll have to start enforcing visiting hours. If Cody were around, she'd have both our hides."

Ray stopped in front of the door to his office, his nose twitching suspiciously. An unfamiliar stench was coming through the closed door. Ray actually wasn't high enough in the bureaucratic scheme of things to rate a private office, but when none of the other agents' personal standards of cleanliness could match his, Ray had made such a fuss that the powers-that-be had bent the rules in the interest of peace, and given him his own room.

It wasn't much. It was just big enough for a spotlessly clean desk, two chairs, and a meticulously organized file cabinet. But it was Ray's own. And he didn't care for anyone to stink it up.

Ray opened the door. A man was sitting in *his* chair, behind *his* desk, smoking a cigar while leafing through *his* private files. The enormity of the outrage left Ray speechless.

The cigar was bad enough, but it was playing only a minor role in the symphony of stenches assaulting Ray's nostrils. A host of other horrible smells emanated from the guy standing behind the man sitting at Ray's desk.

The man slouching against Ray's file cabinet was dressed in a black skintight fighting suit much like Ray's own, except the hood covered his entire face—mouth, nose, eyes, and all. The left eye was covered by a polarized lens that allowed him to see out, but no one to see in. The right eye, though, was covered by black cloth embossed with a small scarlet cross. The cross was the only touch of color about the man.

He was taller than Ray, and broader-built, though he carried no extra flesh on a body that was all taut muscle and prominent bone. He smelled *bad,* as if he never bathed. He also smelled as if he'd just drunk his breakfast out of a whiskey bottle. The distillery odor mixed with his pungent body odor, and something else, some smell that was unidentifiable but disgusting.

The man sitting at the desk looked up, smiled, and stood. He was short and slimly built with a suggestion of a certain amount of wiry strength. His dark hair was receding from his broad, lined forehead and a thick, carefully groomed mustache covered his upper lip. His eyes were large and animated. He smiled a quick, incandescent smile and held out his right hand.

"Agent Ray, glad to finally meet you."

Ray looked at the man's right hand, then to his left where he held the cigar. An inch of dark, fine ash disintegrated from the cigar's tip and drifted into a little pile beside the blotter set in the precise center of Ray's desk.

"Who," Ray said between clenched teeth, "the hell are you?"

"Ah." The man took his right hand away, dipped into the inside pocket of his expensively tailored suit, and took out an ID wallet. He flashed it at Ray. "Special Agent George G. Battle," he said.

Ray studied the ID. He'd never seen one like it before.

"Special duty," Battle said. "Attached to the White House."

Ray nodded slowly and Battle's grin flashed again across his face.

"Have a seat," the special agent said, gesturing expansively as he sat down again behind Ray's desk. Ray remained standing, staring at Battle unblinkingly. After a moment Battle stood again. "Oh, I get it." He sidled out of the chair, around the edge of the desk, between the desk and filing cabinet. The man dressed in black followed him, always remaining at his back. "You want your own chair. I like that. I like a man who knows what he wants and refuses anything less."

He sat cheerfully in the visitor's chair while Ray took the one behind his desk, glancing distastefully at the ashes beside his blotter. Battle didn't seem to notice.

"All right," the special agent said. "Let's get right to the point." He leaned forward conspiratorily. "I like a man I can afford to be blunt with," Battle said, "and I like you. I've had an eye on you for quite a while now. You're a good soldier, Ray. You follow orders well. You're not afraid to obey your superiors. I can use a man with that attitude."

Ray leaned back warily in his chair. He disliked Battle instinctively. He disliked effusive men, and Battle couldn't seem to sit still. He gestured animatedly when he talked, uncaringly flicking cigar ash all over Ray's carpet.

"How'd you like that little piece of action this morning?" Battle asked suddenly.

"It was . . ." Ray was taken aback by the direct question. He started to answer, but then thought better of it. It had been fun. He had felt alive for the first time in months. But he knew that if he said that to Battle he'd only get a weird look. Others rarely understood him.

"Exhilarating!" Battle said suddenly. He locked eyes with Ray and Ray found himself slowly nodding. "Invigorating," Battle added, and Ray nodded again. The special agent's voice dropped again to a conspiratorial whisper. "It was fun."

Ray only nodded again, surprised.

"Well," Battle said. "You have me to thank for it. I pulled some strings to get you there."

"Why?" Ray asked. He certainly appreciated it, but he wasn't used to strangers doing nice things for him.

Battle leaned back in his chair and to Ray's irritation took a long pull on his cigar. "Call it a test. You'd been badly hurt. You hadn't seen any combat in months. Sometimes that takes it out of a man."

"And did I pass the test?" Ray asked tightly.

Battle waved his cigar, dropping more ash on the floor. "Most certainly. I thought you would. I know you're one of the toughest sons of bitches in government service. But I had to make sure. You know how it is."

Ray found himself nodding despite himself, and he felt a sudden warmth at Battle's unexpected praise.

"And it wasn't only a test. Call it"—and Battle's voice dropped an octave—"an introduction to the worst menace facing the nation today: the radicals who have taken over Ellis Island, defied the government, killed and maimed our brave soldiers, and had the actual unmitigated gall to declare themselves independent from our holy union."

"I didn't realize they posed that great a threat," Ray said.

"Few have!" Battle exclaimed. "Few have. But thank God the few that have are in a position to do something about it."

"The military's already tried—" Ray started, but Battle interrupted him.

"They tried, and failed. But they'll try again. This time with some special help." Ray remained silent. He could see that Battle was getting himself worked up. The agent's breathing was agitated. He fidgeted in the chair as if something in it were continually goosing him. "Forces in the media—and even some within the government—have been urging special treatment for those radicals on Ellis Island. But Bloat and his scum are criminal dirt, pure and simple, and the U.S. is about to get out the broom and sweep them into the sea, joker trash and jumper hoodlums alike."

"But what about the peace conference that's been scheduled for today? Surely—"

"You really expect it to resolve anything?" Battle asked.

Ray considered, then shook his head. "Probably not," he said slowly.

"Of course it won't. That scum understands only force," Battle said, leaning so far forward that he almost toppled out of his chair. "I've put together a team of aces to clean out that rats' nest."

Ray pulled at his uneven chin. "And you want me for this team?"

Battle nodded.

"Who else do you have?"

Battle held up a hand without looking back and the guy in black reached down to a briefcase at his feet. He fumbled with it for a moment and finally handed Battle a three-ring binder. Battle opened it to the first page and flopped it down on Ray's desk, facing him.

Ray looked down. The first page was a glossy eight by ten candid shot of a black guy in a cape clinging to a wall. Ray flipped the photo over and read the info on its back and nodded. Then his eye was caught by the photo of a very attractive blonde on the next page. She was young and very cute. He turned the page to read the stats on the photo's back, and saw the picture of another attractive girl. He checked her vitals. "Cameo," he said aloud. "Never heard of her."

"She's new," Battle said, "but we've had our eye on her for a while. Not much gets past us."

Ray nodded and flipped by an unimpressive-looking Asian guy, then stopped at the photo of the man in black standing beside Battle. The only information on the back of the picture was the name "Bobby Joe Puckett: Crypt Kicker."

"Ah," Battle said. "You can meet one of the team right now. This is Special Agent Bobby Joe Puckett. Shake hands with the man, Bobby Joe. Leave your glove on."

Puckett . . . the name was familiar, Ray thought as the agent slowly put his hand out. Ray took it cautiously. The smelly guy had a strong grip, but Ray did too. He put a little more into his handshake and Puckett answered right back. Ray fought to keep the surprise and pain off his face. He put all the strength he had into his grip, but Puckett, seemingly unimpressed, bore down on his hand with overwhelming pressure. Ray clenched his jaw, determined not to give in, but knowing that this guy was way stronger than him. What would happen, Ray wondered, if I kicked the stinking bastard in the face?

"Now, Bobby Joe," Battle intervened, "don't hurt the man. He's going to be working with us."

Puckett let go instantly and Ray took his hand back, determined not to rub it. "He's strong all right," Ray said. "But can he fight?"

Battle laughed. "Oh, that he can, can't you, Bobby Joe?"

"That's right, Mr. Battle, with the strength of the Lord." Puckett's voice was slurred, difficult to understand. He spoke with a southern drawl, but also had a bad speech impediment. It was as if he'd had a stroke or a wound that had damaged his throat.

"So who's leading the team?" Ray asked, making a surreptitious fist in an attempt to get some blood back in his hand.

"I am," Battle said.

Ray looked at him carefully. "Are you an ace?"

Battle drew back with a look of distaste. "I don't need twisted genes to fight that scum. I have something they don't."

Battle didn't seem aware that he'd just insulted someone he was trying to recruit for a dangerous mission, but Ray couldn't resist asking, "What's that?"

Battle pointed a finger at his temple. "Superior intellect backed by an unbreakable will." He saw the skepticism that flashed across Ray's face and smiled a narrow little smile. "You don't believe me?"

"Well—"

Battle's smile fixed and he pulled back the sleeve of his suit coat to show an expensive watch and a muscular forearm splashed by a number of pale circular scars.

"Watch," Battle said. His smile still in place, he puffed at his cigar until the tip glowed a bright red. Then he jabbed it right into his forearm, still smiling.

Ray watched in horrified fascination as the flesh on Battle's arm blistered, blackened, and puckered into a raw circular crater under the cigar tip. The stench of seared meat speared the air and Ray sat back in his seat. Battle removed the cigar tip from his forearm and proudly displayed the wound to Ray. He held his arm steady and his voice was unshaken. "Will," he said. "That is all a man needs to survive, not an unclean genetic heritage."

Battle, Ray thought, is deranged.

Battle's smile turned to something of a grimace as he wrapped his handkerchief around the fresh burn on his forearm and pulled the sleeve of his jacket over it. "I'll have that attended to later," Battle said. He caught Ray's gaze with his own. "Are you in or out?"

Ray hesitated. The guy was a geek. No normal person hurt themselves like that just to impress someone. He looked at Battle. "I'm in," he said, unable to deny the overwhelming need for action that drove him every minute of his life.

Battle smiled and shot to his feet. "Good! I knew I could count on you. Let's get going."

"Where to?" Ray asked.

"You have some recruiting to do. Two of my prospects haven't committed themselves firmly to the team yet." Battle flipped through the book until he came to the picture of the Asian guy. "Him," Battle said, stabbing the picture with his forefinger. Then he turned to the back of the book and a photo Ray hadn't noticed before. "And him. I want you to have a word or two with both and convince them of the desirability of joining our group."

Ray glanced down at the second photo and barely repressed a groan. It was that smartass P.I., Jay Ackroyd.

"All the information you need is in the book," Battle said. He stood and strode from the office, Puckett lumbering after him.

Ray sat at his desk, watching them leave, realizing suddenly that he'd never, ever be able to eradicate the stench of burnt flesh from his office.

Wyungare had been rather impressed by Cordelia's coolness under fire. It wasn't every European woman who could have gathered her self-possession *and* her clothing after being caught naked and impassioned, astraddle her Aboriginal lover, by the doctor. Wyungare wasn't even sure that a woman of the People would have remained so calm under the circumstances.

The lights were on now, and Dr. Finn fussed about the 'gator avatar of Jack Robicheaux. Troll, the clinic's head of security, hulked against the wall just inside the door and looked vaguely embarrassed. Cordelia and Wyungare stood by the head of Jack's bed; the black cat rubbed against their ankles. Their *clothed* ankles.

Finn glanced at Cordelia and smiled faintly. "Your uncle does need his rest, you know."

Cordelia winced. "Okay, I deserve that. Now let's get back to the point here. Wyungare went directly into Uncle Jack's mind. He found my uncle staked out on the ground. That was when the cavalry came in with all four feet."

"Now—" Finn started to say, shaking his mane indignantly. His palomino colors seemed to shimmer iridescently.

"Okay, *Doctor* Cavalry," said Cordelia. "Christ, you spend a couple hundred thou in medical school and you think you deserve respect."

"Just settle down," said Finn evenly. "Is your Australian, um, friend there a trained psychotherapist?"

Cordelia's voice turned fierce and Wyungare smiled. "He's spent the better part of his young life in the dreamtime, you know? He's *lived* in other people's heads. He can navigate the brain like you can find your way uptown on the A train."

Finn's eyes narrowed. He opened his mouth, but whatever he was going to say was aborted as another doctor entered the increasingly crowded room. This one was male, short, and bland-looking. It seemed to Wyungare that the physician's short blond hair must be prematurely thinning. There were no wrinkles on the man's face.

The new doctor glanced from face to face, frowning a little. Then he turned to the bed. "So, how's my patient today?" he said to the large reptile. Jack the Gator slumbered restlessly on. The doctor glanced at the digital readouts, tapping one meter when he apparently didn't get the numbers he wanted at first.

He said to Cordelia, "Looking good, girl. He's floating perhaps a bit too close to the surface, but I'll up the sleepytime doses."

"You do," said Cordelia, "and they'll find you with one of those telemetry gadgets up your ass, and another one square in the center of the dent in your skull that killed you."

The doctor grinned at her.

Wyungare stared. He didn't remember Cordelia ever displaying this much open hostility.

The physician nodded to Finn. "Doctor." He held out his hand to Wyungare. "You would be a friend of the patient, or perhaps of the patient's niece? My name is Mengele, Dr. Bob Mengele. You can call me Dr. Bob."

Wyungare shook his hand. It felt like grabbing a piece of dry, white bone.

"And no," said Dr. Bob, as though answering an expected but unasked question, "no relation. Just a coincidence in names."

"I'm not so sure," said Cordelia nastily. "I'll bet you sing German camp songs in your sleep."

"Cordelia," said Finn, "that kind of remark is out of line. It's beneath you. Dr. Mengele is a first-rate physician. His work here at the clinic has been above reproach."

Dr. Bob smirked.

"He's a fucking butcher," said Cordelia. "If I'd let him, he'd vivisect Uncle Jack. As it is, he's done his best to exterminate Jack's humanity."

Dr. Bob said, "My girl—"

Cordelia's voice rose to something approaching an enraged shriek. "I'm not *yours*, and I am not a *girl*!"

She looked like she might physically attack Dr. Bob. Wyungare took her arm. He could feel the tension tautening the muscles. "I am not entirely sure I understand why you both act like mortal enemies."

"I'm not an enemy," said Dr. Bob. "I'm only here to help."

"The check's in the mail," said Cordelia venomously. "I won't come in your mouth."

"*Cordelia,*" said Finn. He looked as close to embarrassed as Wyungare guessed a centaur could look. His hooves clicked on tile, as he shifted his weight.

"All right, then," said Wyungare. "Tell me the issue."

"Are you related to the patient?" Dr. Bob inspected Wyungare with a merry grin. "I should guess not. Friend of the family?"

"Yes."

"And how conversant are you with this case?" There was an unpleasantly smug arrogance in Dr. Bob's words.

"I am aware that Jack Robicheaux is an AIDS sufferer. I know that he is under treatment here at this clinic."

"You know," said Dr. Bob, "that AIDS is invariably fatal."

Wyungare nodded. "Would that it were not."

"But it is," Dr. Bob said briskly. "Mr. Robicheaux was dying."

"*Is* dying," said Cordelia, voice dropping and wavering a little.

"We all *are* dying," said Dr. Bob, "in one way or another." He reached out and patted Jack's snout. "Mr. Robicheaux is now dying rather more slowly than he was previously."

"You tricked me into granting consent," said Cordelia.

"You were miserable with grief," said Dr. Bob matter-of-factly, brutally. "You agreed because you know I hold the only possibility for his continued existence."

"But he's continuing as an alligator," said Cordelia.

"Give me a translation, please," said Wyungare.

"Heavy drugs," said Cordelia. "Mengele used psychosurgical techniques. He screwed around with my uncle's reptile brain."

Dr. Bob said, "The patient was dying with AIDS. He was shuttling back and forth between the reptile state and the human. To oversimplify, when he was in human form, the AIDS virus was fatal, but that virus meant nothing to the reptile form."

"I think I'm seeing your meaning," said Wyungare.

Dr. Bob nodded violently and triumphantly. "It was a simple stroke of genius. I'm ensuring his life by giving him a permanent form that is safe from viral predators."

Cordelia said, "You're ensuring a life where he'll be murdered as a human being. He'll spend the rest of his born life as a reptile."

"But he will live."

"At such a cost," murmured Finn.

"There has to be another way," said Cordelia stubbornly.

"Acupuncture?" mocked Dr. Bob. "Peach pits? Positive imaging? No, girl, this is the only viable alternative. And in another few days, the process will be permanent. Irreversible."

Cordelia stared back silently. Tears started to well. Finn trotted forward and extracted a Kleenex from his lab coat.

"The human being is still there," said Wyungare. "But he is deep inside. He is a passenger in the alligator's being."

Cordelia honked into the tissue. "There has to be a way to get him back."

"But he will die," said Dr. Bob, as though belaboring the obvious to an audience of simpletons.

"There's *got* to be something," said Cordelia. She added forlornly, "Maybe Uncle Jack wouldn't want to go on living this way."

"Easy enough for the young to say," said Dr. Bob.

For a while they all stared at each other silently or at the floor. The great bulk of the alligator on the table shifted uneasily from time to time. The reptile breathed with an open-mouthed snoring sound.

"You *can* go inside his head?" said Finn, inclining his chin at Jack. Wyungare nodded.

"And deep?"

The Aborigine nodded again.

"Are you a shaman?" said Finn.

"That's a label for others to assign," said Wyungare.

"Then I suspect you are," said Finn. He looked contemplative for a few moments. Then, apparently making up his mind, he said, "I think we all ought to adjourn to the cafeteria. I've got an idea." He turned to Dr. Bob. "And you, I believe, have rounds to complete."

"Oh, I can take a break," said Dr. Bob, grinning.

"You have rounds," said Finn firmly. He led Cordelia and Wyungare through the outside hall. The centaur followed up at the rear of the small procession. The black cat had stayed with his friend Jack. There could be no more faithful guardian, Wyungare thought.

"Do you know of Bloat?" Finn said over his shoulder to Wyungare.

"The fat boy?"

"Succinct." Finn uttered a short laugh. "Yes, the fat boy. Think you could visit his head?"

Wyungare said, "I think I must."

"Then yes," said Finn, "we really *do* all need to talk."

Zappa, the Turtle, and Hartmann were conferring on the first base line. Snotman stood with the other aces near the dugout and regarded Modular Man with wary intensity.

The Turtle and Hartmann would be paying a final visit to the Rox in a few hours to present an ultimatum and talk Governor Bloat and his people into surrendering. If they failed, the rest of the aces would be going in with the armed forces. Cyclone turned to Modular Man. "At least we've got a deadline now. They surrender by sundown or we take care of them."

"Do you think they stand a chance?" the android asked.

"Against *me* they don't stand a chance. Against all of this . . . ?" He grinned. "No jungle to hide in. No international borders to hide behind. No hostages. No chickenshit politicians on their side—even Hartmann's more worried about the political consequences of the Joker Republic than over the fate of these particular jokers themselves. And castles couldn't stand up to artillery even in the Middle Ages, they're not likely to start now, and in any case it's not going to stand up to *me*. They may have a few surprises to throw our way, but it's still going to be very one-sided."

"I hope so."

Cyclone looked over his shoulder at General Zappa. "*That* weirdo, though . . . I wonder why they picked him? He was with the Joker Brigade at Firebase Reynolds, and he said some things afterward . . . I got the impression he likes jokers too much."

"General Zappa's father," said a voice, "died of the wild card."

Cyclone was startled. Modular Man, however, had seen von Herzenhagen's quiet approach on his radar.

Cyclone nodded. "So he's got a grudge, then?"

"That might be inferred," said von Herzenhagen. "Though of course the general has not confided in *me*." His face held an expression of polite attention.

"Modular Man? May I see you?"

The speaker was Zappa, calling from home plate. Modular Man excused himself and followed Zappa and Vidkunssen down a tunnel under the old grandstand and then into the owners' offices. The elegant affect of the plush, tasteful furnishings, the soft carpet, and the rows of pennants and trophies was subverted by military accretions: maps and photographs, communications apparatus, metal shelves holding equipment. A short, powerfully built, red-faced man in the uniform of a lieutenant colonel was scowling at a young officer.

"I did not find that salute *sufficient*, soldier!" he said. His rural Deep South accent was thick as molasses. "I found it careless and negligent in the extreme! I will ask you to repeat it!"

"Knock it off, cracker," Zappa said. "Come with me."

"I'm still waiting for my salute."

The young officer clenched his teeth and raised his hand in a picture-perfect salute. The red-faced man grinned and returned it.

"I *love* this chickenshit Army," he said.

Zappa led the colonel and Modular Man into an inner office, then sat with relief behind the owner's massive desk. There was a thin civilian already in the room. He wore black-rimmed glasses and a necklace of what seemed to be baby teeth. He carried a miniature poodle whose hair was dyed a pastel blue.

"Big Swede," Zappa said, "get me some mineral water. Anybody else want anything?"

"Pepsi," said the civilian.

"Bourbon on the rocks," said the colonel.

Vidkunssen went to the wet bar and opened a commodious refrigerator. It seemed well stocked.

Zappa waved a hand. "Pepsi over there is Horace Katzenback," he said. "I met him in the Nam, when he was with AID. He's my adviser."

"Token intellectual is what he means," said Katzenback.

Modular Man shook his hand.

"Bourbon on the rocks over there is Sgt. Goode, my stepfather," Zappa said.

Modular Man looked at the colonel's uniform. "Sergeant?" he said.

"U.S.M.C.," said Goode. "Retired."

"I got him a light colonel's commission," Zappa said. "If I'm going to have to make a landing on an island, I want to have someone around who was in the first wave on Tarawa and Saipan."

Goode grinned. "I get to make them all salute me. It's quite a change." He looked at Zappa. "Even if I am in the *wrong fucking branch of service*."

Vidkunssen handed everyone their drinks. Zappa took a sip of mineral water, then said, "Let's have some music."

Vidkunssen punched a button on the boom box and Arab music began to wail. Zappa grinned. "The opposition might be listening," he said. "Or our own side. You never know." He looked up at Katzenback. "You've had time to poke around. What do you make of Phillip Baron von Herzenhagen?"

The thin man twitched a smile. "Spook City. I was around enough of them in the Nam. I've got the smell of them by now."

"Von Herzenhagen himself."

"The people around him sure as hell are. The baron himself—" He shrugged. "Hard to say."

"We're ordered to turn any prisoners over to his unit."

"Well, he's a bigwig with the Red Cross, right? So that sort of makes sense. But those guys around him sure as hell aren't Clara Barton."

Zappa gnawed his mustache. "I don't like the vibe. I was with von Herzenhagen when he interrogated Tachyon, and he damn near tore the girl apart. He's either a pro, or he's crazy."

"I don't like the vibe either."

"But the fewer jumpers my men have to handle themselves, the better."

"My guess is that a whole lot of our prisoners are gonna end up working for the spooks."

"If we take any prisoners, that is. If they don't give up, I don't hold out a lot of hope." Zappa leaned forward and put his elbows on the desk. "Anybody here think they're going to listen to Hartmann's appeal?"

There was a long, uncomfortable silence. Katzenback finally spoke. "We'll probably get a few of the more unmotivated types. The ones that wouldn't give us much grief anyway."

Zappa looked up at Modular Man.

"I've assessed the previous assaults," he said, "both in light of my own experience and that of"—nodded at Goode—"the Georgia cracker here. I have no intention of repeating previous mistakes. In the past the goal of the military was to retrieve a national monument without damaging it in any significant way."

"That led to a lot of restraint," Goode said. "And a lot of dead marines."

"But now," Zappa continued, "the national monument simply doesn't exist anymore, and nobody in their right mind wants to protect that freaky castle. I have the authority to use any means necessary to deal with this emergency."

"The island's too fucking small for a landing," Goode added. "You can't put enough soldiers in, and you can't use heavy weapons for fear you'll hit your own people. And that outer wall—well, if we got people on it, we could use them as artillery spotters. But that's about all."

"Therefore," Zappa said, "I'm not putting any more troops on that island until resistance is *over*. Not until I can get my men onto the Rox by walking there on a bridge of spent shell casings.

"They say that Bloat can change physical reality. My bet is that he's not going to be able to change the five hundred artillery and mortar shells I can drop on the Rox every single minute. Or what the Air Force can do to him. Or Tomahawk missiles dropping cluster bombs. One lousy fuel-air bomb will suck the oxygen right out of the defenders' lungs and pulverize their fortifications at the same time. So that means they surrender before sunset or get bombed until there's no one left."

There was another long moment of silence. This was the man, Modular Man thought, who Cyclone thought liked jokers too much.

Zappa looked up at Modular Man. "If I commit the forces available to me, there's going to be a massacre that will make Wounded Knee look like a cotillion. I'd rather not be the man who goes down in history as giving that kind of order."

"Shit," said Katzenback. "A lot of them are just kids. Governor Bloat is just a kid."

"He's a kid who can change physical reality," Goode said. "A kid who killed a lot of police and marines."

"He's dangerous. I fought alongside the Joker Brigade—I know how formidable jokers can be when they're properly motivated, and when they've got a chance to come to grips. I'm *not* going to come to grips. I don't want to hold back when the time comes—that'll just get more of my own men killed. So my men are just going to sit someplace safe and bomb that place till it sinks into New York harbor.

"I want them to surrender before I have to give any kind of final order. There are still phone lines to and from the Rox. They haven't been cut because our intelligence people figure they can learn things listening in. So the leaflets I'm going to ask you to drop over there will contain a toll-free number that Bloat and his buddies can call when they want to surrender. It's 1-800-I-GIVE-UP." Zappa smiled. "My little contribution to communications history. We've got leaflets printed up, but they don't mention the deadline, so we're having more printed off now. Once they're finished, I'll ask you to fly over there."

"Very well," said Modular Man.

"I think the best way would be a low approach over Jersey City," Vidkunssen said. "That's what the Air Force will use on their bombing runs. Your radar profile is going to be lost in the ground clutter of the city buildings, and if you miscalculate your bomb release point the weapons will either fall in the harbor or onto the part of New Jersey that's now occupied by the Rox. . . ." He fell silent for a moment as he realized what he'd just said, then laughed. "I guess with you the bomb release point isn't going to matter much, is it?"

"Is my radar profile?"

"Maybe." Modular Man felt dismay filter through his mind. Vidkunssen's voice was apologetic. "They captured some radars when the Rox expanded onto New Jersey soil."

"How many?"

Zappa spoke up. "Three, along with three complete Vulcan 20-mike-mike antiaircraft systems, four 60mm lightweight company mortars, two .50-caliber heavy machine guns, and a pair of Bradley fighting vehicles. Ammunition for the above, plus assorted small arms. Also some bridging equipment, boats, and plastic explosive."

"Plastic explosive?" the android wondered. "What was plastic explosive doing there?"

"There was an engineer company present, trying to figure out a way to get onto the island. The explosive and the bridging equipment was part of their TO&E. When the castle's curtain wall expanded onto the mainland at Liberty State Park, all the soldiers abandoned their gear and ran for it."

"Do the jokers know how to operate any of this equipment?"

"It's safe to assume that there are a few veterans among them. Pehaps"—he looked troubled—"some of those I knew from the Nam. And they captured maintenance and instruction manuals and the like. We know they've been trying to use the radars because we've picked up their signals."

"What if they try and shoot at me with any of these weapons?"

Zappa frowned up at him. "Take them out. Take out anything that's threatening you. I won't tell my people not to defend themselves just because it isn't in somebody's op plan."

"Thank you."

"Our last photos, taken earlier this morning, show the Bradleys, the fifties, and one of the Vulcans dug in behind the Jersey Gate, with the rest moved to the island. But if you can update that picture we'd appreciate it."

"I'll see what I can do." It should be easy enough, the android thought, to use his radar to spot the point of origin of all the bullets coming at him.

"Any questions?" Zappa asked.

Modular Man tried to think. "I suppose not. It seems straightforward enough."

Zappa turned to Vidkunssen. "Give Modular Man the photo file and an interpreter to tell him what he's looking at."

There was a knock on the door, and an aide reported that Chairman of the Joint Chiefs Powell was calling from the Pentagon.

The conference seemed to be over.

"It's insane," Cordelia had flatly said. They were sitting in the clinic cafeteria, sipping tea and contemplating the green and orange institutional walls. Finn had left them and gone about his business. Wyungare and Cordelia had been allowed space to contemplate their plan of action.

"That's the point," said Wyungare. "It's *not* insane. It may well be that a healer can help."

"You ought to hear the rumors out there," said Cordelia. "I think something big is going down, huge trouble. More trouble than an *army* of healers could cope with."

Wyungare shrugged. "No shame in trying, even if failure follows."

Cordelia giggled. "That sounds like a fortune cookie."

"It is. I received it at a Chinese restaurant in Sydney the night before I left for America."

The woman reached across the table and took his hand tightly. "Understand something, *ma chér*. I know how well you can handle yourself. I haven't forgotten Uluru and our little adventure with Murga-Muggai. You're so damned competent. But you're a healer, and I suspect there's going to be a lot of firepower cut loose if you end up trying to contact Bloat out at the Rox."

Wyungare wrapped her hands in his. "I am more than a healer," he said. "I am a warrior and a magician. I've got some resources I can draw upon."

"I know," she said. "But I just don't want you to die."

"And neither do I wish that." He deliberately smiled at her, trying to relax the tension he felt in her muscles and saw in her face. "Trust me to know what I'm doing."

"And do you?" she said unexpectedly.

He was honest. "No." He added, "But I can vamp like crazy."

That made her laugh. The laughter trailed off uncertainly and died. "Is your mission worth death or worse?"

"Worse?"

"I think there are fates even more terrible."

"I think you're right," said Wyungare. "And my answer is yes."

She put his hand to her lips and lightly kissed it.

"Do you want to get some idea why?"

Cordelia looked at him questioningly, then said firmly, "Yes."

"And, if all goes well, would you like to visit your uncle?"

"You mean back at the room?"

"I mean your uncle Jack—not his avatar."

"Yes," Cordelia said. "Please. Yes." Her fingers squeezed like steel.

Jay Ackroyd's office was a fourth-floor walk-up on 42nd Street, half a block off Broadway in a sleazy section of town that matched, Ray reflected, the P.I.'s personality perfectly.

There were a couple of derelicts hanging around the building's entrance, but they took one look at Ray's snarling countenance and decamped without begging for change. Ray stepped over the snoring pile of rags in the foyer and went up the steps grumbling to himself. He didn't mind the fact that there was no elevator, but he wished that the stairway wasn't so damn filthy. He could hardly wait for the splendor of Ackroyd's office.

The frosted glass on the top half of the office door said JAY ACKROYD in a solid, block-letter arc. Spelled out below that in slightly smaller but just as solid letters was DISCREET INVESTIGATIONS.

Ray opened the door, and stopped, surprised.

The reception room was small, but since there was little furniture, it wasn't exactly cramped. An almost bare desk sat next to one wall.

There was a telephone answering machine on its freshly dusted surface. Sitting in a chair behind the desk was a blond, inflated plastic doll with a round, puckered mouth. Peculiar, Ray thought, but then Ackroyd was a peculiar fellow. A plastic blow-up toy seemed to be just his style. The reception room, much to Ray's surprise—and approval—was spotless. There was no dust on the furniture, no cobwebs in the corners, no grime on the one window that looked out on the grimy street below.

Ray crossed the small reception room and knocked lightly on the door separating it from Ackroyd's sanctum. When there was no answer, he pushed it open.

Ackroyd was sitting behind his desk, his feet resting propped on its spotlessly polished surface, reading a magazine. The P.I. was wearing headphones to drown out the city drone coming from the open window that was letting in the warm late-morning breeze.

"Ackroyd," Ray said, but there was no response. He took two steps into the tiny room, which put him right in front of the desk, and rapped twice on the desktop next to Ackroyd's crossed ankles.

The P.I. looked up, startled, almost dropping his magazine. The alarmed look in Ackroyd's eyes vanished, replaced by one of polite questioning. He uncrossed his ankles and took his feet off the desk. "Yes?" he asked in the too-loud voice of those wearing headphones.

Ray grimly tapped his right ear, and Ackroyd nodded. "Oh, right." He took the headphones off. "What can I do for you?"

Ray choked back a snarl. This had to be another one of Ackroyd's asshole flights of comedy. The two had crossed paths more than once. Ray knew that his face had been messed up badly by Mackie Messer, but there was no way that Ackroyd didn't recognize him.

"It's Ray," he said sarcastically. "Or do I have to show you my ID?"

"Um, no," Ackroyd said, putting his magazine down on the desk. It was the latest issue of *Aces*. "How've you been?"

"How've I been?" Ray repeated, outraged. I've been in the hospital for eight goddamn months, you asshole, he wanted to shout. But he knew that Ackroyd was only trying to set him off. "Fine," he said between gritted teeth. "Just fucking fine."

"Great," Ackroyd said without conviction, staring at the ruin of Ray's face. "Why don't you sit down?"

"No thanks," Ray spit out. "This isn't a social call."

"Business?"

"Business." He paused to gather his self-control. "Listen, gumshoe, this isn't my idea, but the man I'm working for thinks he needs you for a job."

"What kind of job?" Ackroyd asked eagerly.

Now he goes into his eager-beaver act, Ray thought. He leaned forward, put his hands palm down on Ackroyd's desktop. Ray was not one to dissemble. He gave it to him straight. "He's leading a covert assault team onto Ellis Island."

"Ellis Island?" Ackroyd repeated. He shook his head. "You must be from Battle. I've already told him that this isn't my kind of thing."

"You don't get it," Ray said coldly. "I'm not asking your opinion. You've been drafted."

"Drafted? I'm too old."

"None of your fucking wisecracks," Ray exploded. "Battle wants you on the team. You're going."

"I'm a private citizen—" Ackroyd protested.

"Look," Ray said, "I'm just a messenger. As far as I'm concerned, we need you like I need a pimple on my ass, but if the man wants you, you're going. And he's connected. Heavily. You decide you don't want to go on this jaunt and we'll have your ticket pulled faster than you can say 'unemployment line.' You got me?"

"You can't be serious," Ackroyd protested. "You can't take away my license."

"Try me," Ray said.

He glared at Ackroyd, who glared back. The standoff might have held for eternity except for the quiet knock on the open door to Ackroyd's inner office.

Both men turned, stared, and barked out, "What?"

It was an old woman in a domestic's outfit. She looked startled. "All right if I clean now, Mr. Ackroyd? I can come back later if you want."

"It's okay, Consuela," Ackroyd said, still glaring. "Ray here was just leaving. He's got to go polish his medals."

"Polish my medals. Christ, you're slipping, Ackroyd." Ray reached into his pocket, pulled out a card, and dropped it onto the P.I.'s desk. "Be at that address, tomorrow, at six A.M. Or be ready to find a real job."

He waited a moment for Ackroyd's rebuttal, but none came. He left the office muttering to himself and shaking his head.

This time the rite was safe from interruption. Troll stood outside the door, arms folded, daring any intern to attempt to enter Jack Robicheaux's room. He looked like his namesake. Nine feet tall and green-skinned, his appearance was not such that even Dr. Bob would try to move him. Which was good, because he had said things that suggested the blood between Troll and Dr. Bob was bad indeed.

In fact, Dr. Bob Mengele had indeed rushed up to the room when he had somehow found out that Wyungare and Cordelia planned to do something unorthodox with Jack Robicheaux.

"Relax, Doctor," Wyungare said. "It's only a trip the little missy and I are taking. I will perform no unauthorized therapy. All right?" Then he had firmly shut the door on Dr. Bob's dumbfounded face.

He repeated the minor ritual he had set up earlier and alone. Wyungare set the single candle on the head of the bedtable. He changed into his waist-cloth.

"Should I undress?" said Cordelia.

"It would just distract me," said Wyungare. "Actually, you can wear whatever will make you the most comfortable."

Cordelia took off her shoes.

Wyungare hunkered over the skin drum and began to tap out a steady rhythm.

"What do I do?" said Cordelia, hovering close to him.

"Listen to the drum. Watch the candle. Concentrate on your uncle. Remember him as you love him."

Cordelia looked uncertain as she stared at the wavering candle flame. "*Le bon temps . . .*" she whispered.

And then, somewhere in the middle of what she was saying to herself, both Wyungare and she were somewhere else. She stared around them both at the rough stone pillars reaching toward a slate sky.

"Where are we? Are we in Jack's head?"

"We are in the middle world," said Wyungare. "This time we have to climb. Good healthy exercise."

"Wonderful," Cordelia muttered. "I wish I could have dreamed myself a fitter body."

"I think it's plenty fit enough," said her lover.

Cordelia smiled. "You're sweet."

The pair clambered up an increasingly steep slope.

"Can't you dream us a giant eagle to act as a magic elevator and get us up the mountainside?"

Whatever he was about to answer was lost as the reality fabric tore across like ripping silk. The noise echoed in her head, traveled in directly to the core of her bones, started to feel as though someone were scraping the marrow out with a dull metal blade. Cordelia saw something that looked like the squiggle lines when a TV's not on cable and the reception keeps going in and out.

She squinted, concentrated. The picture got a little better, but not much. A buzz-saw whine assaulted her ears and started to cut an entry directly into her brain.

Wyungare knew what she was feeling and thinking. He took her hand. "Come on," he said.

"What is it?" Her voice rose a little. "What's going on?"

"It's like interference," he said. "The signal's scrambling."

She stumbled on the path, her ankle turning as her foot came down on a stone she had somehow not seen. She involuntarily whimpered with the abrupt pain.

"Are you hurt?"

"No!" she said. "Just tripped. Clumsy."

The skies cleared. The metallic whine diminished and then dissipated.

"Better than it sometimes is," said Wyungare. "Let's make time, just in case it returns."

"It?"

"Him," said Wyungare. "He. The boy."

"I don't like what he does." Cordelia still limped.

"This is a minor manifestation."

"What's major?"

"I don't think you truly wish to know," said Wyungare.

"Don't be so sure. Tell me."

They had somehow climbed much farther than the apparent elapsed time could allow for. The two of them were close to the top of the climb. More trees, soft green shade, lush grass awaited as they reached the summit.

"It's paradise," said Cordelia. Their surroundings flickered, somehow rearranged themselves, settled into permanence. Cordelia and Wyungare walked under a thick canopy of twisted tree branches. They skirted a brackish pool. Something surfaced in the center of the water, then went down as fast as it had come up.

The air stifled. It was hot and filled with moisture. Heavy. Wyungare felt like he was trying to breathe underwater without any gear.

"This is Louisiana," said Cordelia, apparently revising her first judgment. "It feels like our parish down south."

"I wouldn't be surprised," said Wyungare, "considering the nature of our host."

They crossed through more thick trees and came upon the sun-grayed frame house. "We used to live here," Cordelia said wonderingly. "Uncle Jack's folks had it before us." She reached out, almost fearfully, and touched her fingertips to the mold-burred wood.

Wyungare listened attentively to something. "Around the corner," he said. "Someone's waiting for us."

They rounded the end of the house. Wyungare saw what he had encountered on the previous trip. He glanced at Cordelia. The young woman obviously was sharing the same construction.

Ahead of them, the young boy struggled weakly with the staked-down screen door pressed tightly over him.

"Move it," Cordelia said, reaching toward the door. "We need to free him."

"Don't be too hasty," said Wyungare. But Cordelia had already bent to one of the steel spikes and had started to prise it loose from the soft earth.

"Well? Don't just stand there," said Cordelia, waving the spike triumphantly. "Dig in. There's plenty for everyone."

Indeed there was. Wyungare pushed and pulled a spike until the head was covered with blood from the Aborigine's abraded fingertips. But finally the spikes were all removed, and together, the pair pulled the screen door loose.

The young boy—perhaps eight—glanced up at them. His eyes were dark and very serious. He shook his head and tried to sit up. At first his arms would not support him. He took a deep breath and started over. Finally he was upright. He toed the somewhat battered screen door.

"Uncle . . . Jack?" said Cordelia. "Are you okay? I mean, is there anything we can get for you?"

The very young Jack Robicheaux said nothing. He cast his vision down, looked up at them from beneath unkempt curly hair.

"Do you recognize me?"

He apparently did not.

"Will you come with us?" said Wyungare.

The boy stared at him for a long time. Then, hesitantly, he reached toward the Aborigine's hand.

But he still said nothing.

Cordelia stared down at him, a trace of tears moistening the skin beneath her eyes.

And that's when the chain-saw howl started to disembowel the world.

Modular Man caught occasional glimpses of the gray towers of the Rox as he flashed above the sweating streets of Jersey City. He increased speed, popped up above street level at the last second as the curtain wall and the bastions of the Jersey Gate came up like an anvil trying to squash him. . . . He soared up above the bastion and emptied one of his two bags of leaflets at the top of his climb. The wind scattered them like a bomb burst as the android dropped down over Liberty Park, then flew at wavetop level for the Mad Ludwig spires of the Rox.

The Bradley fighting vehicles were still in place, he noted. So was the Vulcan. He had observed the barrel of one of the fifties thrust from a cross-shaped slit on the northernmost tower of the Jersey Gate bastion. . . .

A mile-long bridge arched between a huge gatehouse and the mainland. Armored knights, riding flying fish, floated overhead as a kind of combat air patrol. Modular Man crossed under the bridge to help conceal his approach and then popped up again.

A few jokers gaped upward at him, but the rest seemed unaware of his presence. The fish-knights seemed now to be observing him, and they were turning their steeds into slow turns. The android opened his second pack of leaflets.

"I come in peace!" he yelled, and flung a handful of leaflets to the wind. "I'm carrying a message!"

No one seemed to be listening.

Bloat was pissed.

"Damn it, can't anyone shoot him down?" he raged at Kafka. "I want him in little tiny pieces, do you hear me!"

The appearance of Modular Man in the sky above the Rox and the rain of leaflets he'd released had stirred Bloat's kingdom like a stick poked into a mound of fire ants. The mindvoices buzzed with it . . .

. . . *can't be jumped. It ain't no ace, just a machine . . .*

. . . *fucking Bloat can't keep Modular Man out . . .*

. . . *what if those were goddamn bombs and not just pieces of paper? We'd be dead every last one of us . . .*

. . . *Shit, I'm calling that damn number . . .*

Bloat could see Modular Man through the walls of the castle, leaflets fluttering in his wake.

"Governor, we've tried everything. The Vulcans can't seem to track him. He's too fast and too well armored for small-arms fire." Kafka was shaking with fury. His chitinous plates rattled like crockery in an earthquake. Around the room, Bloat's joker guards were clutching automatic weapons at ready, nervous. "Every minute he's here he does more harm to the morale of the Rox than a dozen rumors about the coming attack."

"I know that. I'm *hearing* it, believe me." Bloat watched Modular Man appear over a pair of delicate minarets and then glide behind the thorny spires of the transformed hospital. He glared, listening again to the Rox and knowing that Kafka was right. "Must I always do everything myself?" he sighed. "All right. *I'll* take care of him."

He hoped that he could.

One of the armored knights sped at Modular Man couching a swordfish as a lance. The android added a little lateral impulse, sidestepped the thrust, and stuck a leaflet on the end of the lance as the knight passed by. A gust of foul air, like a million dead fish, followed in the fish-man's wake.

"Don't shoot!" he yelled as a Vulcan mounted on the keep began to track toward him. "I'm not attacking!" He flung more leaflets to the breeze.

The 60mm mortars, he observed, were emplaced inside the inner bailey.

There was a rush of flame and a hissing noise as a shoulder-fired antiaircraft rocket lanced upward from the ground.

"*Don't shoot!*" Modular Man screamed. He added another burst of lateral energy and sidestepped the rocket. The rocket weaved for a moment, then reacquired one of the fish-men and blew it out of the sky in a surprisingly violent burst of smoke and flame.

"*Now look what you've done!*" The Vulcan seemed to be getting a bead on him. Modular Man swung down into the outer bailey, where the 20mms couldn't track, and dumped another bunch of leaflets.

The fish-men began diving on him in a complex pattern that required a lot of twisting flight before he could avoid them. Bursts of small-arms fire crackled out. One of them splashed another fish-man. More fish-men appeared overhead, quite literally out of nowhere. The defenses seemed to be getting much better coordinated. Nobody seemed to be reading the leaflets.

Maybe it was time to go.

Bloat closed his eyes. He brought back the image of Bosch's *Temptation of St. Anthony*, of the writhing, martial deformities that had been on the now-destroyed panels of the triptych, and he reached into that part of him where he dreamed. He opened his eyes again, looking out from the transparent walls to the sky, searching for Modular Man. He found him, a speck racing across the sky, moving closer to the castle and still releasing his propaganda.

"I have you," Bloat whispered.

He brought them forth.

They appeared in the air alongside Modular Man: a squadron of mermen soldiers riding flying fishes. What the android did then startled Bloat. Modular Man performed an astonishing bank and dive, turning acrobatically left and below. The move would have been impossible for a human—the G-forces must have been incredible. The turn would have ripped the wings from a plane.

Bloat, cursing and tracking Modular Man with his eyes, made his dream creatures dart after the android. For several seconds there was a wild aerial dogfight, then Modular Man came to a sudden halt like someone had turned off a motion picture projector; Bloat's gaze went helplessly past for a second, then back. Laser fire raked Bloat's creatures. Several of the fish-mounted knights plummeted to the earth, vanishing before they hit. Then Modular Man streaked off again, scattering more leaflets.

"Damn it," Bloat said. "If I can't catch him, I'll just *ram* the bastard."

Bloat materialized another merman directly in front of Modular Man. The android was moving far too fast to evade. From the Great Hall, they could all see the tremendous midair collision. Modular Man tumbled and fell end over end, slamming into one of the stone walls of the towers in a cascade of granite chips. The android caromed out of sight; it didn't appear that it was still functioning.

Kafka let out a shout. All around the Great Hall, jokers cheered. The mindvoices of the Rox cried in victory. Bloat grinned.

"We've won another skirmish," he exulted. "You see, Kafka? They can't touch us. They ain't *ever* going to touch us."

The android dived down into the inner bailey. The last of the leaflets trailed behind him. He shot across the courtyard, leaving baffled fish-knights in his wake, then climbed again.

One of the fish-men materialized out of thin air right in front of him. Modular Man was going 150 miles per hour and there was no way to avoid a collision.

There was an alloy-twisting crash. Jarred circuits staggered. The knight, the fish, and the android tumbled. The knight's armor was crushed; the limp body vanished in a puff of brimstone before it hit the pavement.

Modular Man slammed into the castle wall, but managed to avoid sliding to the pavement below. Stunned circuits were bypassed or came back on line. The world swayed, then stabilized. Modular Man took off again, popped over the outer wall, then dropped to wavetop level again.

Three fingers on his right hand were twisted into spiral ruin. It was clearly time to leave.

He had accelerated to over 600 miles per hour by the time he reached Manhattan.

He'd talk to Travnicek again.

If he showed Travnicek that he was damaged, perhaps Travnicek would order him to stay out of trouble.

A slim hope, perhaps, but the only one he had.

"I got a real bad feeling about this," Molly Bolt said. She was a slender girl, shaggy hair streaked in a half-dozen colors, inverted cross dangling from one ear.

The bodysnatcher leaned against the back wall, sucking absent-mindedly on a bloody knuckle. Molly had gathered forty jumpers in the onion dome atop the Red Tower. There were 116 jumpers on the Rox the last time anyone had counted, but these were ones who mattered.

Juggler held up one of the leaflets that Modular Man had been handing out. 1-800-I-GIVE-UP. "Amnesty," he read. "It says they'll give us amnesty." He really could juggle pretty good, at least when he was wearing his own body. Other than that, he was a useless little weasel, as far the bodysnatcher was concerned.

"How do we know it's true?" Suzy Creamcheese asked nervously. She was a nervous little fifteen-year-old, no more than five feet tall, but the boys loved her. For two good reasons, at least forty inches of them, barely restrained now in a narrow halter top, fat nipples pushing against the fabric.

"We don't know it's true," Molly told her bluntly. "This is the Combine. The Combine will fuck you every time."

The Combine. That was K. C. Strange talk. She got it out of some book she read. K. C. Strange had been one of the first jumpers. She was dead now. So many dead or gone: David, Blaise, even Prime, who'd created them all. That was Zelda's fault. Zelda had been Prime's bodyguard. It had been her job to keep him safe, and she'd fucked it. Zelda had deserved to die.

With Prime dead and buried, there would be no new jumpers. They were the last.

"They won't dare attack the Rox again," Porker said. He'd squealed like a pig when Prime had fucked him up the ass. "Not after last time. It's just a bluff."

"Maybe," Molly Bolt said. "Maybe not."

"So what if it isn't?" Alvin the Chipmunk said, smiling. "So we'll do it to them again. Fun and games." Alvin had killed both his parents, slitting their throats with his father's straight razor while they slept. Blaise had read about him in the paper and decided Alvin was his kind of guy. They'd sprung him, brought him to the Rox, and Prime had done the rest.

"It's not like last time," Juggler insisted. He rattled the paper. "Amnesty . . . maybe we ought to . . . ."

"Send them home in little pieces," Alvin said, smiling.

"Bloat's not going anywhere," Blueboy said. He'd put on some pants and buttoned up the cop shirt. A half-dozen badges were pinned to his chest, polished until they were as shiny as his mirrorshades. A captain's hat, a size too large, was tilted at a rakish angle across his brow. "So everything's copacetic."

"If you trust Bloat," said Captain Chaos, an anorexic fourteen-year-old with a crazy glint in her eyes.

"We're on the same side," Porker said.

"He's a *joker*," the Iceman pointed out.

"Joker poker," echoed Captain Chaos. "Freak city express."

Juggler glanced behind him nervously. "Don't talk like that," he whispered. "He might be listening."

"Of course he's listening," Molly Bolt said. "He can't *help* but listen. He hears what we *think*, he doesn't give a fuck what we *say*." She looked around the room. "Zelda, what do you think?"

The bodysnatcher moved away from the wall. Everyone stopped talking. She knew they were all afraid of her. They thought she'd gone as psycho as Blaise. The bodysnatcher didn't care.

"Zelda's dead," she said loudly. "A lot of you are going to be dead too before this is over."

Suzy Creamcheese looked like she was going to cry. Juggler started reading his paper again, all about amnesty.

"Maybe not," a new voice said. "Bloat wants volunteers."

Patchwork stood in the door to the long hall. She was brown-haired, slender, freckled. Older than most of the jumpers, twenty at least, the same age Zelda had been before the aces had gotten to her.

Patchwork wasn't a jumper, and she wasn't really a joker either, but both factions on the Rox seemed to trust her.

"Volunteers for what?" Molly Bolt asked her.

Patchwork walked toward her, boots ringing on the stone floor. "To even the odds. He figures, the robot scoped us out, maybe we should do a little recon of our own."

"I'll go," the bodysnatcher said. She'd been itching to get back to Manhattan. And of course it had to be jumpers. Bloat's freaks were too conspicuous for this kind of work.

"Okay," Molly Bolt said. "I'm with you." She looked around the room. "Vanilla, Blueboy, you'll come too. Four ought to be enough."

"Here," Patchwork said, "I've got something for you." She dug her fingers into her eye. There was a soft squelchy sound, a trickle of blood, and the eyeball popped out of the socket. Patchwork handed it to Molly Bolt. Then she popped out the other eye, ripped off her left ear, and handed those across as well. "Better put a move on it," she said. "Charon is waiting, and you know how surly he gets."

FRIDAY
AFTERNOON

September 21, 1990

USING A FEW OF the specialized tools that Travnicek had used to create him, working slowly and with great care, Modular Man managed to bend his fingers back into a shape that would work. But they didn't work as well as they had, and the proportions were slightly different—just a little deformed. At least the plastic skin covering them hadn't torn: the distortion wasn't as noticeable as it would have been if the structural metal were peeking through.

Modular Man had been attending Columbia University for two semesters now, taking courses in advanced physics, metallurgy, and chemistry. He had been hoping to learn ways of repairing himself. He got his tuition free in return for allowing the professors to examine him.

He had learned a lot—he could memorize the textbooks in a single sitting—but he hadn't learned much that could help him. Travnicek was a wild card genius, and no one could duplicate his work.

And Modular Man himself, despite all the facts he memorized, didn't seem able to duplicate the work either. It appeared that the android wasn't very creative.

He was trying to rewrite his programming slightly, hoping it would improve his creativity. He hadn't had much luck with that either.

Travnicek had told him to fix himself, then wait. Having finished his repair job, Modular Man went to Travnicek's room and waited.

He was used to waiting. Usually, to help time pass, he called up pleasant memories from his past and relived them in great detail.

This time he watched as Travnicek watched some of his least pleasant memories on his television. Travnicek was playing the recordings from the android's visit to the Rox. He watched both the video portion and the radar image.

The old Travnicek hadn't known how to read the radar images, or if he did, simply wasn't interested. This one did. Maybe it was similar to one of the ways in which he now apprehended the universe.

Travnicek came to the part of the recording where the merman appeared out of the air in front of the android. Stray alarm programs flickered through the android's circuits at the sight. Travnicek slowed the recording, ran it through the collision, then reversed it. He halted it at the instant in which the merman appeared.

"Toaster," he said. "Do you have the time at which this happened?"

"11:16:31:14 Eastern Daylight Time," the android said.

"Hah." One of Travnicek's trumpet-flowers gave an unpleasant laugh from the base of his featureless head. "I *remember* this happening then," he said. "I remember the *feeling* of that thing coming into being. I sensed it on a southwesterly bearing from the balcony. It was . . . extraordinary." Another nasty laugh. "Very pleasurable. And then only a few seconds later it just came to bits. Annihilated. And *that* didn't feel so bad either. I've been feeling things like that ever since that castle got built. And the castle itself—" Two of his sense organs, facing Modular Man, came erect. The android had the feeling they were peering at him. "That feeling was *immense*. That must be why God creates things. It feels so good." Another laugh. "And why He destroys."

Travnicek rose from the bed and turned off the video and recorder. "Let's go," he said.

"Where?" the android asked.

Travnicek headed out of the room. "The Rox," he said. "We're joining them. I want to *feel* the place firsthand."

"Sir." The android followed, his self-preservation programming shattering hopelessly against the overriding hardwired command to obey his creator. "Sir. Do you think that's wise?"

"Fuck you, Toaster." Walking rapidly through the living room. "*I'll* decide what's wise around here."

"Sir. They think I'm an enemy. They'll probably open fire the second they see me. And if I'm carrying you, you'll be in danger. You could be . . ." One of those thoughts he wasn't allowed to think shot through his circuits, then slammed to a halt against hardwired circuits. "You could be killed," he said.

"We'll do some fast talking."

"Sir. Ellis Island is coming under heavy assault if they don't surrender. If I'm damaged, you'll never get off. I don't think this is . . ."

"If you're damaged, I'll fix you." Breezily. "Do as I say."

There was no point, the android knew, in reminding Travnicek that he'd lost his abilities to repair his creation. Travnicek was obstinate in claiming that his second dose of the wild card had enhanced rather than diminished his capabilities.

"And you've got that Zapper's battle plan," Travnicek added. "Bloat would give a lot for that, I betcha."

"Zappa." Hopelessly.

Travnicek stepped onto the balcony and raised his blue-skinned arms to the sun. "It's a good day for flying," he said.

◆

Sometimes it pays to have a private office, however small. This was one of those times.

Ray sat down at his desk and took out the can of Glade—natural pine scent—that he kept in the upper right-hand drawer of his desk. He squirted the air, which was still contaminated by the smell of cigar smoke, burned flesh, and Bobby Joe Puckett. He wished the office had a window, but opening it would only have let in equally disgusting city odors. The air freshener smelled as much like real pine trees as anything from a test tube could, but it was hardly adequate.

He put the can away and flipped on his computer, asking it to search for the names "Bobby Joe Puckett" and "George G. Battle" among various law agency and newspaper files. He keyed in half a dozen data bases, and then sat back to wait, memories of Puckett's handshake rising unbidden in his mind.

If there was one thing Ray despised it was bullies. Puckett, Ray was sure, fit that category big time. He was begging for payback. Ray was just playing the opening sequences of such a confrontation in his mind when a line of words crawling across his computer screen brought him back to the here and now.

It was, he saw, the info he'd requested on Puckett. And it wasn't good. Reading it first brought a sense of disbelief, then a frisson of fear. Something was wrong here. Definitely wrong.

FBI records listed a Bobby Joe Puckett born June 5, 1959, in Cross Plains, Texas. He was arrested for car theft at fourteen. The case was dropped due to lack of evidence, but he'd been before the judge three more times in the next two years for car theft, again, and B and E. He spent seven months in a juvvie home, and three weeks after being released was arrested for armed robbery and assault with a deadly weapon for pistol-whipping a 7-Eleven clerk. He'd spent the next three years in jail.

All of this was unremarkable and wouldn't have deserved inclusion in a national data bank, except that it provided the backdrop for the next stage of Puckett's career. He apparently drifted through the early 1980s, occasionally in trouble for more small-time stuff, then the highlight of his life of crime came down in 1987.

Ray clenched his misshapen jaw as he read the details of a liquor-store robbery gone wrong. This time Puckett killed the clerk instead of only scarring her for life. The killing snapped something in Puckett and he took a deer rifle and .45 Magnum handgun to the top of a tower at the University of Texas in Austin and spent an afternoon sniping at passersby. He got twenty-six students and cops before the police charged his stronghold. To avoid capture he put his Magnum in his mouth and blew away the right side of his face. Shot himself as dead as any of his victims.

Only Puckett wasn't dead. Ray had shaken hands with him just a few hours before and he could attest to the strength of the man's grip. But, with a chill running down his spine, Ray remembered the odd, misshapen silhouette of the man's face under his all-enveloping hood. Given the state of his own face, Ray hadn't thought much about it then. But now . . .

And the smell . . .

His file said Puckett was dead. Maybe, Ray thought, Puckett hadn't really killed himself. Maybe, for some reason, he'd been brought into government service and the suicide story was leaked as cover. Ray could see why the government would want to recruit him. He was an ace, after all. But was he?

Ray stopped and reread the file. There was no indication that Puckett was anything other than another petty criminal whose stupidity had driven him to a horrible death.

But Ray had felt Puckett's grip. Maybe he hadn't been an ace before his purported death but he sure was one now. He'd been a scumbag then, and was one now. Except now he was a scumbag for the government.

And speaking of government scumbags, the file on Battle was coming on-line.

Ray studied it intently, but there were no hints of the bizarre like those that abounded in Puckett's story.

Battle came from a prosperous family. He was now a lawyer, but he'd started out in the army. He'd been too young for World War II, but he hadn't served active duty in Korea or Vietnam, either.

After graduating from law school, Battle had gone into government service rather than private practice. He started out in the FBI, but stayed there only into the early 1960s when he disappeared into a haze of agencies, committees, and staff positions that was enough to give a headache to anyone who tried to sort it all out. There was one agency that Ray was familiar with. Battle had been special counsel to CREEP—the Committee to Re-elect the President—when Nixon was running for his second term. After that there seemed to be a gap in his career. His next official posting was in the middle 1970s, and he'd also served on both of Reagan's election campaigns. Currently he was attached to something called the Special Executive Task Force headed by someone named Phillip Baron von Herzenhagen, which sounded like a Nazi name if anything did. The Task Force was headed by Dan Quayle.

Great, Ray thought. Just fucking great. It looked like wheels within wheels time. He thought about it for a second and then dumped the files. He went throught his requests meticulously making sure that no trace of them survived in the computer system.

Ray usually didn't worry about covering his ass, but very definitely something whacko was going on here. And he had put himself right in the middle of it.

He sat at his desk for a moment, thinking. He'd never paid too much attention to office-politics bullshit. His job had been guarding bodies and kicking ass, and he'd been good at it too, until the business with Hartmann.

The senator's face suddenly filled Ray's mind and he felt a flash of anger. All those years he'd spent with the bastard, and then the prick had never even come to see him in the hospital when he'd literally had his guts spilled trying to keep Messer from him.

Ray'd done everything he could for the senator, even turning his face the other way when the man had stepped out on his wife all those times, even acting as his personal messenger boy when the man wanted someone summoned to his presence. And then, the first time he failed him, Hartmann shut him off, just like that.

Ray still felt a sense of loss, a void that ached to be filled by the simple touch of Hartmann's hand on his shoulder. But he hadn't seen Hartmann since the day he'd been carried out on a stretcher from the Atlanta Convention Center trying to stuff his guts back into his stomach cavity. He'd heard nothing from the senator, no word, no visit, not even a lousy phone call or a stupid card.

Ray caught himself, realizing he was standing on the brink of a very treacherous abyss, and pulled himself back with great effort.

That was then, he thought. This is now. He had Battle to worry about, and their upcoming mission. He looked at his wristwatch. He just had time to head for the second place on the list before he was due to meet with Battle.

It was someplace in Chinatown. Looked like an apartment address, belonging to a guy by the name of Ben Choy.

Modular Man dived out of the sun with Travnicek in his arms. Wind whipped at Travnicek's organ lei, and the organs folded in on themselves. The jokers at their posts down below didn't see him. The lacy spires of the Rox waited ahead.

The android crossed over the outer wall. Travnicek suddenly clutched at him. "Wait!" he screamed. "Stop! Go back!" The words came from several trumpet-flowers at once with a curious harmony effect.

Relief flooded through the android. He began to slow. He'd head back upsun and get away before anyone noticed him.

"No," Travnicek said. "No, hold on here." The panic faded from his voice. "Keep going."

The android kept slowing. "Are you sure?"

"Yah. Just felt a little frightened there for a second. But I'm okay now."

Just wait, the android thought, till the fish-things come at you with lances.

But in that he was disappointed.

They were back in Jack Robicheaux's clinic room. Cordelia's nails were buried in Wyungare's upper arm nearly to the point of drawing blood.

"Mon dieu," she said shakily, "what happened?"

The Aborigine turned toward her and gently disengaged her fingers. He enfolded her into his arms. Just above her head, he said, "That was only a taste of the madness."

She tilted her head back so she could look at him. "Whose madness? Bloat?"

"At one time, I would have said yes. Now . . ." He shook his head. "There is a contagion, and it is spreading like a physical disease, except this one's not—it's psychic."

The black cat whined from beside Jack's bed. Cordelia suddenly shook her head violently. "Jack! The boy—where is he?" She stared about the room.

"Calm yourself," said Wyungare, stroking her hair. "He's still inside there." He gestured with his chin toward the bed where the great reptile wheezed ponderously and the massaging rollers moved endlessly up and down the mottled body. "We got him out of his initial captivity, but he is still there in the upper world. I don't think there's a way to manifest him back here in this physical reality."

Cordelia looked stricken. Her dark eyes started to glisten. She pulled free of Wyungare's hands and moved toward the bed, bending down and taking hold of the black cat's head with her fingers. The cat meowed deep in his throat. "Can't we do *something*?"

"We can go back," said the man. "But we must first have a council. We need to sort things out."

"The madness," said Cordelia, not yet turning to look back. "What did you mean by that?"

"The boy Bloat is powerful. On the psychic plane, in the dreamtime, whatever you want to call it, his power has obeyed no rules, confined itself to no boundaries."

Cordelia nodded silently.

"There's something you have to understand," said Wyungare. "In this world there are many, many cultures who have a greater appreciation of these things than do most of the Europeans. With my people, the dreamtime is not just a part of reality, it *is* reality." The man hesitated. "Imagine a group of villagers spending most of their lives living in a delicate, balanced environment like a grove of trees and flowers, with a crystalline stream running past their homes. Imagine that one day, without warning, an enormous steel bulldozer bursts through the brush and cuts a swath of destruction through all the green things and through the houses. It pushes all manner of debris into the stream. The shock to the people who live here is incalculable. They can no longer reach what they know is their reality. Some are maddened. Some are hurt in lesser ways. But no one is left unaffected."

Cordelia continued unconsciously stroking the cat, her face averted toward Wyungare. "Bloat is doing all that?"

Wyungare nodded soberly. "He is not simply giving scattered sleepers nightmares. He's destroying them—he's blasting their realities."

"Whole peoples?" Cordelia whispered.

"He has to be stopped. If he can be healed, then that will happen. If not . . ." Wyungare spread his hands in a universal gesture.

"You can do this?"

The Aborigine chewed his lip. "Perhaps. I have some allies. There is a Peruvian holy man named Viracocha. I hope to draw aid from Buddy Holley here in your country. There are others. It is possible I—we—can help the boy."

"And heal the dreamtime," said Cordelia. The cat had started to relax, butting his black snout into her hand.

Wyungare nodded. "To attempt this, I need to meet with the boy in person."

"You can't just, uh, call him up on the psychic telephone, you know, find him there in the dreamtime?"

"Remember the interference," said Wyungare. "It's something like sunspots and radio broadcasts. I need to be close to him physically."

"That won't be easy. There's a wall. CNN's been carrying it all morning. You can't get through."

"It's fundamentally a psychic barrier," said Wyungare. "I've got a plan I've stolen from Homer. It worked for the noble Odysseus; I think it will work for me. But I'm going to need your uncle."

Cordelia stood up, shocked. "You're going to manifest him in this world?"

Wyungare shook his head violently. "No! I thought of this while we were inside him, within the dreamtime. For this, I need him in his alligator form. I must get him to the water."

Cordelia stared, at first as though her lover were utterly demented, and then as a grin started to quirk around the corners of her mouth. She began to giggle, then to laugh outright. "You're crazy too," she said. "I saw that movie. Circe's island. The hero was tied to the mast, and the crew put wax in their ears." She shook her head and wiped away tears.

"Just like the movie," said Wyungare. "Jack won't need wax in his ears."

"Good!" said Cordelia. "I wouldn't relish trying to put it there. How are we going to get him to the bay?"

Wyungare shrugged. "Walk him. Wake him up and point him in the right direction. Alligators can move rather fast when they wish to."

Cordelia giggled again, a little hysterically. "How are you going to steer him, dangle a poodle in front of his snout?"

The Aborigine shook his head quite seriously. "Just as I contacted his human self, I can do the same with his reptile brain." He looked down. The black cat had ambled over in front of the man and sat down on his haunches. He looked up expectantly at Wyungare. "Our friend here will help, I think. He has a bit of a bond with your uncle."

"Rub-a-dub-dub," said Cordelia, cracking up again. "Three men in a tub. No, one man, a gator, and a pussycat. But no owl . . ."

"An owl would be handy," said Wyungare. "But first we must get the alligator to the shore."

"I think not," said a new voice. Both Wyungare and Cordelia turned. The black cat hissed and showed his claws, the fur rising up along his tail.

Dr. Bob stepped all the way into the room. He wasn't smiling. "Rounds bring me back every once in a while," he said, "and sometimes my timing seems to work out." He smiled again, but managed to make the expression look disapproving in the extreme.

"You might knock," said Cordelia.

"This is a hospital," said Dr. Bob. "I am a physician. Normal rules are, shall we say, a bit suspended."

"What happened to Troll?" Cordelia looked puzzled, realizing that the head of security should have kept Dr. Bob out.

"There was a code zero," said the doctor. "Our *lumpen* green friend's services were required in matters of more urgency."

"Granted," said Wyungare. "Could you excuse us, please?"

"You mean, would I leave?" The doctor shook his head. "Under the circumstances, assuming I heard correctly, that would seem to be unadvisable."

The three of them stared at each other.

"We seem to be in a bit of stalemate," said Wyungare finally. He smiled humorlessly. "Time is wasting. I suspect I could settle this matter quickly by taking up my nullanulla and cracking your skull smartly, Dr. Mengele." The physician seemed to take an unconscious step back. "But we should probably pursue a more civilized course."

"You want *me* to hit him?" said Cordelia.

Wyungare shook his head. "Channels. To ensure peace and good karma, as you say here, I think we shall consult the good doctor's superior. Let's go."

"Fine," said Dr. Bob. "Let's."

On the physician's way out the door, the black cat hissed and lightly struck with his forepaw. The claws ripped through Dr. Bob's expensive slacks and the man recoiled.

He bent and probed his ankle with a forefinger. "I do believe," he said mildly, "our friend drew blood."

They traipsed down a floor to Dr. Finn's disarranged office. There was no one there. Cordelia picked up a phone and had the doctor paged. In about thirty seconds, an answer came back.

"Up," said Cordelia. She gestured with her index finger. Her look at Dr. Bob suggested a wish to use a very different digit.

In the elevator, the woman punched the button marked ROOF. Wyungare looked questioningly at her.

"I should have thought," said Dr. Bob, "it's our administrator's exercise hour."

"What about the code zero?" said Cordelia. "Don't those emergencies draw on everyone?"

"Perhaps," said Dr. Bob, "I exaggerated a bit."

"Perhaps," said Wyungare, "you lied altogether."

"Perhaps."

The car chimed, the door drew back, and the three stepped out. They walked through an open doorway and found an exercise track laid out crudely on the clinic roof. Finn loped around the nearest turn and drew up, chuffing loudly, in front of them. The doctor was holding a stopwatch.

"Not bad," he said. "Not Derby quality, but pretty good for a man of my age." Finn grinned and snorted. He picked up a white towel from the graveled roof and wiped at the profuse sweat. "Frankly, I just don't give a damn about the Triple Crown anymore." He glanced at the three. "Let me guess. Problems?"

Dr. Bob explained the problems.

Then Wyungare and Cordelia told their side of it.

Finn stood silently, taking it all in. At the end, Finn uttered a sigh. He said, "Obviously we cannot lightly discharge a patient in Mr. Robicheaux's condition."

Dr. Bob nodded vigorously and smirked.

"He is in no condition to leave the clinic without a thorough set of evaluations," added Finn.

"Absolutely," said Dr. Bob.

"Perhaps you can now excuse us," said Finn to Dr. Bob, "while I explain certain facts of medical life to our guests."

Dr. Bob frowned, looking quickly at his superior. Then he offered his unctuous smile and nodded. As he turned to leave, he winked at Cordelia. The young woman balled her fists, but said and did nothing.

After the elevator door had sucked shut after Dr. Bob, Finn cleared his throat. "Listen up, you two. I've got a clinic to run and I need the confidence of my staff. But I am not blind. I'll say this just once. Give it a rest for a time, perhaps an hour. *Exactly* an hour. I will make sure Dr. Bob Mengele is occupied. It will be up to you two to finesse the smuggling of a fourteen-foot alligator from his room. I don't know anything about this."

Wyungare said gravely, "We shall do our best."

Cordelia said, "We'll have to wake him up."

"It can be done," said Finn. "Remember something: I can't give you permission. But I can give you one shot at the gold ring." He smiled.

"Good," said Cordelia. "I wasn't looking forward to buying every Mylar helium ballon in the gift shop, tying them on, and floating him out like a zeppelin."

Even Wyungare cracked a smile.

It all went very smoothly. Modular Man didn't know whether to be pleased by that or not.

He hadn't known that Bloat could read the minds of people inside his domain. Bloat had read Travnicek as soon as Modular Man had carried him across the outer wall—read his intentions, and called off the castle's defenders.

"I want some things," Travnicek said. He stood, blue-skinned and featureless, below the vast creature that was Bloat, pale body pulsing beneath the broken arm and torch of the Statue of Liberty. Armored mermen stood guard, lances at rest. The giant carp on which they rode were propped on the floor on splayed fins. Marble columns rose on high.

"I want a place of my own," Travnicek said. "A tower, so I can get up and down when I want, arranged to my specifications. You can build it the way I want, yah?"

"Just visualize it," Bloat said, "and I'll try to put it somewhere." His voice was high-pitched and adolescent.

Travnicek turned to Modular Man. "This is the damn life, right?" he said. "I think it, and White, Fat, and Ugly here builds it."

A joker named Kafka made an angry, chittering sound, but Bloat only giggled.

"You don't care what people think, do you?" he asked.

Travnicek's voice was defiant. "Why should I?"

Bloat looked down on him. There was a touch of sadness in his tone. "Welcome to the Rox," he said, "I think you'll fit right in."

"Of course I have a plan," said Wyungare. "Do you think I'm bluffing?"

Cordelia raised her eyes ceilingward. They stood again in room 228, Jack's room. "Give me patience, Lord."

The black cat moved restlessly about their feet, stalking fluidly between their legs in a slalom pattern.

"I need to borrow your Walkman," said the Aborigine. "Please."

Cordelia looked curious, but extracted the small black box from her handbag. "You want some tunes to go with it?"

"I have my own, thank you." He dug into his dilly bag and took out a tape cassette.

"So what are you going to do?"

"I'll take a quick journey into your uncle's reptile mind and attempt to establish some communication. This will be quick and dirty, no time for ceremony."

"You're not going to strip?"

He shook his head. "No time."

"Good," said Troll. "Aesthetics are important here."

Cordelia jerked around. "None of you ever knocks."

"Sorry. I'm used to just barging in. Besides, as I gather your Australian friend was saying, we don't have a lot of time for social niceties. Dr. Finn really cannot afford to be seen helping you. I can."

"So what's the tape?" said Cordelia as Wyungare clicked it into the Walkman.

He adjusted the ear-buds and handed her the box.

"Gene Krupa? Cool. Not exactly traditional," she said.

"I'm not going to bother with my own drumming," said Wyungare. "I need what's called a sonic driver. This will do admirably. I find Mr. Krupa's approach to rhythm quite impressive."

"I'll go ahead and disconnect the sleep probes," said Troll. "The moment the voltage stops going into the alligator's brain, he should start to wake up." He set the medical case down on a chair. "I've got some stimulants that should help accelerate the process."

"You know how to do all this?" Cordelia shook her head. "Gator uppers."

"Precisely." Troll hesitated. "Hang around this place long enough and you either have to learn something or go bug-fuck. I sure don't have an M.D., but please trust me anyway."

Cordelia laughed. "You *sound* like a doctor."

Wyungare sat down cross-legged. "Carry on," he said to the two. "I'll be back with you soon." He punched the tape player's ON button and closed his eyes.

Bloat's Wall towered a hundred feet high. Brokers on Wall Street could look out their office windows and count the demons on its ramparts. The Staten Island Ferry passed right under its battlements, or had before service was suspended.

But above the physical barrier was another wall. Invisible. Intangible. A wall of fear. A wall of loathing cold as stone, of hatred hard as iron. The wall of terror had the same boundaries as the other, but it was higher, much higher. To get to the Rox took courage and a strong stomach. Most people didn't have either.

The previous month, when the Turtle had tried to take Dr. Tachyon out to the Rox in search of his stolen body, the stone wall hadn't been there, but the invisible wall had stopped him dead. On the second try, Tom had discovered a very important fact: the wall ended around two thousand feet.

This time he came in high, and it was candy.

The powers-that-be had decided it would be undignified for the rest of the peace delegation to sit on top of his shell. The vice president had volunteered his limousine. Tom couldn't help notice that he hadn't volunteered himself.

The limo floated under the shell, gripped tight by Tom's telekinesis, the two moving as one. It was long and black and bulletproof. A little flag emblazoned with the vice presidential seal flew from one fender, a miniature stars and stripes from the other. The delegates sat in back. Nobody sat in front. The Great and Powerful Turtle was all the driver they needed.

The demons moved in as they passed over Bloat's Wall.

Tom watched them approach on his screens. Mermen riding on flying fish, carrying lances shaped like swordfish. They took up positions around the shell, and escorted him in, surreal outriders in a procession out of nightmare.

The Rox grew stranger the closer they got. Inside the Wall was more bay. Slender stone causeways connected the castle with its outer defenses. On Ellis itself, the castle bulked huge as Gormenghast. Tom glimpsed stone walls twenty feet thick, a confusion of towers and turrets and courtyards, crystalline fairy bridges delicate as spun sugar, onion domes carved in obsidian and ruby, black iron portcullises, huge wooden doors banded in steel, and in the center of it all a high golden dome as wide across as three football fields.

When they got above it, Tom saw that the golden dome was fashioned in the shape of a tremendous face, staring up at the sky. The eyes were skylights, but they seemed to follow them as they approached. One of the mermen dipped his spear. Tom understood the gesture. *Down.*

He thought of falling leaves.

The shell and the limo drifted downward. The face swelled larger and larger on his screens. When they were almost on top of it, the mouth opened wide, swallowing the limo. Tom followed.

He found himself in a vast, airy chamber full of golden light and jokers. There were hundreds of them, maybe thousands, staring up at the peacemakers as they descended. And from the middle of that human sea rose a mountain of pale flesh.

Bloat.

The governor was even bigger than Tom remembered. Still growing, it seemed. The chubby, boyish face and the two small arms that grew from the top of his monstrous body looked like flyspecks. Tom pressed a button; his cameras tracked and zoomed in. Bloat's features filled his screens. The boy governor was smiling.

It was the face of the golden dome, Tom realized.

The torch from the Statue of Liberty stood behind Bloat's throne, mounted on an iron frame. In front of him, a landing area had been cordoned off with velvet ropes. Tom teked the limo down to a gentle landing, and hovered ten feet above it.

A handful of VIPs had been allowed inside the ropes. Tom swung some cameras toward them. A humanoid cockroach stood protectively in front of Bloat, a penguin at his side. A magnificent antlered joker towered over both of them, shaking out a red-gold mane as he watched the limo. On the fringes stood groups of normal-looking teenagers who had to be jumpers.

The penguin skated forward and opened the back door of the limousine. Senator Gregg Hartmann stepped out, looked around for a hand to shake, found none offered, and cleared his throat. Father Squid squeezed out after him, struggling with his bulk and the folds of his cassock.

High above them, Bloat giggled. "Welcome to the Rox."

"Governor," Hartmann said politely. "Thank you for seeing us. We've come in the name of peace."

"Peace?" the stag-man said. He had a deep voice and a British accent. "You mean surrender."

"My children . . ." Father Squid began, spreading his hands.

The stag-man moved forward, cloven hooves ringing on stone. "Bugger that," he interrupted. "We're not your bloody children."

Father Squid's voice was drowned out in a chorus of obscenities.

Hartmann appealed to Bloat. "You agreed to this peace conference, Governor. The least you can do is hear us out."

The cockroach stepped toward the senator. "The governor knows everything you have to say. You can't lie to him. You can't keep secrets."

Bloat giggled. "Yes, Senator," he said to Hartmann, "the smell in here *is* appalling. Even in my throne room, there's no escaping bloat-black. *Especially* in my throne room."

The shell had its own air-conditioning. Tom couldn't smell a thing. But Hartmann paled and hesitated for a moment.

"Go on," Bloat urged. "Wrinkle your nose, you want to. Use your handkerchief if you must. Silk, isn't it?"

Hartmann had actually started to pull out the handkerchief tucked in his breast pocket, but now he froze. Tom heard scattered laughter at the senator's discomfiture.

"Governor," Father Squid said, "think of your people. Of the price they'll pay if this mission fails."

Hartmann tried to recover himself. He took out the handkerchief after all, mopped at his forehead. "You may know what we're going to say," he said loudly to Bloat. He looked around the vast room at the sea of joker faces. "But your people have the right to hear our terms for themselves. Don't they?"

One of the jumpers spoke up. "You're offering amnesty?"

"Full and unconditional," Hartmann replied. He tried to tuck the handkerchief back into his breast pocket, and missed. It fluttered lightly to the floor. Hartmann ignored it. "Forgiveness for all past crimes, regardless."

"You guarantee it?" another jumper asked.

"You have my word, and the solemn pledge of the United States government," Hartmann declared.

Several of the jumpers exchanged glances.

Bloat tittered. "Oh, that's good, Senator. That's very good." He giggled again. "So your government will forgive us all for being criminals. Well, that's fine for our jumper friends. But tell me, Senator. My people would like to know." He took a long dramatic pause. *"Who's going to forgive us for being jokers?"*

The silence in the hall was profound.

"Yeah," Bloat said smugly. "That's what I thought."

Tom could feel the tension in the pit of his stomach. He turned his exterior volume all the way up. But Bloat spoke up before Tom could find the words. "The man in the can's got something to say," he announced.

Tom pushed with his teke, floating up, until he was higher than Bloat, higher than the balconies, higher than the torch, commanding the whole room. He wanted them to look up at him. "THIS ISN'T A FUCKING GAME. IF YOU DON'T SURRENDER, THEY'LL KILL YOU."

"They've tried to kill us before," Bloat said.

"LISTEN TO ME. YOU ONLY HAVE TILL SUNSET . . ."

"Then we all turn into pumpkins, right?" a jumper put in.

"Then they send more soldiers," the stag-man said.

"NOT JUST SOLDIERS," promised the Turtle. He had to make them understand. "THE AIR FORCE AND THE NAVY WILL HIT YOU FROM BEYOND THE WALL WITH EVERYTHING THEY'VE GOT."

"Let them try," the antlered joker said, "we'll hit them back." He stepped toward Hartmann and Father Squid, bent suddenly, scooped up the senator's fallen hankie. He clenched it in his fist, raised it high over his head like a banner. *"Five for one!"* he shouted, his deep voice ringing off the rafters.

"Go on," Bloat said, giggling. "Tell us about the aces."

He's reading my mind, Tom realized in panic. He'd known Bloat was a telepath, but knowing it and experiencing it were two different things. "THEY'RE RECRUITING ACES TOO. YOU HAVE NO IDEA THE KIND OF POWER YOU'LL BE FACING. CYCLONE AND MISTRAL, DETROIT STEEL, PULSE, ELEPHANT GIRL." He was blanking. He licked his lips. "FORTUNATO." He couldn't think of anyone else. He lied. "J.J. FLASH, STARSHINE . . ."

"Flash *and* Starshine," Bloat said merrily. "I can't wait to see that."

Fuck, Tom thought wildly. You can't bluff a telepath. Another name came to him. *"MODULAR MAN,"* he blurted.

The whole Great Hall erupted into laughter.

Bloat jiggled and rumbled, pipe-stem arms slapping helplessly against his sides in a paroxysm of hilarity. The stag-man was laughing thunderclaps. Jokers and jumpers on all sides were roaring and falling down. The penguin was twirling figure-eights in the air. Even the human cockroach looked like he was smiling. The dome overhead rang with laughter.

Tom's eyes went wildly from screen to screen to screen. They were all laughing, everyone but Hartmann and Father Squid, who looked as baffled as he was. He didn't get it.

"WHAT THE FUCK IS SO GODDAMN FUNNY?" he asked.

The laughter died away slowly, like the ebbing of a great tide. Out from behind Bloat's immensity stepped a solitary, sheepish figure. A handsome man in a blue jumpsuit, with guns mounted on his shoulders.

"Excuse me," Modular Man said. "Senator, Father, Turtle." He sounded as embarrassed as an android could sound. "I don't know how to tell you this but, well . . . I met the enemy, and he is me."

The jokers laughed at the Turtle, Father Squid, and Hartmann's discomfiture; Modular Man looked as bemused and uncomfortable as an android could. Bloat made no effort to cut them off. He stared at the peace delegation and grimaced. Hypocrites, every last one of them—and one of them especially.

Bloat knew about Hartmann—he'd figured out months ago that the senator must be a hidden ace. Several of the jokers on the Rox carried painful memories of actions that were entirely out of character for them; old, loyal Peanut most prominent among them. And like Peanut, most of those jokers had associations with Hartmann; as with Peanut, the circumstantial evidence indicated that someone had manipulated them, had taken control of their actions for a brief time.

The information Black Shadow had given him a few months ago had confirmed that suspicion in Bloat's mind. Bloat figured Hartmann was an ace "up the sleeve." He also suspected that the ace had much to do with Tachyon's betrayal of the senator at the Democratic National Convention. It all made sense. Bloat knew, but he'd never met the man, never had the opportunity to prowl through his thoughts.

What Bloat had found in the last hour was a stench worse than bloatblack, a deformity uglier than any joker's.

Hartmann had been paranoid from the moment he entered the Rox's boundaries, knowing Bloat's reputation as a mind reader. The fear had made it difficult for the senator to pass the psychic barrier of Bloat's Wall. Once forced through, his mind sagged open like a rotten fruit.

. . . can't even think about Puppetman . . . he'll know . . . can't even think about it at all . . . but of course that only opened the gates of Hartmann's memory. Through all the talk, through all the nice little speeches about how he had the best interests of everyone at heart, through all the entreaties for reasonableness, Bloat listened to that interior voice, those old memories.

A sickness, a charnel house of putrefaction, spilled out. Bloat had gagged at the taste of it in his head, unbelieving. *This* was Senator Hartmann, the hero of Jokertown, the almost-president, the friend of the jokers? This *thing*?

Any optimism that Bloat had harbored concerning this meeting dissolved under the barrage. Hartmann was not a good man, a compassionate one, or even a misguided one. Jokers were human beings whose bodies were twisted by the wild card into something inhuman. Hartmann was a joker in reverse—a normal form with something horribly inhuman inside.

The realization made Bloat angry. The deceit of *all* of them made him furious.

"You're all liars," he said suddenly, and the hilarity around him ended as if it had been cut off by a switch. The anger in him made his body writhe around the inlet pipes that impaled him like a mounted insect. Bloatblack oozed from the scabrous pores and the miasma of raw sewage filled the room. The inhabitants of the Rox might be used to the stench; the thoughts of the others were quite expressive.

"Don't you like Eau de Bloat?" He giggled, and then frowned. "Can't you taste the shit that's coming out of your own mouths? God, such a fine trio of hypocrites. I listened to all this crap and there's nothing in your words. Nothing at all."

Father Squid gaped, his tentacles wriggling over his open mouth; inside the shell of the Turtle, Bloat could hear Tudbury gasp as if struck; Hartmann looked like he wanted to run. Around the room, automatic rifle bolts clicked back; Kafka waved angrily at the joker guards.

"GOVERNOR," the Turtle began. He'd turned up the volume on his speakers, trying to gain in decibels what he couldn't in fervor. Bloat could hear the turmoil and sudden guilt in the man-boy's mind. "PLEASE—"

"I hear you," Bloat interrupted, waving his helpless stick arms. "I hear the thoughts, not the words. I know all your secrets. I know your *name*, Oh Great and Powerful Turtle. You can't hide from me behind the shell, and you can't hide from the world in it, either. You don't really like what *your* side is doing in this, do you? That's an armored shell you ride, not a fucking white horse. Your own little Wall, and you the Bloat behind it."

Bloat's gaze went to the priest. "And you, Father Squid? Are you a saint?"

"I'm at peace with myself," the large joker answered, but Bloat could hear the skittering memories inside. Bloat followed their sounds into dark places.

"No, you're not at peace, Father," he cackled. "Not when you spend some nights kneeling by the bed asking God for forgiveness—and you still have those nights, don't you, Father? Don't the faces of the ones you killed with your own hands haunt *your* dreams? You protest that you were young then and caught up in something you've since found to be wrong, but don't you still find that you look the other way when violence just happens to benefit *your* side, even now? You want the names, Father? You want the dates and places? I can get them for you. I can tell *everyone,* just like I could tell everyone the Turtle's real name."

Father Squid was silent, clutching the crucifix of Christ the Joker to his huge chests. He made soft, wet sounds deep in his throat, as if he were sobbing.

"And *you*, Senator . . ."

Hartmann visibly startled. He looked old suddenly, and frail. He wiped sweat off his brow with the back of his hand. "Governor . . ." he said pleadingly.

Bloat guffawed. "Wow, the great senator wants a little goddamn compassion. C'mon, Senator, you're the sickest one of all. Sure, I can see that in your mind as clearly as you can. You even agree with me. The great friend of Jokertown certainly did *love* the jokers, didn't he?"

The ugly pores along Bloat's flanks flexed and pouted like circular mouths; great turds of bloatblack emerged from them, sliding down the stained hills of his flesh. His body was trembling again, as it had when the *Temptation of St. Anthony* had been destroyed and he'd first brought forth the demons from his mind. Bloat forced the energy back down, tried to still the turmoil inside the vastness of his form.

Bloat looked around the room. He could feel the rising enmity against the delegation. The torrent of voices inside his head made him grin. Their massed support sparked the dream-energy inside him. He could feel it rising once more, chaotic, and he reached out with mental hands to channel that vitality. For a moment as he first grasped the power, there was a whirling disorientation—like he remembered as a kid, spinning with arms outspread in the living room until the room danced around him. In that split second, he thought he could hear angry voices calling him . . . *Teddy* . . . and there was a wisp of cold mountain air; an impression of a flat, dark-skinned, wide-nosed face; a sense of outraged invasion from watching minds.

Then he was back. The cold air was only the warm stink of his own bloatblack and he was speaking with the resonant, compelling tones of the Outcast, causing everyone to look up at him in astonishment.

"You don't want to help me, Senator," he said, banishing the residual dizziness. "You don't care about the jokers at all. You don't give a shit about the Rox or what we've done here. None of you really do."

From around the room came shouts of agreement, loud enough that the huge torch on the wall behind him rattled in sympathy.

Father Squid and Hartmann had moved back close to the Turtle and the limousine, and their mindvoices chattered in panic. "All the three of you want to do is save yourselves the guilt of having to fight with the nats against your own kind, and you don't care that you sell out the Rox and all the people here to do it." More shouting: jokers and jumpers alike added their voices. But when he spoke, the Outcast's voice sent them all silent again.

"You can tell Bush and General Zappa this. If anyone wants to leave here, he or she can do so. Governor Bloat doesn't chain his people up against their will—hey, I've got Liberty's torch right behind me, after all. But all I'm hearing is the same old shit from you. All I hear is that . . . that those who the wild card touched are lepers: diseased people to be shut away, sterilized, and kept watch over. Man, I didn't *choose* to be this way. It ain't my fucking fault. I didn't *want* to put up the Wall—it's just there and I can't turn it on and off at will. All I'm doing is using what I was given in the best way I know. That's all *any* of us here are doing, and I think we're beginning to make progress. I think we're beginning to put something together for jokers."

More shouts. Bloat laughed, and this time it wasn't his adolescent, shrill giggle, but something deep-throated and full. "But you don't care. Huh-uh. We're just pieces of bloatblack to you, to be disposed of or put somewhere out of sight."

More cries erupted around them. Captain Chaos, standing next to Bloat, reached down and plucked one of the pieces of bloatblack from the floor. She flung it; the fecal blob bounced off Hartmann's shoulder and left a brown stain on his gray suit coat. Hartmann flinched back, startled. "Here's an answer to take back with you," Chaos said, and suddenly several of the jokers in the hall were running to Bloat's side, grasping the filth there and flinging it at the delegation.

Bloat laughed. Hartmann and Father Squid scrambled into the limousine for shelter. The jokers ran to the car and began rocking it side to side. The suspension squealed in protest; the tires sagged like the waists of tired old men. "GET BACK!" the Turtle roared, and lifted the limousine straight up. Bloatblack missiles thudded dully against the bottom of the car and the Turtle's shell.

"GOVERNOR . . ." the Turtle began, then the speakers crackled and went silent. Bloat could hear the man's thoughts racing, trying to find words and coming up with nothing that seemed appropriate. Finally, the ace gave up. Hartmann stared at Bloat from the window of the car . . . *ugly little thing. If I had Puppetman* . . . Father Squid looked down from the opposite side.

"I understand," the priest said softly, and the faint smell of the sea came to Bloat. "I really do."

Then the Turtle and his burden moved softly away as the bloat-black barrage continued. To the jeers of the Rox, the Turtle and the limo left through the open mouth of the Bloat-face in the ceiling of the Great Hall.

The light was red.

The Buick idled in the middle of the Jokertown intersection. The bodysnatcher tapped on the driver's window. The man inside looked at her, hesitated. He must have decided she looked harmless enough. The window came rolling down. Power window. Very nice.

There was a family inside. Daddy was tall and balding, wearing a gray suit. His wife was a plump woman in a polyester pants suit. In back was an ugly little girl in blue jeans and a Smurfs T-shirt, maybe three.

"Yes?" Daddy asked. "Can I help you?"

"Your little girl isn't wearing her seat belt," the bodysnatcher told him. "What kind of parents are you?"

The man didn't know what to make of this. His wife said, "The light's changed," nervously. She was smarter than he was. She knew you don't stop and talk to strangers in the middle of a Jokertown street.

"It's not just a good idea," the bodysnatcher said. "It's the law. Watch this." She took the bottle of Drāno out of the pocket of her trench coat, twisted off the cap, and drank.

The pain was a purifying fire inside her, burning out all the filth. She heard them gasp. When the bottle was empty, the bodysnatcher tossed it aside, wiped her lips, and smiled down at Daddy. She had to lean against the car to keep from falling. She would have said something, but her throat was too badly burned.

Daddy was staring up at her in horror, knuckles white where they gripped the steering wheel. The bodysnatcher blinked back tears, and jumped.

Inside the car, inside Daddy, he raised the power window and watched the face outside twist in sudden agony. Mommy was whimpering in the seat beside him. The bodysnatcher hit the accelerator, heard a *thump* as the body hit the street. The screams began before they were halfway across the intersection.

"Oh, God, oh, God," the wife was saying. The Buick's handling was flabby. The bodysnatcher turned a corner hard. "We have to call the police," the wife finally managed.

"Blueboy would like that," the bodysnatcher told her.

The wife looked at him strangely. "John?" she said. She still didn't get it. By then the bodysnatcher was turning into the alley, and it was too late. They went down past the dumpster, to the dead end way in back, under the fire escape. Blueboy and Vanilla and Molly Bolt were waiting there, in the shadows.

"No," the wife said as they came toward the car. "No, no, no." She locked all the doors, closed all the windows, frantic with fear. As if windows could stop a jumper.

Molly Bolt shook her head in disgust, and jumped.

Mommy sat back, adjusted her pant suit. "Polyester," she complained. "I hate polyester." She looked over her shoulder at the girl in the backseat. "How you doing?"

"Motherfucker," the little girl said, squirming. "The brat isn't even toilet trained yet. This is disgusting."

Outside, Molly and Blueboy had both collapsed. Vanilla carried them under the fire escape, and tied them at wrist and ankle in case they came to. It wouldn't do for them to run off. Molly and Blueboy had a sentimental attachment to their original flesh. "Where to?" the bodysnatcher asked impatiently.

"The Empire State Building," said Mommy, counting the money in her purse. "I think we got enough for lunch at Aces High."

♥

The world into which Wyungare plunged was dark.

The dull thudding of the drum was not what he remembered of the complex jazz rhythms. He didn't know where he was.

Wyungare raised his right hand and snapped his fingers once, twice, and then on the third attempt, a flame sprang up on his palm. It was cool and blue and did not burn his flesh. Instead, the flickering illumination crept out around him until he could see that he stood on a springy carpet of dark moss in the midst of huge trees. The trunks of those trees descended into tangled puzzles of winding, interconnected roots.

The Aborigine turned until he saw an opening among the trees, a path that led through that gap. He began to follow it, his hand held in front of him like a torch.

He walked perhaps a quarter of a mile until he saw the path blocked by a hillock; more properly, it looked like the flank of a mountain. Bare of vegetation, the stony surface seemed to shine.

Wyungare blinked. The mountainside had now become the mouth of an enormous cavern. The top and bottom of the opening was lined with sharp, curving stalactites and stalagmites. The man couldn't remember which of those was supposed to grow from the top down, and which from the bottom up. He supposed it didn't matter, since the formations jutted everywhere around the opening.

And then the cave spoke. "So, my star-seeking cousin, you travel in company with unusual and fine drums." The words vibrated low, shaking inside Wyungare like ocean tides sweeping up an estuary and into the coastal swamplands.

Wyungare stopped in his tracks and slowly began to grin. "Cousin Kurria, is it you? The crocodile guardian?"

"None other." High on the flank of the "mountain," two huge eyes abruptly blinked open, staring down at the man. "I watch over all such as the one you seek, even if their forms are a bit alien, something less sleek than the cousins in our home."

"Then you know my mission."

The laugh sounded like the toppling of tall trees. "I have spoken with Viracocha and others. I know of your need to encounter this one called Jack Robicheaux."

"Will you aid me?"

"Come right on in." The laughter rolled out again. "I will help you."

Wyungare walked up to the huge spikes he now understood to be teeth. He slipped between two of the largest and sharpest. He climbed up into the jaw of Kurria. He stepped upon the resilient tongue and walked forward, toward the back of the guardian's throat.

Then the jaws closed and there was utter darkness, save for the blue flame still flickering from Wyungare's hand.

The man walked farther. He didn't know how long he traveled, or how long it took. But finally, he found himself in a room darker than the passage through which he had come. He could feel impressions: sleep, hunger, pain. The walls around him pulsed. A pair of invisible eyes opened behind their armored, protective lids.

"Cousin," said Wyungare. "Friend."

Hunger, came the response.

Hunger can be fed. Wyungare projected the image of fish. Enough fish to sate.

Hunger.

Wyungare projected the image of the black cat, of Cordelia. He received back flickers of recognition, but still one overriding response.

Hunger.

Wyungare sighed. It looked to be a long, though not especially sophisticated conversation.

The hallway was narrow and filthy. The walls looked like they hadn't been washed, let alone painted, in Ray's lifetime. He couldn't understand how anyone, particularly an ace, could live in such an environment.

He stopped before the warped door. Light spilled through the gaps in the frame from the apartment beyond. Ray paused, smelling the exotic fragrances wafting through the floor from the Chinese grocery below. A mysterious touch of the Orient, he thought, rapping authoritatively on the door. How appropriate.

There was silence, then he heard light footsteps.

"Yes?" It was a woman's voice.

"I'm looking for Ben Choy," Ray said.

The door opened. A dark-haired, dark-eyed Asian woman stood in the doorway. Ray glanced past her. The tiny apartment beyond was empty. It was, he noted in approval, spotlessly clean. He focused on the girl. She was young, maybe in her mid-twenties, cute without being beautiful, serious and somehow disapproving as she looked silently at Ray.

"You Choy's girlfriend?"

"His sister," she said.

She looked like him, Ray thought. "Where is he?"

She shook her head. "He's not here. I don't know where he went."

Ray nodded. Ben Choy, also known as Lazy Dragon, was an ace who frequently worked on the wrong side of the law. He wasn't wanted for any specific crimes, but he'd been associated with the Shadow Fists when they were the preeminent criminal organization in New York City. But, as Dragon's dossier indicated, he sometimes disappeared for long periods of time. This looked like one of those times.

"I'm from the government," Ray told the girl. "Special Executive Task Force." She looked at him blankly. He didn't know what that meant either, but it sounded as impressive as hell. "It'd be to your brother's advantage to get in touch with me. I'm prepared to offer him a full executive pardon for all crimes he may have committed."

"Why?" the girl asked.

"What's your name?" Ray asked, flashing his best lopsided smile.

"Vivian."

"Well, Vivian, it's a secret actually. A secret mission you might say."

She nodded her head, apparently unconvinced. "A full pardon?"

Ray handed her his card. "That's right. But there isn't much time. He has to call tonight, before midnight."

Vivian still looked doubtful.

"By the way," Ray said, "you busy next Friday? The new Bruce Lee movie is opening. It's supposed to be great."

That she was busy she had no doubts at all.

Daddy's body was flabby and out of shape, pale little gut pressing against the buttons of his shirt. The way the air felt against the bald head made the bodysnatcher feel vulnerable, and when he tried to move, he found he was slow and clumsy.

The restaurant pissed him off too. Aces High was supposed to be this high-class place, with four-star service and famous aces at every other table. It was all hype. They'd been hanging around for more than a hour, spending Daddy's money, and the only thing scarcer than aces were waiters.

"Where's the fat guy?" Molly-Mommy wanted to know. "This is his place. He's supposed to be here."

"Maybe he'll come in later," Bluebaby said in a little Shirley Temple voice.

The waiter finally appeared with their drinks. One Chivas straight up, one extra-dry martini, one tall glass of milk. "So where are all the aces?" Molly-Mommy asked him. "The guidebook says this place is always full of aces."

"Some days are slow," the waiter said, like he could give a shit. He nodded toward two men at the far end of the bar. "You got a couple right there."

The bodysnatcher glanced over in that direction. The aces didn't look like much. An average-looking white guy drinking beer, and a slender black guy in a gray suit and an orange domino mask. Except for the mask, they could have been a couple of insurance agents. "Are they famous?" the bodysnatcher asked.

The waiter shrugged. "This is New York. Everybody's famous. That's nine seventy-five."

The bodysnatcher pulled a ten out of Daddy's wallet and gave it to the waiter. "Keep the change."

The waiter made a sour face and moved off. Molly-mommy leaned across the table. "I think the white guy is Pulse."

"So?" the bodysnatcher asked.

Bluebaby picked up the Chivas and took a sip. The tumbler looked huge in the tiny three-year-old hand. "Jesus, Zelda, don't you know nothing? He was in the Swarm War, I read about him in *Aces*. Guy can turn himself into a fucking *laser*."

"Even better than Hiram," Molly-Mommy said. Her eyes sparkled. She took the olive out of her martini with her fingers and popped it into her mouth. "This is more like it." She opened Mommy's purse, took out one of Patchwork's eyes, and dropped it into the martini in place of the olive.

The bodysnatcher sipped his milk. He had too much respect for the human body to pollute it with alcohol. He glanced over casually at the aces. "What about the other one?"

"Beats me," Molly-Mommy said. She put the martini glass under the drooping leaves of a potted plant, where the busboy wouldn't spot it. From there, Patchwork ought to have a good clear view of the whole room.

The bodysnatcher wiped milk off Daddy's upper lip with the back of his hand. "I'll find out," he said, rising.

The aces were deep in conversation. Even up close, Pulse didn't look like much. He had little love handles bulging out above his belt, and his dark hair was going gray.

"Sorry to bother you, Mr. Pulse," he said, "but we're big fans, and well, we don't get to New York real often, you know. My little girl would sure like your autograph."

"No bother," Pulse said, smiling. He put down his beer and scrawled a signature on a cocktail napkin.

"She's just going to be thrilled," the bodysnatcher said. He looked at the black man. "Say, don't I know you too? You're somebody famous, right?"

"Wall Walker," the black man said. He had an accent. Jamaica, maybe.

"Really?" the bodysnatcher said. "And what do you do? If you don't mind me asking?"

"I walk up de wall." Wall Walker didn't seem nearly as friendly as Pulse.

The bodysnatcher bobbed Daddy's head up and down and grinned like an idiot. "This is terrific," he said when Pulse handed him the cocktail napkin. "Say, I was wondering . . . would you mind posing for a picture with the wife?"

"Not at all," Pulse said. "If you'll excuse me," he said to Wall Walker.

"Got to be going anyway," Wall Walker replied. "Good luck, mon. By and by, you going to be needing it." The black ace tossed some change on the bar and left.

"Why doesn't he just walk down the side of the building?" the bodysnatcher asked Pulse.

"The Good Lord gave some of us super powers," Pulse replied, "but He also gave us elevators." The bodysnatcher decided he was really going to enjoy killing this asshole.

He led him over to their table. "Honey, this is Mr. Pulse, the man we read about in *Aces*."

Pulse extended a hand. "Cy."

Molly-Mommy twinkled at him. "It's nice to meet you. I'm sorry your friend had to leave."

"That was Mr. Wall Walker," the bodysnatcher told her. "He walks up walls. Sometimes. When there's no elevator." Everyone chuckled happily. It would have made a great Norman Rockwell scene, so long as he left out the eyeball in the martini glass.

"So where do you want to take this picture?" Pulse asked in a genial tone of voice.

"Let's go outside," Molly-Mommy suggested. "Then we can get the view."

Aces High was eighty-six stories above the street. You could see all the way to the Rox. "Magnificent," Molly-Mommy said when they stepped out onto the terrace.

"Jesus," Bluebaby said as her hair whipped around her face. "What's with this fucking *wind*?"

The bodysnatcher shot her a look, but Pulse didn't seem to notice. He looked up, shaded his eyes, smiled. "You're in luck, folks," he said, pointing. "See there."

The bodysnatcher looked up, glimpsed a parachute falling toward them, white against the deep blue sky. But it was moving wrong, circling the building in a graceful spiral instead of coming straight down. Then he realized it wasn't a parachute at all. It was a woman, dressed all in blue, riding the winds on a huge white cape.

"Mistral," Pulse told them as she glided down toward the terrace. "Beautiful, isn't she? Sweet girl."

Mommy and Daddy exchanged glances. "We'll have to get a picture of her too," said Mommy.

◆

There were no rumors on the Rox. Not, at least, for Bloat. No gossip, no secrets. Bloat *knew*.

In a perverse way, it was mildly interesting to listen to the jumpers' sinking confidence. That damned 1-800-I-GIVE-UP number kept flitting through their minds like a mantra for AT&T executives. Most of the jumpers—nearly a hundred of them—had gathered in one of the halls across the island. Without the strong leadership of Molly and Bodysnatcher, the impromptu strategy meeting was turning into a rout. It was an ugly scratch on the surface of the Rox's thoughts.

"You'd really let them go, wouldn't you?" The penguin was gazing up at Bloat as it skated in nonchalant circles around the lobby floor. Outside, the sun was lowering itself gingerly onto the spires of his Wall.

"Anyone who wants to throw themselves on the mercy of Hartmann and the nats can go ahead. I'm not keeping anyone here against their will. That's not why I created the Rox."

"Uh-huh." The penguin did a quick twirl and a high leap, landing gracefully just below Bloat's head and shoulders and then skiing down the steep slope of his body to the floor once more. The joker guards stationed around the balcony applauded; the penguin gave a grinning bow. "Good ol' kindly Bloat. Compassionate Governor Bloat. Doesn't want *anyone* to get hurt."

"All I've ever wanted is a joker homeland," he told the penguin. "That's all. A place where we can be whatever it is we need to be. The nats can have the rest."

"That ain't gonna happen, Your Immensitude," the penguin cackled. "I've told you that a hundred times before." The penguin canted its head and the funnel hat tilted dangerously to one side. "You stay here and you're gonna haveta fight."

"So what are you saying?"

"Don't *stay* here. I should think that's obvious."

"Right. Excuse me. I've been *so* stupid. I'll just get up and walk away." Bloat giggled; on cue, so did the guards who had been half listening to the conversation. The penguin put on an aggrieved look and pouted.

"Tell me, Gov, why is it that idiot nats with paranoia complexes use every last ounce of power they got, and a joker with more ability than ten aces put together just sits here and waits for them to take potshots at him? I *swear* I don't understand it. Can't you *feel* it, fat boy? All that power . . ." The penguin sighed. Flippers folded behind its back, it skated off down one of the side corridors.

Bloat watched his creature leave, pondering as he listened to the continuing disagreements in the joker compound. He *could* feel the degeneration of the Rox's morale; more with each passing hour, it seemed.

The answer came to him suddenly.

This morning, Kafka looking at the side corridor where the penguin and the Outcast stood and *seeing* them . . . The way his voice had sounded during the meeting with Hartmann's delegation . . .

He *could* walk away. He actually could.

With the thought, his vision shimmered. Bloat yawned; his body began to tremble and the odor of bloatblack arose. As his mind relaxed and Bloat began to slumber, a surging violet tendril fanned up from somewhere deep within him, turning and sparking, dividing and dividing again.

The Outcast laughed. He knew this feeling: the power of dreams. He took the electric force and shaped it. He shaped it, he put himself into the vessel of energy and told it where to carry him.

The transformation didn't happen immediately. For several moments he felt himself lost in some limbo. Pulsing cords of self led back to Bloat, drawing sustenance from that immense form and keeping him irrevocably tethered to it. There was a sensation of falling. A fierce brightness made him shade his eyes with his hands. He was in the dreamworld again. He saw creatures of all kinds in a landscape like a Chinese brush painting, skeletal trees and steep round hills. A slavering ogre lurched by with a struggling young girl flung over its hunched back. A naked young boy waggled his newly severed, bloody foreskin before the Outcast's face. An androgynous, six-armed figure in a headdress danced by. A lion strutted past, bearing a man holding a glowing orb that was as bright as the sun.

Voices assailed his ears as the sights invaded his eyes, alternately pleading and threatening. . . . *go back! . . . Don't you know what you're doing? . . . You have no understanding. None. . . .*

The Outcast pulled power from Bloat and from the dreamworld itself. He willed himself to return to reality. The Rox snapped into existence around him.

". . . I say we leave."

"You do, Juggler? Why? Are you frightened of *nats*?"

The jumper named Juggler had literally leapt into the air at the unexpected voice behind his back. "Who the fuck are you?" he snarled, his hands fisted. At the same time, the Outcast heard the thought . . . *jump the mother* . . . and felt the force of the boy's mind recoil off the perfect alabaster shield of his own ego.

"No, *I* can't be jumped," he told Juggler and the others. Captain Chaos took the challenge; she failed. So did Iceman, then Suzy Creamcheese. The Outcast smiled. "You already know me," he told them. "Just not in this form. I'm your governor, after all."

"Governor Bloat?" Juggler snorted. "Fuck, man, you sure as hell lost some weight. You on Nutrisystem?"

"Yeah," Alvin said from farther back in the room. "This guy could be one of the aces Modman says Hartmann's got."

"No." The Outcast smiled, and he let the power of his presence leap out. *"I am Bloat,"* he said to them, encasing the words within his power. *"In this form, you can call me the Outcast. Like you. Like all of us cast from society by the wild card."* The energy touched each of them, calming and soothing them, dampening their skepticism. "And you still haven't answered my question. Why are you so frightened? There's no reason for it. None at all. Let me show you."

He rapped his long wooden staff against the floor. The amethyst flared.

They were all crowded on the ledge near Bloat's Moat. The heat from the rushing lava far below made the jumpers gasp; the ruddy light rendered the Outcast's features fierce and stern. "I built the Rox. I shaped it. Did you think I would make it *easy* for them?"

The Outcast slammed the base of his staff against the rocks. They were now arrayed along the north side of the Wall facing Manhattan. The glass eyes of the skyscrapers glittered at them mockingly; behind, the Disney-meets-Escher fairyland of the new Rox stuck out spired tongues in return.

"This is our land," the Outcast told them. "It grows every day in size and strength. Just as the Wall's now visible, so is my power. You see it in what I've done with the Rox. You see it in the demons and strange things that walk in the caverns. And—I promise you this—you'll see it if the nats are foolish enough to attack."

As he spoke the words, a flare shot from across the bay, near where the Wall touched the Jersey shore. It quickly resolved into a cylinder trailing a line of billowing smoke. The weapon shot directly toward them at immense speed. The jumpers cried out, but the Outcast laughed. In the instant before the glowing missile would have struck them, he waved his staff, the stone at its summit glaring, and the jumpers were showered with pink and white petals.

"In this world, things are as I wish them to be." The Outcast laughed and flung his arms wide.

They were back in the hall once more. The Outcast brushed bright petals from his shoulders and folded his hands across the top of his staff, resting his chin atop his hands as he gazed at the jumpers, a hint of a smile on his lips. "I know you're worried. I understand that. If any of you want to leave, no one here will stop you. You're free to go if you think that's what you should do—I've told you that before. But I want you to know how much we need you. I'm Bloat, your governor. I'm also the Outcast, the one who calls demons and who builds the Rox. Molly and Bodysnatcher will be back soon with more aces. Croyd will wake up any moment, and his form is very, very promising. But all that's not enough. I need *all* of you. The Rox is your land; I'm asking you to stay with me to help protect it. It's up to you."

♥

"The governor says he's ready." Kafka gazed at Travnicek from his insect face. His expression was unreadable, but the rest of his body radiated disapproval. "All you have to do is visualize what you want."

Travnicek leaned back and threw out his arms. "All right, fat maggot!" he said. "You listening?"

Kafka quivered in anger. Jumpers, standing in the courtyard, snickered among themselves.

Kafka and Travnicek and Modular Man stood in the inner bailey, facing the semitransparent inner wall of the Crystal Keep with its delicate gingerbread balconies and stained-glass eyes. Mortar crews, lounging around their pits, watched from behind sandbags.

Modular Man's eyes focused on the inner keep wall. Something was happening there.

Even replaying the event later he found it difficult to follow. Something shadowlike crawled up the inner wall, something silent and purposeful. One second there was nothing on radar, the next there was. But *what* it was wasn't clear until a few seconds later, until it *firmed* from the ground up like a tree growing in fast motion.

Travnicek gave a high cackling laugh. All the clustered organs around his neck were swollen and erect.

"Jesus," one of the mortar jokers said. "Never saw a *neck* get a hard-on before!"

Bloat's creation stood clear in the light of day. "Hey!" the mortar joker said. "*Another* goddamn boner!"

"Not bad, eh?" Travnicek gloated. "Home away from home."

What it looked like was a thick tube welded to the inner wall of the keep. The tube thickened as it approached the ground, like a bulbous plant, disappeared below ground level, and on top blossomed into an armored, conical roof.

Travnicek's tower.

Travnicek looked at Kafka. "Thank the Stinkworm for me, will you?" he said, then walked toward the tower. He planted a foot on its vertical surface, tested it, then began walking up the outside of the tower. His body was reflected in its glassine surface. He paused partway up and turned to Modular Man. "Come with me," he said. "I want you to know how this works."

The android floated up next to him as Travnicek finished his climb, then slid through one of the upper story's armored shutters. Modular Man followed, floating through the window feetfirst. The upper story consisted of a floor with a hole near the wall that led down into the tower. The heavy metal shutters could be dropped into place at the touch of a lever. Travnicek threw out his arms. "Great!" he said. "I can feel everything from here! Right to the horizon!"

He moved to the hole in the floor and sat in it, then planted his feet against the wall again and began walking down. His voice came hollow from the hole.

"Follow."

Modular Man floated down the hole. Daylight shining through the semitransparent tower wall provided enough light to see.

"No stairs, see?" Travnicek said. "Nobody's gonna follow me down here."

The tower seemed to extend some distance below ground level, where the walls became opaque black stone. The floor was bare flags. On the inner wall was a heavy metal hatch with a wheel in the center, like something from a submarine. Travnicek spun the wheel and swung the door open.

Inside was a room about twenty feet square. There were shelves with canned goods, plastic bottles of water, candles and matches, fantastic Rox furniture, all carved baroque dragons with lolling tongues, including a bed with a headboard made of carved intertwining monsters. Even a chemical toilet behind an oriental screen. Travnicek had visualized things pretty thoroughly.

"I can stay down here *forever*," Travnicek gloated.

The android let his boots touch the soft carpet on the floor. He glanced around. Calculations sped through his brain, slammed up against one of his hardwired imperatives.

"Sir?" he said. "Is that door airtight?"

"Air- and watertight!" Travnicek said. "*Nothing's* getting in here I don't want in."

"Is there concealed ventilation?" Modular Man asked. "Because if there isn't, you'll smother in here. More quickly if you light any of those candles."

Travnicek stiffened. "Good you thought of that," he said.

The android really hadn't had any choice. The welfare of his creator was his highest priority.

He couldn't *not* try to preserve Travnicek's life.

Travnicek stood stock-still, concentrating.

The walls shimmered. Ventilation shafts appeared at headlevel, leading up to the tower's exterior.

Travnicek cackled. "Thanks, big maggot."

The ventilation shafts were another problem, the android realized, another way to get in. But he didn't think there was an alternative, and anything coming down the shafts would have to be very small.

"Sir?" Modular Man asked. "How long are we going to stay here? You don't actually think the governor is going to win, do you?"

"I don't much care who wins, toaster," Travnicek said. "And as for how long we'll stay—" He gave one of his little laughs. "We'll stay till it's over. Till Bloat's dead and can't do these interesting things anymore."

"But if Bloat's dead—"

"When Bloat's dead, you get me out," Travnicek said. "Nobody has to know I've ever been here."

"They'll know *I've* been here."

Travnicek turned. "That's something *else* I don't care about," he said.

The tape ended.

Wyungare was jerked back from the dark world, from the swamp, from the inside of the crocodile guardian's head, from the company of Jack the alligator. He opened his eyes, blinked, looked up into the concerned faces of Cordelia and Troll.

"How do you feel?" said the security man.

"Like that chap in *My Dinner With Andre*," said Wyungare, "except I was attempting to converse with a reptile, and a famished one at that."

"The patient's received plenty of nutrients."

"He wants meat," said Wyungare. "I tried to bargain on that basis."

"And?" said Cordelia. "You really contacted him? How is he?"

"He is an alligator," said Wyungare. "There is very little of the human aspect of your uncle at home on that side. But I believe we have come to something of an agreement."

"Good," said Troll, "because he's starting to come awake. Time for me to go invisible again. I don't know anything of what's happening. Remember that."

"That's Dr. Finn's line," said Cordelia.

Troll smiled. "You're right. Actually, I've got an appointment." He started for the door. "Good luck, you two." His tone got serious. "Don't let him hurt anyone." He indicated the alligator. "Except maybe Dr. Bob, that kraut son of a bitch. And don't let him hurt himself. Please?"

"We shall do our best," said Wyungare.

"I love him," said Cordelia.

Troll looked at them a moment longer, then turned and was gone.

"Now what?" said Cordelia.

Wyungare looked down at the outside window. He smiled. "The clinic deals with laundry several times a day."

"The clean comes in, the dirty goes out so?"

"There is a truck downstairs now, apparently loading soiled laundry."

"So?" Cordelia said. "You proposing to smuggle Uncle Jack out in a laundry hamper? That's another movie I've seen more than once."

"I think not. He's just a little large for a hamper." The alligator was beginning to writhe on the bed platform. The black cat jumped onto the chair at the platform's head and stared at the alligator, nose to snout. "We are on the third floor," said Wyungare. "We have to get past the second to the ground floor. I saw some reconstruction going on on the second level. We have to get Jack down there." He quickly outlined the rest of his plans to Cordelia. "I'll accompany you for a ways, then I will go down to the ground floor and maneuver the truck in place."

The Aborigine went to the alligator, whose eyes were now fully open. Fetid breath whistled in and out of the powerful jaws. Wyungare placed the heel of his hand on the reptile's forehead. His palm seemed dwarfed by the armored plates. He concentrated for a few seconds. "All right," he said, "let us go."

"Thank God," said Cordelia, once they were out in the corridor. Jack took up a considerable amount of that corridor. Wyungare looked at her questioningly. "I'm afraid there'll be more witnesses a floor down," she said. "The elevator?"

Wyungare shook his head. "I don't think so. Your uncle's flexible, but I don't think he'll bend *that* much." They came to the door to the stairwell and the Aborigine pulled it open. He held it for the others.

"We could just walk all the way down to the first floor," said Cordelia.

"There are many more people there," said Wyungare. "Our answer is a floor above them."

"You're the shaman," said Cordelia, flashing him a brilliant smile. She went ahead, the cat bounding down the steps as though on point. The alligator wheezed and cantilevered his body down the concrete flight. Wyungare followed.

The midfloor landing was a squeeze, but the alligator got around it. The party approached the second-floor access door. Cordelia slipped it open a few inches, looked out, turned, and motioned the rest to follow. She opened the door as far as it would go. The doorway was close to the juncture of two main halls.

"To the right," said Wyungare, "to the renovation work."

"Ssh," said Cordelia.

The alligator's short legs pumped and the reptile squeezed into the hallway. The other hallway led to the physicians' office wing. The elevator bank was about halfway to the offices where they had searched in vain for Finn.

A bell chimed and elevator doors hissed open.

"Oh, shit," said Cordelia.

Three people exited the car and turned toward the offices, and away from the escape party. One of them was Finn, prancing a little as his hooves clattered on the tile. One was Troll. The other was Dr. Bob Mengele.

Troll ushered the party along the hall, away from the escapees. Finn carefully kept his eyes to the fore. Wyungare couldn't see Dr. Bob's face, but it sounded as though he was talking through clenched teeth.

"Tonight," said Dr. Bob. "I will disassemble our Cajun friend tonight. There is no question of ethical ambiguity here. I will be vivisecting only an alligator, *not* a human being. I will find things out. The gay community will thank me. I may, as well, discover things of great importance to the joker community as well."

"I don't think this will be possible," Finn said.

"It *will* be possible," said Dr. Bob tightly. "Trust me."

The doctors and the security man reached an office door at the end of the hall. Finn and Dr. Bob went first. Wyungare was sure he saw a flash of one huge Troll eye winking back at him. Then the door closed.

He started, realizing the explosive rush of fetid air beside him was because the alligator had been holding his breath too.

"You can take Jack the rest of the way," said Wyungare. "I will find another stairwell and go to the ground. Wait for my signal."

Cordelia nodded. She looked appraisingly at the alligator and then kissed Wyungare. "Hurry," she said.

The Aborigine sprinted down to the end of the corridor, noting with approval the placement of the mouth of the waste chute to the street. He found the stairwell access and sped down the concrete steps silently.

On the ground floor, he found the street exit. Outside, the laundry truck was still there, and only a few yards from the spot he wanted. Wyungare sprang into the back and started throwing armloads of dirty linens out onto the street. He had a small mountain of soiled laundry piled up when the driver came out of the clinic.

"Hey, muthuh!" he yelled. The driver was short and spindly, skin looking like it had been crisped in a waffle iron.

Wyungare grunted and tossed another armload of sheets out the back. "Please leave me alone," he grunted. He fixed the driver's eyes and grinned in what he hoped was a maniacal way.

"Um, sure, man," said the driver. "Take all the filthy sheets you want. No problem." He turned and walked toward the clinic door. "Honk when you're done. I'm gonna shoot up some java."

Wyungare *was* done. He glanced up at the second floor, then reached forward past the driver's seat and punched the horn rim three times. Then he got out and waited.

Like many other buildings renovating on the cheap in Manhattan, the builders used a simple plank-and-timber chute to convey all the broken wallboard and plaster and scrap down to the street, where it could be carted off.

Wyungare saw the snout of the alligator first, then the rest of him as he wiggled into the chute and started to flow downward like a mossy, green tidal wave. The alligator hit the mounded laundry with an audible *whoof* and an impact that shook the sidewalk.

The Aborigine saw Cordelia staring down from a window. He motioned to her. Then he stood clear as the large reptile whipped his tail back and forth, struggling free of the sheets and towels.

"Let's go, my cousin," said Wyungare. He glanced about, getting his bearings. He knew which way was the Rox.

Cordelia and the black cat burst out through the door of the clinic and followed after them, on the run. Wyungare was trotting now. "Uncle Jack can really motor," gasped Cordelia, catching up.

Man, woman, alligator, and cat, they escaped together. Nobody seemed to notice.

After all, this was Jokertown.

And it was New York.

Do whatever the Great White Worm wants, Travnicek had said. Just check with me every couple hours.

What the Great White Worm wanted was information.

"Your memory is very detailed, yes?" Kafka leaned forward to peer at Modular Man from only a few inches away. The android had noticed that Kafka kept his distance from everyone else but didn't seem to mind getting close to him.

Maybe he liked machines, Modular Man thought. Or disliked people.

"Yes," Modular Man said. "My memory is very detailed, though I frequently edit unimportant parts to save space."

"And you've been in Zappa's headquarters."

"Yes."

"Did you see the maps?"

"Yes."

"Describe them."

"I wasn't paying any particular attention to them."

"But the *memories* are very detailed. Pay attention to *them*."

"I will." He brought the images scrolling out of his memory banks. "I don't know what most of the symbols mean," he added.

"That doesn't matter. We do."

Modular Man, since the rout of the peace mission, had spent most of the afternoon being debriefed by Bloat's assistants. Zappa's plans for overwhelming the Rox with a barrage of missiles had both impressed and angered them. It appeared they had been expecting another attack by ground troops, much like the last.

"Come with me," Kafka said. "I'll show you *our* maps."

Kafka led Modular Man up several flights of stairs, into a part of the castle made of gray stone instead of glass, and then down a long corridor tiled in black-and-white slate. Graceful Romanesque window arches were supported by columns painted in spirals of white and blue. Stained-glass windows showed heroic, legendary scenes, identified in strong Roman letters: LOHENGRIN DISPLAYS THE GRAIL, YSVELT MOVRNS FOR TRISTRAM, THEODEN DEFEATS THE ORCS OF SARVMAN. The panicked, screaming orcs all looked like jokers in armor. Kafka didn't seem to notice.

The end of the corridor was less impressive—the bare stone was fused and scabbed, as if it had been melted, and a misshaped door was set into it. Apparently Bloat hadn't thought out this part of the building very thoroughly. Kafka led Modular Man inside.

Inside, high in a tower, was what looked like a medieval version of Zappa's headquarters. Communications equipment was stacked on shelves; maps were pinned to the wall; a large reel-to-reel tape recorder spun on a desktop; an intent four-eyed joker worked a court reporter's stenography machine; a legless joker in a wheelchair frowned at pins in a map. Light was provided by fluorescents and cross-shaped arrow slits.

In the center of the room was a thin young woman, maybe eighteen, lying on a couch. The arms of the couch were carved to look like swans. The woman wore combat fatigues, a wide cloth band across her eyes, and a floppy black beret down over one ear. As the door opened her head turned toward the sound.

"It's Kafka, Patchwork," the joker said. "I've got Modular Man with me."

The woman gave a thin smile. Modular Man noticed a spray of freckles across her nose. She held out her hand, not toward Modular Man but in his direction. She was blind.

"Hello," she said. "I'm Modular Woman."

The android didn't quite know what to make of this. He took the hand. "Hello," he said.

"Call me Pat."

"Okay."

She turned toward the stenographer and tilted her head back. "I just heard about the location of another platoon of 155s. Inside the perimeter of Newark International, northeast corner. They're digging them in."

"Mobile or towed?"

A hesitation. "Towed. I think."

A labeled pin went into the map. Kafka turned to Modular Man. "Patchwork can't get a full view of a lot of the maps," he said. "She's vague on some of her information. But if your data can be cross-referenced with hers, we can get a pretty good view of Zappa's dispositions."

The android looked at Patchwork. "How are you getting this?" he asked.

Patchwork lifted the bandage covering her empty eye sockets, and the beret covering another socket where her ear should be. "One of my eyes and my missing ear are sitting on a shelf in Zappa's communications center. One of our people put them there."

"Modular Woman." The android nodded. "I get it now."

Patchwork slid the bandage down over her sockets again. "The other eye isn't getting much," she said. "Not since Pulse and Mistral left. Maybe you could send somebody to get it back?"

Kafka made an agitated movement. "Let's get this debriefing over with," he said. "We've all got plans to make."

Not quite, the android thought.

Everyone was making plans but him. And he didn't have any choice but to try to fit into whatever plans were made.

Detroit Steel's armor stood in center field like Gort in *The Day the Earth Stood Still*, but it didn't look like anyone was home. None of the other aces were in evidence.

"WHERE IS EVERYBODY?" Tom asked one of the officers working on the Rox model.

"General Zappa's down in command HQ with his staff," a captain told him. "Some of the aces went out to get dinner."

There was nothing to do for it but wait. Tom drifted out over the outfield and set the shell down on the grass beside Detroit Steel. He popped his seat belt and stretched. It felt good to relax. He could feel a mother of a headache coming on. Sometimes that happened when he overdid the telekinesis for a long period of time.

He turned off his cameras to let darkness fill the shell. There was a can of Schaefer in his miniature fridge. He washed down two aspirin with a swallow of beer. Then he reclined his seat all the way, and stared at the darkness. Sleep would have been nice, but there was no way. He wished Dr. Tachyon hadn't run off to the stars. Bloat respected Tachyon; he might have listened to him. As it was, the jokers had left them with damn little choice.

It was easy to lose track of time as he lay there in the dark, sipping his can of beer and thinking. The sound of someone knocking on his shell brought him out of his reverie.

Tom sat up, turned on the nearest camera. A bald woman was outside, leaning into his lens, a little white cardboard container in one hand. The only hair on her shaved head was a buzz-cut purple lightning bolt right down the center. Her skintight red leather jumpsuit glittered with golden studs, and she wore a tiny gold skull in her right nostril.

For one awful second Tom thought the jumpers had found him. Then he realized that the girl was Danny Shepherd.

It was the smile that gave her away. The hair, the clothes, everything was different, but her smile was the same. Tom pressed a button to turn on his exterior mikes.

". . . one home?" She glanced over her shoulder at a man standing behind her. "I don't think he's in there, Mike."

"I'M HERE," Tom boomed. Danny winced. Tom twisted a dial to lower the volume. "I was, ah, resting," he explained.

Danny waved the cardboard container. "We went over to Chinatown, got some Chinese food. Come on out and join us."

Tom found himself staring at the skull in her nose. He felt like Rip Van Winkle. When had Danny found time to get her nose pierced? Never mind getting a haircut and a new leather wardrobe. He'd only been gone a few hours. "I, uh, don't do that," he said.

"You don't do what?" Danny asked. "You don't come out? Or you don't eat Chinese food?"

"I don't come out," Tom explained.

"Ever?" said the man behind her. He was a big guy about Cyclone's age, with close-cropped blond hair and a beer gut. His arms were full of brown paper sacks. "That's no way to live. I ought to know."

Tom got it. "You're Detroit Steel."

"Mike Tsakos," he said. "*That's* Detroit Steel." With both hands full, he had to use his chin to gesture toward the armored suit. "I got to put this stuff down," he said, moving off camera.

"You sure you're not hungry?" Danny asked. "We've got a real Chinese feast here. Egg rolls, pot-stickers, moo shu pork, lemon duck, hot shredded Hunan beef, three-flavor shrimp, fried rice . . ." She looked behind her. "What am I leaving out, Mike?"

"Chicken chow mein," Mike Tsakos called out.

Danny made a face. "Right. I was trying to forget."

"General Tso's chicken," a woman's voice called. "Extra hot." It sounded like Danny.

But Danny was right there in front of Tom's camera. "Just who is this General Tso, I wonder, and why are we eating his chicken?" she said lightly.

Suddenly Tom was very confused. He threw a row of switches, one after the other, turning on the rest of his cameras. His screens blinked on, giving him a 360-degree view.

On the other side of the shell, in the shadow of Detroit Steel, Mike Tsakos and Danny Shepherd were laying out cartons of Chinese food while two other women spread a picnic blanket on the outfield grass. Startled, Tom looked from Danny in red leather to Danny with the ponytail and the baseball cap, and back again. *Twins*, he thought, for at least a moment . . .

. . . until it dawned on him that the two other women were *also* Danny Shepherd.

One was in uniform, with her black hair cropped short and a corporal's stripes on her sleeve. The other one looked like a yuppie: business suit, big round glasses, carefully styled hair, gold Rolex. But the faces were the same.

"Danny," Tom said. All four looked toward the shell. "What the fuck is going on here? Are these your sisters, or what?"

"Sisters," said punk Danny. "That's good. I like that."

Ponytail Danny stood up. "I should have introduced you," she said. "This is my sister Danny, and my other sister Danny, and my other sister Danny. My sister Danny would have been here too, but she had to pick up my sister Danny at the airport." She grinned.

"They're all the same girl," Mike Tsakos added.

"Von Herzenhagen told you I was an ace," punk Danny said.

"Wait a minute," Tom objected. "You weren't even there."

"We were all there," Corporal Danny said.

"Her name is Legion," Mike Tsakos put in.

Ponytail Danny stuck out her tongue at him. "Her name is Danny," she said. "Is anyone going to eat this Chinese food before it gets cold?"

Tsakos started filling a paper plate with chicken chow mein. The other Dannys all moved in too. When they were close together like that, you could see they were more than twins. Something about their movements, their conversation, the way each one seemed to know exactly what the others were doing. And yet they were *less* than twins too, Tom thought as he watched them. Maybe it was just their clothes, but Corporal Danny looked at least two inches taller than the others, and yuppie Danny definitely had larger breasts.

"Are you sure you don't want to come out?" ponytail Danny asked him. Her plate was heavily laden with shredded beef, moo shu pork, and General Tso's chicken. "It's going to be a long night. You must be hungry."

"I'm fine," Tom said. "I've got food in here." There was half a bag of nacho-flavored Doritos around somewhere, he knew. His stomach growled at him. Fortunately, the microphones didn't pick it up.

"Okay," two Dannys said in chorus.

Tom sat inside his shell, watching Mike Tsakos and the four girls put away a ton of Chinese food. They seemed to be having a great time. He got hungrier and hungrier.

After a while, the rest of the team began to drift in. The Reflector came up out of the dugout from command HQ, and looked at the picnic in confusion. Punk Danny rolled him a moo shu pork burrito. He accepted the plate, stared at it suspiciously for a moment, then ate it with his fingers. Tom had to make a conscious effort not to think of him as Snotman.

Two more Dannys joined them a little later. One was a young starlet with a cascade of honey-blond hair that fell past her waist, long slender legs in tight jeans, a low-cut lace blouse that hinted at breasts most Playmates would kill for. The other one was pregnant. She wore a blue maternity dress and a gold wedding band, and looked like she was ready to give birth any moment now. Both of them talked like Danny, moved like Danny, smiled like Danny.

The food was pretty well gone by the time Zappa, Hartmann, and von Herzenhagen emerged from command HQ to start the briefing. With them came a gaggle of brass in assorted uniforms, Cyclone and his daughter Mistral in matching blue-and-white flying suits and a slight, green-eyed, Irish-Indian woman named Radha Valeria O'Reilly. Radha had a strange beauty: deep auburn hair, dark lashes, skin like burnished gold. She wore a green, spangled acrobat's costume and a caste mark in the center of her forehead.

"All of you know Elephant Girl, I believe," Hartmann began. "Once Pulse arrives, our team will be in place." He glanced at his watch and frowned. "He should have been here by now. It's not like Cyril to be late."

"I saw him at Aces High an hour ago," Mistral said. She had her helmet cradled under one arm. A light wind riffled through her hair. She'd dyed a bright blue streak down one side, to match her costume. "He was having pictures taken with some tourists."

"Just mark him tardy and get on with it," Cyclone said irritably. He didn't look nearly as good in his cape and Kevlar as his daughter did in hers.

Zappa agreed. "Major Vidkunssen, perhaps you'd care to go over the layout of the Rox with the team?"

"WHAT ABOUT MODULAR MAN?" Tom wanted to know.

Von Herzenhagen took a puff. "What about him?"

"HE'S CHANGED SIDES," Tom pointed out.

"Unfortunate," von Herzenhagen said, "but hardly a fatal blow. If he gets in our way, we'll simply have to destroy him. It's not as if it hasn't been done before."

"Leave him to Detroit Steel," Mike Tsakos put in cheerfully. "I got no use for turncoats."

"Get in line, tin man," Snotman snapped. "I trashed him before. I can trash him again."

Tom was aghast. "A COUPLE OF HOURS AGO, HE WAS ONE OF US."

"He made his choice," von Herzenhagen said. "Now I'm afraid he'll have to live—or die—with the consequences." He waved his pipe at Tsakos and Snotman. "Gentlemen, we appreciate your eagerness to get in there and grapple with the enemy, but we don't want to distract ourselves with personal vendettas. Let's just leave Modular Man to Pulse, shall we? He should be able to burn through that cheap plastic skin just like *that.*" He snapped his fingers. "You can't dance with a laser. The robot won't even see it coming."

"Poor Mod Man," the pregnant Danny said.

Time had stopped.

The bodysnatcher rose through a silent sunlit sky. He had no body now. He was fire, he was light. He was a burning arrow, ascending. It seemed as though he were moving in slow motion. But around him, nothing else moved at all.

The towers of Manhattan dwindled beneath him. Everything was strangely distorted. Objects seemed to stretch away, receding into infinity when he looked at them. Ahead of him, everything was tinted blue; behind, the world was awash with sunset, as if seen through a red filter. His passage etched a burning line through the sky, like a tracer frozen in flight.

The endless music of the streets was gone now. There was no wind, no words, no sound at all. The silence was endless. There was no sense of movement. No sensation at all.

Below, stretched and reddened, were the shoreline of the Battery, the waters of the bay, the twisted towers of the Rox, small as a child's toys. Indigo clouds appeared above him. He knifed through them. For an instant he felt a vague heat. Around him, the cloud stuff turned red and orange. It was over so fast it was almost subliminal. Then the bodysnatcher was above the clouds.

He saw a jet high against the blue, its fuselage as long as a freight train, stretching back to infinity. Slowly, ever so slowly, he drifted up toward it. The jet hung dead still in the sky, frozen in space and time, a big 747 with KLM markings. Pale round faces peered out of the windows, little Norman Rockwell faces looking down on the city. The bodysnatcher wondered what they'd think when they saw him, realized that he'd never know. He'd be a hundred thousand miles into space before their vapid little mouths began to open in surprise. He'd be past the moon before the pilot could turn to the copilot to say, "What the fuck was *that?*"

This was what it was like to move at the speed of light.

Intoxicated, the bodysnatcher rose higher and higher. He could see all of Manhattan and Staten Island now, and most of Long Island. The sky was growing darker, and the stars were coming out. Maybe he *would* go to the moon, he thought.

Except . . . it seemed he was rising so slowly . . . time turned subjective when you moved at lightspeed . . . a laser might reach the moon in minutes . . . seconds . . . but it would seem like weeks to him. And if he got tired . . . how long could the Pulse body stay in its lightform before it ran out of energy?

The bodysnatcher felt a twinge of sudden panic. He was high enough now to see the curve of the earth. He would have flailed his hands against the empty air, if he'd had hands to flail. How does a laser *turn*, he thought wildly.

And as he thought it, it happened.

He curved downward, watched the line of his ascension grow into a glowing arc, a rainbow painted in a single color. The colors all shifted around him. Now the earth below was blue, the sky a red sea above him. He fell as slowly as he'd climbed. He willed himself to veer right, then left, then right again. It happened. His ascent had been straight as a ruler; his fall was frozen lightning, jagged and bright.

A hundred feet above the Rox, a sea gull was frozen in time, white against the dark water. The bodysnatcher altered course. He went through the bird's head. The heat was sudden and intense, scalding water on bare skin, gone as quickly as it came. For an instant he was surrounded by walls of flesh and blood and bone. He saw them blacken and burn around him. Then he was gone.

By the time the gull began its fall, the bodysnatcher had burned through the eye of the dome's great golden face into the throne room, and willed himself back to human flesh.

That was the hardest part. He fell the last five feet and bloodied his knee on the rough stone floor. The world came crashing in around him: noise, smells, pain. He realized he was naked. The smell of bloatblack was enough to gag him. His legs trembled as he got to his feet beneath the looming torch.

"Zelda?" Bloat squeaked in astonishment. His joker guards swung their weapons to bear. Kafka gaped at him. Only the penguin seemed unperturbed.

"The bitch is dead," the bodysnatcher said, laughing. "Leave her rot. I'm Pulse now."

Kafka asked, "What about Molly and—"

Bloat took the answer out of his head. "Vanilla and Blueboy are bringing back her body," he told Kafka. "Her guest may be conscious by the time Charon comes in. Take her down to the dungeon. We may need a hostage or two to bargain with."

The bodysnatcher looked up at Bloat, and pictured himself turning to light, burning into the governor's mountainous flesh, lancing through him again and again, until blood and pus and bloatblack oozed from a hundred smoking holes. He savored the thought, turning it over and over in his mind to give the governor a good long look. For once, the fat boy had nothing to say.

The bodysnatcher laughed hysterically. Let them come. The nats with their guns, the aces with their powers. Let them all come. He would be waiting for them.

The bodysnatcher finally had a body he liked.

"There's no more information coming in," Patchwork said. "Everything seems to be in place or nearly. All Zappa's people are eating pizza. I think we can take a break."

Kafka looked at the maps; his chitin made a scraping sound. "I should talk to the governor and the others. Decisions have to be made." He turned to the other jokers. "Help me carry these maps."

The jokers carried the maps away, leaving Modular Man with the blind woman. Modular Man turned to her. "What are they going to do?"

"I don't know. They don't tell me much." She leaned her head in the direction of the big reel-to-reel. "Would you mind turning that off?"

Modular Man snapped off the recorder. Patchwork leaned back on her swan-necked sofa.

"They don't tell me much because I don't think Bloat believes I'm loyal."

"Are you?"

She smiled vaguely. "Some things I'm loyal to, some things I'm not." She gave her head a toss. "1-800-I-GIVE-UP. Was that serious? Can we really surrender?"

"So far as I understand."

"Because I've never done anything criminal other than *be* here, y'know? But if I give up—" She gestured toward the band across her face. "How do I get my eyes and ear back?"

"I don't know."

She drew up her legs. "I'm not normally blind and I have a hard time tracking people. Would you mind sitting down? That way I'd know where you were."

He settled onto a cushion. "As I understand it," Patchwork said, "you're not here voluntarily."

"No."

"But you just can't fly away."

Modular Man hesitated—a human mannerism he'd picked up. It wasn't as if he hadn't explained this before. "I can't even *think* about flying away. I have to obey my creator."

"Funny about not thinking. Because that's what people here have to do, so the governor can't pick up our thoughts. We have to sort of keep our minds far off, way in the atmosphere like. Scramble up our thoughts. And even then we can't know for sure if he can hear us."

"Can Governor Bloat hear all of you all the time?"

"I think he can hear anything he really wants to. But it's work for him, and usually he doesn't want to bother. And when he sleeps— well, he sleeps a *lot*. But I don't really know how it is with him. Or anybody." She grinned faintly. "I got a better line to Zappa than to anybody here."

"What do you think is going to happen?"

"What's gonna happen?" She shrugged. "I don't know, man. But I've been reeling off these statistics for the last few hours. Tanks and helicopters and fighter-attack squadrons and Hellfires and LAWs and 155s and 105s and 120s—all those numbers. And LCACs and AAVs and MLRs and ATACMS—initials, okay? Just like the numbers, only letters, and lots of them. A whole *fuck* of a lot of them. And the *New Jersey*, which I know is a battleship. A carrier task group built around the *John F. Kennedy*. And a Los Angeles submarine with cruise missiles. So—" She took a breath. "I have no idea what a 155 is, and I wouldn't know an MLR if it bit me, but I have a feeling I'm gonna get bit pretty soon. We're *all* gonna get bit. So all I can do is hope that the governor can do something brilliant, or that the phone lines stay open so that I can call that 800 number once things get serious."

From having worked with the military in the past Modular Man knew what a lot of those numbers and letters meant, and he hadn't seen anything here that could stop them from doing their work.

"I hope the lines stay open too," he said.

Patchwork frowned a bit, as if concentrating. "I'm thinking dirty thoughts," she said. "Real porn. It embarrasses the governor, you know—he's just a kid."

"You're not so old yourself."

Her concentrated look deepened. "I'm thinking about something really disgusting. I don't want the governor listening in."

"He's probably more interested in Kafka talking about MLRs and 155s."

"Yeah. Maybe." She relaxed against the swan couch and put a hand over where her eyes had been. "No fucking eyes," she said, "one ear. I can't go to the toilet without someone leading me, and plumbing wasn't one of the governor's major concerns when he built this place so it's a long goddamn walk from here, and when I get there there isn't going to be any toilet paper." She laughed again, cynically this time. "That'll teach me to fall in love."

"Are you in love?"

"I was. He's dead." She said it lightly, as if it didn't matter.

"I'm sorry."

"I'm not." Defiantly. "The bastard was stepping out on me when he got killed. Neck snapped and the body turned to a block of ice—him and the bitch both. They said Black Shadow did it. That cold bastard."

"Ah." Not certain what else to say.

"I met Black Shadow myself just a few weeks ago. Here on the Rox." She shuddered. "He knocked my block off. And all because I fell in love." She waved her hands. "I thought about it you know. I mean, sometimes you fall in love with the *person*, and sometimes it's just with the person's *style*. And it was his style that I fell for."

"Ah."

"Diego was a jumper, right? And we were both gonna be jumpers together, and rich, and he'd have a black Ferrari and I'd have a red one, and we'd both have great clothes and drugs and parties, and we'd have *adventures*. But Diego got killed, and so did the Prime, so I never got made into a jumper. And now I'm sitting here in this tower and *I haven't got any eyes*." She reached up into her bandage and made swabbing motions with her fingers. "Still got tear ducts, though. Yep. Still do." She shook her head, then looked up blindly. "How come I'm doing all the talking here?"

"Probably because I haven't got a whole lot of news you haven't already heard."

"Oh. Okay." She laughed again. "Just wanted to find out." She paused, licked her lips. "Would you mind taking me to the toilet?"

"I'll take you, I don't know where it is."

"I'll give directions, you do the steering." She put her feet on the floor and rose hesitantly. Modular Man stood and offered her an arm.

"Thank you," she said. "Anything here we can use for toilet paper?"

"A spare roll of paper for the stenograph machine."

"Great. That'll do."

Modular Man reached for the roll and handed it to her. "I'm glad the toilet paper shortage is one problem I'm not going to have to face," he said.

Patchwork laughed. He escorted her out the misshapen door and then down the black-and-white-tiled corridor. At the top of the stairs they turned onto a long balcony that overlooked the stairwell, then turned off onto the battlements.

The toilet was a little shed built onto the massive wall of the inner bailey, a two-holer that simply dropped waste out into the mile-wide moat. Patchwork said thank you, patted his arm, and disappeared inside, pulling the door shut after her.

Modular Man waited. Both his radar and his optics reported a lot of air traffic overhead.

The door opened and Patchwork reemerged. She stuffed the roll of paper into a pocket and held out her arm. Modular Man took it and led her carefully back inside.

"The governor can make all sorts of things appear," she said, "but there are some necessities he can't be bothered with. I've got a couple unused tampons I'm guarding with my life."

A pair of young men dressed in a mix of military gear and black leather with zips were waiting just inside the keep. One had a buzzcut and one didn't. Both carried guns. One had a roll of computer print-out under an arm. Apparently they were heading for the toilets.

"Yo, Pat," buzzcut said as he passed—he stuck out an arm and clotheslined Patchwork with his forearm.

Electronic hash sizzled through the android's macro-atomic circuits as Patchwork's head came off and bounced. Her jaw came loose and skiddered over the hard surface.

Patchwork's body staggered, then recovered. Headless, it bent down carefully and began to search for its head with its hands.

Knocked my block off. Now Modular Man knew what she'd meant.

"I love it when that happens," buzzcut said.

"Don't do it again," said Modular Man. He picked up Patchwork's head and handed it to her. With a practiced gesture she reattached it. Eye sockets gazed blankly from under the disarrayed bandage. The android retrieved the jaw—the tongue was still attached and flapped frantically—and gave it to Pat.

"Don't do it again?" Buzzcut smirked. "What happens if I do?"

Modular Man grabbed him by the throat and hung him out over the balcony.

"We find out if you can fly," he said.

The boy's arms and legs flopped wildly. His friend made a move, but Modular Man saw it on radar and the servomotors on his right shoulder swung his microwave laser up and pointed it straight between non-buzzcut's eyes.

Non-buzzcut decided not to continue moving.

Buzzcut was turning purple. Evidence of a savage effort showed in

his face. He stared at Modular Man and narrowed his eyes menac-
ingly.

"By the way," the android said, "I can't be jumped."

Buzzcut passed out.

The android hauled the boy in and lowered him to the floor. All
through his movements, Modular Man's laser remained focused on
non-buzzcut. Then he straightened and took Patchwork's arm.

"As you were," he said. "The toilet's free."

Though, judging from the smell, it was a little late for the toilet in
buzzcut's case.

Modular Man led Patchwork back along the walk overlooking the
main stairs. He glanced down and saw someone climbing it.

Astonishment didn't come easily to him. He was a machine and
for the most part he accepted the readings he got on reality. He'd seen
some pretty strange things and accepted what he'd had to.

Still, seeing Pulse climbing the stairs was the cause of the first
double take in his life.

Bodysnatcher was performing a relentless series of pushups. The Outcast could hear the steady counting inside his head: . . . *seventy-six . . .
seventy-seven . . .* He could also tell that bodysnatcher was as disappointed in this body as with any other, finding it soft and flabby in
comparison with his old body, the one the aces had destroyed. . . .
seventy-eight . . . seventy-nine . . . eighty . . .

The right arm spasmed and went out from under him. He slammed
hard onto the wooden floor. "You'd never have made a hundred anyway," the Outcast said. The penguin appeared alongside him. It was
doing curls with a set of tiny barbells as it skated around the Outcast's
feet.

"Jesus—" The rage inside Bodysnatcher's head went to sudden
fright and then cold. He rolled to a fighting crouch, sweat raining on
the floor. His eyes narrowed but hands relaxed. "You're the one Juggler
was talking about. The Outcast. You really the governor?"

"You really Zelda?"

"Zelda died, motherfucker."

The Outcast ignored that. "Oh, he's the gov, all right," the penguin told her. "Same old weenie, different package. Like you."

"Shut up," they both told the penguin at the same time. It shrugged, doffed its funnel hat, and skated out the door, still doing reps. "Juggler's going to surrender," the Outcast said to Bodysnatcher.

"Thought you had talked him out of it with those fancy pyrotechnics, *Governor*." Bodysnatcher managed to put an edge on the word as he went over to a bench press, grabbed a towel, and started to dry off.

"I did, for a while. I didn't think it'd last and it hasn't. Juggler's talked several of them into it: Creamcheese, Porker, Rain Man, the twins, some others. I can't really say I blame them."

"Yeah? So what do you want me to do? Go give them another goddamn pep talk? Let the little fucks surrender. We don't need 'em."

The Outcast smiled. "No," he said. "I've said that I'd never hold anyone here who didn't want to be here, and I meant that. I don't keep slaves. If they want to go, I'm not going to let anyone stop them. But . . . I've been thinking about it. What do you think the Combine's going to do with the jumpers when they give themselves up?"

Bodysnatcher shrugged, but the Outcast heard the sudden curiosity the question aroused. "I don't know," he started to say, then he—almost—grinned. "You're thinking that maybe we should find out."

The Outcast allowed himself another smile. "Exactly."

"Then send Needles up here," Bodysnatcher said.

"Why?"

"I want to look nice for the man when I surrender," he said.

"So," Battle said after Ray summarized his meetings with Ackroyd and Vivian Choy, "I think we can count on Ackroyd. You did a good job there." He hmmmed for a moment. "I guess we can forget about Lazy Dragon. I don't think he'll call. That's all right. We should have enough muscle for anything that freak Bloat might throw at us."

"That's it then?" Ray asked.

"Not quite," Battle said. "We still have one more visit tonight. To Our Lady of Perpetual Misery."

"The Church of Jesus Christ, Joker?" Ray asked.

"Not the church. The graveyard."

Ray looked at him. "Christ. Not another deader."

"How's that?" Battle asked.

Ray was being as subtle as he could. "Well, Puckett's dead, isn't he? And he's on the roster."

Puckett was waiting outside Ray's office, ostensibly because Ray said there wasn't room for the three of them inside, but really because Ray couldn't stand the sight or smell of him. The government ace acquiesced easily enough and Battle didn't seem to be missing his company either.

"Puckett is a special case," Battle said slowly. "And I see you've been checking on us."

"Not really," Ray lied. "I just recognized the name. It took me a little while to remember where I'd heard it. The Texas sniping incident."

Battle nodded. "We should really use Puckett's code name, Crypt Kicker. And you're quite right. He's dead."

Somehow hearing Battle say that in such calm, reasoned tones made it seem even worse. "I didn't know tower snipers were usually recruited into government service," Ray said with distaste.

"They're not," Battle explained, "but Puckett, as I've said, is a special case. Oh, he's had his problems with the law in the past. Haven't we all?" Battle asked. "But Bobby Joe has seriously repented for his wrongdoings. When he—well—woke up, he knew that the Lord had given him a second chance to do right with his life. He accepted Jesus as his personal savior and decided to devote the rest of his life—or whatever—to upholding the law."

"Christ!" Ray said.

"Exactly."

This was getting too weird. "Just where did he 'wake up'?"

"In the potters field where he'd been buried by the state. It seems the grounds had also been used as a toxic waste dump. PCBs, insecticides, industrial acids, light radioactives. That sort of thing," Battle said, leaning forward with a tight little smile. "And Puckett—that is, Crypt Kicker—found that he'd absorbed the toxic wastes into his body and that he can now secrete them. Couple this with the fact that he's also extremely strong and extremely hard to hurt—he is dead, after all— and extremely, extremely loyal to the government and its properly appointed representatives, and you can see that he makes the perfect soldier."

"Too bad he smells so damn bad."

"Well, almost perfect."

Ray nodded. This was all as crazy as he had feared. Worse even. "What about this graveyard stuff? Are we counting on another convenient resurrection?"

"Oh," Battle said, a twinkle in his eye, "in a way." He stood and checked his watch. "I've got to be going, but I'll meet you at the graveyard in six hours. And bring a shovel, will you?"

The military was deploying again, and Patchwork was busy reeling off their movements to the crew of the Joker Situation Room. The Rox, however, was making its own preparations.

Cruise missiles, for example, were supposed to be incredibly accurate, but they guided themselves to the target through a radar image of the target locked into their guidance systems.

So, with Modular Man's help, the Rox was changing its radar profile.

Bloat was creating rafts with radar reflectors. Building them out of thin air so that jokers in rubber boats could tow them out into the bay and anchor them there. Some of the reflectors were hollow masts filled with lead foil, some were odd structures that looked like step pyramids covered with aluminum.

"Right angles," Kafka kept saying. "We want lots of right angles."

Modular Man's radar had several times picked up the *New Jersey* offshore. The funny step pyramids and hollow masts gave off radar profiles almost as large as the battleship.

High above the Rox, looking at its reflection in his radar image, *he* was certainly confused.

He could only hope it would confuse the cruise missiles.

As the skies had darkened in the west above New Jersey, the pair with the black cat and alligator in tow felt more confident about crossing the financial district and the southern tip of Manhattan to Battery Park.

The small groups of humans and beasts continued to attract little attention. The onset of night helped. The major exception was an elderly lady walking her two poodles. As Wyungare and the others crossed Chambers, the old woman, apparently noticing them from a block away, pointedly crossed to the other side of Park Row. Once there, she ignored them as she tottered abreast of the fugitives. Both dogs, attired in matching red sweaters, yapped as they pulled at their leashes. The old woman jerked them back into line, eyes still fixed straight ahead.

Jack started to veer into the street. Wyungare set his hand on the gator's snout and the reptile returned to his original course.

"I think he's hungry," said Cordelia.

"We'll be at the water soon."

"*I'd* never eat anything from that cesspool."

"You're not an alligator with a four-meter metabolism." Wyungare paused thoughtfully. "Come to think of it, I could do with a snack myself."

"I thought you people could trek for weeks without eating," said Cordelia.

"'You people'?" said Wyungare. He reached and lightly touched her hip with his index finger. "Perhaps you might try that regimen yourself, Euro-girl."

Cordelia slapped the finger away. "You weren't complaining earlier."

White teeth, major grin. "I must admit I enjoy some meat on a woman."

Cordelia matched his smile tooth for tooth. "Me too, love, depending on whose meat it is."

Wyungare, a bit embarrassed, let his hands swing at his sides. "Ah, look, our destination." They could see the elms of Battery Park.

"Listen, mon cherie," said Cordelia, "I have a question."

Wyungare looked at her quizzically. Beside them, the paws of the black cat padded steadily; the alligator grunted in hoarse accompaniment.

"I'm helping the three of you make a break and embark on this fantastic voyage to the Rox. For whatever good it will do, you know? I hope you'll accomplish some good. But the question I still have is, what about Uncle Jack?"

Wyungare said, "I will continue searching him out. I shall talk with him."

"So?" said Cordelia. "That sounds like the same sort of rigmarole I got from the clinic staff. At least Dr. Bob Mengele, asshole that he is, actually tried to *do* something." The grit in her voice edged her words. "I know you're not just bullshitting me, love; if you were, that would be it for us. So just tell me what you think you can do. Please." The metal in her voice dulled. Wyungare saw tears in her eyes.

He stopped and gripped her shoulders, confronting her face-to-face. Wyungare carefully side-kicked the alligator; Jack whuffled and looked around confusedly, but stopped too. The black cat turned his head and burred curiously from deep in his throat.

"Cordie, it's not that I won't tell you my plan, it's that I cannot. There's a fundamental principle that says that now is the moment of power. Not yesterday, not tomorrow. Now. I am not planning a long-term strategy because, simply, I cannot."

He hesitated and, for the first time, avoided her look. "What?" she said. "What's wrong?"

"The tuckonies taught me something." Wyungare shook his head. "The tree-spirits, the spirits of growth," he said by way of explanation. "I assume you have your own definition of karma?"

Cordelia looked puzzled. "What goes 'round . . . All that kind of thing?"

Wyungare nodded slowly. "Most Europeans see it as a function of the distant past. Sins of your childhood come back to haunt you as an adult."

Cordelia nodded.

"Try it this way," said her lover. "You, me, all of us, represent a huge gene pool, both physically and psychically. Our resources span an enormous inventory. Karma is not some ancient instrument of vengeance. It is *now*. Each moment we re-create who we are and what we do." He gently raised his hands to her face, cradling her chin between thumb and forefinger. "Perhaps this is all simply an elaborate way of saying that karma is the ongoing process of winging it."

Cordelia smiled. "I don't think that's what a lot of the sensitive New Age folk want to hear. What you just said means that we all bear a burden of responsibility for our actions."

"See, young missy?" said Wyungare. "An easy lesson to comprehend."

"But hard to carry out." Cordelia shook her head. "Karma is now."

"The past distances things. People let that soften their responsibilities."

She took his hands into hers and dug in her nails. "So connect this with Uncle Jack."

He didn't flinch. "I believe I have three tasks to perform within a day. The first is to speak with the boy, Bloat, and help him pass from warrior to magician. The second is to draw upon *mana*, to help Jack Robicheaux draw strength from the power within, and to define a condition of healing. The third—" His voice dropped off and he shook his head. "The third I must not speak of now."

She regarded him puzzledly. "Does it have anything to do with us?"

Wyungare dropped his head so that his chin tucked into his chest. He was quiet for a moment. Then he looked straight at her again. "Whatever happens, Cordie, remember this: I feel a great amount of affection for you."

"*Merde*," she said, eyes flashing dangerously. "Guys are such wimps, even if they're revolutionaries and shamans." She leaned toward him, up on her toes, face close to his. "So do you love me?"

Wyungare regarded her gravely. Then he smiled. It was as though a gate had opened. "Yes," he said. "Yes. Very much. I love you."

"Then that's enough." She drew his lips down to hers. Parting from his mouth at last, she said, "I will love you always." The seriousness in her voice suddenly moderated. "This is no teen crush, wombat-boy." She grinned. He kissed her again.

The black cat rubbed around their legs, purring. Then Jack rushed past them, reptilian patience apparently at an end.

"Boat's leaving," said Cordelia. "Wait, Uncle Jack!" she called. They both followed.

The cat bounded ahead, as though acting as a forward observer. He yowled triumphantly and cut right, past some anonymous statue covered with pigeon droppings, then in front of a phalanx of empty green benches. He bounced almost as stiff-legged as a kitten through some brush and then they were at the water's edge. Wyungare set a restraining hand on the alligator's head. He was no physical match for Jack's reptile avatar, but he directed a sensation of soothing well-being into the creature's soul. That should last just long enough, he thought.

Gray water lapped unappetizingly against the ornamental rocks. Directly ahead they could see the dark wall that surrounded the Rox.

Cordelia stooped and touched the water with one finger. Then she rubbed it vigorously on her denim-clad hip. "Yuck. Bad stuff. Are you sure you can't just translate out there through the dreamtime?"

Wyungare shook his head. "Interference from the boy is making that too chancy. Believe me, I'd rather fly than swim."

Cordelia took his hand and held it as though it were a direct line to sanity. "Is there any way we can communicate while you're out there? I'd like to try."

The Aborigine shrugged. "Perhaps in the dreamtime. You've had a bit of experience now in getting there. Just be cautious. The worlds are not altogether safe."

"I'll be careful," she said.

"We must leave." Wyungare disengaged himself. The alligator roared, a cry of challenge, of hunger and impatience. He shuffled forward into the water, looking suddenly like a huge, rough-barked log floating low in the Upper Bay.

The black cat rubbed against Cordelia's calf and then leapt onto the alligator's back. He stalked along the ridge of the reptile and settled himself on Jack's armored skull. The cat sat on his haunches and regarded the distant view of New Jersey. The alligator didn't seem to mind.

"My turn," said Wyungare. He gave Cordelia a sudden, fierce hug.

"Come back to me," said the young woman.

"One way or another."

"What?" she said, confused.

He kissed her a final time. "Remember me."

Then he turned and stepped onto the back of the gator as though boarding a gangplank. Balancing, he strode forward and then settled himself astraddle the alligator's midsection with both brown legs trailing into the disgusting bay water. He ran his fingers along Jack's dorsal line.

"I feel like I should be tying you to the mast," said Cordelia, "and stuffing beeswax in your ears."

Wyungare turned back toward her. "Just like Odysseus." He tapped the fingers of his right hand against Jack's armored hide. "That's your uncle's job. He's not human now. He can get me through the barrier."

Like a warship pulling away from its dock, the alligator smoothly and sinuously launched himself toward the deeper water.

Wyungare again turned and saw Cordelia standing on the shore watching them. He felt a sudden empathic flash. To Cordelia, the image of her three friends leaving the land was weirdly reminiscent of Gilbert Stuart's famous iconographic American painting of George Washington crossing the Delaware.

She wishes she had a camera, Wyungare thought. But she has her memory. That will be enough.

But before turning back to their course and the waiting Wall, Wyungare couldn't help himself. Silly, maybe; melodramatic, definitely. He waved.

And Cordelia waved back.

FRIDAY
NIGHT

September 21, 1990

THE BODYSNATCHER WAITED BY the Jersey Gate with the cowards and weak sisters. A fog was rolling in off the bay. The light from the setting sun brushed a hundred-odd silent, frightened faces as the small clot of jokers and jumpers waited.

A few stragglers were still crossing the causeway, lugging whatever they could lug. Most had bedrolls or blankets. A few were carrying their pathetic little sacks with all their worldly possessions. No one had any weapons. Bloat's joker guards had relieved them of guns and knives. They could leave if they wanted to, but the guns stayed behind to defend the Rox.

Pulse's body was all the weapon the bodysnatcher needed. No one dared to say a word to him.

He looked at the crowd around him. A bare hundred jokers had shown up, out of the thousands on the Rox. Old women, the sick and feeble, a few mothers with small children. Nobody who'd be missed.

The jumpers were clustered together under the watchful eyes of Bloat's demon guards. The bodysnatcher counted them twice, and came up with twenty-one. Twenty-two counting him. The world's only middle-aged jumper.

He was taking a risk. Someone might recognize the Pulse body. But the bodysnatcher had made it hard for them.

He'd shaved his head, plastered tattoo transfers over his face. A death's head moth spread its wings around his eyes. He was wearing a filthy pair of denims and a leather vest. Under the vest he was bare-chested. There was a safety pin through his right cheek, and another in his left tit. His nipple leaked blood like a mother leaking milk. That was all right. The pain kept him sharp. He didn't think anyone would want to look at him too long.

Finally the huge gate swung open. Jokers on the walls stared down with contempt as they raised the portcullis. Outside, the bodysnatcher glimpsed men in uniform, trucks, a yellow school bus.

For a long moment, no one moved.

Then Juggler took a step forward. He was carrying a beat-up old suitcase in one hand, and the amnesty leaflet in the other. He looked back over his shoulder. "Let's go," he said.

The parade of cowards shuffled slowly out through the castle gate. Up on the ramparts, one of the guards unzipped and began to piss down on them as they passed, moving the stream back and forth as jokers and jumpers tried to scramble out of the way.

The bodysnatcher waited until almost the end, when the guard had run out of piss. Then he mixed in with a sorry bunch of jokers. Outside the gate a grizzled sergeant was directing traffic. "Jumpers left, jokers right," he droned, over and over.

The trucks were parked to the right, military troop carriers, a double row of them. Uniformed soldiers were helping the jokers up inside. Father Squid was there too, tending to his flock. There were way too many trucks. The Combine had grossly overestimated the coward count. Off to the left, the jumpers were boarding a battered yellow school bus. The bodysnatcher studied the setup for a beat, then decided to go right, with the jokers.

He hadn't taken more than three steps when two soldiers fell in beside him. One put a hand on his arm. "Excuse me, sir," he said. "I think you want to go that way." He pointed.

The bodysnatcher imagined all the ways he could kill him. "Where are you taking us?" he asked.

"Routine debriefing," the soldier said.

The bodysnatcher went to join the other bozos on the bus.

♠

The Outcast had orders for Modular Man. The Outcast was supposed to be Bloat in another form.

Which was certainly on par with all the surrealism Modular Man had seen so far.

"We need to get some messages out," the Outcast said. He held an amethyst-headed staff with the same casual, elegant sense of power with which a king held his scepter. "There are teams of jumpers and jokers we have waiting in the city and in Jersey. The only secure method of communications is by messenger."

"The orders are important," Kafka said. "We want you to carry them for us." His mouth parts worked. "The governor has decided we need to take political action."

"Political action?"

The Outcast gave an apologetic giggle that completely undermined his nonchalant air of authority. "Hey," he said, "we're gonna blow things up. Okay?"

"You're certain?" Herne asked. "I mean, this is something you really want me to do, Governor?" His voice was eager, as were his thoughts—this was Herne the Huntsman speaking, not the daylight personality of Hardesty. The inner transformation had already begun.

"Yes," the Outcast replied. He looked at the jokers gathered in the courtyard in front of the Crystal Castle. Bloat's white body, snared in a web of spotlights, could be seen sleeping there, guarded as always by a few dozen jokers and a squadron of fish-knights. In the gathering darkness, the lights of the skyscrapers shone beyond the ebony stones of the Wall out in the bay. The Outcast raised his staff as if in benediction, the glittering rays from the amethyst touching the faces: Mustelina, Andiron, One-Eye, Squirt, Bumbilino, a handful more—all of their minds set and firm.

Angry.

Anxious.

"You want to know about Hartmann?" the Outcast said, and he let his power bleed into the words so that they sparked in the minds of the listeners. "You want to hear what I've heard in his mind? Let me tell you. Hartmann's an ace, or he once was. A powerful ace and an evil one. He could make you dance to the strings of the power in his mind, and he used that power. He used it to get his kicks, to take pleasure from the pain of the jokers he controlled. He *used* us, his own little pet slaves. He used us to kill and maim and torment, and he let us be blamed for the things he made us do. Oh, Hartmann *deserves* this. Believe me."

Herne pulled a handkerchief from his pocket. An ornate "H" was stitched on the cloth. He tossed it on the ground.

"Now," the Outcast said to Herne.

This was a power the Outcast had never felt before. Most aces seemed to have powers that affected only their own bodies, made them stronger or faster or able to project energy in some way. Like Bloat himself. Hardesty/Herne affected the very shape of reality around him. As it had with so many others, the wild card had taken something from Hardesty's mind and given it form. In the dark of night, Hardesty could become a figure from Celtic mythology: Herne, the leader of the Wild Hunt.

Herne took the battered silver horn that hung around his huge chest and inhaled deeply. He lifted the horn to his lips and winded the instrument. The note that emerged was pure and crystalline in the night air; as the sound lingered, storm clouds began to gather far above. A wind rose from the east, and the horn shimmered in the joker's hand, the patina changing from tarnished silver to rich, polished gold, the dings and dents filling in until the surface gleamed and threw back the lights of the Crystal Castle. The Outcast's skin prickled, the hair on his forearms lifting as if with static electricity. The long call continued to sound, impossibly loud and vast, like a celestial horn calling the end of the world.

But the world didn't end. Instead, the heavens answered with a barrage of lightnings. As the mournful sound faded, it was replaced by thunder and wind and the wild howling of dogs. A mist rose around the courtyard, incandescent with its own light. The Outcast shivered, but Herne laughed, deep and resonant.

They came, the Hunt.

The mist coiled and folded; from the tendrils issued the shape of the Gabriel Hounds, fierce and glowing-eyed. Herne reached down and plucked the handkerchief from the ground. He threw the cloth toward the pack, and they pounced on it, sniffing and tearing, howling all the while. A lightning flash momentarily blinded the Outcast—when he could see again, Herne was leaping astride an enormous black stallion, and a herd of like beasts paced alongside.

Andiron clashed his steely fists like a gong against his chest and clambered onto the nearest steed, the other jokers alighting a few moments later. "Away!" Herne shouted. The hounds leapt and growled in response, the stallion reared underneath him. The others in the courtyard shouted with the Huntsman, and the Outcast heard his own voice join with them.

A great power here, one that tugs at you like an addiction.

The mindvoices raged like the storm, a cyclone of rage and fury and blood lust, all linked to the madness of Herne. The jokers, the jumpers—they howled like Herne's beasts; they shouted and raised fists.

"Ride!" exclaimed Herne.

"Ride!" echoed the Rox, and dug their heels into the sides of their horses.

"Ride for Hartmann!" Herne exclaimed. His stallion screamed, the hounds bayed; like an onrushing stormfront, the Wild Hunt tore from the gates of the Crystal Castle, leaving the sleeping Bloat and the Outcast behind.

"Wait!" the Outcast cried, knowing he was snared in the web of fury that Herne spun but finding himself helpless to resist it. He wanted to be with them, he *had* to be with them.

"I'm coming too. *Wait!*"

The Outcast spoke a word of power and became lightning himself, streaking above the Hunt as they pounded from the shore of the Rox onto the frothing water of the bay, the mounts and hounds riding over the waves as if they were nothing more than rolling, transient hills. The Outcast followed, his breath fast, the wind of his passage ruffling his hair and making him squint. In a few minutes they came to the stone edifice of the Wall itself. Herne looked up, and the Outcast grinned back. He sent his power down to the Wall and opened the great gates facing Manhattan, letting the immense doors of oak and steel swing out to loose the Hunt. He flung himself forward to keep pace, crying as Herne sounded the horn again.

And he found that he could go no farther. The air became a solid fist and pushed back at him. He could not pass his own boundary. His world would not let him go.

"No!" the Outcast wailed, almost weeping. "Please!"

But the lust was already fading, his mind emerging from the spell of the Hunt as it moved farther and farther away from him. He could feel the strings that bound him eternally to the great form of Bloat. Those bonds were far, far stronger.

He could not ride with the Hunt. He was a prisoner in the Rox, confined to his own land.

The Outcast materialized on the top of the nearest tower. He pounded his fists on the stones there—they seemed substantial enough, cutting his flesh so that he bled and cried out. There, his hands gripping the cold blocks of granite, he watched the green fire and the blue lightnings of the Hunt recede over the bay, the turbulent cloud of death riding toward the city.

He found that he was crying, and there were too many reasons for the sorrow for him to sort out why.

Once, almost in another lifetime, it seemed, Wyungare had visited OutbackDisneyland. The experience, business aside, had been horrifying. It all came back. The stately voyage to the Rox rapidly evolved into Mr. Goanna's Wild Flume Ride.

First, there was the environment. The skies, what he could see of them through the swirls of fog, were ablaze with lights, most of them moving at speed. No missiles, heavy shells, or other bombardment, at least. But glowing streaks of exhaust that might be reconnaissance craft. There was a *lot* of air traffic behind him over Manhattan. Many helicopter landings. A couple of times he saw what looked like human figures moving through the air rapidly, without benefit of craft.

Then all hell burst loose as a sudden thunderstorm seemed to brew over the approaching island. Wyungare blinked and averted his face as lightning forked and linked sky and earth. It looked like a radiant vision tree impressed on his retinas. The thunder rolled past a fractional second later, the concussion shoving the air before it like the blow of a nullanulla.

Wyungare thought he heard howling, as though from rather larger predatory throats than he cared to encounter in the middle of the Upper Bay. *Madhi?* he wondered. Perhaps extremely *large* dingos. Lightning blazed again.

Further speculation was lost as the alligator dipped his snout like a diving plane and water sheeted across Wyungare's fourteen-foot reptilian vessel. The black cat leapt backward and the Aborigine found himself with nearly two stone of soaked cat wound around his chest.

Does this reptile fear thunder and lightning? he wondered. It couldn't be. It wasn't.

Jack's massive jaws opened and closed like a medieval portcullis. The webbed, slightly glowing tail of some unknown fish flopped frantically outside of the teeth. The alligator gulped and the tail disappeared within.

Ah, thought Wyungare. *Supper.* Jack was a mighty engine that needed fuel. Feeding could not easily be denied.

The alligator jigged through the bay waves with remarkable agility considering his size. Jaws opened. Jaws closed. Some of the prey screamed.

The Aborigine tried to hook his strong toes around the curve of the reptile's body. He leaned forward, keeping his center of gravity as low as he could, attempting not to be thrown loose into the frigid water. Crushed between Wyungare's and Jack's rough hide, the black cat wailed.

Then Jack's particular feeding frenzy ceased. His teeth clicked together decisively a few more times as he turned his snout back toward the Rox.

Wyungare tried to let communication sink from his fingertips into the armor protecting Jack's head. You're doing fine, he wanted to say. Now let us make land. It will aid your digestion. And mine, he thought.

The feeling of approaching Bloat's psychic barrier crossed a spectrum of apprehension. It's like—Wyungare thought a bit fuzzily—it's like approaching a glass wall at speed in a Land Rover. He thought of insects squashed on windscreens. He felt an unaccustomed dread, and then a sudden terror, the abrupt image of shattering glass smashing around him. He felt as though he were breathing in a cloud of microscopic shards. They stung like ice, like invisible razors, like venomous, stinging mites. *Wundas*. Evil spirits.

The Wall was closer than it had looked. Suddenly it loomed directly in front, the waves slapping against the peculiarly textured gray stone blocks. The Aborigine's head cleared.

Wyungare touched the alligator and *suggested* that he follow the curve of the Wall in the direction the Aborigine believed a gate to be.

Indeed, the Aborigine, gator, and cat arrived at the gate after the voyage of only another hundred yards. Jack docked as smoothly as the Staten Island Ferry pulling into its slip. The side of the alligator bumped up against what appeared to be oaken beams, but sounded more like heavy steel ringing like a gong.

Wyungare gingerly rapped his fist against the door. It did feel like metal. And it rang like metal. His head throbbed. He pounded harder.

With a rusty creak, the gate swung inward.

Wyungare said to the darkness, "Thank you, I was afraid I was going to have to bloody my knuckles."

Light grew within the gateway. The entrance was lined with truly grotesque Boschian creatures. Beside them, the intermixed jokers looked like matinee idols.

"You a nat or what?" said one of the jokers.

"What," said Wyungare. He motioned. "This is an alligator. That's a cat."

"I know the nursery rhyme," said the joker. "So where's the owl?"

Wyungare stopped, bewildered for a moment.

"Don't worry, you'll catch on," said the roller-skating penguin, suddenly weaving its way through the crowd of guards. "So. You have business with his Bloatitude? Or just another version of the Circle Line cruise way off course."

"That is correct," said Wyungare. "The first hypothesis. I have important business with the one called Bloat."

"Well, he's pretty busy," said the penguin. "The war and all. Could you perhaps come back tomorrow?"

Wyungare felt like he was in Lewis Carroll Land. "Tomorrow, no. It is essential I see your . . . governor now."

The penguin spun on the tip of one skate. "It helps me concentrate," he said once he'd stopped. "All right, then. It's off to the castle with you."

Wyungare stepped into the gateway.

"Them too," said the penguin, dipping its beak toward the cat and the alligator.

The guards, joker and simulacra alike, drew back when Jack hauled his long, armored body out of the bay and into the opening in the Wall.

Suddenly the cat sprung from Jack's back and grabbed the penguin in his paws. Bird and beast rolled over and over as the guards glanced at one another.

Wyungare shook his head. "They are just playing," he said reassuringly.

The penguin sat up, laughing uproariously. The cat purred and rubbed against the penguin's feathered haunches.

"Perhaps we should go," said Wyungare. "We're off to see the wizard."

"I don't know how I do it," Danny told him. "I mean, I do know, but there's no good way to put it into words."

She was perched on Detroit Steel's right shoulder, legs crossed, Giants cap pulled low, looking down on Tom in his shell. They were alone with the empty armor. The soldiers had turned on the floodlights, and the outfield grass was a deep, rich green.

Zappa and von Herzenhagen had been taken off by helicopter, to supervise the surrender at the Jersey Gate. Pulse still hadn't shown. The other aces had gone inside to get some rest. No one was saying when they'd be sent into action. There was no way Tom could get his shell down the narrow tunnel under the grandstands, so he'd been left behind to guard center field. The ponytail Danny had stayed to keep him company.

"There's six of you, right?" Tom said.

"There's one of me," Danny corrected him, "in a bunch of different bodies."

"So," Tom said, "so one of you is in New York, and three are in Minneapolis, and one's in Chicago, and . . . I mean, you're in six different places at once. Doing six different things at the same time. Seeing different things. Feeling different things. I mean, how do you make sense of it?"

Danny pushed back her Giants cap, shrugged. "You ever eat and watch TV at the same time?" she asked. "Well, how do you do that? I mean, you're doing two things at once, right? Doesn't it get confusing?"

Tom thought about that for a moment. "I see what you're getting at," he said. "Have you always had six bodies?"

"Remind me never to introduce you to my mother. Giving birth to one baby was distasteful enough to hear her tell it. She'd be mortified at the suggestion that she popped a litter." She grinned. "There was only one of me at first. I hardly remember what that was like. I drew my wild card when I was three. They thought I was going to die. I got very sick, and very big. You should see the pictures. I looked like Bloat's little sister. Then I started to split. Mom was set to have kittens. The family wasn't ready for a Siamese twin. When I turned into two perfect little girls, the relief almost killed her."

"Only two?" Tom said.

"At first," Danny said. "Would you believe it, they made *both* of us go to school. What's the use of being two people if both of them are stuck in Miss Rooney's class reciting the multiplication tables? My parents even *named* the other me. Michelle. I never paid any attention. I knew both of us were Danielle, even if nobody else did."

"And your other, ah, sisters? When did they—?"

"When I hit puberty, I hated myself. I wanted to be taller. With beautiful long dark hair. No freckles. And boobs. I was thirteen and neither of me had any boobs at all."

She had boobs now, Tom reflected silently as he watched her on her screens. They were right there under her shirt, giving a hint of curve to the bulletproof vest.

"Next thing I knew," Danny said, "one of me was getting big again. The splits take about a month. Fortunately, there was another me to go to school, so I didn't miss anything."

"Did you get, ah . . . everything you wanted?" Tom asked delicately. He couldn't quite bring himself to say "boobs." All of a sudden he felt strangely shy.

Danny grinned. "Oh, yeah. No freckles at all. Or were you thinking of something else?"

Inside the shell, Tom found himself blushing.

"You should have seen me in a bikini," Danny said. "After that, it was easy. My dad tried to pretend we were triplets, but I'd started to see the possibilities. One of me kept on with school, one took up dance full-time, and one helped out down at Dad's store. After a while, I decided the world was too big for three of me to handle, and I split again. For a few years there, I gave myself a new body every year for my birthday. I stopped when I hit my lucky number."

"Six," Tom said thoughtfully. "Do all of your bodies split off the original?"

Danny polished Detroit Steel's tailfin idly with her sleeve. "Nah," she said. "Any of me can make a new me."

"Which one of you is the original?"

"That would be telling," Danny said coyly. "Besides, I'm not sure I remember. It was a long time ago."

"How old are you anyway?"

"Free, white, and twenty-one," she replied cheerfully.

"You don't look more than nineteen."

"Tell me about it. I still get carded everywhere I go." She made a disgusted face.

Tom remembered when he'd been twenty-one, half a lifetime ago. Even then, he didn't have a fraction of Danny's energy or optimism. All of a sudden, he felt old, tired, and depressed.

"So there you have it, Mr. Turtle Sir," she was saying, "the story of my life." She flashed a crooked grin. "Your turn."

That took Tom aback for a moment. Then he laughed. "Nice try," he said, "but no way."

"No fair," Danny protested. "I showed you mine."

Tom was glad she couldn't see him. He was blushing again. Forty-six years old, and all of a sudden he felt like he was in high school again. "I prefer to remain an enigma," he said. "Don't you read *Aces*? Mystery is the Turtle's middle name."

"And what are the Turtle's first and last names?"

Tom laughed again. But Danny made a short, sharp gesture with her hand, cutting him off. Her head was cocked to one side, listening. "What's wrong?" he asked her.

"Do you hear that?" she asked.

Tom couldn't hear a thing. He turned a dial, boosting the volume on his exterior mikes, filling the shell with the familiar sounds of the Brooklyn night: a distant roar of traffic, a horn blaring, the rumble of a tank.

Then he heard it.

Far off and small, yet somehow it cut through the street noise to bring a chill to the blood. A baying, as of . . .

"Dogs," Tom said. "A lot of dogs."

"Hounds," Danny said. Suddenly she was all business. She jumped down off Detroit Steel, landing with catlike grace on the balls of her feet and snatching up her M-16. "I grew up in the north woods. I know the sound of a hunting pack."

High, high overhead, a lightning bolt crashed across a clear sky. The thunderclap came an instant later.

It was warm and close in the steel confines of his shell. But Tom Tudbury shivered.

♠

"Croyd, wake *up,* would you?" The Outcast shook the form on the bed. The bedsprings rattled, but Croyd continued to snore. From the doorway, the two guards that Kafka had set to watch the Sleeper stared silently.

"Bet if he got those adenoids fixed, he wouldn't snore like that." The Outcast turned to see the penguin, doing tight little figure eights on the ledge of the high tower window. The guards grinned; the penguin waved back at them.

The Outcast sighed and straightened up. He exhaled loudly. "He's *gotta* wake up," he said. "We need him." He gestured at Croyd. "Look at that body. Those orifices have to do *something.*"

"Well, I have other visitors for you, Your Largeness. They came to help."

"More aces?" the Outcast said, suddenly eager. "Who—"

"An alligator, a cat, and an aborigine."

"Oh, them. I heard. Thought there was supposed to be an owl along with that."

"So they didn't quite get it right. Are *you* perfect?" The Penguin attempted a triple axel, failed, and did a pratfall to the floor. It grinned up at the Outcast. "So you coming or not?"

"I'll be there in a moment." The Outcast looked down again at Croyd and sighed once more.

The penguin clucked at him. "You might try an alarm clock. Hey, okay, I'm going, I'm going."

Tom's fingers tightened on the armrests of his chair. He pushed with his mind. The shell rose slowly off the ground.

There was another flash of lightning. He heard rolling thunder. Then the baying came again, louder this time, closer. There was something terrifying about the sound. The way it lingered on the wind and chilled the soul. It was a dark, primal sound. It turned his bowels to water.

Tom turned up his speakers to drown out the distant hounds. "GET TO HQ," he told Danny. "WARN HARTMANN AND THE

OTHERS." She didn't move. She stood there listening, cradling her M-16. "*NOW!*" Tom thundered. "WE DON'T HAVE MUCH TIME."

Danny turned her head slightly, looked up at him. The wind was rising. Her baseball cap went sailing off her head. "I've told them already," she said. "They're on their way up."

Her sisters, Tom remembered. Before he could reflect on it, the others came boiling out of the tunnel beneath the grandstands. Cyclone and Mistral in their fighting suits, Snotman in army fatigues, Mike Tsakos in his skivvies, Radha O'Reilly in a sari, a bunch of Dannys and a larger bunch of uniforms. Hartmann stopped by the dugout. He looked scared. Somewhere off to the west, thunder rumbled, and they heard the stutter of machine-gun fire.

The Turtle crossed the infield, his shadow rippling across the model Rox, the rising winds buffeting his shell. "WE'RE UNDER ATTACK," he told them. He wasn't sure how he knew, but he did.

A grizzled, red-faced old man in a lieutenant colonel's uniform was the first to gather his wits. "Cyclone, Mistral, do something about this wind," he ordered in a southern accent so thick you could cut it with a knife. "Tsakos, get your skinny butt in those iron long johns and go reinforce the main gate." Tsakos went running off toward center field. "We need to find out what's happening out there. Turtle, you—"

"*Dear God,*" Hartmann interrupted, his voice shrill with sudden fear. He looked around wildly. "They're after *me.*"

A lightning bolt crackled toward the west, underlining his words. The call of a hunting horn shuddered through the night, faint but distinctive.

"We don't know who they're after," Vidkunssen began.

"Can't you *hear* it?" Hartmann screeched. "Dear God." He sounded close to hysteria.

The thunder was louder, the lightning flashing all around. But under it, you could hear the eerie baying of hounds, coming closer and closer.

"Corporal Shepherd," the lieutenant colonel drawled in his grits-and-bourbon tones, "the senator's a little upset. Escort him back to headquarters and get him a warm glass of milk." He looked around at the aces. "You, Booger—"

"My name is *Reflector,*" Snotman insisted.

"You let anything happen to the senator, boy, and your name is Shit, you got that?" the old man snarled.

Corporal Danny put a gentle hand on Hartmann's arm. "Come with me, Senator. We'll keep you safe."

He wrenched away from her violently. *"No,"* he said. "They'll *find* me. They'll *get* me."

The cracker colonel spat. "Shit, boy, get a hold of yourself. It's just someone out walking his dawgs."

Hartmann backed away from them. His head twisted back and forth, like a rabbit about to bolt. *"Run,"* he shouted over the wind, over the sounds of automatic weapons fire from the street outside. "We have to run. We have to get away from them . . ."

A lightning bolt flashed down and touched one of the light towers. For a moment a brilliant shower of sparks lit the night. Then the field went dark. The hounds were very close now. Outside the walls, someone screamed.

Even the grizzled old colonel looked shaken by that scream. He spit, and made a decision. "You up there," he shouted at Tom. "The senator's a little nervous. Maybe you should get him someplace safe. Can you do that?"

"NO PROBLEM." Tom thought of a hand. Invisible fingers closed gently around Hartmann, lifted. Tom deposited him on top of the shell. Hartmann was hyperventilating, his eyes wide. "HOLD ON, SENATOR," Tom told him. "THIS COULD BE A BUMPY RIDE."

"I just don't have time for this," said Bloat. "I don't. I really don't." He rolled his head distractedly.

Wyungare gazed up at the immensity that was the overgrown boy. The joker called Kafka set one chitinous appendage on the Aborigine's shoulder. Wyungare shook it off.

"Sorry," said Kafka. "That's it for the audience. I'm afraid there's a war on."

Wyungare ignored him. "You have to listen to me," he said to

Bloat. "What I described to you about the destruction wrought to the dreamtime is, if anything, understated."

"Later," said Bloat. "I can't worry about it now."

"There are millions, *many* millions of human beings around this world whose lives are being destroyed by you, however inadvertently."

"*No!*" said Bloat. "There are hundreds on this island whose lives will be destroyed if we don't figure a solution. They count more to me than your millions. Sorry."

Bloat's advisers murmured, mumbled, nodded appreciatively.

"I can appreciate that," said Wyungare. "Your loyalty to your friends here, your colleagues, is admirable. But is it possible that both our purposes can be served? Perhaps if we simply reason this out . . ."

Bloat said, "How many penguins can skate on the head of a pin?"

The penguin performed a series of tight infinity signs, each one precise and equal to the one before it.

Bloat nodded. "We will talk, but another time." He pointedly directed his look toward Kafka.

Agitated, the joker looked from Wyungare to Bloat. He took a step forward. The sound of his body was like the sound of a barrel of steel flatware rolling downhill. "So where do you want I should take him?"

"A cell, I think," said Bloat. "For tonight, anyhow. Tomorrow, we'll talk. I promise," he said to the Aborigine.

"I think it will be too late."

"Can't be helped," said Bloat. "The feds didn't consult me before setting up their offensive."

"What about the gator?" said Kafka.

Bloat rolled his eyes. "Put him in the moat. He can earn his keep as one of the guards."

"How we gonna get him there?" said the joker practically.

Bloat thought for a moment. "I'll have one of the guards waiting out front on his fish mount. If that doesn't work as bait, I don't know what will."

"What about the cat?" said Kafka.

"What cat?" said Bloat.

Kafka glanced around the huge chamber confusedly. "He was right over—shit, I don't know where he went."

The Aborigine smiled. No one but he had seen the black cat depart.

"I'm ready to go to my room," Wyungare said. He held out his wrists as though expecting iron shackles.

"Just go," said Kafka disgustedly. "I'll tell you which way to turn and when to stop. If that doesn't meet with your approval, well, then I'll just fill you with nine millimeter." He hefted his rifle suggestively.

"It's not too late to discuss this," said Wyungare over his shoulder.

"Yes, it is." Impatient, Bloat clearly turned his attention to other things. Kafka gave a shove to his prisoner and Wyungare moved toward the door.

Wyungare sensed the presence of the black cat as Kafka and he moved up a spiral climb of stone steps. Good.

The cat would know the Aborigine was confined. And thus, so would the alligator. And that seemed, to Wyungare, to be important.

Out in the streets of Brooklyn, nature had gone mad.

The street lamps were shaking in the grip of gale-force winds. Thunder was booming all around. Down below were screams, shouts, howls, a tank rumbling around a corner, the chatter of machine guns and the whine of rifles. Soldiers were scrambling everywhere like frantic cockroaches. The hounds were among them, dozens of them, more than he could count, huge pale wolfhounds with glowing eyes.

A spear of lightning flashed down, throwing everything in sharp relief for a split second, etching the scene forever in Tom's memory. The images seemed frozen on his screens. Blood swirling into a gutter. A white hound as big as a pony, tearing out the throat of a downed soldier. Another bounding after a jeep, dissolving into mist as a stream of tracers ripped it open.

The light faded; darkness closed in. It took his eyes a moment to adjust. The thunder slammed into the shell with an almost physical force. For a moment it broke his concentration. Twenty-three tons of steel and armor plate dipped, then plummeted down like a dropped saucer. Hartmann yelled something incoherent into his mikes. Tom jerked the shell to a sudden stop, tasted blood in his mouth where he'd bitten his tongue. Too close, only ten feet off the ground, he had to get higher. He saw motion from one corner of his eyes, glanced back . . .

The hound smashed up against the glass, snarling. *"Jesus!"* Tom said. If the TV lens had been a window, the thing would have come right through. The shell slid sideways. Tom heard claws scrabbling for purchase against his armor as they began to fall again. Hartmann shrieked. Tom was breathing hard. The sound was deafening; thunder, gunfire, howling. On top of the shell, Hartmann was on his knees, fighting for his life. The hound had his right hand in its jaws. Its eyes glowed a baleful green. Other hounds were closing in.

Tom reached up with his telekinesis. He reached deep inside the hound, wrapped a telekinetic hand around its heart.

He thought of claws, and *squeezed.*

The beast's massive head snapped back, and it howled in sudden agony, shuddered . . . and then it was gone, melting away into green mist, dissolving on the wind. Tom pushed up, hard and fast. The hounds leapt after him, missed the rising shell by inches.

"Senator," Tom said. Hartmann had collapsed atop the shell, sobbing, cradling his mangled fingers. "I'm sorry," Tom said, not even knowing if Hartmann could hear a word. "I didn't know they could jump so high, I . . ."

Another lightning bolt blew apart a street lamp ten feet below him. He had to get the fuck out of here. The shell would draw the storm better than a lightning rod. All it would take was one hit to fry his electronics . . . not to mention the senator.

Tom pushed and the shell rose straight up, a steel balloon. The thunder battered at him. He turned off his exterior mikes. The sudden silence was a blessed relief. He was pushing higher, higher. He never heard the horn wind, but when he scanned his cameras again, the Hunt was coming down the street.

There were a dozen riders on huge horses with glowing green eyes. They flowed down the center of Bedford Avenue like water. Behind came a ragtag mob of animals, some with two feet and some with four. Feral dogs, poodles, and cocker spaniels with glowing eyes, street punks and winos and *cops,* for chrissakes, a whole phalanx of bikers on chopped Harleys. His sound was off, but Tom could see how their mouths twisted as they screamed, and he knew they were screaming for blood. There was nothing human left in any of those faces. Ahead of the mob, ahead of the armed jokers on the horses, *he* came. The Huntsman . . .

It was the joker he'd seen on the Rox, the stag-man with the antlers, but now he seemed transformed. He was naked, his shaggy red mane moving in the storm winds, his eyes glowing green. A golden dragon horn hung across his chest. Green fire played along his antlers and flickered around the great spear he held.

"Holy fuck," Tom said aloud.

Somehow the Huntsman seemed to hear him. He pulled up suddenly, the great black stallion rearing as if it were about to prance into the sky. The hounds seemed to go wild, leaping, snapping. Then the street in front of the Huntsman exploded.

Horses, hounds, and riders went tumbling through the air. A burst water main fountained upward. Somehow the Huntsman kept his mount, leaping nimbly over the torn pavement, then moving toward the ballpark at a full gallop, more hellhounds coming hard at his heels.

In front of Ebbets, the tank had settled into position. Tom let out a cheer. A thin tendril of smoke trailed from the turret gun.

The Huntsman threw his spear without breaking stride.

It sliced through the air like a cold green thunderbolt, dead on, right up the barrel of the turret gun.

The gunner must have fired at the same instant, that was all Tom could think. The tank exploded. A huge gout of orange flame and green witchlight flowered in the street.

When the fire faded so Tom could see again, the Huntsman had his spear in hand once more. He gestured with it, pointing upward.

Pointing at the shell.

"You're late," Battle said flatly at the entrance to the graveyard of Our Lady of Perpetual Misery. Crypt Kicker stood slackly behind him, slumped against the moss-covered rock wall that cordoned off the tiny cemetery from the rest of the church lawn.

"You know how hard it is to find a shovel in New York?" Ray asked, dropping it at Battle's feet. "I had to go all over the damn city looking for one. Who the hell ever digs in the ground in New York City?"

Battle gestured to Puckett who bent over slowly and laboriously to pick up the implement. The dead guy may be as strong as shit, Ray thought, but that's also about how coordinated he was. The battle computer that was Ray's mind filed that tidbit away for future reference.

"This way," Battle said, leading the way into the graveyard. "And quickly. I've got to be someplace very soon."

It was quiet inside, and peaceful except for distant thunder to the south. Ray looked up at the sky. It was clear above them, but there seemed to be a hell of a storm brewing in Brooklyn. Ray hoped that it'd stay there. The last thing he wanted was a rainstorm when he was screwing around in a graveyard at night.

Many of the cemetery's headstones were small and plain. Only jokers were buried in the confines of Our Lady of Perpetual Misery, and most jokers couldn't afford elaborate graves. The stones were also crammed closely together. A lot of jokers had been planted within the cemetery's walls.

Battle stopped. He'd found the grave he'd been looking for. The tombstone was a simple one, with a grinning death's-head chiseled into its top with the name "Brian Boyd" engraved below it. Boyd had been dead for two years.

"This who we're looking for?" Ray asked doubtfully as he leaned against another tombstone that read simply "Chrysalis."

Battle nodded. He gestured at Puckett and the ace began to dig. He was strong and he could move dirt fast. Ray, knowing the man had been dead once, considered asking him what it was like to lie in the ground. But then he decided it would be better not to know. Besides, he had a more pertinent question for Battle.

"What do you expect to get from this guy, anyway?" Ray asked.

Battle looked at him. "Boyd was known as Blockhead when alive—" Battle began, but his jaw slung open wordlessly as a ton of bricks landed on Ray's back.

Ray had time to think only, *Christ, now what?* then all conscious thought fled as he flowed into action.

He grabbed one of the arms that encircled his chest and pulled at it, but whoever had grabbed him was stronger, and that meant he was a strong fucker. Ace category. But Ray could also tell from the distribution of weight on his shoulders, back, and legs that whoever was holding him from behind was relatively human-shaped, unlike the flying squirrel man he'd fought that very morning. Human shape meant human weaknesses.

Ray fell forward, bringing his attacker with him, using him to break his fall. Whoever had him still wouldn't let go, but Ray twisted like an eel, turned, and butted hard enough with the top of his head to bring tears to his eyes.

His head connected with the bottom of his attacker's chin. Whoever had him pulled back at the sudden pain and Ray wriggled free.

Ray hit the guy three times before he realized who it was.

"Christ," he said, and stood up.

Quasiman, Father Squid's handy joker, lay on the ground, bleeding from his lips and nose. No wonder, Ray thought, he hadn't heard anyone sneaking up on him. Quasiman was a teleport. He'd probably swooped down on Ray from his favorite position atop the church's roof like a hawk on a pigeon, stepping off into space and materializing right before landing on Ray's back.

"What are you doing?" Ray asked the joker-ace.

Quasiman straightened up slowly. He was big and ugly, hunchbacked and half-witted as well. But in the strength department he was up there with heavyweights like Modular Man and the Golden Weenie.

"Guarding the cemetery," Quasiman said, "from grave robbers."

"Well, shit," Ray said, "we're not grave robbers. We're federal agents."

He turned to Battle and Puckett. Battle was watching with a guarded expression. Ray found it as difficult as ever to read what was going on in his devious brain. Puckett was also looking on, frozen in midmotion with a shovelful of dirt. The events of the last few seconds had totally overwhelmed what passed for his mental processes and he was still trying to figure out how to react. He came to a decision and resumed shoveling.

"We have a court order to exhume this body," Ray explained. He turned to Battle. "Don't we?"

"Indeed we do," Battle said. He reached into his jacket pocket, extracted a folded sheaf of papers, waved them at Quasiman, and then put them away again.

Quasiman nodded slowly. "Why do you want the body?"

"It's not the body," Battle explained impatiently. "It's—ah!"

There came the scrape of shovel on wood, and everyone gathered around the grave as Puckett scraped dirt off the top of the casket. He tossed his shovel on the back-dirt pile, then horsed the coffin out of its hole using brute strength. He tipped it over the lip of the hole and pushed it onto the ground. He clambered stiffly out of the grave, somehow looking very much in his element.

"Open it," Battle commanded.

Puckett didn't need a crowbar. He hooked one hand under the coffin's lid and pulled. There was a squeal of protest as nails were yanked from holes they'd been in for two years. Ray screwed up his nose, expecting a hideous odor, but it wasn't too bad.

There wasn't much left of Brian Boyd, a.k.a. Blockhead. He hadn't been a big guy to begin with and his remains had shrunken down to the size of a withered child.

Battle peered closely at the body, bouncing up and down on the balls of his feet like he did whenever he was excited. "There," he said, bending down and pointing. "The ring."

Puckett bent stiffly and reached into the casket. There was a brittle cracking sound and he offered Battle the corpse's desiccated left ring finger, ring still attached.

Battle shook his head. "I don't want the goddamn finger. Just the ring."

Puckett stripped the gold wedding ring off the finger and tossed the digit back into the coffin. He gave Battle the ring. Battle took it and put it into his coat pocket, smiling, happy as a goddamn clam.

Ray looked at Quasiman and suppressed a shrug. He still didn't get it. But Battle was the boss.

The boss checked his watch. "Ah, good," he said. "I still have time to make my appointment. Ray, I have one last thing for you to do tonight."

He swept out of the graveyard, Puckett following him. Ray paused and looked at Quasiman, but found nothing to say. He followed Battle and Puckett from the graveyard. He looked back when they'd reached the gate and saw that Quasiman had retrieved the shovel Puckett had discarded. He was standing by the open coffin and empty grave, a bewildered expression on his sad, ugly face.

It took Modular Man hours to deliver the messages to all the joker combat groups hidden in various parts of the New York area. Most of them had been hiding in small apartments for days and—when he could read the jokers' expressions at all—they seemed happy at last to have a chance to get out of their claustrophobic surroundings and attack something.

All the groups seemed to have television sets, and CNN's bluish glow illuminated their crowded apartments full of sleeping pallets and weaponry. The rooms were crowded with the mingled scents of Cosmoline and unwashed bodies.

"They're just discussing you," said one adolescent. He was part of the last group to be visited, thin to the point of anorexia and pale enough to remind the android—with a private shudder—of the albino Croyd. He dressed all in gothic black and wore shades even at night. He seemed to be this group's jumper.

Modular Man glanced up at the set and felt something flutter through his macroatomic heart. The screen was full of a close-up of a blond woman named Cyndi. The television identified her as *soap opera actress*.

"I *know* Modular Man," she said. "I know he's not doing this from choice."

"You tell um, bitch," laughed one gray-skinned joker. He brandished his k-bar suggestively.

"Maybe he's been jumped," Cyndi said.

The interviewer's response was reasonable. "How do you jump a machine?" he asked.

"Are you kidding? How do you jump a *human?*"

Modular Man had to admire her.

"He's got to do what his creator tells him," Cyndi continued. "He has to have been ordered to do this. Or maybe somebody's messed with his programming. But if he's fighting the government, I know it's not from choice."

The adolescent grinned up at Modular Man. His teeth were bad. "That true?" he asked.

"More or less."

"Life sucks, huh?"

"That interpretation has occurred to me." Images of Cyndi floated through his memory.

"And now you're stuck on the Rox." The kid laughed. "Man, I'm glad I'm not on that island being a target for napalm an' cruise missiles an' shit."

"Your sympathy is noted."

The kid laughed again, then jumped as lightning struck nearby and a blast of thunder rattled the windows. "Shit," he said again.

Modular Man left to return to the Rox.

A strange, dark storm was hovering over Brooklyn, more or less where Zappa had his headquarters at Ebbets Field.

Modular Man didn't want to know.

The Aborigine realized he was not the only prisoner in the drab cell block as Kafka led him down the narrow passage. At the very end of the hall was a young woman. She slumped against the barred door of her cell. Wyungare caught a glimpse of dark spiked hair and stained leather. He could smell her hysteria, a pungent odor that ate corrosively at his nostrils.

Two doors farther, the joker jammed a key into a lock and twisted. Then he tugged at the door. Wyungare helped him wrestle it open. Kafka stared at him sideways. "Thanks," he said. "You're weird, guy." He shut the door after the Aborigine and locked it. "Sleep tight, people," he said to the two prisoners.

Wyungare looked around at his new—temporary, he hoped—home. It looked like a medieval monk's cell, or something out of a dungeon, which figured, considering what he could deduce about Bloat's maturity level and range of interests. He put his palm against the wall. Hard, cold stone blocks. Unyielding.

The cell had no furniture. The only amenities were a hummock of loose straw in one corner, a galvanized steel bucket in the corner opposite. Wyungare shook his head. Obviously Bloat wasn't expecting many guests.

But the environment didn't matter. It was time to work.

He would make the formal acquaintance of his fellow prisoner later. Then he stopped. He heard the woman weeping softly and his heart went out to her. It didn't take supernormal powers to pick up her feelings. The dark terrified her. So did the loss of power that came with imprisonment. Wyungare took a deep breath and let his soul range out.

The black cat yowled low in his throat just a short distance away. He had followed Wyungare and Kafka first up, then down to the cell block. Wyungare *pushed* just a little, made a suggestion.

The cat purred and ambled up to the barred door of the woman's cell. He flowed between the bars almost as fluidly as quicksilver.

There was silence for a few seconds. Then, "Kitty?" said the woman. Wyungare felt the sense of arms wrapping tightly around the cat, hot tears spotting his warm fur. Wyungare offered thanks to the mirragen's spirit.

Then he sat cross-legged on the stone, conscious of the fissures of the irregular surface imprinting in his flesh. He took a deep breath, another, began deliberately to control his respiration. Wyungare let the rhythm of his breathing fall into synch with the cycles of his body. One breath, four beats of his heart, then six beats.

He slapped the stone with the heels of his hands. If he had no drum, he could make one.

And he descended into the lower world.

Wyungare found himself in something that looked like swampland. Good, that was what he had hoped for.

In the distance, he heard the mournful cries of a harmonica. He walked toward the sounds.

He had to circle the huge complex trunks of cypress. Most of the sun was shut out by the foliage canopy. The water now lay on either side of him, brackish and green with moss.

Finally, as the music grew louder—it was a French ballad, he finally decided—Wyungare rounded a clump of scrub oak and found a young boy, perhaps eight or ten, sitting on a fallen log and playing his juice harp.

The boy stopped when he saw Wyungare.

"You can keep on if you like," said the Aborigine.

"I don't mean to bother you, sir," said the boy shyly. His hair and eyes both were the black of starless nights.

"It's no bother," said Wyungare. "Hello, Jack."

"Do I know you, sir?"

Wyungare nodded. "We'll take a walk, young man. We need to talk. I have a favor to ask of you."

Jack looked at him curiously, but got up from the log.

By the time he neared the Brooklyn Bridge, Tom knew what he had to do. Hartmann was curled up on top of the shell, his bloody hand pressed to his chest, moaning. "Hospital . . . my hand . . ."

"I *can't*," Tom said. "They'd be on you in no time. The Hunt's only five blocks behind me. I've been doubling back, dodging through alleys and over rooftops, trying to lose them, but they've got the scent, I can't shake them."

Thunder pealed behind them. The storm went before the Huntsman, it seemed.

". . . hurts . . ." Hartmann whispered.

"I'm sorry. Hang on a little longer."

There was no reply. Tom glanced up at his overhead screen. The senator's eyes had closed. He started to slide down the curve of the shell. Tom caught him with his teke, shoved him back up top. Hartmann whimpered in pain.

The great stone arches of Brooklyn Bridge loomed ahead of him. Tom slowed, hovered, looked around. There wasn't much to work with, except . . .

"This is going to make me real fucking popular with the natives,"

Tom muttered. But he didn't see that he had a whole lot of choice. He summoned all his concentration.

A half-dozen cars parked along the bridge approach floated into the air, yanked upward by his teke. One slipped from his mind's grasp. The windshield shattered as it hit the ground. "Fuck," Tom said. The sound of the Huntsman's horn came echoing through the night, and he heard the baying of hounds. There was no *time*.

He thought of a net.

He held it high in the air, above the street lamps, and began scooping parked cars into it, fast as he could. Three, five, ten, twelve, he grabbed them with his teke, shoveled them up into the net, where they slammed together. Twenty, twenty-five, thirty . . .

A dozen hounds came howling around a corner, a block away.

Tom fled, dragging his net behind the shell. Metal screeched, glass broke, and sparks shot off concrete as the jumble of cars bounced along in his wake.

The Hunt came howling after him.

He pushed harder. The shell picked up speed. He started gaining on his pursuers. The baying grew more frantic.

At the approach to the bridge, the Turtle stopped, hovered, and began to slam the shattered cars into place.

By the time the hounds reached him, the wall was there: a solid barrier of twisted metal, not as high as the one in his junkyard, but high enough to shut off the roadway.

A yellow cab, coming on too fast and braking too late, fishtailed and sideswiped the barrier. "GET THE FUCK OUT OF HERE," Tom roared down at him. The cabbie must have seen the hellhounds in his rearview mirror. He smoked his tires backing up, then lit out of there. One of the hounds bounded right over the taxi, staving in the hood as it bounced off.

Tom flew back over his barrier, onto the bridge.

More traffic was coming from Manhattan. "TURN AROUND," the Turtle told them. "YOU DON'T WANT TO BE HERE." A big limo saw the wall, slowed, stopped. "MOVE IT," Tom thundered down. A taxi swerved around in a sudden U-turn. The limo began to back up. It got rear-ended by a Mercedes. "OUT OF HERE!"

If the drivers had any doubts, the sight of the first hound coming over the cars made up their minds.

The wall of wrecks barely slowed them. They were climbing it in the blink of an eye, leaping down the far side, baying up at the shell. The Mercedes reversed, backed, fled. The limo followed. Other traffic was turning back halfway over the span.

More hounds were bounding onto the bridge now. Behind came the Hunt. The Huntsman sounded his horn again, and took the barrier in full gallop. The great black stallion leapt clean over it, with a good five feet to spare. The other riders followed.

"OKAY, YOU CAN JUMP," Tom said. "BIG FUCKING DEAL."

He pushed higher, taunting them, way up in the air out of their reach, watching his cameras until the mob came into view.

Tom zoomed in on the faces. Cops, streetwalkers, bums, bikers, old women who'd taken their poodles out for a walk and gotten caught up in the blood lust as the hunt went by. People, that's all. They had no part in this.

He thought of a portcullis. Made it a gate. Wide, solid, heavy, strong as iron. He pictured it in his mind's eye. Then he brought it down. The metal barrier jumped with the impact. Cars *crunched*. A biker tried to ride his Harley over the wrecked cars, hit the invisible wall, and went flying. The mob found they could go no farther. They groped at nothingness, hit it, clawed at it.

"NO WAY PAST," he told them. Nobody listened. This bunch wasn't going to give up and go home.

Lightning fingered the cables of the bridge like a demon harpist. Close, too close. Thunder swept over the shell. Beyond the wall, the mob was howling louder than the hellhounds.

He had to keep the wall in place, Tom thought wildly. He moved the shell out over the span. "The wall," he muttered to himself, a frantic mantra. "The wall, wall." The microphone caught his plea, sent it booming out into the storm. He held the wall firmly in his mind even as he left it behind.

The Hunt came howling after him.

He'd never moved the shell so fast before. He was forty feet above them, skipping along like a twenty-ton Frisbee. The massive stone arches of the bridge loomed overhead. Far below, the East River churned and foamed. The storm was whipping the river into a frenzy. Whitecaps danced a madman's frenzy, waves crested and broke against the huge stone pylons. Lightning played among the drooping cables and lashed at the waters. The world had gone mad.

"The Wall," Tom prayed. He clung desperately to the image.

The Huntsman had outdistanced the hounds and the other riders. For a moment it almost seemed as if the great bridge was shaking beneath him. His eyes were fixed on the Turtle's shell, burning like two green stars. He blew his great horn, and now the bridge *did* shake. The hellhounds and the other riders followed, hot for blood.

"COME ON, YOU MOTHERFUCKERS," the Turtle roared down at them. "COME TO POPPA."

The Huntsman drew up beneath him, lifted his spear, threw.

There was a flash of green light that burned the eyes, and Tom felt his shell shudder, heard the scream of tortured metal. He blinked. Four feet of spear was sticking out of the floor, not a foot in front of his face. Smoke was still rising from the carpet where it had punched through. He could smell fused metal. The spear was golden, ornate, crackling with green fire. Without thinking, Tom reached for it, but it faded and dissolved before his fingers could touch it.

Wind whistled through the hole in the floor. Solid battleship plate, Tom thought numbly. He was too stunned to be afraid. The wall was forgotten. He only prayed the mob wasn't on the bridge yet.

He thought of a hammer.

Bigger than that.

Bigger than *that*.

The biggest fucking hammer in the world.

He pictured it, half as wide as the East River, hanging in the air above the bridge. The hammer trembled. It was heavy. It was too fucking heavy for him to support it. He made it heavier still. Down below, the Huntsman raised another spear.

Tom let the hammer fall.

The center span of the Brooklyn Bridge exploded.

Stone, steel, and pavement blew apart like paper. The cables snapped with a screech straight out of hell. A huge fragment of roadway came spinning up past the shell. Tom barely had an instant to savor his glimpse of hounds, horses, and hunters all tumbling toward the river.

Then the shock wave hit, and swept him away.

Once Modular Man returned he reported to Bloat, who he found awake, with a few members of his staff and a bodyguard of fish-knights. Travnicek was nowhere to be seen. Modular Man made his report, then looked up at the vast figure. "May I speak with you, Governor?"

"Is it important?"

"To me."

"Very well."

"You know," the android began, "if you've been in my creator's head, that I'm here involuntarily. Seeing as that's so, I'd like the same opportunity to surrender as was given your other followers."

Bloat looked startled, then confused. "That's Dr. Travnicek's decision," he said. "Not mine."

Travnicek. So Bloat knew Travnicek's name, presumably having plucked it from his mind. The android wondered if Travnicek would even care.

"As I understand it," Modular Man continued, "your society on the Rox is based on ideals. Presumably your ideals don't condone slavery." The next piece had to be run several times through the android's macroatomic mind so that he could phrase it properly without disobeying his creator's orders. He found himself having to phrase it as a theoretical problem.

"If someone brought a slave onto the Rox," he said, "you could make it a condition of that person's presence that the slave be freed."

Even that was misleading: there was no way, short of ripping out circuits, that Bloat could "free" Modular Man from Travnicek. But Bloat could refrain from assigning him to any dangerous tasks.

"This is ridiculous!" Kafka said. "You're a machine! The governor might as well free a Mixmaster!"

The android turned to him and tried to put quotes in his voice.

"'The governor might as well free a roach.' I am a sentient being, as are you. Either we are equal under Rox law, or we are not."

"We are a society of ideals," Bloat said. His high-pitched voice did not point to justice. "We're fighting for our freedom, for our new country. All we ask is to be left alone."

"*I* will leave you alone, if I can."

"We hope you will join us of your own free will."

"I am programmed to fight the enemies of society, barring my creator's intervention. You would seem to be society's enemy."

"The enemy of *what* society? Have you noticed there's more than one? How do you know George Bush ain't the enemy of society?"

"I'm very careful in assigning those labels, if it's left up to me."

"That's big of you, Mister Judge Your Honor Sir. We want nothing from the outside, let alone your labels."

"You want nothing except the money you've stolen. The bodies you've stolen. The drugs and arms you've brought in illegally. The criminals to whom you give shelter, and the kidnap victims you permit them to bring here. And of course you want *me* to fight for your right to do that."

Bloat's voice was getting more insistent. "We've only taken what we're owed. The outside doesn't *care* about jokers! We do! That's why we came here! We are a principled people."

"If you wished to act with principle, you could have come out here with your group of idealistic jokers and occupied the place and issued your proclamations—"

"And starved to death." Kafka's voice was scornful. "That's what happened to us—no one gave a damn. We needed those others to make it work."

"As I understand it, idealists often suffer for their beliefs. It would seem to be part of the job description. And *if* you had starved here, you might have attracted favorable attention to your cause, sympathy, perhaps aid. But you didn't want to suffer that way, so you let in the jumpers and the murderers and the drug dealers and the kidnappers and the arms merchants and the fugitives from the law."

"The signers of the Declaration of Independence were criminals in the eyes of the British government," Bloat said. "I don't see any difference."

"With respect, Governor, I see a number of differences between Thomas Jefferson and Governor Bloat. Not the least being that Jefferson and his allies were fighting to keep a land they already possessed, and hold it free from tyranny, while the other is trying to steal a land owned by others, with money he's filched from strangers who have nothing to do with him, and in doing so is imposing tyranny on a rather wide variety of people, including myself, and I presume Pulse, and all those other people whose bodies the jumpers have stolen and hold in bondage."

"*Jefferson* had slaves."

"He didn't create that system; he inherited it, and he had the decency to be embarrassed about it. What is more to the point, he didn't demand that they fight for slavery."

"Yeah?" There was a sneer on Bloat's face. "Since you admire Jefferson so much, I tell ya what—I'll follow his example. Jefferson didn't free his slaves till after his death, right? I'll give you the same consideration. Once I'm dead, you can leave."

If that's the way you want it. The cold thought rolled through the android's circuitry. He knew better than to say it.

He had used the wrong approach, he knew. He had expected to argue with an idealist, a figure knowledgeable on political and revolutionary theory. He hadn't quite realized that Bloat was a barely educated adolescent whose political thought derived more from MTV than the *Federalist Papers*.

He was the pawn of a willful, desperate, and ignorant teenager.

If that's the way you want it. That was always an option.

"Go away!" Kafka made shooing gestures with his hands. "We've got important things to consider! Go help your creator!"

"I am not aware that my creator needs any help."

"He's with the Wild Hunt! Go help him kill Hartmann and make yourself useful!"

Calculations snarled through the android's circuits, ran into brickwall hardwired imperatives. "That storm?" he said. "You let him go?"

"Hey, it wasn't my idea." Bloat laughed. "The guy jumped down from his tower, knocked Rolypoly right off his horse, hopped on, and rode off. He must have been susceptible to Herne's message."

Modular Man's programming lifted him into the air and fired him out of the room like a gunshot. He had an image of Kafka and Bloat gaping in surprise and then the night and fog enveloped him.

He shot straight up to get out of the radar clutter and the fog, then took visual bearings. The dark storm was prowling over the eastern approaches to the Brooklyn Bridge, and Modular Man fired himself straight for it, streamlining his guns back over his shoulders to decrease air resistance.

He didn't know what to hope for.

The storm seemed to lose intensity even as he raced for it—the lightning ceased to crackle, and the thunder died away. There was the brief radar image of a small flying object—the Turtle?—racing off to the north.

And then Modular Man was above the broken bridge, absorbing the shattered image of the shattered span, watching as emergency vehicles poured up the bridge approaches.

What if his creator was dead but never found? he wondered. He'd have to obey the dead man's orders forever, defending the Rox till there was nothing left.

In cold panic he spiraled toward the water. A few figures splashed forlornly in a boiling tide that carried them toward Sandy Hook. The android floated down over the cold, choppy water, saw hands raised toward him in pleading. Stag horns jabbed high above the water, and the android sped toward them.

"*Where is my creator!*" he shrieked.

"Ah dinnut ken!" This did not seem to be Received Standard English. Herne gulped water, spat it out. "*Find the hoern!*"

Both Herne's horns seemed to be all right. Modular Man ignored the frantic cry and began a swift spiral in search of Travnicek.

He found him close to the Brooklyn shore, swimming strongly across the tide toward land. Modular Man dropped into the water beside him, lifted him with arms across the chest, and brought him to the end of Brooklyn Pier 5.

Travnicek stood on the end of the pier, water pouring off his torn clothing. "Magnificent!" he shouted. There was a gloating tone in Travnicek's voice; he didn't seem injured. "I never knew how glorious it was to kill!"

"Sir? Are you hurt?"

"Pah!" He gave a contemptuous wave. "The horse broke my fall." He tilted his head back and gave a howl. "Magnificent! I snapped that woman's neck! I *felt* the shock run through her brain! I *felt* her terror. I tore at her neck with a piece of broken glass and licked her blood before she died."

The android was appalled. His mind was refusing to process any of this. "I should return you to the Rox."

"Lemme tell you something," Travnicek said. He sounded exalted. "I learned an important lesson when the Krauts machine-gunned my family back at Lidice, okay? As I was lying under a bloody pile composed of my second cousins, I realized something. There are two kinds of people in this world—the shooters and the shootees."

He gave a laugh. "The shooters are the ones with authority, and they have authority because they control the guns. The shooters kill other people, or they get other shooters to do it for them. And the rest—they're bullet fodder. Bloat's a shooter—you don't see him out on the front lines risking his ass, do you? Even as the Outcast? Zelda's a shooter—she's got a whole other body to do the killing for her. And—" He pointed at himself with his cilia. "I'm a shooter too. I got the best gun in the world—that's *you,* toaster."

Travnicek leaned closer to the android. His sensory necklace pulsed with emotion. "Are you a shooter or a shootee, toaster? A winner or loser? That's what you gotta decide." He pointed commandingly back out at the East River. "Find Herne and bring him here. I'll want to ride with him again."

"Yes, sir."

There were fewer swimmers now, and the huge rack of horns made Herne easy to spot. The big joker was racing frantically toward the lights of the Brooklyn Bridge, but the tide was carrying him away faster than he could swim.

The android grabbed him by his shaggy mane and began to pull him toward shore.

"No!" Herne was almost sobbing. "Find thee the hoern! The hoern!"

"Your horns seem to be intact."

"The *hoern*, the *hoern*! Aa lost me goelden hoern! Aa kinnut sommon th' Hoont!"

Modular Man lifted the ace from the river, hauled him to where Travnicek waited by the pier. "Where is it?" he asked.

"Oonder thon bridge!" Herne pointed desperately.

Somehow Modular Man knew that, even with a featureless face, Travnicek was leering at him.

"Fetch, doggie!" Travnicek said.

The android arrowed toward the bridge, calculating distances, flow rates, wind velocity. The storm cloud overhead had completely dispersed, and only a few people were still swimming. Modular Man dove into the water and propelled himself toward the bottom.

Radar was useless under the water and the water was completely black. Even infrared vision revealed only crumpled ruin, huge chunks of bridge span lying in opaque clouds of bottom mud.

Finding the horn took him almost twenty minutes, working methodically, by feel alone. He was lucky he didn't need to breathe.

When he rose from the water with the battered old hunting horn, the water was empty of survivors. So far as he knew, only Herne and Travnicek, of those who had fallen, had survived the end of the Wild Hunt.

Modular Man deposited Travnicek, a naked Dylan Hardesty, and a weed-snagged horn on the floor of the Crystal Castle. The Outcast was waiting there, below the dreaming Bloat, below the spectacle of Liberty's torch. A bit of dirty East River water dribbled from the bell of the horn onto the tile floor.

The Outcast stared at the scene grimly. "So many gone . . . One-Eye, Bumbilino . . . God*damn* it!" His nostrils flared, the amethyst gleamed in purple fury. "How?"

Modular Man answered before Herne could speak. "Moose Man here did his best. Morning traffic's going to be hell, that's for sure."

"Ye Tuhtle . . . destroyed the Hoont." Dylan shuddered. The Out-cast made a gesture with his hand; a large blanket appeared around the huge figure. In Dylan's mind there was residual horror—remorse for what he'd done as Herne, fear from the memory of the bridge. The Manchesterian accent was thicker than usual. The coloring of dialect drifted into Dylan's usual impeccable cultured British. "Ah dinnut see anything, but alla soodden sommting cum a'smashin' inna oos and yonder bridge was toomblin' . . ." He pulled the blanket tightly around his shoulders. He paused and corrected his speech in his head. "Some-times I hate myself, Governor. I really do."

"I saw it," Travnicek said. "A hammer of gravity and air. Excite-ment. Blood lust. It was . . . pleasant." There were odd images in the man's head—he was seeing with some other sense than any the Out-cast had ever experienced. It made for extremely confusing but very colorful images, like falling into a whirling Mandelbrot set.

"Hartmann?" the Outcast asked, and then plucked the thoughts from Dylan. "Still alive, yet my jokers are dead . . . *Damn* it!"

The Outcast pondered. Teddy was getting tired. Staying in the Out-cast's form for the last several hours had drained him. He could feel all the links: to Bloat's body sleeping above him, to the demons, to all the physical changes he'd made here. They weighed on him, as if the Rox were a shell that he carried tortoiselike on his back. It would be very easy to fall into dreams right now. He could fall like a ghost through the cav-erns and gawk at the strange creatures there; he could maybe find Kelly and talk to her again, maybe even kiss one more time . . .

Ted shook his head, bringing himself back to the present. Travnicek had brought those strange eyeless tendrils around toward him. *Yes* . . . he was thinking, as if in sympathy. Dylan, with the mournful de-meanor of an alcoholic regarding an empty bottle of Mad Dog, had picked up his horn from the floor.

One of the guards had gone to wake Kafka; Ted could hear his adviser rising, his thoughts still confused with the vestiges of dreams.

"The Hunt has failed," the Outcast said slowly as Kafka scuttled in from his alcove. "I think we can still gain something from this. I really do. We forced an ace and the political leader of the mili-tary to run from their own headquarters. We caused panic and fear

throughout New York for most of the night." The Outcast was nodding, more because he could sense the uncertainty in the thoughts
around him than because he believed what he was saying.

"Kafka—I want you to prepare a statement. Tell them that this was
just a little of what they can expect if the Rox is attacked. Tell them
that the Wild Hunt wasn't destroyed, that it can return each and every
night. Say that unless Hartmann and General Zappa and the others
are reined in and any plans for attacking the Rox are shelved, we will
continue to defend ourselves. We're willing to talk, to negotiate, to do
whatever we can to live peacefully here in our own country, but we
won't tolerate threats. We won't be responsible for the destruction or
the deaths that will occur if President Bush and the government of
the United States persist in their current course of action."

The Outcast waved a hand at Kafka. "Or something like that,
anyway. You know how to word these things. Maybe they'll reopen
negotiations."

"Governor, there isn't going to be a political solution to this,"
Kafka said. "I'm sorry, but I don't see it happening."

So tired . . . "Well I do," Ted said, more harshly than he wanted to,
then softened his tone slightly. "I have to, Kafka. I don't want any
more people to die than already have."

"Nobody dies if you surrender," Modular Man pointed out quickly.
"We just dial that number—"

"Shut up, tinface," Travnicek snarled. Modular Man's mouth
clicked shut audibly.

"We have a chance," Ted continued. "We made Hartmann and the
Turtle run; we've beaten off the two previous attacks."

"And they beat off the Hunt," Dylan said. "From their perspective,
they're probably calling it a victory."

"Then let's get our own victory," the Outcast said loudly. "We
know where the ammo dumps are located, where they've placed the
artillery batteries. Let's take them out. We can use Modular Man,
Pulse, some of the jokers who served in the Brigade and have experience. We can do it."

If they hadn't been so tired, he might have been able to rouse them.
They just looked at him dully. Even their thoughts were dull. Only

Kafka was moving, barking orders at the guards. Dylan clutched his horn to his breast and walked out of the hall like a wounded, dripping stag. Modular Man looked at Travnicek. "Do I have to, boss?"

"You heard the governor." Travnicek chuckled. "Go hit some ammo dumps for your poor father, would you?"

As Modular Man took off, Ted felt the weariness overtaking him. He willed the Outcast's body to dissolve, expecting that he would find himself back in Bloat's form again.

Wyungare regarded the other boy, the one who lay dozing beneath the tree. He showed little sign of who he eventually would grow into. But he was clearly dreaming.

The Aborigine watched with fascination as the dream generated within the dream. It was almost like watching a werewolf movie, one with decent transformation special effects. The boy's figure blurred and lengthened and solidified. Now a man's form stirred on the moss, a man dressed in a cowled medieval robe.

"Outcast," said Wyungare. "Wake."

The man opened his eyes, stared in confusion. His eyes narrowed and he struggled to his feet.

"You?" he said. "You're in a cell."

"Indeed," said Wyungare. "And so are you."

"I don't understand." Outcast yawned and stretched his arms.

"You will."

"I don't have time to understand," said Outcast a little petulantly. "I've got so many things I have to do."

"Don't worry," said Wyungare. "The time you're spending here is a series of tiny bits of being that fit very comfortably into your normal time stream. Believe me, this is hardly taking any time at all."

"Oh," said Outcast uncertainly. "Okay . . . I guess."

"Let's walk." The Aborigine led the way. "Tell me about yourself."

"There's really not much to say," said his companion.

But Wyungare made encouraging noises and what seemed half

an eternity later, Outcast was still elaborating out all the things that comprised "really not much to say."

"Let's talk about your parents," said Wyungare. Outcast looked back at him suspiciously, fearfully. "Let's talk about loneliness."

After a while, Outcast did.

Dead Nicholas was dead.

Ray had been to the club a couple of times before. They grilled a decent steak and a certain amount of excitement could be found in the gaming rooms in back. Usually Dead Nicholas was crowded. To-night, though, the pale-skinned waitresses dressed in tattered shrouds that gave tantalizing glimpses of their smooth white flesh were mostly standing around the bar gossiping. There were few customers to serve. Dead Nicholas had always relied on the tourist trade. And now tourists were staying away from Jokertown in droves.

Ray got a table in the lounge. He leaned over its glass top to see who was interned in the coffin that formed its base. It was a woman, no more than a girl, a beautiful and lifelike Sleeping Beauty. The figures were supposed to be waxworks, made by the Bowery Dime Museum, but they looked damned real. Ray found himself staring intently, try-ing to see if it was breathing, as two waitresses raced to the table. The one with the white streak through the middle of her long black hair beat the ash-blonde. "What can I get you?" she asked.

"A babe named Cameo," Ray said.

The waitress frowned. "She expecting you?"

Ray reached into his pocket and pulled out a twenty. He held it up, showing it to the waitress. "What do you care?"

"Right this way."

Ray recognized Cameo right away from the photo in her dossier. She was young, maybe twenty, maybe less, with long wavy blond hair and big brown eyes. She was dressed in an outfit from an old Cagney gangster movie. She looked good in it. She also wore an antique cameo on a black ribbon choker around her long, graceful neck. Ray wondered what kind of lingerie she preferred. Something old and lacy and expensive, Ray thought. Something about this girl suggested money. Lots and lots of money.

"Cameo?" Ray said. "Or would you rather I call you Ellen?"

She looked at him and frowned. "How do you know my name?"

"Shouldn't I? It's in your dossier." Ray sat down in the chair opposite her. There wasn't much else in Cameo's private back room. The table that they sat at was small and round, well suited for intimate conversation. Atop it was Cameo's beaded clutch purse, a cordless phone, and a crystal-stemmed goblet that she toyed with as Ray sat opposite her.

"If you've read my dossier," Cameo said, "you must be from Battle."

"That's right. My name is Ray." He flashed his lopsided smile. "You can call me Billy."

"Well, Mr. Ray, what exactly do you want?"

All business, no banter, Ray thought sourly. "I have something for you."

For the first time eagerness showed on Cameo's face. "Did you bring the jacket?"

"Which jacket is that?" Ray asked with a frown.

"The jacket that was my price for going on this expedition of Battle's. The leather jacket that once belonged to the ace called Black Eagle."

Ray frowned. "What, you collect clothes from dead aces? Weird hobby."

Cameo frowned back. On her, it looked pretty. "I thought you read my dossier."

Ray shrugged. "I did. It said you were a psychosomatic trance channeler."

Cameo rolled her eyes. "A *psychometric* trance channeler, Mr. Ray."

"Oh. Okay. What's that?"

"I didn't know that my discussion with Mr. Battle would lead to my secrets becoming common knowledge," Cameo said frostily.

"Hey, you can trust me to keep my mouth shut. Besides, we're both on the team. I'll see you in action tomorrow. It won't hurt to tell me what you can do tonight."

Cameo nodded. "All right. I read psychic impressions from objects and then channel the psyche of the dead from the things they once owned."

"Wow," Ray said. "Sounds like fun."

Cameo shrugged.

"Exactly how would that help us take Ellis Island?"

"Well . . . this is not something that's widely known, but if the deceased is an ace—"

Ray snapped his fingers. "Then you can channel his powers!"

"If," Cameo said, "the powers were mental in nature. I couldn't channel, say, the Harlem Hammer's strength, but I could channel Dr. Tachyon's telepathy."

"If," Ray said, "Tachyon was dead and you had a pair of his socks or something."

Cameo pursed her lips. "Yes. Interesting example."

Ray reached into his pocket and pulled out the ring they'd taken from the graveyard earlier that night. He put it on the table between them. "That explains this, then."

"Whose is it?"

"It belonged to a guy named Brian Boyd, an ace also known as Blockhead. He's dead now."

Cameo reached out, not quite touching the ring.

"I guess Battle wanted you to have it so you could do your mumbo-jumbo and be ready first thing tomorrow."

Cameo nodded abstractedly, still looking closely at the ring.

"I guess he has the jacket and he'll give it to you tomorrow."

Cameo looked up at him. For the first time there was uncertainty in her liquid eyes. "That when everything starts?" she asked. "Tomorrow morning."

"Well," Ray said, leaning close, "if you want we could have some real action tonight. Just the two of us."

Cameo looked back at him steadily. "Tomorrow will be quite soon enough, Mr. Ray, thank you very much."

♠

"It's another cunt," the bodysnatcher said. "Someone's cut it with a straight razor. You can see where it's bleeding."

The psychologist sighed and put down the Rorschach card. "We've looked at fourteen cards now. You've seen images of sexual mutilation in every one of them."

The bodysnatcher tilted back his chair. "I'm a twisted mother-fucker, what can I say? Too bad you gave me amnesty."

"I don't think there's any point in continuing with this test," the psychologist said.

"Don't give up," the bodysnatcher told him. "Come on, show me the rest of the inkblots. I promise, I won't see anything but butterflies and puppy dogs."

The psychologist opened a drawer and put the cards away. "Why don't we just talk instead."

The bodysnatcher yawned, like he could care less. Or maybe the meat was just tired. Pulse was an old fuck, after all. The bus had delivered them to a low cinder-block building behind an electrified fence somewhere in Jersey. Inside, the place was bigger than it looked, with at least four levels hidden under the surface. It had airlocks instead of regular doors, and closed-circuit TV cameras everywhere. The jumpers had been fingerprinted, photographed, run through a physical, then split up for a battery of tests that reminded the bodysnatcher of college entrance exams. After that he was given to this shrink.

"You look to be much older than the other jumpers," the psychologist said.

"I'm young at heart. And this isn't my original body."

"I see," the psychologist replied. He didn't let any reaction show on his face. "Where is your real body?"

"Worms are eating it," the bodysnatcher said. "It was a great body. I kept myself in shape. Not like you. When's the last time you did a sit-up?"

The shrink ignored that. "What happened to your body?"

"An ace threw oven cleaner in my eyes," the bodysnatcher told him. "Then some weights fell on me and broke my back. The ace left me there and killed the man I was supposed to be protecting."

"I see." He made a steeple of his fingers. "How did that make you feel about aces?"

"I want to kill every last one," the bodysnatcher said.

The psychologist made a notation.

"I'd like to kill all the nats and jokers too," the bodysnatcher added.

The shrink wrote faster.

"They finally found me," the bodysnatcher said. "They took me to some hospital. It was too late to save my eyes. Being crippled, that didn't matter, but I *needed* my eyes. You can't jump what you can't see. All I could do was lay there and wait to die. You know what saved me? My cunt."

The psychologist stopped writing and looked up. "Are you telling me you used to be a woman?" He licked his lip, like the idea got him excited.

"What do you think, Doctor?" the bodysnatcher said. "I'd been in that hospital maybe a week. One night I was lying in my own shit, waiting for someone to come clean me up. Finally an orderly shows up. He wiped me off, changed the sheets. Then he spread my legs and raped me." The bodysnatcher gave a savage smile. "I jumped while he was in me. No one had ever done a blind jump before, but he was close enough for government work."

"I see," said the shrink. "So this body originally belonged to the orderly."

"Fuck no," the bodysnatcher said. "That jellybelly? His feet always hurt, I couldn't stand it. I used him for a few days. Then I filled a tub, opened his wrists with a razor blade, and phoned 911. I jumped the first paramedic through the door. The meat arrived DOA."

The psychologist sat very still after he had finished, then gave a nod. "I see. Very well. I think we're just about through here." He stood up. "If you'll come with me."

The bodysnatcher followed him downstairs, where the shrink turned him over to a nasty-looking old fuck who said his name was George Battle. Battle looked over his file, then escorted him to a small bare room in the lowest subbasement. There was nothing in it but a large glass window opening on another small room. On the far side of the glass an old man in a flannel shirt sat at a table, working a crossword.

"One final test," Battle told him. "We'd like to see if you can jump that gentleman over there."

The bodysnatcher looked through the glass at the geezer. He was about eighty. Loose skin dangled under his chin, and there were liver spots on the back of his hands. He didn't seem aware that he was being watched.

"Why should I?" the bodysnatcher asked.

"A good soldier never asks why. He follows orders," Battle said. "But I'll tell you, this one time. We want to get a better understanding of how your jumping power works."

"Why don't I just jump you instead?" the bodysnatcher asked.

Battle was as cool as Prime used to be, he had to give him that. "I certainly can't stop you, but it won't establish anything. This experiment is designed to ascertain whether jumpers can use their powers on a visible target even if a physical barrier interposes. Like that window."

"Windows can't stop jumpers. Take my word for it."

"I'd rather you show me. If you can." Battle gestured.

The bodysnatcher moved to the window, studied the geezer lost in his crossword. He drew a fingernail down across the glass. The geezer looked straight up at the window, blinked. Not a television hookup, then. It had to be one-way glass.

The bodysnatcher turned. "Fuck you," he said.

"Save the vulgarity," Battle said. "I've heard it all before. If you'll follow me, you can rejoin your friends."

Wyungare knew he was still in the cold, drafty, starkly austere cell. No question about that. But he simultaneously knew he remained in the dreamtime. No discrepancy, there. You *can* be both a particle and a wave. No contradictions.

"Let me show you something," he said to the Outcast.

The man looked uncomfortable.

"Is something wrong?" Wyungare said.

"I have to get back." His voice shook a little.

"You *are* back," said Wyungare. "You don't have the ground rules down yet. You're still there as well as here. And *here* is taking virtually no time. It's like Mr. H. G. Wells's 'The New Accelerator.' The times are different, here and there."

"I still don't see," Outcast muttered.

"Please trust me," said Wyungare. "Now come on. I've something to show you."

"More of this swamp?" said Outcast, more than the hint of a complaint in his voice.

"Not much more." The pair came out from under what had seemed an endless canopy of overhanging tree branches, both broad-leafed and pine. They entered a clearing, a space where the scars of clearing were long since muted by time and the wear of human usage. The low frame house squatted at the edge of the water. A ragged curl of smoke drifted from a crooked, rusted vent pipe in the roof.

Wyungare whistled a few bars of "Blue Bayou." Outcast didn't seem to get it. The Aborigine stopped. "All right, we're going visiting now. Just follow me and watch." He glanced back at Outcast.

The man nodded. "Okay. But please make this quick. Back in . . . the real world . . . I'm sending people—" He hesitated.

"—out to die." Wyungare finished the sentence for him. "I know. Don't worry, you'll send them all out in plenty of time for their respective appointments in Samarra."

Outcast looked puzzled.

"Don't worry," said Wyungare. "I'll explain someday. You need to read something more than game-playing novels." He led the way around to the front of the house. The two men climbed rickety steps and crossed the sun-bleached plank porch. The door stood open.

They heard sounds of pain from within.

"After you," said Wyungare. He motioned inward. Outcast went.

And stopped, dead in his tracks.

"Go ahead," said Wyungare. Outcast resisted the urging. Wyungare gently pushed him forward anyway.

"Oh, no," said Outcast. "Please, no. I don't want to watch this."

"I'm afraid you must," said Wyungare. "Just a bit. Just enough to make an impression."

They stood just outside the doorway into the small living room.

"No," said Outcast.

"I'm afraid so," said Wyungare.

They saw a young boy tied facedown across a rough wooden table. His wrists were lashed with clothesline cord to the table legs at one end, his ankles secured to the wooden legs at the other side. His hair was very black. He rolled his head from side to side with pain. When he turned toward the pair in the doorway, they saw how dark his eyes were.

"That is Jack," Wyungare said.

"Do I know him?" Outcast sounded puzzled.

"You've met." The Aborigine chuckled. "You didn't recognize him because his outer appearance has changed just a bit."

On the table, the boy's thighs were spread. A cloudy figure stood between the boy's legs, pumping in a violent pounding rhythm.

"What's that?" said Outcast, alarmed.

"Just what you think." They heard the brutal sounds of flesh slapping flesh.

"But . . . who—"

"Someone you might have known well, at least in a slightly different context," said Wyungare. "Recall your cousins. Think of their father."

Outcast moaned. Then he rushed forward past Wyungare, striking out at the phantom figure pistoning between the imprisoned boy's thighs.

Fingers through smoke.

It did no good. The rape continued.

"I commend your attempt," said Wyungare quietly. "At least you tried to do something." He took Outcast by the shoulders and steered him back toward the door. "Jack would thank you if he could."

"Jack?" said Outcast. "That boy? Jack?"

"Indeed."

"But can't—"

"—we help him?"

Outcast nodded frantically.

"Perhaps," said Wyungare. "But there's nothing we can do about the past. Jack found his own solution."

"What?" said Outcast, voice as desperate as a man trying to pull his feet out of quicksand.

Wyungare said, "After a time, Jack killed him."

Outcast gasped. "Killed his daddy?"

"Stepfather."

Outcast looked shocked and sober. "And then?"

"Things just got worse," said Wyungare.

Outcast shuddered. "How could they?"

"Take my word for it."

"Tell me."

"Prurient interest?" said Wyungare gently.

Outcast said slowly, voice shaking, "I have to know."

"And why is that?"

Outcast shook his head. "I can't tell you. It's . . . a family secret."

"I think I already know," said Wyungare.

Outcast began to cry.

SATURDAY MORNING

September 22, 1990

BLOAT AWOKE BACK IN Bloat's body. Echoes of the dream still reverberated in his mind. *Family secrets, yes . . .* Teddy wasn't sure who he hated most, Wyungare for dredging up those buried memories, or himself for letting the story pour out to the Aborigine. *I'm sorry. I promised I'd never tell. I'm sorry . . . It was just that seeing that boy reminded me . . .*

He made me do it, he wanted to add. But that wail was not only childish, it wasn't true. Teddy hadn't realized just how much he'd wanted to lance that particular mental wound.

He sat there for long minutes, mostly feeling sorry for himself. Now that he could use the Outcast's body even while awake, it was quickly becoming home—that young, handsome figure was certainly more desirable than this, this enormous slab of immobile fat and skin, pinned like some gargantuan specimen to the floor of his castle and fed on shit and garbage.

He was tired, so tired. So sleepy.

The mindvoices of the Rox ebbed and flowed in his mind, a backdrop to his misery.

Kafka rattled in; evidently the guards had alerted him to the fact that the Bloat-body was awake again. "Governor?"

"I'm beat, Kafka. Leave me alone."

"I thought . . . Excuse me, Governor, but I thought you would stay as the Outcast." The rest of the sentence followed, unspoken. *. . . . why would you WANT to come back to this horror if you could get out?*

"I would if I could, believe me. But I always come back here when I'm tired. Always. I'm linked with this body." His voice was so mournful that he ended up giggling harshly at himself. "We jokers are so damned ugly," he said. "We don't like the way we look any more than the fucking nats. Ain't that a trip? If we could, we'd cover all the goddamn mirrors in the world." Bloat yawned, the pimply fat cheeks stretching like uncooked dough. "I was inspecting the Wall emplacements. We've picked up a fair amount of stuff from the Jersey shore. There's a couple radar units. We got anyone who knows how to use them?"

"I think so, Governor. I'll find out and get them set up. We can certainly use them."

Kafka's voice sounded weary, and the roach-man's thoughts were pessimistic. *Maybe they'll give us a few seconds warning before the missiles hit. Just long enough to scream . . .*

"Is it really that bad, Kafka?"

Kafka looked around. They were alone except for the ring of guards around the balcony and at each of the entrances into the main lobby of the castle—half of them jokers, half Boschian mermen seated on flying, armored fish. Outside, the Rox was slumbering as false dawn lightened the eastern sky. The towers of Manhattan shivered in the waters of the bay.

"I . . ." Kafka began. Stopped.

Kafka sighed, a high and thin wheezing. "I *am* worried, Governor. This time they won't try a ground assault. If what you're hearing from Patchwork is true, then it's going to be a long-range bombardment. The *New Jersey* is stationed suspiciously close to the bay. Governor, a Tomahawk cruise missile comes in low and fast maybe 500 mph— how quickly can we detect it, and can we respond to the attack in the four or five seconds we might have? A Lance missile moves at Mach 3, *much* faster than a Tomahawk. They have missiles that can be fired from Apache helicopters; some of the jets can fire from as far away as three miles and put a missile straight down a chimney . . . You want me to go on? Governor, they don't have to commit any troops to this assault—not this time, not if they don't want to. They can just bang away until there's nothing left here but rubble."

Kafka left one thought dangling, but Bloat heard it. . . . *and you're the prime target, Governor. We already know that. What the hell chance do we have if you're gone? If you're dead, there's no Wall, no caves, no fairyland castle, no demons from Bosch. There's nothing but a bunch of jokers with stolen weapons and the jumpers. It isn't going to be enough.*

The thoughts from the joker guards weren't much better. More than one of them was thinking of that fucking 800 number and of the jokers who'd left yesterday under the amnesty. He knew he had to do something—talk like this would lead to flashfire rumors, and he couldn't afford that.

Bloat shook his head at Kafka. "You are about the most pessimistic roach I've ever seen." Kafka glared up at Bloat at that. "No man, I mean it. You must think that every cloud is the bottom of a shoe. Look, everything you said is true. Okay, fine, it's all true. But look at what *we've* got. Modular Man's here, Molly's in place, Croyd's likely to wake up any minute, Hardesty's banged up but he can call up the Hunt tonight if we need them. We have the caves and the Wall and a lot of goddamn equipment. We have a *lot* of jumpers. We have Patchwork's eye and ear in Zappa's goddamn *headquarters,* so we stand a good chance of knowing in advance every move he's going to make. There's a lot of protesters out there right now walking the streets in J-town and making noise about how Bush's 'kinder, gentler nation' is just a crock of bloatblack. Manhattan's practically a ghost town, from what we've heard. Put enough pressure on Congress and they might demand that Zappa and his people get pulled back out. Half the aces they asked to join refused, didn't they?—maybe they'll even show up on our side if things get ugly. Maybe this Wyungare fellow can actually *do* something. If the military's targeting buildings the way they are, then I can *change* them—every day if I need to—so their targeting systems are fouled up. We have some radar, we have some jokers with useful powers. C'mon, Kafka. *Think.* Give me advice, not sob stories. If you were me, what else would you do?"

Bloat's shoulders sagged back against the rubbery skin of his body. The long speech had made him more tired than before, but he could hear the difference in the mindvoices. Even Kafka stood up a little straighter under his carapace.

"I'm sorry, Governor," he said. "I—"

Bloat waved a weary arm. "What else would you *do?*" he repeated. He plucked the answer from Kafka's mind before Kafka could speak it. "If all it takes is a little foul weather . . ." Bloat said.

Bloat giggled and looked out from the transparent walls of the castle. The sun was just rising over the bay. Deep black, long shadows crawled like ebony fingers over the lower buildings of Manhattan while bright sun was glinting from the upper windows. The moat between the Wall and Ellis was dark and still, with wisps of dawn steam rising from the surface of the water. Untroubled by Bloat's Wall, a gull glided in over the Manhattan Gate, swooped low over the wavelets, and plunged into the cold water. It came out with silver wriggling in its beak. The gull raised its head and swallowed the fish whole.

It all looked so damned peaceful . . .

"Get me a phone," Bloat said. Kafka snapped his fingers; one of the Boschian mermen leapt atop his fish-steed and left the room, returning a moment later with a cordless receiver. The merman glided up to Bloat's head; hovering, he held the phone out to the boy. Bloat took it in his stick-thin hands and nearly dropped it. He giggled, then slowly and deliberately punched the buttons. ". . . I . . . Give . . . Up," he said aloud, then cleared his throat.

"Joker amnesty," said the voice at the other end. "Who are you and where and when can we pick you up?"

"You couldn't pick me up with a fucking derrick," Bloat shrieked. "This is Governor Bloat. Listen, I got a message for your goddamn General Zappa. Tell him that I figure the whole problem is that you nats hate the sight of us out in the bay. Well hell, I can fix *that*. Tell him to go look out his window."

Bloat disconnected in the middle of the spluttering from the other end and let go of the receiver. The merman flicked the reins of its fish and did a power dive, scooping up the receiver just before it hit the floor. Around the room, Bloat's guards applauded.

Bloat paid no attention. He had his eyes shut, humming to himself and imagining . . .

He visualized each of the hundreds of gargoyles he had so carefully placed along the roofs of the Rox—those leering, obscene little creatures. Then he thought of fog, a pea soup that London would have been proud of, a mist that might have wreathed the macintosh of Sherlock Holmes, one that would set the lighthouses along the Maine coast to wailing mournfully to unseen ships. Images of old horror movies came to mind: the Ripper stalking the streets of Whitechapel, bursting through ropes of fog to attack an unsuspecting woman of the streets; Frankenstein trudging stiff-legged through a smoky Bavarian village; Castle Dracula blanketed in stuff so thick it looked like coils of soiled cotton. He thought of fog so dense you could cut it and slice it and serve it for dinner.

He thought of that fog belching from the open mouths of all the gargoyles on all the rooftops and all the towers in his domain.

Bloat imagined it. He opened the gates and let the power flow through. It was so much easier now; if nothing else, Wyungare had done that for him. Now he *knew* where the power came from. He could find the path quickly, could tap the energy anytime he wanted. Voices from the dreamworld screamed at him in outrage as thick streams of cloud vomited from above.

Bloat opened his eyes! He chuckled. All around the Crystal Castle, from everywhere in the Rox, the wreaths and tendrils fell and spread, like thick gray velvet being pulled over the sun and sky. In moments, there was nothing outside the transparent walls of the castle except wisps of dark sullen cloud.

"So much for my great view," he said. "This is really gonna cut down the value of the property."

He yawned. A feeling of exhaustion overwhelmed him. Bloat slept.

♥

The basement lounge was full of old people.

The bodysnatcher did a quick count while they locked the doors behind him. He saw three faces he knew, still wearing their own flesh, and fourteen geezers. Seventeen total, eighteen counting him. They'd started out with twenty-two jumpers.

The youngest geezer was maybe sixty. The oldest looked like he'd been embalmed a decade ago. A few seemed pretty spry, but one old fuck struggled with his walker, and there were a couple in wheelchairs.

The bodysnatcher studied the room. No windows, only the one door. A pair of television monitors were mounted high on the walls at either end. Sprinklers dotted the ceiling. A folding table had been set up, supporting a steel coffee urn and a dozen boxes of assorted donuts. Most of the donuts were gone. Not that he cared. Caffeine and sugar were poison.

"Zelda." A hand clutched at his arm.

The bodysnatcher pulled away. "Don't touch me." He looked down at a cripple in a wheelchair. She was an ancient, withered stick of a woman whose ghastly blond wig couldn't conceal almost total baldness.

"You didn't jump," the dried-up old cunt in the chair said in a high, quavery voice. She sounded like she was going to cry.

The bodysnatcher recognized her. Something about the way she whined. "Suzy?" she asked.

Suzy Creamcheese bobbed her head up and down. Her wig almost fell off.

"She'll love your tits," the bodysnatcher said. "Did you tell her about the herpes? I hope she has a warranty."

Suzy blinked vague, watery eyes. "What do you mean?" She clutched at the bodysnatcher's sleeve. "Why are they doing this? When will we get our bodies back?"

The bodysnatcher didn't waste his breath answering. Behind them, the door opened. Juggler was ushered inside the room. They heard the door lock behind him. Juggler was still wearing his own body. The bodysnatcher went up to him. "Maybe you're not as stupid as I thought."

Juggler had a look of dismay and confusion on his face as he saw all the geezers. "It was one-way glass, wasn't it?"

"One-way glass, one-way jumps."

Suzy Creamcheese began to cry.

Juggler said, "They promised us amnesty." He took the leaflet out of his back pocket, unfolded it.

"I take it back. You are as stupid as I thought." The bodysnatcher looked around. "We're three short. Who's missing?"

"Gyro Gearloose, Hari-Kari, and Mam'selle," Monkey-face put in. She hadn't jumped either. She looked just like what she was a frightened sixteen-year-old girl.

The bodysnatcher thought about the missing jumpers. Then it all made sense. Mam'selle was French. She spoke four languages fluently. Hari-Kari was a twelve-year-old nip who understood electronics better than Kafka. Both had IQs up in the genius range. Neither one was going to give anybody any trouble. And Gyro was a congressman's son.

"This is bullshit," Juggler told the geezers. "No way they can keep you in those bodies." He held up the leaflet, shook it for emphasis. "We got amnesty *in writing.* If we need to, we can jump the guards, the doctors . . . whoever we have to, until we get our own bodies back."

"You see anybody here but us chickens?" the bodysnatcher asked him.

Juggler glared at him. The bodysnatcher could see him struggling to come up with a nasty reply.

They all heard the sound at the same moment.

The bodysnatcher glanced up. Gas was hissing out of the overhead sprinklers. Someone screamed.

"Not very fucking original," the bodysnatcher said. Then it was showtime. He went to his lightform.

They were four floors deep. It took him half of forever to burn his way back to the surface, and he felt weak as water before he finally got there, dangerously low on energy. He reverted to human form and hid in the bushes just inside the electric fence, naked and shivering. It was his own fault. He never should have stopped to kill the shrink.

By the time the guards came out of the building, the bodysnatcher had rested long enough. He lasered out of there at lightspeed.

It wasn't until he was almost back at the junkyard, coming in low and fast through the fog, that Tom finally lost it. He tried to concentrate, but it was no use. The shell slid downward. He felt faint.

The shell plowed into the wall of junkers along the shore, crunched through them, slewed heavily to the right and crashed. Tom was slammed forward violently by the impact. He must have blacked out. When he came to, the shell was canted at a sixty-degree angle, and he was suspended in his chair. He knew he'd have bruises across his chest where the seat harness had caught him.

Tom freed himself, dropped two feet to the floor. His hands fumbled as he punched the hatch controls. There was a *hiss* as the hatch unsealed. He crawled out into the night, left the shell half-buried in rust and iron, and limped back to the shack.

Inside it was dim and still. The severed head of the first Modular Man sat on the television, staring at him. The dead eyes seemed to follow him across the room. "Stop looking at me that way," he told it.

Exhaustion weighed heavily on him. The dull throbbing behind his eyes wasn't going to go away anytime soon. He had flown sixty miles up the Hudson before finally dropping Hartmann off at a hospital. Even that far upstate might not be safe. The trip home had been endless. He'd had to detour around the Rox to get to Bayonne, and the fog was getting so thick that he almost overflew the junkyard.

When he was running before the Hunt, there hadn't been time to be afraid. But the fear had found him now. He could still see the jaws of the hellhound as it slammed up against his shell. He could feel the impact as the Huntsman's spear punched through his battleship plate. Another foot to the side and . . .

Tom didn't want to think about that.

He hadn't dared look at the Brooklyn Bridge on the way back. When he closed his eyes, he saw them tumbling . . .

In almost twenty-seven years as an active ace, the Turtle had never killed anyone. Until now.

Maybe they weren't real, Tom thought. The hounds didn't bleed, he remembered. When they died, there were no bodies. They just vanished. Maybe it was the same with the horses and the hunters who rode them. Not *people,* just demons off the Rox, like the mermen and the knights on the flying fish.

Only Bloat's demons couldn't go beyond the Wall, and the Wild Hunt had ridden through deepest Flatbush. And he'd *seen* some of those jokers out at the peace conference. The antlered man had even spoken.

Tom buried his face in his hands. His head was pounding.

Was this what war was like?

He needed to talk to someone. But Joey was in North Carolina, Tachyon was on his way to another planet, and Barbara had cried at his funeral, years ago.

They hadn't given him any choice, Tom told himself. The hounds were ripping men apart. Hartmann's hand had looked like something pulled from a meat-grinder. At least he had been able to lead the Hunt away from Ebbets Field, maybe that had saved a few lives, maybe he'd helped protect Danny and the rest . . .

He went to the medicine chest, dry-swallowed four aspirin. Then he turned on the shower. He stood under the spray for a long time, soaped and scrubbed until his skin was raw. It didn't make him feel any cleaner.

The Outcast was wrenched from dreams by the thundering of the Rox's thoughts. He found himself standing in the Great Hall, under Liberty's torch, below the slumbering Bloat.

Pulse—Bodysnatcher—kept throwing images of Bloat at him: Bloat skewered, great gobbets of Bloat-meat cooked by Pulse's laser. Bloat chopped and diced and dead. The Outcast rubbed the smooth facets of the amethyst on his staff, looking up at the sleeping, pimply face of Bloat far above them. He stroked the monstrous flanks of Bloat's body affectionately.

Outside, there was nothing. Just the fog.

"They fucking offed all the jumpers," Zelda raged, stalking up and down the lobby. The others in the room watched him, silent, though their head-voices shouted in the Outcast's mind. "They played with them, tricked them into jumping some fucking old codgers, and then gassed them all. That's the kind of goddamn amnesty they're offering the Rox. Anyone else feel like calling that fucking number now?"

"We'll contact the media and let them know what happened," Dylan said. "Enough bad press and they'll be forced to call off the assault."

Zelda snorted. "Call the reporters in and Battle will parade out all the nice teenage bodies his friends are now in, and they'll answer all the questions just the way they were briefed, and all the controversy turns into more propaganda against the nasty old Rox. It's almost beautiful the way he set it up. He's got the jumper bodies for the old folks, and the jumpers themselves are dead. One less threat. That fucking *stupid* Juggler."

They were all a little frightened: Kafka, Shroud, Dylan, most of the rest. There were images: images of war that looked like they'd been pulled from old pictures from Korea or Vietnam, the most graphic images from Shroud, who had been in the Joker Brigades in Nam. Kafka had even scarier scenes in his head—missiles streaking over the Wall and into the fog, disappearing down the flues and spires of the fantasyland he'd made here, buildings exploding one after another and the jokers running screaming with blood-streaked bodies . . .

"We could just leave," the penguin said. No one paid any attention.

"Kafka?" the Outcast said.

"I'm worried, Governor. I didn't think . . ." Kafka shivered, sending a dull ringing through the vast crystalline hall. "They're going to land on us with both feet. I don't even know if we can rule out a tactical nuke at this point—a 'clean' weapon that could take out the Rox, delivered in one of a hundred ways. Maybe they'd even dare the outrage that would cause. They want us dead."

Kafka's words fell into brooding silence. Even the head-voices went still for a moment. Shroud was remembering Nam: a village still smoldering from a direct napalm hit, a buzzing cloud of black flies rising from distended bodies strewn like broken dolls across the open space between the huts.

"I will not let this happen to the Rox," the Outcast declared. "I hear what you're all thinking. I will not let that happen."

"How you gonna stop it, Bloat—oh, excuse me, *Outcast?*" Zelda asked. "You gonna turn all the missiles into pretty little flowers like that trick you pulled last night with the jumpers? You gonna bring on enough demon armies to take out the whole frigging Marine Corps? C'mon, Bloat, can you think at transsonic speeds!—'cause that's how fast they're gonna be comin' in."

"I can't promise that there won't be deaths here," the Outcast said. "I ain't stupid, Bodysnatcher. Yes, jumpers are going to die; jokers are going to spill their blood on our soil."

"Great. A bloody campaign speech," Dylan muttered. The Outcast ignored him.

A hero could make them believe . . . He didn't know where the voice came from, but the words lingered long after the voice had faded, and he realized that it was true. A touch, just a touch, of the Outcast's power, of the dreamtime's energy . . . His staff began to glow faintly. The purple radiance glimmered from the crystalline walls, touched the edges of the fog with color.

"All that happened the last time too. Yes, they're going to throw everything they have at us this time. But I'm far, far stronger now. Then I couldn't project myself out of that ugly body"—he pointed to the Bloat-mountain behind him—"then I didn't have the power to transform the Rox, as I have since. We didn't have the physical Wall, the fog, or anywhere near as many caverns. We didn't have the Jersey shore or Liberty Island. We didn't have the weaponry that the Twisted Fists have brought in, we didn't have Modular Man, Pulse, Herne, or the Sleeper."

"If he wakes up," Shroud muttered.

"No. *When* the Sleeper wakes," the Outcast answered. "Croyd is stirring already, showing signs that soon he'll rise and join us. We have power. We have more power than even we believe or understand or can use."

The Outcast listened to the mindvoices and realized that his words were beginning to weave a kind of spell. Even Zelda was listening, and the angry doubt in Pulse's mind was slowly dissolving under the tidal impact of his speech. The Outcast found the power, followed the thread of it back into the world of dreams; and widened the channel, so that the energy poured through like molten gold. The penguin had stopped skating around and between the others and was standing watching him. He clenched his staff tightly, and the amethyst arced and flared, holding all of those gathered before him in a globe of light.

"There's no need for this dissension," the Outcast told them, and each word seemed to explode from the air. "Our bickering is exactly what they want. I am telling you as your governor, as the creator of the Rox: *We are stronger than they are.* We have the power of my magic, we have the power of the wild card, and we have the power that comes from being right. What we do here in the next day or so will be heroic, and we will prevail. We will keep the Rox as a homeland for all oppressed people; we will grow despite everything they do against us.

"They. Cannot. Win."

The Outcast emphasized the last three words, slamming the end of his staff down on the tiles with each one, and with each, the staff sent out streamers of light that pierced the thick fog gathered around the castle, illuminating the roiling cloud with sapphire, ruby, and then coruscating emerald hues.

"Now go," he spoke. "Go and get your people ready. I'll be sending defensive plans to each of you in the next few hours. We're going to hit everything we can before they use it against us. I need Pulse, Bodysnatcher; I'll need Modular Man too. I'll have to have joker and jumper volunteers to go outside the Wall through the caverns. Kafka, send Wyungare to me as soon as you can, would you? We're going to hit them first this time."

They nodded. The spell slowly faded as the intense hues faded in the fog, but they remembered. One by one, they nodded to the Outcast and left the Crystal Castle. Even Zelda's mind was cleansed of violent, sick images for a moment, and he shaped Pulse's body into light and sped away like a lightning bolt. The Outcast smiled grimly.

"Not a bad little speech." The Outcast glanced up at Bloat's body. The penguin had somehow moved from the floor to the sleeping

Bloat's shoulder. "Jim Bowie to the troops at the Alamo, wasn't it? Just wait until ol' Santa Anna opens fire."

The penguin cackled and skied away down the far side of Bloat.

Distant concussions battered the windows of the Rox. Kafka's strike teams were hitting at Zappa's supplies.

Modular Man, waiting for news in Patchwork's high room, tried to stand out of the way of the crowd of jokers who'd shown up and ended up being shoved back behind the mapboards.

The big reel-to-reel rolled on, recording all for posterity.

"News coming in," Patchwork said. "Somebody's reporting jumpers hitting sentries at Prospect Park. The ammo dump at Clove Lakes has just gone up."

"We can *hear* that," said one of the jumper aides.

Patchwork's chin lifted in the strange way that blind people had, as if she were trying to perceive the world with her chin.

"Just got another report. Somebody's firing self-propelled grenades into the battery set up at Newark International."

"That's Giles Goat-Boy," the joker said smugly. "Three jumpers on that team—nobody's gonna stop 'em."

"*That* got Zappa out of his office," Patchwork said. There were cheers from the jokers. "He's on the phone to . . . somebody named Ferguson?"

Jokers flipped through computer printout that listed military units and their officers. "I think this is him," one said. "Colonel, U.S. Army Intelligence and Security Command, last stationed at Fort McPherson, Georgia . . ."

"Got another Ferguson here," said another. "He's a brigadier in the Marines."

"*Hold it! Hold it!*" Patchwork said. "We've got a request from something called Oscar Red to commence hostilities."

"Oscar Red." Kafka jabbed at a map. "That's the rocket battery set up down at Fort Lee on Sandy Hook. MLRS."

"Zappa's thinking about it," Patchwork said.

There was a respectful silence. Kafka had impressed everyone with the capabilities of the Multiple-Launch Rocket System, capable of saturating an area the size of the Rox with no less than 8000 submunitions—nasty little exploding bombs—in less than a minute. The location of any MLRS unit was one datum that Kafka insisted be reported before anything else.

"Permission denied," Patchwork reported. Her voice had taken on a slight Zappa inflection. "Our ammunition reserves are too depleted on the Jersey side to be certain of sustained action."

There was a collective sigh of relief. A big joker bit the top off a can of Spam and began squeezing the contents into his mouth as if it were toothpaste.

"We don't have anyone near that unit." Kafka was still looking at the map. "Modular Man." His eyes swung, in their chitinous sockets, to the android. "Zappa might change his mind. I want you to take that battery out. That one and the other MLRS unit we know about."

"Very well," Modular Man said.

There wasn't much else he could say.

The PATH station on the Jersey side of the bay was deserted except for a squad of poker-faced soldiers. No one wanted to go into Manhattan today, what with last night's series of unexplained disasters.

One of the soldiers saluted as Ray approached. "Mr. Battle is waiting downstairs, sir."

"We taking the subway to Ellis Island?" Ray asked.

"I don't know, sir," the soldier said, deadpan.

Ray nodded and went down the stairs. The vacant subway platform struck Ray as vaguely creepy. There was something about the vast, echoing expanse of concrete overlooking a silent tunnel that made Ray feel like he was in some cheesy post-holocaust sci-fi flick where a mutant form of the wild card virus had killed everyone or turned them into vampires or something.

The platform was not entirely deserted, however. A single soldier stood at its edge, looking down the silent tunnel, ignoring the people clustered around the battered vending machines and neighboring concrete benches.

Battle was wearing Kevlar armor and full battle regalia, shadowed, as always, by his evil-smelling henchman. Cameo, also in Kevlar and with a backpack at her feet, was speaking very earnestly to him. He seemed to be impatiently ignoring her. A dejected-looking Jay Ackroyd was sitting with his gear piled around his feet, sipping vending-machine coffee from a plastic cup. Ray guessed that he had put the fear of God into the P.I. the day before. He didn't know whether to be happy or sorry.

He started to go over to join the group, then stopped to stare at the final team member sitting by herself on the second concrete bench.

She had blond hair and blue eyes and skin that was tanned a deep, flawless bronze. Her black sleeveless T-shirt bared arms with muscles like bundled wires that bunched and coiled with her every move. Ray unconsciously licked his lips as he watched her buffing the stock of the gun she held in her lap.

"Nice rifle," he said as he approached.

She looked up at him for the first time, regarded him closely with penetrating blue eyes. "You don't know much about guns, do you?" she asked.

Ray shrugged, knowing that he'd fucked up again. "I know which end to point. I carry one," he said, slapping the Ingram pistol holstered at his side, "but I never need it much."

She nodded. "I know. You're Billy Ray." Ray grinned his crooked grin. She knew who he was. "I thought you were dead," she added. "That Mackie Messer fellow sure messed you up in Atlanta. I saw it on TV."

Ray's smile froze in place, becoming more of a grimace. The girl didn't seem to notice. She went back to polishing her gun, whatever the hell it was.

"Took a lot of guts, the way you kept coming after him, I mean, after he sliced off your fingers and the bottom part of your face and all." She looked back up at him. "I see everything grew back."

"Yeah," Ray said.

She stood up gracefully, the muscles in her arms rippling as she moved. Her breasts were small, but their large nipples stood upright against the soft fabric of her black T-shirt.

"My name's Danny. Danny Shepherd. This isn't a rifle. It's a shotgun." She held it out for Ray to inspect. Ray took his eyes off her long enough to glance at it. Now that he looked closely at it, he could see it wasn't an assault rifle. There were a few differences. It was longer than an M-16, and its magazine box was also longer and wider. Overall it looked sleeker than an assault rifle.

"It's a Smith & Wesson AS-3 automatic combat shotgun," Danny explained. "It fires ammo cartridges with flechette, high explosive, and armor-piercing rounds. I didn't have time for a lot of weapons training before this expedition. The armorer thought I'd be more likely to hit something with this than an automatic rifle. Pretty sexy, isn't it?"

"Not as sexy as you," Ray said.

She looked him over with a lazy smile. "Not many men like women with muscles."

"I'm not like many men," Ray said. "Maybe we could pump some iron together sometime."

"Maybe."

Slow down, Ray told himself. He nodded. "Sure. Anytime. When we get done with this little job." He hesitated. She'd been in Battle's book, but she'd looked different.

Not as lean or as hard-edged as she looked in person.

"What's your role on the team?" he asked.

"Communications."

Ray frowned, but before he could question her further a curtain of blackness suddenly descended over them. Ray panicked for a moment, imagining scything hands coming out of the blackness to cut him to shreds, but then he realized what was happening as Battle called out, "All right, Black Shadow, you can cut the cheap theatrics."

"I'll cut the theatrics, Battle, when I see my pardon." The voice was that of a black man. It was deep, vibrant, and cultured.

"Cautious, aren't we?" Battle said dryly.

"I've got reason to be."

"I suppose you do. Well, turn on some kind of light so I can find the damn thing."

The darkness shrank, contracting until it became an inky bloat that coalesced into a tall, well-built man in a tight-fitting suit, black cape, and domino mask.

"Here it is," Battle said, holding out a sheaf of papers to the vigilante.

Black Shadow took the papers from Battle, unfolded them, and quickly read them.

"Satisfactory?" Battle asked.

Shadow nodded.

"Signed by George Bush and everything," Battle said with something of a smirk. He turned and looked at the others. "I suppose that everyone has heard about the events of last night, the attack on the command post at Ebbets Field, the attempted assassination of Senator Hartmann, the destruction of the Brooklyn Bridge?"

Ray, like the others, nodded. It had been an eventful evening.

"The peace initiative has failed," Battle said. If it was possible to be grim and happy at the same time, Battle managed. "The mutant-coddlers have left the field. It's up to us to clean out that nest of vipers on Ellis Island." Battle now unquestioningly looked very, very happy. "It's time to go kick mutant ass."

Ray took a deep breath to calm his racing nerves. He was ready. And so, as best they could be, were the others.

It was time to party.

Von Herzenhagen was pontificating. "This creature, this Bloat, is twisting the fabric of reality. No one knows the limits of this power. The danger he poses is immeasurable, unthinkable. If he can transform the Rox, what happens when he turns his attention to Manhattan . . . or even the world?"

There was a huge helicopter in center field. The soldiers were loading it with corpses as the briefing began. Last night's assault had left twenty-six dead. The body bags were laid out in orderly rows across the outfield grass.

Zappa stood near the center of the miniature Rox. The castle was as tall as he was. "We've seen Bloat's reply to our peace offer." The general used his map pointer to gesture at the bodies in the outfield. "I have twenty-six families to phone. Twenty-six grieving mothers to talk to. I'd choose combat any day."

Tom looked at the body bags. Maybe he should offer to swap assignments. Zappa hadn't seen the hellhounds. Tom would take the grieving mothers every time. But he said nothing.

"We're going to soften them up first," Vidkunssen said. "Air strikes, missiles, artillery. It won't be as surgical as we'd hoped, so long as this fog lasts. Our optical guidance systems are useless in that soup, and it even seems to be fucking up our radar. But we can still get their attention."

"Then we hand off to you," Zappa said.

"About time," Cyclone said.

"*Yes!*" yelled the Reflector, punching the air.

"No one expects you to conquer the entire Rox," Zappa said. "All you have to do is break through the Wall, brush aside any defenders that may confront you, and proceed to the castle to deal with Bloat. We'll do the rest."

"Terminate his rule," said Phillip Baron von Herzenhagen. He took his pipe out of his mouth. "With extreme prejudice."

There was a long silence.

"I'M NOT A KILLER." Tom's words echoed off the grandstands.

Zappa nodded as if he understood. "No," he said gently. "But last night you proved you were a soldier."

Tom fell quiet, weighing Zappa's words. Maybe he was right. Somehow the thought made him feel a little better. If this was war . . . if he was a soldier . . .

"What about the jumpers?" Corporal Danny asked.

Von Herzenhagen fielded that one. "Twenty-two jumpers surrendered last night at the Jersey Gate. According to our best intelligence, that should leave no more than a hundred on the island, possibly as few as eighty or ninety. I don't need to tell you how dangerous their power makes them. *However . . .*"

He paused, flashed them a broad, chubby smile, and gestured happily with his pipe. "The jumpers can only switch bodies with those they can see. The Turtle in his shell and Detroit Steel in his armor ought to be proof against their power.

"Intelligence tells us that one jumper died when he tried to take the Oddity, and become trapped inside that creature's multiple mind. Another girl jumped a polar bear. The bear turned into a bar of soap and the jumper died. That should give them second thoughts about jumping Elephant Girl, wouldn't you say? And if one of them should attempt to jump Legion . . ."

". . . I've still got six bodies to spare," said the punk Danny in red leathers.

Tom sat up. "WHAT IF THEY GET ALL SIX OF HER?"

"There's no risk of that," General Zappa said.

"I've been assigned here to headquarters," the pregnant Danny explained.

"And I'm being flown out to the *New Jersey,*" the yuppie version added. She was dressed in a jumpsuit and bulletproof vest today, but she still wore her Rolex.

That wasn't enough for Tom. "SO SHE ONLY LOSES THREE OR FOUR BODIES. WHAT EFFECT WILL THAT HAVE?"

"I'll risk it," Danny said. The one with the baseball cap and the ponytail.

"DANNY, LISTEN TO ME," Tom said urgently. "THEY DON'T KNOW WHAT WILL HAPPEN IF YOU GET JUMPED. YOU'VE ONLY GOT ONE MIND. YOU COULD WIND UP WITH SOME MANIAC IN YOUR HEAD FOREVER. YOU COULD WIND UP INSANE. EVER HEAR OF BRAIN TRUST?"

Danny looked annoyed. All six of her. They frowned in an eerie unison. "I didn't ask for a history lesson."

Tom appealed to von Herzenhagen and Zappa. "THIS IS NUTS.

SHE'S A KID. YOU THINK SIX GIRLS WITH GUNS ARE GOING TO MAKE ANY DIFFERENCE? SHE'LL GET IN THE WAY, WE'LL HAVE TO PROTECT HER—"

"You *asshole!*" three of the Dannys said in perfect chorus.

"Come on out of that iron catbox and I'll show you what six girls with guns can do," Corporal Danny added in counterpoint.

Everybody started talking at once. Von Herzenhagen winced and raised his hand. "Please," he said. "These factors have all been considered. Agreed, Legion adds little to the team's offensive capability. Her primary function is communications."

"I'LL GET YOU A GOOD DEAL ON SOME RADIOS," Tom argued.

"Radio transmissions can be intercepted. Legion is the perfect communicator. Every one of her is instantaneously aware of what all the others are seeing, hearing, and experiencing."

"Bloat's a telepath," Mistral pointed out "He'll know—"

"Nothing," said von Herzenhagen. "Legion has frustrated our best government peeps. This isn't ordinary telepathy. Legion cannot be jammed, cannot be scrambled, cannot be intercepted—"

"SHE CAN BE KILLED," Tom insisted.

Von Herzenhagen's plump round face went cold. "The decision had been made," he said flatly. He turned to Zappa. "General."

Zappa lifted his pointer. "We'll hit them simultaneously at three gates." He pointed. "Here, here, and there. One Legion with each squad . . ."

Out in center field, the last of the body bags was being loaded into the waiting chopper. Tom watched them sling it aboard, then looked back at Danny, surrounded by her sisters.

Ray didn't care for the smell of oil and machinery compounded by garbage and must that permeated the subway tunnel. Puckett's presence wasn't helping. Danny hung back once the group was well into the tunnel and said to Ray, "What's with that guy dressed in black? He smells funny and he never says anything."

"He's dead," Ray said. He felt it best not to elaborate.

Danny looked at him as if she were trying to decide if he was making fun of her, then shook her head and moved up next to Cameo.

They marched through darkness lit only by their flashlights, hiking down a curved section of tunnel that opened up onto an area illuminated by portable spotlights. A dozen soldiers moved in and out of the light beams like gigantic khaki-colored moths.

A sentry called out a challenge and Battle responded. He must have gotten the password right because they were waved forward.

"This the place?" Battle asked.

A soldier with captain's bars nodded. "Our instruments indicate a corridor parallel with the subway tunnel right beyond that wall." He pointed to a section of wall on which shaped gelignite charges clung like gray leeches.

"Blow it," Battle said.

"Yes, sir."

One of the soldiers shepherded them back down the tunnel. The explosion wasn't nearly as impressive as Ray had imagined it would be. There was a muffled *thunk,* and that was it. They went back around the bend and saw that the spotlights trained on the wall were now illuminating a nearly circular hole about two feet off the ground and six feet or so in diameter. Half a dozen soldiers surrounded the hole, automatic weapons pointed at it, ready for just about anything to come charging through. The dust stirred up by the explosion was still settling. Everything else was quiet and calm.

"Kill those lights," Battle snapped at the captain. "Do you want every damned mutant on Ellis Island to know we're coming?"

"No, sir." He gestured, and the spots were turned off. The corridor was now eerily illuminated only by the flashlights carried by a few of the soldiers.

Battle nodded. "All right. Shadow, you've been here before. What can we expect?"

"Right off," the ace answered, "fear."

Battle frowned. "What do you mean?"

"Bloat's got some kind of spell—"

"Spell!" Battle scoffed.

"Call it what you want," Shadow said defensively. "It's like a watchdog.

After a while, it knows you're there. It goes into your mind and finds what you fear the most. Then it shows it to you—but only as images, as phantoms that have no physical presence. They can't hurt you, but if you don't know what's coming they can scare the Jesus out of you."

All right, Ray said to himself. Phantoms. Images. Buzz-saw hands that can't hurt . . . I can deal with it.

Battle nodded. "Right. Here's the marching order. Black Shadow, you go first. Ray, you follow Shadow. I shall bring up the rear with Legion, Popinjay, and Cameo. Crypt Kicker will cover our backs. All right?" Everyone nodded. "Then let's go!"

Black Shadow nodded again and, darkness draping him like a cloak, stepped through the hole in the Wall that led to Bloat's domain.

Shooter or shootee? The android didn't want to make the choice.

Using the Army's lost plastic explosives, hoping to destroy equipment and not people, Modular Man succeeded in mining the third tracked MLRS vehicle before a sentry spotted him. There was a shout and shots. Modular Man accelerated straight up.

Below him, below the arcing tracer rounds trying to find him in the night sky, the first vehicle blew up. An instant later one of the missiles ignited and blasted loose from the launcher. It hadn't received any computer guidance and went straight up, its rocket flaming, before beginning to corkscrew wildly across the night sky.

Another rocket flamed upward, took a wild yaw, dropped into the Atlantic, and detonated. Seawater, carried by the brisk offshore wind, spattered over the sand spit.

The second vehicle exploded and all the rockets went off at once, not firing, just blowing up. A wave of pressure and heat swept through the android's sensory scans. Submunitions lofted high, thousands of them, and fell to earth.

From above it looked like many strings of firecrackers going off at once. Firecrackers that killed.

Sand blew high, masking the target. Beneath the cloud, things kept blowing up, the cascade of concussion obliterating the sound of screams.

Modular Man headed for the second battery he'd been told to eliminate.

He didn't want to think about what that was going to be like.

The second missile battery had moved by the time Modular Man got to its location. Probably just a random shift, unconnected to the Rox's preemptive strike, but lucky for the crew in any case.

The horrid memory of Sandy Hook floated through the android's mind. He couldn't think of any way he could have kept the casualties down.

He'd become a shooter without ever meaning to.

He didn't spend much time searching for the battery. Instead he returned to the Rox.

Once there he found out his tasks weren't over. One of the strike groups was pinned down in Grand Army Plaza, after having attempted an attack on an ammo dump and instead having walked into a Special Forces ambush.

The battle was garish and weird, fought in an environment illuminated by searchlights, flares, and twisting spirals of tear gas, and filled with joker bodies sprawled beneath old, green statues of Civil War heroes. The android managed to extract the remnants of the team, he hoped without killing anyone himself.

It was, he suspected, just a matter of time.

There were other missions on Modular Man's agenda, first an attack on a division of Apache helicopters parked at Teterboro Airport. He blew them up without being seen, and without (he thought) any casualties among the crews, who were sleeping under tents off at the far edge of the field.

He blew up more helicopters at the Coast Guard heliport in Jamaica Bay, then was ordered into an attack on the missile battery again, in what Kafka thought was its new location in Great Kills Harbor. Instead Modular Man found Great Kills Park filled with the ballooning plastic tents of a field hospital. He thought of submunitions cascading down on the hospital as they had on Ft. Hancock.

He couldn't find the missile battery. He was happy to leave the hospital alone.

By that time it was dawn. An aerial view of the Greater New York Area showed, on all points around the vast foggy murk expanding from the Rox, towering plumes of smoke from fires still burning.

He thought of the massive U.S. war machine he'd witnessed in combat against the Swarm. He measured the damage done by Governor Bloat's strikes against the military that he knew could be brought to bear.

Almost zero. A company or two of helicopters wrecked—there were battalions more. A few dozen missiles destroyed—there were thousands in inventory. A few ammo dumps blown up—millions of shells remaining. Maybe a few hundred Americans had been killed.

There were 250 million more.

Modular Man dropped onto the Rox, reported to Travnicek, was told to make himself scarce. He went to the intelligence group, where Patchwork and Kafka were still gathering information. Kafka was as far away from everyone as he could get in the small room. Patchwork, seen even through the bandages, was completely exhausted.

"The brass are really pissed," Patchwork reported. "Zappa's delayed any action until the ammunition from Clove Lakes can be replaced."

The jokers seemed pleased. "We've shown 'em," someone said.

"He's talking about something called 'shoot-and-scoot' tactics."

Kafka saw Modular Man and scuttled closer to him. "That could be a problem," he said. "The artillery batteries set up, fire a few rounds apiece, then pull out and set up somewhere else. That means we can't preempt them, because we won't know where they're going to be. And we'll have a hard time retaliating, because they're running away before we can get a fix."

"Not fast enough for Pulse and Modular Man," said one joker. He was grinning hugely with three rows of pointed teeth. "Am I right?"

Eyes turned toward Modular Man. "You're going to lose," he said.

There was a long moment of silence. Patchwork lifted her chin toward Modular Man, as if once again sniffing for his presence.

"I'll do what I can," the android said. "We caught them by surprise last night—they weren't expecting you to have so many of their units located. But they'll get better. Your strike teams are going to get killed or go to ground or get arrested. There's only one of me, and one of Pulse, and Pulse's energy is limited—during the Swarm invasion he ended up in a near coma with a glucose feed in his arm because he'd burned himself out fighting. My energy is limited as well, and I can't be everywhere, and in any case Snotman can beat both of us with one hand tied behind him."

The others looked at Kafka. "We're working out every contingency," the roach said.

"Up to and including getting everyone killed? Because there are over a million soldiers under arms *right now,* and lots of wild cards out there who will fight for the government, and—how many do you have here? A few thousand, and you're all concentrated on a *very small target?*"

"We've got the fog, and the radar spoofers, and—"

"How many million rounds of artillery ammunition do you have? How many rockets? How many fuel-air bombs? *One fuel-air bomb could kill everyone here!* That's what Zappa told me, and he's right. You can't hide underground—a fuel-air bomb will suck the air *right out of the caverns.* Everyone below ground will asphyxiate, everyone in the open will burn to death. And if that doesn't work there's nerve gas, and even tactical nuclear weapons. . . ."

"We've got Herne and the Wild Hunt," one joker said. "We can kill *anyone.* . . ."

"How well did that work with Hartmann?"

"Enough," said Kafka. "We're planning for everything." But the other jokers in the room looked stricken.

A moment ago they'd been congratulating themselves on a battle won. Now Modular Man had told them their victory was meaningless.

The android pressed his advantage. "I think you should call that 800 number and work out the best deal you can."

"We have our governor," Kafka said. "He gave us the Rox, and he'll keep us safe." He looked at his staff. "I'll prove it to you," he said. "Come with me. To the Great Hall."

The jokers began filing out.

"Hold on!" Patchwork clapped a hand to her missing ear as if trying to hear better. "There's something going on!" For a few seconds the big reel-to-reel was the only thing moving in the room.

"It's that Katzenback guy," Patchwork said. "He's talking about security breaches. Wondering about how we knew where so much of their equipment was parked . . ."

"Hide your eye," Kafka said.

"I *am*. I'm just *hearing* this."

"Katzenback, Horace." One of the jokers read from a computer print-out. "Former AID official, now college professor, assigned to Zappa's staff with the rank of—"

"Will you *shut up*!" Patchwork said. There were overtones of panic in her voice. Her head moved back and forth as if aiming her ears at a sound source. "Vidkunssen is agreeing. He's wondering about whether their communications are secure. Maybe somebody's broken their cipher." She took a breath. "Good," she said, "that's—"

Her head jerked up. It was clear that someone else was talking. "Oh, shit," she said. "Katzenback's talking about bugs. And Zappa's come out of his office. He's listening. He's—he's going to call the techs for a sweep."

"Good," Kafka said. "They won't spot you that way. You don't transmit on FM."

"*Shit!*" Patchwork screamed. "Katzenback's telling everyone to give a visual search first!"

"Get your stuff out of the way," Kafka said.

"It *is*, it *is*." She put her hands over her invisible eyes. "But it's just lying there on the top shelf, behind a stack of folders. My eye can roll around, but the ear . . ." Her voice trailed away. "Oh, shit, I can hear them moving stuff around. Zappa's telling everyone to be thorough."

Modular Man stepped to her couch, sat by her, and took Patchwork's hand. She clutched at him. "I'm going to be blind," she muttered. "Blind, with half the U.S. shooting at me. *Shit!*"

Terror filled her face. "*They found me!* Oh, fuck . . ."

"Run for it!" Kafka urged.

"Eyeball's rolling!" Patchwork shouted. "I'm off the shelf and trying to get under a desk!"

The android's olfactory sensors could scent her terror. She seized his hand in both of hers.

"They're jumping around and yelling! Oh, fuck, I hope I don't get stepped on!" Her voice rose to a shriek. *"Jesus they're moving the desk they're moving the desk . . ."*

Her body swayed in a circle, imitating the frantic rolling of her eye. "I'm getting covered in dust, I can't see. I'm rolling—*oh fuck they shut the door!"*

She shuddered. Her face showed total defeat. "Everything just went dark. They dropped something on me. A wastebasket or something." Rivers of sweat poured from under her bandages. "I can still hear, though. *Something's touching my ear!"* She gave a little wail. "Somebody get in there and get me!"

"I'll go," Modular Man tried to make his voice soothing. "Just keep listening and looking, and find out where they put you. Then I'll see if I can get you out."

"They dropped me!" Patchwork gulped air. "They dropped my ear into a container or something. I can feel cold, like glass or metal." She bit her lip. "They're all gathering around the . . . around my eye. I'm trying to creep the ear out while they're not looking but it's not working—the container's too slick. *Daylight!"* Her voice rose to a shriek. "I'm rolling—oh, shit!" Her free hand pounced the sofa. "They've got me! They've got their fucking fingers on me!"

Modular Man kept up his reassuring tone. "I'll get you loose."

Patchwork's voice changed. She stared defiantly into an empty space where she assumed Kafka and the jokers were. "I want the other eye *now!* There's nothing going on at Aces High for me to see. I never should've let you make me blind in the first place."

"I'll get it," Modular Man said. "But let's see what they're doing with your other eye and ear first."

"I'm in a jar. There's slime all over everything and it's hard to see." A spasm of disgust shuddered across her face. "It's a peanut butter jar! And there's still peanut butter in it!"

"What can you see?"

"Not much. I'm looking through peanut butter smears. Everyone's staring at me. They're passing me from hand to hand."

"Just wait." Modular Man stroked Patchwork's arm. "They'll have to put you somewhere. And once we figure out where that is, I'll go get your eye and ear for you."

Zappa's staff searched his room and office for at least ten minutes. Then they stood around staring at the peanut butter jar for another few minutes, conversing in low tones so that Patchwork couldn't hear.

"Somebody picked me up." Her voice had grown calmer by now. "I'm being carried out the door. I think it's that Katzenback guy. He's walking down a corridor. We're outside of the stadium—I see a burned-out tank. We're walking up to one of those jeep things—"

"A humvee?"

"I guess."

"He just jammed me under the passenger seat. I can't see anything."

"I'm gone." Modular Man didn't bother to stand up; he just levitated up and started moving for the door. He paused in front of Kafka.

"You've just lost your edge," he said. "From now on, jokers die."

And then he was out and up into the fog-strewn sky.

The corridor was natural rock, unimproved by human hands. The floor of beaten dirt was strewn with stones the size of pebbles to small boulders and was nearly blocked in places by rockfalls from the roof and walls. Some of the falls looked recent, perhaps caused by the explosion that had given them access to the corridor.

Black Shadow was a three-dimensional ink spot, the darkness that was part of him soaking up the beams from their flashlights. "Which way?" he asked, his whisper echoing eerily off the tunnel's ceiling and walls.

The corridor ran due north and south from the point they'd broken into. As far as Ray could see it was dead-dark in both directions. Neither could he hear anything. Battle, however, didn't hesitate. "North. If we go any farther south we'll miss Ellis Island when we turn east toward the bay."

Black Shadow nodded and moved silently off into the darkness. Ray let him get ten or fifteen yards ahead before following. Shadow was good, Ray thought. You could hardly hear him moving in the darkness that was his natural element.

Shadow suddenly hissed. Ray stopped and held out a palm to signal the others. He crept up to join Black Shadow and found him standing in front of a door set into the east wall of the corridor. Shadow had turned off his personal darkness, satisfied with the natural blackness that surrounded them all.

"What is it?" Ray whispered. Something in the tunnel's atmosphere made him automatically lower his voice as he pointed at the door and the face carved into the rock beside it. The door was made of wooden planks banded with iron strips. The stone face had a certain rough-hewn majesty to it, but underneath it all it was just the face of a teenage boy.

"Bloat," Shadow and Ray said in unison.

They looked at each other and nodded.

"I'll get the others," Ray said.

They inspected the door carefully, trying to decide what to do. Battle finally nodded at Puckett. "Pull it out of its frame," he told the ace. "Shepherd and Ray, cover him."

Ray nodded, but said, "Maybe you try the handle first. It might not be locked."

"Not locked?" Battle said.

Ray shrugged. "Who knows? Have *you* got this Bloat character totally figured out?"

"No," Battle admitted reluctantly.

Puckett looked at him and he nodded. The ace tried the handle, and the door creaked slowly forward, Puckett standing unconcernedly in the center of the entrance.

Ray heard a sound over their heads like stone grating against stone, and shouted, "Look out!"

But it was too late. A trapdoor opened and something red and viscous flowed out, totally enveloping Puckett, splashing on Danny and also on Ackroyd. Ray dodged the deluge as he tackled Danny, but was too late to pull her totally out of the way. The liquid coated the front of her right leg from the knee to the ankle, and also splattered her left leg. After a moment of stunned silence a white envelope fluttered down out of the trapdoor and landed right on Puckett's head. It stuck there in the thick liquid. Puckett turned to look at the others, holding his hands up and out in a gesture that bespoke of his bewilderment.

"What the hell—" Ray began. He reached down and gingerly touched the liquid running down Danny's calf. He rubbed his fingertips together. "Paint," he said. "Red paint."

"Give me that envelope," Battle said angrily.

Puckett reached up with paint-soaked fingers and carefully took it from the top of his head. He handed it to Battle, who tore it open impatiently.

"'I could have killed you just now,'" Battle read aloud, "'but I didn't. Remember that. Next time it won't be for fun.'" Battle looked up, outraged. "He's playing with me. The fat bastard thinks he's playing with me!"

Ray looked at Danny, his face inches from hers, her hard body half under his.

"I think you can let me up now," she said.

Ray scrambled to his feet, giving her a hand up. She thanked him.

It had really begun now. The score was Bloat 1, Battle 0, even though no one had been hurt. But that didn't matter to Battle. Ray could see that he was seething. He wanted Bloat's ass, if Bloat had an ass.

Still, no matter how pissed he was, Ray noted that he was careful to set Black Shadow ahead on point, put Ray second, and station himself, covered by a paint-soaked Crypt Kicker, well to the rear.

Modular Man was halfway to Brooklyn before he was out of the fog. The stuff was enveloping the entire city. He banked high and came down on Ebbets Field out of the sun. He could see Katzenback in a moving humvee—it looked as if it was heading for the Verrazano Narrows Bridge approaches.

Modular Man dropped out of the sky like a fighter ace, tucked, came down feetfirst, landed neatly in the passenger seat.

Katzenback gave a yelp and sideswiped a cab. The taxi driver howled obscenities in Arabic and slammed on the brakes.

"Sorry, Horace," Modular Man said. "I didn't mean to frighten you."

Katzenback pulled over into a loading zone. He recovered quickly, though he was still a bit wild-eyed. "What do you want?"

"Peanut butter jar."

"Heh heh." Katzenback grinned nervously. "What peanut butter jar?"

Modular Man groped under the seat and pulled it out.

Katzenback shrugged. "At least I tried."

The Syrian taxi driver stepped up to his door and began shrieking abuse.

"I want you to know this isn't my idea," Modular Man said. "I'm obeying orders, same as you."

"Whose orders?"

The taxi driver kept screaming. Modular Man, without result, gestured for him to be quiet. "I can't say. But switching sides wasn't my idea. Please tell General Zappa."

"You got *jumped*? Look, if you got jumped and are back now, we can work something . . ."

"Later. I hope."

Modular Man rose into the sky and sped north, toward Aces High.

Even that didn't make the taxi driver shut up.

Warm air caressed Ray's face as he moved into the narrow corridor behind the door. He stopped and put his hand against one of the walls. The rock was warm to the touch when it should have been cool. He didn't like the feel of it. He didn't like the way the air smelled. It was hot and sweaty and tasted like fear.

He wondered if this was the result of the spell that Black Shadow had warned them about. He glanced back at the rest of the team. Despite the poor lighting, he could see the strain on the others' faces. Strained expressions wouldn't be totally unexpected under the circumstances, but was it natural stress, or was Bloat playing with their minds? Black Shadow might know. He'd been through it before.

Ray hurried up the corridor, catching up to the man in black.

"Shadow," he hissed in a stage whisper. "Wait up, dude."

The ace stopped and turned, his face shielded by the darkness that enveloped him like a mother's arms.

"That fear you told us about," Ray asked. "Can you feel it now?"

The darkness shifted, as if Shadow were looking about. "Yes." His voice was deep and unshaken. "There it comes."

A hand pointed out of the blackness, up-tunnel where two figures were approaching. They were young men, probably in their teens, and even in the dim light Ray could see crazed expressions on their ugly, manic faces. One had a garrote dangling from his hands, the other carried a large, shiny knife upraised and poised to strike.

"Christ," Ray said, "they're ugly fuckers. No wonder they spooked you."

"You can see them?" Shadow asked. "Last time only I could—"

He was turning, but it was too late. The schitzed-out one with the knife struck, plunging the weapon into Black Shadow's back above the right shoulder blade. The ace screamed in pain, anger, and surprise. The maniac crooned in pleasure and pulled his knife out of Shadow's back. He raised it above his head again, eyes gleaming brighter than the knife blade.

Shadow pivoted off his right foot, falling backward, and kicked with his left, catching his assailant in the stomach, but the maniac just bounced off the tunnel wall and came back after him.

Ray jumped between the two. The crazy guy with the knife seemed fixated on Shadow as Ray grabbed his knife wrist and broke it. The maniac dropped his blade and focused on Ray for the first time. Ray wasn't taking any chances with this supposed phantom. He crushed the nut's windpipe with a knife-hand blow, then kicked out both his kneecaps while he stood there wheezing.

Ray turned as his opponent collapsed. Shadow was a puddle of blackness against the tunnel wall, leaking red. The knife must have cut something important, maybe a lung. There were shouts of consternation and surprise coming from the other team members, but they were all too far away to help as the second nutcase leaned over

Shadow with his garrote stretched tight, looking for a neck to twist it around.

Ray surged forward, kicking the apparition between the legs from behind. It was gratifying to discover that even apparitions had balls. The specter screamed and collapsed forward, falling unto Black Shadow. Ray went after him, but recoiled from the wave of killing cold that blasted out from the impenetrable blackness that was Shadow and the crazy guy.

Ray motioned the others away as they ran up, then he cautiously reached out to test the air temperature around Shadow and the supposed apparition. It had warmed up to the bone-chilling range.

"Shadow, you all right?" Ray asked cautiously.

"Been better," came a weak voice from the darkness. The black dissipated slowly like squid ink in water, to reveal Black Shadow and the flash-frozen corpse of the second assailant. "Think he got a lung."

Ray knelt down beside him: "Take it easy. We'll get you back."

Battle loomed over them, looking more annoyed than concerned. "I thought you said these things were only immaterial manifestations." He kicked the frozen corpse that lay next to Black Shadow. "This one feels pretty real to me."

Puckett squatted by the one whose throat Ray had crushed. "This one's real too. But he's dead as shit now."

Black Shadow shook his head, then closed his eyes in pain. "They *were* only ghosts the first time I was here."

"Bloat must be getting stronger," Danny said.

"How come these phantoms—or whatever they are—aren't attacking us?" Cameo asked.

"Takes a while," Shadow said through gritted teeth, "before they zero in on you. I been here before. I guess they were ready for me."

"Right," Battle said crisply. He looked at Ackroyd. "Send Shadow back to the mouth of the tunnel. He's no more use here."

Ackroyd looked at Battle, then Black Shadow, and wet his lips with his tongue.

"Well?" Battle said. "We don't have all day. Get popping, man."

Ackroyd smiled apologetically and shrugged. "I can't."

"What?" Battle said. "What the hell are you talking about?"

"I'm not Jay Ackroyd."

Ray closed his eyes and rocked back on his heels. "Jesus Christ," he said in a low voice.

Battle blustered wordlessly. "Are you serious?" he finally spluttered. "If you're lying to me—"

"I'm not," the ersatz Ackroyd said in the same quiet, apologetic tone. "Jay Ackroyd has disappeared. I'm also a detective. I've been trying to figure out what happened to him. I'm an ace too. I can change my appearance," he explained unnecessarily.

"Jesus Christ," Ray repeated.

"Who the hell are you?" Battle barked.

The Ackroyd-imposter shrugged. "I don't think you need to know that. You can call me Nemo."

"Can you do anything besides change the look of your face, or are you totally useless?" Battle asked.

"Look, I didn't want to come along on this thing. You made me." Nemo looked thoughtful for a moment. "But maybe I can come up with something useful."

He frowned, concentrating, then everything went black. All their flashlights went dark and the fear crawling around the back of Ray's head turned to panic. Then the lights came back on, dimly at first, then brighter.

"Shit," Ray said in a low voice.

Battle, for once, was speechless.

The Frankenstein Monster stood before them. "How's this?" it asked in a growling rumble.

"Right," Battle said, unconvinced. He turned his attention back to Black Shadow. "Well, there's nothing we can do for you."

"We can't just leave him," Danny said.

Battle looked at her coldly. "We can't take him with us and we can't spare anyone to escort him back to our lines."

"You're all heart, man," Shadow mumbled. He made a move to sit up. "Don't worry. I can make it on my own."

Battle nodded crisply. "Good."

Danny looked at Ray, who slowly shook his head. As much as he hated to admit it, Battle was right. They couldn't afford to weaken the team any further by having someone nursemaid Black Shadow, and they couldn't wait for someone to escort him back and then return. They had to move on through this area before their fears ate them away mentally or, worse, came to life and ate them up physically.

"At least," Danny said, kneeling down by Shadow, "let's bandage his wound." She shrugged off her backpack, cracked it open, and rummaged through it for the first-aid kit.

Battle sighed. "All right, but hurry up."

"'Preciate it," Shadow said.

Ray, who had a certain amount of practical knowledge about field-dressing wounds, helped Danny, half the time glancing over his shoulder for a glimpse of his own personal ghosts of fear and failure to come haunting. He didn't know what form they would take. He didn't want to know. Hartmann, maybe, whom he'd failed in Atlanta. Or maybe Hartmann's wife who'd fallen down a stairway and lost their child after Ray's desperate lunge missed her as she'd stumbled. He made himself look at the ugly wound they were bandaging, forcing himself not to think of the things that scared him so he wouldn't give them shape and substance. It was hard, very hard.

Danny helped a shaky Black Shadow to his feet. The ace's face was almost white with pain and shock.

"Can you make it?" Ray asked quietly.

"I'll make it," the ace said.

"Good luck," Ray told him. Danny echoed the sentiment while Battle, Puckett, Nemo, and Cameo looked on as Shadow stumbled off, leaning heavily against the tunnel wall.

"All right," Battle said crisply. He beckoned Ray to his side. "Good luck," Battle repeated with a snort. "He'll need it all right. I suppose it'll just make it easier for the soldiers to handle him, if he even makes it back to their lines."

"What do you mean?" Ray asked in a low voice. "You sound like you expect them to arrest him or something."

"I do," Battle said with one of his bright little smiles. "Indeed I do. He's a wanted criminal, after all."

"What about his pardon? The one signed by Bush and all?"

Battle looked at him. "Signed by Bush? Really now? Do you know what George Bush's signature looks like?"

"You mean it was a fake?" Ray hissed.

Battle shrugged blandly. "Black Shadow is a wanted criminal. And after all, what good was he to us here? He got himself hurt at the first sign of danger and then limped off. I don't think he fulfilled his part of the bargain, do you?"

Ray clamped his mouth shut so tight that his misshapen jaw ached. Bastard, he thought. Dirty, lying bastard.

Battle nodded. "With Shadow gone and Ackroyd, that is, Nemo . . ." He gestured helplessly. "You'll have to take point." Battle looked around at the others, his face sharp with what Ray recognized as worry and fear. "Let's get the hell out of here," he said. "We don't have all day."

What fears, Ray wondered as he set off at the head of the team, were nipping at George Battle's ass?

Modular Man found it easy to get Patchwork's second eye. He kicked his way through the balcony door of Aces High, found the eye behind the potted plant where it had been hidden, and—while buzzing alarms punished the air—ran some clean water from the bar tap and washed all Patchwork's various parts.

He tried to be gentle. He knew the eyes were watching him. They were brown, with little gold and green flecks. The ear had a gold stud in the lobe and two delicate gold rings on the upper flange.

The android hoped the ear didn't mind the alarm buzzer overmuch.

The eyes and ear were sealed in a plastic container meant for maraschino cherries. From midtown it took longer than the android expected to return to the Rox. The fog had covered the southern tip of Manhattan, and the Rox was absolutely lost in it. He triangulated off the tall buildings surrounding the harbor, then dropped down until ramparts and battlements became visible.

It occurred to him that if he could accomplish that, sooner or later so would the military. It didn't improve his state of mind.

Patchwork was alone in her room high in the keep, sitting patiently on the swan couch. The maps and stacks of printout had been moved, leaving only the couch and an empty desk.

"They're moving the intelligence center somewhere safer," Patchwork said. "It occurred to them that a bomb could drop right through the ceiling and—"

"It occurred to me as well."

He took her hand and put the plastic container into it. Eagerly she tore away the lid. Her two gleaming brown eyes stared at her.

Patchwork handled her parts with far less care than had Modular Man. The android cringed mentally at the sight of the way she jammed her eyes back into place, then poked and prodded till they were comfortable.

Despite how they got there, the eyes looked very nice once they were back where they belonged.

The ear, which contained the organs of the middle and outer ear in a kind of twisted tube, had to be sort of screwed back into the side of Patchwork's head, with little noises that sounded like two blocks of Styrofoam being rubbed together.

Patchwork took the beret off her head, rearranged her brown hair, and looked up at Modular Man.

"Very attractive," he said.

"Jesus. *You* must be the blind one."

"What would have happened if I hadn't got them back?"

"The detached parts die after a week or so. Then they'll grow back, but that takes weeks. Months sometimes."

"You sound as if it's happened before."

She just gave him a look. Then she stood, reached behind the swan couch, and pulled up a heavy pack, an M-16 rifle, and a new military-issue Kevlar helmet. She put the helmet on, shouldered the rifle, and grinned bravely.

She was far too young, too pale, too thin, to make a convincing soldier.

"Now that my special functions are over," she said, "I'm just another damn grunt-on-the-ramparts." She shrugged. "At least I don't need help to go to the toilet anymore."

"Where are you stationed?"

"The Iron Tower. That's the one on the south side that's sort of rust-colored."

"Shall I walk there with you?" He took her pack.

"Don't you have something else to do?"

He ordered his face to assume a rueful grin. "If I don't *know* I have something to do, Pat, then I don't have to do it."

Patchwork assessed this, then nodded. "You're an old soldier, all right."

He followed her out onto the battlements. The fog was dark and cold and slicked the walkway with wet. Their footsteps echoed in the mist.

Modular Man looked at the crenellations atop the walls, put a hand on their damp, cold surface. "Does this seem like the work of an idealist to you?" he asked.

Patchwork considered. "I wouldn't know. Guess I haven't met many idealists."

"The thing that keeps occurring to me is how much of all this benefits the governor. He's deformed, and unhappy, and maybe eighteen years old, and he can't move easily from place to place—so he gets himself an island where he can live. All his rhetoric is about freedom and independence and so forth, but get down to the bedrock, it all seems to benefit *him*, to serve *his* needs. *He* needs a place to stay, so he takes the Rox. He wants to be king of his own kingdom, so he builds *this*." He slapped the wet stone. "If he had any sense, he would have built a geodesic dome of battleship plate. But it had to be a *castle*. Because he's got some adolescent notion of what being a hero and a leader is, and it's all tied up with—" Words failed him.

"*Dungeons and Dragons*, I guess," Patchwork finished. "Or Tolkien. But I've never read that kind of stuff, so I don't know."

"I've not, either. But the Rox—somehow it doesn't seem to me like a *real* castle. Why a mile-wide circular moat? Everyone on the outer Wall is out of support of the main structure—they're all alone out there. It's like an *idea* of a castle from someone who's never actually seen one."

"I wouldn't know. I haven't seen one either."

"Bloat talks about giving people a refuge from oppression, but he let the jumpers in. The jumpers weren't oppressed, they were *criminals*. But they were *rich* criminals, with access to things Bloat needed, and their presence here enhanced his power, so he let them in. And the jumpers have brought their victims with them, like Pulse, and he lets those in too.

"And now Bloat's taking on the entire U.S. military. It's not *possible* for him to win. It's just not. But he's going ahead with it, even though it doesn't make any *sense*. And why—" He searched for words carefully, found them. "Why does this suggest to me that the governor has a way out of here? That if he doesn't win and become the king of New York Harbor, that there'll still be a Bloat out there somewhere . . ."

Patchwork looked at him in surprise. "How?" she said. "Bloat's here with the rest of us."

"What seems to be characteristic of the governor is that he wants it both ways. He wants to be a noble idealist fighting for his freedom, and at the same time acquire money and power through the most vicious means. He wants to have slaves and be a freedom fighter. He wants us to feel sorry for the jokers but not think about the people the jumpers have killed. He wants to live in a castle and have fantasy servants but he doesn't want to think about who the country under this domain actually belongs to. And he wants to be Bloat and the Outcast both."

Patchwork stared at him. "The Outcast? You think—"

"The Outcast could put on a suit of normal clothes and walk right out at any time."

"My impression is that the governor's emanations can't cross the Wall."

"Maybe I'm wrong. I'm not reasoning from knowledge. I'm only saying that Bloat's behavior would be consistent if he had some kind of escape hatch. Maybe it's the Outcast, maybe not."

Patchwork thought about it. The Iron Tower loomed ahead.

Something flashed in the distant periphery of the android's radio consciousness.

Something falling.

He picked up Patchwork in his arms and flew at top speed to the

Iron Tower, then down the spiral stairs to the dank thick-walled room beneath.

The shells began landing a scant few seconds later.

It began as a whisper . . . *Jesus, there's something on the screen—*

. . . shifted to a shout . . . *Hey! Someone's—*

. . . and ended in a roaring conflagration. *They're firing! Oh, shit, they're really . . . !*

With the first tentative hint, the Outcast had slammed the end of his staff down on the tiles and disappeared in a gout of smoke. All over the Rox, from the thousand open throats of the gargoyles perched on every roof, came the ululating wail of alarm. The Outcast appeared in rapid succession to Travnicek and Modular Man, to Zelda in Pulse's body, and to Kafka. To each of them, he had said only one word: "Showtime!" and was gone. He spent no more than ten seconds in doing that. Even so, the first barrage hit as he materialized on the Wall facing out into the bay.

Something brilliant and glowing white slashed through the fog several meters from the Outcast and then disappeared again. He heard it twice, once with the dull concussion as it slammed into earth behind him, then again in his head—in the mindvoices of the Rox.

The Outcast heard pain and loss and death. He heard wordless screaming and pleading; he glimpsed bloody images that he knew he could never again forget.

. . . *omigodomigodomigod where's my leg where is it why can't I feel it please let it be there please oh please . . .*

. . . *Jesus so much blood it can't be mine can't be . . .*

. . . *Tom please Tom don't be dead answer me love please get up oh God get up . . .*

The Outcast screamed with them, raising his staff high. The crystal blazed like a nova. Reality shifted around him dizzily, everything slowing down. He opened the channels of power wide within Bloat, drawing at the power deeper than he had ever dared before. Dreamtime voices screamed at him in outrage, battering him with words of power. The blows were like the fists of a child against a parent. Teddy laughed at them; they annoyed, but they didn't hurt.

Thief! they shouted. *Fool! Idiot!* Teddy giggled. "Fuck off," he answered back and drew the power into him. What happened then was something new.

He was no longer Teddy or the Outcast or Bloat. He was, instead, everything that he had ever made here on the Rox. He was Crystal Castle and minaret towers, penguin and demon, underground caverns and Wall. The energy coursed within him and he was no longer a flesh-and-blood body living within the confines of the Rox. The Rox *was* him; there was no difference. Teddy could feel the incoming missiles like needle pricks in an immense skin, and he stretched forth fingers shaped of wild energy to pluck them out.

He could not catch the quicksilver things. Inside him, more jokers died.

Raging, he did with them what he'd done with Modular Man—interposed Boschian apparitions between the missiles and the Rox.

The missiles went through them like paper, their courses altered from the collisions but too little. Inside, more death and a burning conflagration.

Thief! Fool! Idiot! "Shut up!" he screamed at the voices of the dreams. "Shut up!"

Desperate now, he could think of only one thing to do. He snatched at the power, holding the sizzling, burning threads in the hands of his mind, and cast them to the sky. Where they struck the Wall of the world, sparking, he willed small openings to appear, ugly holes between the realities. He could not hold the gateway open long, could not enlarge them much at all.

But they were large enough. The incoming bombardment fell through. For an instant, in this slowed and distorted spacetime he inhabited, he thought he saw the warheads and shells changing as they passed the boundaries of the dreamtime, becoming strange warbirds or immense blue lightnings or writhing monsters consumed in flame.

Then they were gone.

He was exhausted from the exertion. So tired. Other than the wordless cry of the gargoyles, there was a strange waiting silence over the Rox. A quiet everywhere . . .

. . . but inside . . .

The figure of the Outcast wavered, then solidified. Back in the dreamtime.

"Guess what?" said the Outcast.

"Even here in the dreamtime," said Wyungare, "there may be no time for twenty questions." The two men stood in the shadows of a bayou glade. Herons flapped and cried out behind them. Through the thick canopy, Wyungare sensed the flickering uncertainty of clouds rushing in ranks across the southern sky.

The Outcast's heroic features frowned in what—for a moment—looked like a small boy's grimace of displeasure. And for just a split second, Wyungare thought, perhaps fear. "All right," he said patiently, regardless of the flash of impatience he felt. "What?"

The Outcast took a deep breath. "Peace is out," he said. "So's compromise. Sorry, healer-man."

"Why's that?"

The Outcast started to explain about the reports of the jumper massacre back across the river.

"No," said Wyungare, "that one I can figure out. Tell me why you're sorry that the peaceful way seems impossible. Or was that mere politeness?"

The Outcast looked startled. He appeared to concentrate, gathering his thoughts.

Good, thought the Aborigine, finally an apparent brain activity.

"Okay," the Outcast said. "I was being a smartass. I guess I've never really thought that anything else except combat's going to settle this."

The cries of the herons rose in intensity. Wyungare ignored them. "Perhaps you're right. But battles can still be picked—or declined."

The Outcast shook his head. "I don't think so—not anymore. Up until now, I figured we could hold our own. I was strong enough. Now . . . it's like a do-or-die thing, you know? They're gonna kill us all if they can."

Wyungare nodded. "It's probably good that you've begun to register that harsh reality." He smiled. "So tell me, what isn't this like?"

"Isn't?" The Outcast thought about that one for a long while. Finally he said hesitantly, "It isn't a game anymore."

"Good," said Wyungare. "Extend that thought."

The Outcast stared down at the water's edge. Ripples formed as though rain were beginning to sprinkle onto the bayou. "Okay," he said. "I know what you're getting at. Life isn't a game where things come about because of a roll of the dice."

"You've got it," said Wyungare. "What happens in your reality happens because you—and all around you—take hold of responsibilities. Virtue's not going to work miracles. Luck's just about as undependable. What you accomplish, you'll achieve because you do it."

"You're sounding like my uncle from Maine," said the Outcast.

"Sorry," said Wyungare. "I don't mean to sound like a sermonizing Yankee uncle."

"I liked him."

"Good," said the Aborigine. "Then listen to his memory."

"Listen," said the Outcast. "There's something else."

Wyungare looked at him expectantly.

"I *know* it's no game. I'm sending my friends out to die, some of them. Maybe all of them. It's not like a videotape where I can rewind it." His voice was sad. "I don't want to think about that."

Something whistled overhead like a banshee. Both men looked up. Blood burst across the sky in a spray of crimson droplets. As the dispersal sank in a rippling curtain toward the earth, the color muted to brown, then to a dirty black.

"Is that what I think it is?" said Wyungare. He had a feeling he knew already.

Something new burst. Bits of flesh, stinking of corruption, rained down. A third umbrella of light, then—excrement, brown and redolent, sank toward the swamp surrounding the two men.

The Outcast nodded. "I guess so. I didn't know what they would do."

"They can do much more," said Wyungare. "But for now, ignore them."

"It seemed like a good idea at the time."

"It always does." Wyungare shaded his eyes, staring up at the proliferating air bursts of translated missiles. He shook his head.

"I'm sorry," said the Outcast. "I thought better they should come here than kill more of my people." He hung his head.

"All right," said Wyungare, "then let me give you something to distract you." He reached over and passed his right hand across the Outcast's eyes.

"I don't think I'm going to like this," said the Outcast glumly.

They stood in the dimly lit tiled hallway of a hospital. All in white, two nurses and a doctor bustled past them without a glance. The medical personnel pushed hurriedly through a pair of swinging wooden doors.

"What's this?" said the Outcast. "I already know it's a hospital."

"Specifically it's Atelier Community Hospital," said Wyungare. "We're in Jack's province of the dreamtime, remember. Follow me." He led the Outcast toward the swinging doors.

"Shouldn't we stay out of there?" said the Outcast nervously.

"It's the emergency room," said Wyungare, "but we are effectively ghosts. Come along."

They passed a boy sitting miserably on the bench outside the double doors.

"It's Jack," said the Outcast.

"Stay close to me," said Wyungare. The wooden door felt hot against his fingertips, as though the pores of the wood itself were sweating.

The young girl's scream stopped the Outcast dead in his tracks. He halted just inside the emergency room's doors and stared. Then he looked away. "What is this?" he said. "She's so young."

"Eleven," agreed Wyungare. "Not even a teen and she is bearing a child herself."

The girl lay with the sheet across her chest, one nurse holding her right hand tightly. Her sticklike legs were spread wide, and there was a dark tide of blood.

"Who is she?" said the Outcast, looking back at the girl, then glancing quickly away.

"Jack is her older brother, but not *much* older. Considering that their stepfather sired the child, I have no idea what that turns Jack's relationship to her baby into."

More piping screams from the soon-to-be mother ripped through their ears. The Outcast looked back toward the table and shook.

"Hemorrhage," said Wyungare neutrally. "There are complications. She was beaten. This is a small hospital with a competent staff, but I'm afraid—"

The wail from the table was echoed by the cry from out in the hallway. The boy's sorrow continued. His sister's did not.

"The baby is dead as well," said Wyungare quietly. "Come." He took the Outcast's arm firmly and steered him toward the door. In the hall, they passed unnoticed by the boy. He looked suddenly as though he carried the weight of mountains on his back.

"What . . . happened?" said the Outcast.

"Before now? Simply the sort of family violence you know in your own fashion."

"And what's going to happen next?"

"Jack has no magic sword," said Wyungare. "He will fight his demons inside himself. He will blame himself for the rest of his life, unless—"

The Outcast looked over at the Aborigine with sudden hope. "Unless what?"

Wyungare stared back for a long moment. "Unless there is a gesture of healing."

"Like what?"

"Empathy," said Wyungare. "Like to like."

The Outcast stared, mute. The surface of his eyes glistened.

"Think about it," said the shaman.

"Empathy . . . Think about it . . ." The echo of Wyungare's voice drifted through Teddy's thoughts, relentless.

"I don't *want* to think about it," Bloat wailed. "I don't want to re-member any of it. Stop making me."

He suddenly realized that he was back in the throne room, that he was Bloat once more. It was difficult to keep his eyes open—a sapping weariness held him, made it nearly impossible to concentrate or move. Something was going on—jokers were scurrying across the mosaicked tiles of the floor like ants whose nest had been stirred with a stick. Kafka was directing traffic under the stained-glass central dome. The mindvoices of the Rox were yammering and shouting; Bloat was too exhausted to even try to sort them out.

Kafka had stopped waving his arms to glance up at Bloat. Under the carapace, his eyes glistened. "Governor?"

"I'm going back to sleep, Kafka," Bloat said. "I don't want to have to think about it, okay? I need . . . need to find the Outcast . . ." Bloat's eyes closed, but he kept mumbling, not quite sure what he was saying. "Don't want to go back with Wyungare again . . . need to find some-thing pleasant . . . something of mine . . ."

He realized that he wasn't in the throne room anymore.

He fell into memory . . .

"I'll . . . I'll tell my dad," Teddy said. "Really. He'll do something about it." Teddy didn't know what his dad would really do. Actually, he couldn't imagine his father doing *anything,* not really, especially not standing up to Uncle Alan, who looked like the brawny steelworker he was. Teddy's father looked like, well, Teddy: soft, overweight, and not very brave.

A slug.

Teddy just wished he were back home. He wished he'd never come to stay overnight with his cousin.

"*No!*" Rob half shrieked, half whispered in the warm darkness under the covers. His voice sounded like Jack's. Teddy hoped desper-ately that his uncle and aunt didn't hear them. "If you tell, then your dad'll say somethin' to mine, and he'll just make it worse for me. So shut up, Teddy."

"Rob—" The image came back to Teddy, the quick frightful glimpse of Rob's tear-streaked face crushed against the bed, of his uncle . . . *I should have said something but you never say anything to grown-ups.*

They can do whatever they want. That's why I just went back downstairs to the porch and waited until I saw Uncle Alan come downstairs buckling his pants. I didn't mean to see it. I didn't want to see it.

"Just shut up, I said. There's nothin' you can do about it. Nothin'. Don't your dad never hurt you?"

"Yeah, I guess. He's spanked me before."

"Well, what would your dad do if my dad told him to stop spankin' you?"

Teddy knew the answer to that. His dad would give that stupid, nervous half laugh and say, "Sure" because he wouldn't want to fight, but it wouldn't change anything. "Nothing much."

"Yeah. Right." Rob huddled in a fetal crouch under the covers, hugging himself. "So don't you say nothin', you hear? Never."

Teddy heard. And he never said nothin', even though he somehow knew he should and even though the guilt gnawed at him and even though it was awfully hard to joke with Uncle Alan the way he used to. He stopped asking to see Rob. He never asked Rob to spend the night with him, not after that night. After a few years, when Uncle Alan and Aunt Eileen and Rob moved away, Teddy even believed he'd forgotten the entire incident.

Damn Wyungare. Damn him for making me remember. Damn him for expecting me to do something.

◆

There was a continuous roar from the Jersey Gate. Things sounded pretty bad there.

But still the bombardment was not as effective as it might have been. Patchwork's prediction of shoot-and-scoot tactics had been correct: each battery fired no more than five shots per barrel before shifting position. And the fire hadn't been terribly accurate—the fog and the radar spoofing had diminished accuracy considerably.

Travnicek was on top of his tower, enjoying the show. Fog and spoofing didn't seem to affect his perceptions much.

Modular Man stood with Travnicek. Waiting for orders.

The android's radar detected more shells arcing toward the Rox, saw a discontinuity appear, a strange little gap in the world that gave off radio emissions rather than let them pass. . . .

So far Bloat hadn't been so busy that his abilities were in danger of being swamped.

So far . . .

Pulse zipped overhead, burning a few shells that the Outcast missed. So far the job hadn't required a dangerous amount of energy.

So far . . .

But despite all efforts a few shells got through. The ramparts shook; battlements crumbled; a few people died or bled.

Still, no damage was critical. So far, despite the trickle of injured to the hospital tunnels, the Rox was perfectly secure.

So far . . .

Travnicek's neck organs shifted, as if scenting a new breeze. "I think we're being painted with a laser," he said. "The fog's diffusing it, but there'll be missiles any second."

His neck organs gave a little twitch, and then Travnicek flung himself on the floor. Modular Man thought that was a good idea and imitated it.

Hellfires shrieked overhead, slammed into battlements. The android could hear screams.

"More coming," said Travnicek.

The air cracked as Pulse lasered through it. Missiles detonated in his wake. Several still hit the outer wall. A mortar bomb, unnoticed in the tension, dropped into the middle bailey and briefly turned the fog red.

"More coming," said Travnicek.

The attackers turned out to be a flight of helicopters firing full loads of sixteen missiles each. One of the outer towers took a pair of missiles that punched through the stonework and sprayed white-hot superheated metal through the interior. Another three slammed harmlessly into the wall of the inner bailey, and one hit the Crystal Keep itself, turning one of the upper rooms into an inferno.

Travnicek rose, walked toward the hole in the floor. "Chubs and Pulse are getting tired. Life gets dangerous from this point on." He turned to Modular Man. "Go to the slug. Find out what he wants and do it."

"Yes, sir."

It was all he could say.

Bloat was going to turn him into a shooter again.

The tunnel was hotter. Sweat ran down Ray's forehead and into his eyes, making them sting. There was a distinct smell of sulfur to the musty-tasting air. Where the hell, Ray wondered, was the tunnel taking them?

He stopped in front of a huge open archway that looked like it'd been taken from some old church. It was backlit in dramatic fashion by a lurid, ruddy glow that cast flickering shadows on the leering gargoyles clinging to the niches within the archway's elaborate fluting. Ray watched the carved stone figures for a long time before he was convinced that they were only carved stone figures, and even then moved quickly through the arch lest one of them suddenly pounce on him.

Clinging to the shadows, Ray found himself at the edge of a large platform jutting over an abyss that went way, way down like a knife wound in the flesh of the earth. Running in the wound was a river of molten lava, red and shining and damn hot. All around the side of the canyon was a stone ledge. It wound off north and south into darkness. It looked rather narrow and crumbly.

Running east, spanning the chasm, was a narrow stone bridge that arched high over the glowing river. There was a man standing in front of the bridge, wooden staff in hand. He was an old joker, with a seamed and wrinkled face and a wild mane of crazed white hair. He had two pairs of skinny, veined arms and he was wearing a T-shirt that proclaimed I SAW THE BIG BLOAT MOAT. Hanging over the T-shirt was a big, shiny gold medallion like the ones Wayne Newton wore in Vegas. Ray watched the old man closely. He didn't move much, except to pick his nose and then wipe the booger on his tattered cloak. That convinced Ray that the geezer wasn't one of Bloat's apparitions. He was real.

Ray withdrew to where the others were hidden in shadow.

Battle looked at him impatiently. "He doesn't appear to be much of a threat, but there's no way to sneak up on him now that Black Shadow is gone and Ackroyd turned out to be an imposter." He spared Nemo a bitter glance. "If he's not a construct, then Bloat can detect us through his mind. It's time for a diversion." Battle turned to Danny. "Tell your sisters to go."

"*Go,*" Danny whispered urgently. Somewhere off in the fog, a church bell was tolling the hour.

Tom pushed off with his mind. The shell lifted and slid silently out of the ferry slip where they'd lain concealed. Not that they needed much concealment. Not in this fog. The Staten Island Ferry could have been twenty feet in front of him, coming dead on, and Tom wouldn't have had a clue.

The Turtle moved out low and fast, like a stone skimming across the waves. A bare foot below him rolled the cold green waters of New York Bay. On his rear screens, Battery Park and the ferry terminal vanished in the fog. Then his cameras showed nothing but the strange, cold, gray-green fog that had swallowed them . . . and Danny, stretched out on her stomach atop his shell.

She was still pissed. "*Go*" was the first word she'd spoken to him since they left Ebbets Field an hour ago. Nothing Tom said got past her icy silence.

Somewhere off in this too-dark morning, the rest of the assault force was moving in simultaneously. Back at Ebbets Field, Zappa or von Herzenhagen had given the order to the pregnant Danny, and her sisters had all whispered, "*Go.*"

Punk Danny had whispered it to Detroit Steel and the Reflector, in Liberty Park over in Jersey. Now they were charging the Jersey Gate, while a detachment of heavy armor provided supporting fire.

Starlet Danny had whispered it to Mistral and Cyclone in the old fort on Governor's Island, and watched their capes fill out like parachutes as they summoned the winds, and flew.

Corporal Danny had whispered it to the elephant perched atop the Stock Exchange. And Radha had leapt off the roof, flapped huge gray ears, and began to climb, spiraling up above the fog, above Bloat's Wall of fear.

"Danny," Tom said. The volume on his speakers was turned way down, but in the eerie silence of the fog the word rang.

"Not now," Danny said, her voice soft but urgent. She had traded her baseball cap for a helmet and infrared goggles that made her look like some strange species of insect. The Army had welded brackets on top of the shell. A net of canvas webbing strapped Danny in place, for safety during violent maneuvering. But just in case, she was wearing a parachute. Her hands were tight around the stock of her M-16.

Tom sighed, turned. His screens were empty. There was nothing to see but Danny's face. The wall of fog receded before them and closed in behind. It was like being in a small gray-green room. Without the water sliding by beneath them, even the sense of motion would be lost.

The Rox was out here somewhere. Tom checked the compass, consulted a harbor map. He veered off toward the southwest.

"Hurry," Danny urged him. "Steel and Snot just hit the Jersey Gate. They're under fire."

Tom pushed harder, driving silently into the fog.

"Radha's still climbing," Danny whispered. The elephant made a slow, cumbersome flyer, and they had to reach two thousand feet, to come in over Bloat's Wall of fear. "Mistral and Cyc are circling, whipping up the tornado. C'mon."

The fog seemed darker in front of them, as if hinting at some looming presence just out of sight. Then the gray-green curtain tore, and there it was.

The Wall rose out of the bay like some vast cliff, a massive construction of dark stone that towered a hundred feet above the waves. The fog took away all sense of scale; the Wall seemed immense, impregnable, endless. Up top, Tom knew, wary jokers waited behind well-oiled machine guns in the watchtowers and nightmares out of Bosch prowled the ramparts. But the top of the Wall was lost in fog now, the enemy as blind as they were.

Tom stayed low over the water, and followed the curve of the Wall toward the west. It would be easy enough for him to fly above it, but those weren't the orders. The idea was for him to make as much commotion as possible at the North Gate, like Detroit Steel and Snotman were doing at the Jersey Gate, like Mistral and Cyclone would be doing when their tornado blew apart the East Wall. Meanwhile, Elephant Girl could reach the Rox undetected, and with luck Corporal Danny would put a rocket right down the throat of the big bloatface atop the golden dome.

"There," Danny whispered urgently.

On Tom's forward screens, the barbican took shape out of the fog. The gate was fifty feet high, deep-set in stone, heavy dark wood banded by black iron. He could see guards watching through the slit windows of the gatehouse.

He thought of a battering ram.

Except for the continuous booming at the Jersey Gate, quiet fell over the Rox. Bloat's staff moved restlessly beneath his pulsing form. Miss Liberty's torch hung over them all like the Sword of Damocles.

"The Jersey Gate's getting pasted," Kafka was reporting. "They're taking serious casualties. The bastions are starting to crumble under shellfire, and I don't know if the gatehouse will hold. If we don't get someone there to knock out those tanks and rocket launchers . . ." He looked at Modular Man, and the android felt his heart sink.

"Lemme get my breath back," Pulse said. "I'll handle it."

"Wait." Bloat's head jerked upright. "Something's going on . . . *all the gates are being attacked!*" He spun toward Kafka. "Pulse to the Jersey Gate!" He pointed at Modular Man. "Something's going on at the East Gate—I can't tell what. Defend it!"

Modular Man's response was inevitable. He glanced upward into the murk.

He'd been right. It was shooter time.

◆

He had finally found the energy to become the Outcast once more when it began again.

Mental voices began shouting for the governor: there was an assault at the East Gate; at the Jersey Gate, Snotman and another ace like a gigantic robot were approaching; someone had spotted Elephant Girl through the tendrils of high drifting fog, climbing far above the Rox; now the Turtle was hitting the North Gate as well.

Teddy was suddenly reliving the terror of a few months ago when the nats first assaulted the Rox, when he wasn't sure of himself or his power. He remembered the fright and the feeling of utter helplessness. This was just like that; no . . . this was far worse. This time he *knew* his power and its limits, and he was very afraid that it wasn't anywhere near enough for *this*.

"Oh, piss," the Outcast said. It sounded very unwizardly and the words dissolved the link. Exhausted, he fell back into himself. Teddy felt dislocated, torn apart. He didn't know if he was Teddy or Bloat or the Outcast. *Governor!*

The power was still there, but it was simply the old channel he had always used before, and he did with it what he'd always done. He called the demons up from his subconscious, had them strike the Jersey Gate in a massive suicidal wave to bury the aces there; he imagined the Manhattan Gate closing, closing, becoming a structure of thick steel and impregnable stone despite the horrible battering it was taking from the Turtle. He caused new fogs to belch from the gargoyles' straining mouths. He let the lava river underneath the Rox surge with newfound force against any possible attack from that area.

Even that, which was too little for the Rox, was too much for him.

There were so many places to watch, so many locations under attack. Teddy felt schizophrenic, his attention scattered. A thousand mindvoices screamed at him.

The Outcast screamed back wordlessly, a paean of anguish. He rapped his staff against the flagons and left the ramparts.

♥

There was a howling at the Brooklyn Gate. The fog twisted and roiled as if it were alive. Even the light seemed effected by whatever was going on—the darkness was pierced with strange flashes of green.

Modular Man followed the thin ribbon of causeway leading from the castle to the Brooklyn Gate. The radar image ahead was confused, giving him an impression of turbulence without any clear indication of what was causing it.

He knew he was approaching the gatehouse with its four round bastions, and he dropped his speed. He didn't want to get into trouble before he had some idea of what the trouble was.

There was another brief green flash. Something boomed ahead, a sound like lightning.

The fog was torn apart. A buzz-saw roar filled the air, and Modular Man burned energy as wind gusts buffeted him. The air was a sickly green and filled with a furious, fine salt spray.

Two pillars of water hovered over the gatehouse, coiling and bending like snakes. Waterspouts. Lightning crackled around and through them. Spray and white water boiled over the ramparts.

Bloat's fish-knights circled furiously over the gatehouse, unable to cross the Wall to get at their attackers. No other defenders were visible, though some abandoned weapons were scattered on the battlements.

Above and far away, hovering in the air, were two bright figures.

Cyclone and Mistral. They were living up to Cyclone's name.

One waterspout was nearer the gatehouse than the other, and seemed larger and more powerful. The other waterspout was thin by comparison and hovered uncertainly behind. Perhaps, the android reasoned, Mistral hadn't had as much practice as her father.

The first waterspout screamed as it lurched over the gatehouse. Debris spun upward as one of the covered bastions imploded. Water spilled over the walls. Several of the fish-knights disappeared into the funnel or were flung into the water with back-breaking force. One of the giant carp flopped in the moat, apparently drowning in its own element.

Modular Man rose, his weapons tracking on the nearer figure. The radar image was confused but he had a decent optical track. His microwave laser pulsed. A line of steam lanced toward Cyclone as the fine sea spray vaporized in the ionized air.

Lightning flashed from the funnel. Modular Man felt air sizzle against his plastic flesh. He wondered if his laser had somehow triggered it.

The laser burst didn't seem to affect Cyclone. Modular Man had fired a microwave laser—a maser, actually—tuned to one of the water frequencies. In the Columbia physics department they called it the "chicken band," because it was used in microwave ovens.

All of the beam's energy had gone into vaporizing the mist. Not enough had remained to impact on the target.

Modular Man was going to have to get closer. He rose, trying to stay inside the Wall till he was at Cyclone's altitude.

One wall of the gatehouse crumbled. The gate itself had been reduced to kindling—foaming water surged right through the gatehouse tunnel. One joker ran madly on four centaur legs from the gatehouse onto the walls and was swept away.

Cyclone began to dance through the sky, cape billowing. Clearly evasive action.

That jetting spear of steam, or maybe the impact of the remaining microwave energy on Cyclone's armor, had given the android's attack away.

The funnel cloud veered for Modular Man, howling like a chain saw and spitting debris. It was an awkward weapon. Energy surged from the android's flux generators and he easily avoided the waterspout as he spiraled higher. He fired a short burst from the Browning just to distract Cyclone, but the bullets were torn away by the furious wind.

The funnel cloud seemed to lose energy; then a torrential wall of wind smashed into Modular Man from above. His flight path staggered downward. Saint Elmo's fire played around his figure as energy surged through his generators. He fought the wind shear, reeled upward, then realized that there had to be a better way to do this.

He ceased struggling against the wind and, tumbling, allowed it to cast him downward. He flailed with hands and feet. He hoped he would look completely out of control. Trajectory calculations flashed through his macroatomic mind. The gray surge of the moat spun nearer. Spray leapt up as the wind struck the water. The android called on his flux generators to sideslip him out of the grasp of the wind shear, then called on his full energies to stop his descent. Gravity tugged at him as his descent slowed. Spray filled the air. The android streamlined his weapons over his back and gave himself maximum lateral thrust. He shot out of the wind shear's grasp like an orange pip squeezed between finger and thumb.

With any luck Cyclone thought he'd been smashed into the moat—the spray might have concealed his escape. Modular Man raced back into the fog bank, then sped north at wavetop height, following the curve of the outer curtain wall. Once he was thoroughly hidden in the fog, he rose, skimmed over the wall, and began a long ascending curve toward the Brooklyn shore.

He should be well behind Cyclone now. He shot straight up into sunlight, seeing the boiling fog below, the waterspouts dancing over the water, the ruined gatehouse. Cyclone and Mistral were facing away from him. He rose above Mistral in a curving arc, calculations flashing through his mind.

He was in the perfect bounce position, above and behind the two aces. He was dropping out of the sun and their billowing cloaks prevented them from checking their six o'clock.

He couldn't lose. Mistral was going to fall, then Cyclone.

This was going to be murder.

He reached the top of his arc, began to descend. Deployed the laser.

He didn't have a choice.

He'd been ordered to defend the gate.

He couldn't think of a way to do that without killing Cyclone and his daughter.

He remembered how he'd fought against the Swarm alongside Mistral, the way she'd hovered over the scenes of the worst disaster, her wind power tearing at the invaders.

He thought of what the microwave laser would do, stimulate the water content of Mistral's body until her flesh exploded in a blast of steam.

He didn't want to do this.

And then the rearmost of the two waterspouts, the one that hadn't hit the Wall yet, lurched forward.

Heading straight for Cyclone.

There was a lengthy moment when Modular Man couldn't comprehend what his sensory apparatus was telling him.

The funnel took Cyclone from behind and swallowed him. There was a brief impression of arms and legs spinning, of fragments of costume being torn away.

Modular Man hovered, undecided.

The funnel spat Cyclone out and began to disperse. Cyclone tumbled, his famous cloak in rags. His arms and legs fluttered in air.

Then a wind picked him up, buoyed him slightly, altered his trajectory. His arms and legs moved feebly, as if he was trying to move—or perhaps that was just the wind.

The wind increased in velocity. Cyclone began to tumble. He picked up speed very rapidly.

The wind smashed him against the outer curtain Wall of the Rox. Modular Man almost winced at the force of the impact.

Cyclone slid off the Wall into the angry, wind-whipped sea. It swallowed him instantly.

The two waterspouts faded. The fog began to roll in again.

Mistral began to fly toward the Rox. Modular Man was still high and behind her, undetected.

Jumped, Modular Man thought.

Mistral penetrated Bloat's Wall without hesitation and Bloat's remaining fish-knights parted to allow her to pass.

Modular Man followed her all the way to where the governor waited.

The huge wooden gate grew stronger by the moment.

Inside the barbican, jokers were jeering at him through the slit

windows. Tom ignored the taunts, summoned his telekinetic battering ram once more, and hit the gate again.

The crunch of impact echoed through the fog. On his screens, he
saw the center of the gate give under the blow. The cracks in the wood
widened visibly. Another dozen hits and he'd smash through . . . except . . .

The gate was healing itself. Tom watched it happen. Wood reached
out to wood; the great, gaping cracks narrowed, faded, and were gone.
He zoomed in tight, saw black iron veins creeping slowly through the
grain, groping toward each other, thickening. Veins of metal deep in
the wood.

"HE'S TURNING THE WHOLE THING TO IRON," he told Danny
through his speakers, his voice thick with frustration.

He heard the voices jeering down from fog-shrouded parapets
above, glimpsed joker faces peering out through the slit windows.
Someone tossed a Molotov cocktail down out of the fog, but the shell
was too far back. He watched it arc out and hit a good ten yards shy. A
fireball blossomed briefly on the water.

"The Jersey Gate is down," Danny told him. "Detroit Steel's inside
the gatehouse. Snot took a direct hit with an armor-piercing shell. You
ought to see him now. So are we going to the dance or what?"

A machine gun opened up somewhere above them, firing blindly
through the fog. Danny swore and returned fire.

Tom frowned, tightened his grip on the arms of his chair, and
hit the gate again. The crash sounded more metallic than wooden
this time. Again the gate gave a little, then held.

"Radha's high enough," Danny reported. "She's moving in. The
windy twins have a nice tornado going in the east, that ought to hold
Bloat's attention awhile."

On screen, Tom watched random fire kick up the water of the bay.
Another Molotov cocktail came spinning out from the gatehouse.
The iron snakes were melting into each other, mating, becoming solid
metal bars.

Shots went *pinging* off the steel plate.

"*Shit!*" Danny cried out in alarm. "Too damn close!"

"YOU ALL RIGHT?" Tom asked.

"For now," she said. "How long you planning to park here? Not that I'm complaining, but one of us isn't wrapped in armor plate, remember?"

Tom grimaced. He could smash the fucking gate. He knew it, even if the jokers inside did not. He could imagine what it would be like. It left a bad taste in his mouth. He twisted the volume of his speakers up to maximum. "LISTEN UP IN THERE. YOU GUYS IN THE GATE-HOUSE. ANYONE UP ON THE WALLS. GET OUT OF THERE. NOW."

Hoots and catcalls were all the reply he got. The gate was almost whole now, solid iron fifty feet high.

"That scared 'em," Danny offered. "Good idea, they're laughing too hard to shoot."

"I MEAN IT," the Turtle insisted. "YOU ASSHOLES WANT TO LIVE, GET THE FUCK OUT OF THERE."

"Look at the third-floor window, over on the right," Danny said. "I think they're trying to tell us something."

Tom zoomed in on the window. One of the joker guards was mooning them. The window was very narrow. Fortunately, so was the joker's ass. "Just hold that pose," Danny said. She aimed and squeezed off a careful round. The joker in the window shrieked, and suddenly vanished.

"Good news and bad news from Jersey," Danny told him, a little breathlessly. "The good news is, Pulse just showed up."

"About time," Tom said, relieved.

"The bad news is, he's on their side. He's fighting the Reflector. You ought to see it. It looks like Snot's inside a cage of light, wrestling with a hundred glowing snakes. His clothes are on fire. I think he's pissed."

Tom sighed. All right, enough. "Hang on," he told Danny. "I'M THROUGH PLAYING AROUND HERE," he warned the defenders. "NO MORE KNOCK-KNOCK ON THE GATE. THIS TIME, I'M BRINGING IT DOWN."

"Tell them you'll huff and you'll puff and you'll blow their house down," Danny suggested. "Or is that Cyclone's department?"

It was all an adventure to her, Tom realized. Suddenly his anger flared. He turned down his speakers to a whisper so only Danny could hear. "What the hell do you think this is, a Rambo movie?" he barked at her angrily.

She looked down at his camera. "What are you so upset about?" She sounded puzzled.

"Those are *people* in there, and if I hit that wall as hard as I hit the bridge, they're going to *die*. You ever seen anyone die? Ever killed anyone?"

"No." Her voice was smaller, subdued.

"They don't have any spare bodies," he told her. Then he turned away, disgusted at his anger, at her, at the whole situation.

"Turtle," she said softly. He looked back up at the overhead screen. The infrared goggles hid her eyes, but Tom could see that he'd hurt her. "You're right. I'm sorry."

She was. Tom could see it in her face. "Me too," he said gruffly, feeling awkward. He wrenched his attention back to the gatehouse, twisted his speakers back to full volume. "ALL RIGHT," he announced. "NO MORE MISTER NICE GUY."

He forgot about the battering ram.

He thought of a freight train.

He laid the tracks with his mind, straight across the water, running dead on into the gatehouse. Not at the gate. The gate was solid iron now. At the stone wall just to the right of it. He closed his eyes, summoned an invisible train twice as big as any real train had ever been, sent it hurtling forward. For a moment he could see it in his mind's eyes, hear the iron thunder of its wheels against the rails, the doomsday wail of its steam whistle.

But it was all teke. The enemy couldn't see a thing. The defenders were still jeering and hooting when the train crashed head-on against the base of the gatehouse.

The whole barbican shook with the force of the impact. The entire bottom half of the gatehouse collapsed inward. Huge stones came tumbling off the parapets to crash into the bay. Tom heard screaming. The immense iron gate still stood, but now there was nothing to anchor it on the right. Tom grabbed it with his mind and *pulled*. He heard the shriek of tortured metal. The gate resisted, twisted slowly, then gave all at once, ripping free of the stone in an explosion of dust and rubble. He flung it backward; it arced over the shell and splashed down in the waters of the bay behind them.

Through the huge gap he'd torn, Tom glimpsed deep water, a long stone causeway stretching back to the Rox.

But only for an instant.

Then the gatehouse fell in on itself, and a whole section of Bloat's Wall came crashing down.

"Jesus Christ," Danny said softly from atop the shell. Tom lifted the shell higher. It was raining stone and bodies. An immense chunk of masonry hit the bay and sent up a sheet of water twenty feet high.

Tom felt sick at heart. It was an effort to push the shell forward. Now the hard part . . . he had to punch through the second Wall, the invisible Wall, before the fear got hold of him and made him turn back. Maybe if he built up enough speed . . .

"Turtle," Danny screamed in warning. Tom could hear the sudden fear in her voice. "Demons!"

He scanned his screens quickly, saw nothing. "Where? I don't—"

Danny shook her head violently, jerked a thumb upward. "Not here. It's Radha. She's in trouble."

Tom hesitated only a second, then pushed hard with his mind. The Turtle shot upward.

Ray frowned. "We still have to deal with the geezer without letting Bloat know we're here."

"Of course," Battle said. He turned to Cameo. "Here's where you start earning your pay."

Cameo nodded. She took her pack off and set it at her feet. She rummaged in it for a moment, then removed a small package that she unwrapped to retrieve Blockhead's ring. She slipped it on the middle finger of her right hand. It was as simple as that.

She changed instantly. She drew up, backing away from the others. Her eyes grew large and tinged with fear. Her mouth clamped shut and she carried on a whispered, one-sided conversation with herself.

"What am I doing here? I don't want—no. No, I said!" Her voice rose as she continued to speak aloud. It was her voice, yet it wasn't. It had the same pitch, but the patterns and inflections were those of a dead man: Brian Boyd, a.k.a. Blockhead. It took a while, but Cameo finally managed to convince him to cooperate. "Okay, if you say so."

"Blockhead?" Battle asked.

Cameo's face stiffened into a frown. "I detest that name," the ace said. "My name is Brian Boyd. You may call me Brian, or you may call me Boyd. But do not use that awful sobriquet again."

"Fine," Battle said. "How do you feel, Boyd?"

"How do I feel? Why, imagine—"

"I can't," Battle said. "I mean, are your powers functioning?"

Boyd looked outraged, then calmed down as if he were listening to some soothing inner monologue. "All right," he said to himself. "All right. Yes. Certainly." He took a deep breath and shut his eyes. After a moment he nodded. "Yes. The mind shield is up."

"Excellent. Ray, take the joker."

Ray looked at Battle. "That's not much of a plan. I could be in trouble if the geezer's some kind of ace."

"You're paid to face danger," Battle reminded him. "And Bloat doesn't have many aces in his entourage. Not yet, anyway." Battle fixed Cameo with his hard stare. "Make sure you maintain the mind shield over Ray and that joker."

Cameo—or Boyd—nodded. Ray moved off into the shadow, and then simply stood and walked out onto the middle of the path leading to the bridge. The geezer had fallen asleep while leaning on his staff. He was snoring gently to himself. Ray, irritated, woke him up.

"Hey, Gramps, which way to Bloat?"

The guardian of the bridge snorted, started, then regarded Ray with a bright, old man's stare. "To cross the bridge and enter Bloat's domain," he intoned in a low, cackling voice, "you must be prepared to answer the question perilous."

Ray frowned. "All right," he said in an uncertain voice.

The old man leaned forward and pointed with his staff. His voice was deep with authority and expectation as he intoned, "What's your favorite color?"

Ray was struck not only by a sense of total bewilderment, but also of *déjà vu*. This all seemed somehow familiar to him.

"Uh, white," he said.

"Wrong!" the old man cackled, showing his snaggled teeth in a wide, triumphant smile. Ray just stared back at him in bewilderment and the old man pulled himself up with a gruff frown. "Well, what do you want then?" he asked grumpily.

Ray shook his head, as if to clear it. "I told you. I, um, have to see Bloat."

The old man sighed. "Half a mo', then. Let me check in with the guvnor." He fell silent, frowning in concentration. His frown deepened. "Something's wrong. I can't seem to contact him." He reached down to his side and came up with a walkie-talkie that was hanging from a strap around his neck. "I'll try with this."

Ray lunged, grabbing it from the old man and pulling it away before he could make contact. "I don't think that's a good idea," Ray said.

He turned and waved an arm vigorously over his head and the others arose from the shadows and joined them at the threshold of the bridge.

"It's an invasion," the old man yelped.

"Did he get through to Bloat?" Battle asked.

Ray shook his head. "The shield held. He was going to call someone on this"—he held up the walkie-talkie—"but I got it away from him in time."

"Good work," Battle said. He turned to the old man. "Which way to the tunnels leading to Ellis Island?"

The old man drew himself up defiantly. "I'm not telling. And there's no way you can make me."

"You're probably right," Battle said. He looked at Puckett.

The ace lumbered forward, grabbed a fistful of the old man's I SAW THE BIG BLOAT MOAT T-shirt, and yanked him up off his feet. He tossed him over the edge of the chasm, down screaming into the lava river below.

"Hey!" Danny said.

Battle turned his narrow gaze on her. "This is war, Corporal. Or do

I have to remind you? We couldn't leave him behind and let him alert Bloat and we couldn't take him with us."

"We could have knocked him out—"

"And taken the chance that he'd wake up at any time and betray us?" Battle shook his head. "I think not."

"But—"

"Let's go, Corporal Shepherd," Battle said coldly.

"But—"

Ray stepped between them, facing Danny. He shook his head and she subsided when she saw the closed, set look on his face. "Not now," he said quietly. He turned back to Battle. "I suppose you want me on point again?"

"Right you are, Agent Ray," Battle said, cheerful again, a false twinkle in his cold, cold eyes.

"My ass," Ray muttered to himself as he made his way carefully onto the naked rock span. He looked over the edge in the glowing, sputtering lava, and was glad that he wasn't afraid of heights.

The Outcast materialized in Wyungare's cell. First, a roaring, spitting fireball flared like an exploding sun on the back wall of the room, then the Outcast stepped through the aching white glare like a movie wizard.

"Great special effects, huh?" He grinned, and snapped his fingers. The nova shrunk to nothing and popped out of existence with a sound like a light bulb exploding. The Outcast brushed flecks of clinging radiance motes from his cloak to expire on the stone-flagged floor. "I always did love a good entrance."

The Aborigine stared at him with wide, veined, coffee-brown eyes. The gaze was appraising, but whatever Wyungare was thinking was shut away behind the ebony shield of his mind. Wyungare said nothing. He just stared. The steady, critical gaze made the Outcast uncomfortable and the head-silence was perturbing. Suddenly it was very difficult to pretend nonchalance. Suddenly it was difficult to joke. His false humor fell from him like a cloak.

"You have to help me," the Outcast admitted at last. His body sagged, the shoulders slumped and defeated.

"Mate, you look horrible."

"I'm losing people out there." A basso rumble shook dust from the ceilings and shivered the floor. A second concussion followed the first. "My head hurts. I'm being pulled apart."

"I'm sorry." Wyungare glanced up at the Outcast from the corner of his cell. His nut-brown skin was difficult to see in the gloom. All Teddy could see were the moist highlights of the eyes.

"You're *sorry*? That's it?"

"What do you want me to do? I don't have your powers. That's not how I can help you."

Another explosion rumbled through the ground, vibrating underfoot. The Outcast heard a chorus of screams in his head, and he wanted to scream with them. Instead, he sobbed. The crying hit him hard—great, gulping gasps of it. He could no longer feel the staff in his hand, and through the tears he could no longer see the Outcast's trim, muscular body. He was simply Teddy. Just Teddy. Just an overweight adolescent. "I'm wiped. I hurt and I'm tired and I can't be tired. Not now. They're screaming and dying and in pain and I can't get rid of the voices."

Wyungare had risen silently to his feet. Teddy felt the man's hand on his shoulder, and then he was hugging Wyungare fiercely, clinging to him like a child to his father—no, for he'd never embraced his father in that way. Never.

Sniffing, Teddy pulled away. He wrapped the Outcast's body back around him like a cloak as the noisy clamor of the Rox came back into his head. Kafka was calling him; the jumpers were in chaos; at the gates, the jokers were overmatched. "If you won't help me, I have to go. I can't stay."

"You won't let me help you."

"When have you tried?"

"I've told you. You haven't listened. You are the one with the power, why do you stay here and let them hurt you?"

"You and the penguin . . . Where am I supposed to *go*? Hawaii?"

"To the dreamtime. To the place that feeds you," Wyungare answered.

Irritation flooded through Ted with that. "Yeah, great. Even if I could do that, then what have I accomplished? Damn it, this is *our* world too. Why should the nats be able to run us off just because we were unlucky enough to be infected by that damn virus? Why should *we* have to run away with our tails between our legs." The image made him laugh sarcastically. "And some of us even have the tails to do that, don't we? Listen, you can keep your damn advice, okay? I can beat these assholes. I don't care if I have to pull every last fucking erg of energy from your precious dreamtime or break all the barriers between that world and this. I don't care what leaks out or what happens. I'll do it."

"Always the hero," Wyungare said softly.

"You're damned right." The Outcast took a deep breath. With it he pulled in power, feeling the energy course from the shadow world to Bloat's body to him. With the power came the cacophony of the Rox—the pleading, the terror, the anger.

The sons of bitches—I'll kill them! I'll kill them all!

That fucking Snotman just tore the gates down . . .

Where the hell's the governor? Where's the demons? I need help . . .

"I have to leave," the Outcast said. "Thanks for nothing."

"You don't have to be Bloat forever, you know. The way I see it, you have three choices." Softly again. Quietly. The Outcast stared at him. "With the help of the others like me, you could sever the link. All of us together could do it. You could stay as you are right now—in that form, but without the power. You'd be a nat. Normal."

The Outcast blinked. "Or . . . ?"

"Or we could move you fully into the dreamtime—the entire Rox. It would take all of us, each of us calling on the powers of our own portion of the dreamtime, but we could take the Rox and move it away from this shadow plane and take you to the source of your power."

"Where you can deal with me on your terms? Where I can be *handled?* Where I wouldn't be stealing power from your precious dreamtime—in either scenario: me as nat or me in the dreamtime?"

"All of that's true," Wyungare admitted. "And there's another sacrifice to that. It's going to take *you,* as well. You won't be the Outcast in the dreamtime, or even Bloat."

"What will I be?"

"You will be. That's all."

Teddy could read nothing in those mahogany eyes, nothing at all. He strained to hear Wyungare's thoughts in the maelstrom of the Rox: silence.

"What's the third alternative?"

"Don't do anything. Stay here and let them bomb you to hell."

Teddy snorted laughter. "I've already met one of your shamans; he tried to kill me. Why would Viracocha and the rest of your friends turn around and help me? The Rox and me seemed to be a threat to you just like I am to the nat world—why should I think you're going to deal with me any differently?"

"Maybe you shouldn't. I don't come with guarantees, mate."

"Then why the hell *did* you come?"

"I told you. Because the dreamtime brought me here." Wyungare sighed and squatted down again in the corner of the cell. "We can give you the body you want at the cost of your power, or we can take you to safety in the dreamtime, or you can stay here and let them kill you—at which point you won't hurt the dreamtime anymore. Make your choice."

"Why are you telling me all this? Why now?"

"Every hero has to have a temptation."

The Outcast laughed. "Fuck you. Fuck all of you shadow-walkers." Another explosion rocked the caverns; the Outcast broke his gaze away from Wyungare. "I can't waste any more time with you," he said. "I have to go."

The Outcast left in a gout of purple flame.

"The Jersey Gate is down," the Outcast said. His face showed the strain of trying to comprehend the fight everywhere at once. "And the Turtle's just smashed the North Gate. Molly—" This to Mistral. "I need you there right now."

Mistral/Molly nodded. Winds filled her cloak and she rose into the darkening mist.

There was a burning in the misty air. Pulse materialized, his face pale. He fell to one knee.

"We're fucked," he said.

"All my Bosch creatures have been killed," the Outcast said. "I don't know what's happening out there. I can't read the man who's killing them."

Pulse gasped in air. "I've been trying to burn the guy, but nothing works. He's killing everyone. Blew up our tanks, wiped out the troops." He waved an ineffective fist. *"It's just one man!"*

The Outcast turned to Modular Man. "Get to the Jersey Gate. Try to retrieve the situation."

The android turned to Pulse. "Who is it?"

He was afraid he already knew.

"I dunno, man," Pulse gasped. "He's young—brown hair, not even carrying a gun. We've been throwing everything at him and—"

"Snotman," Modular Man said. Despair roiled through him.

"And a big robot."

"Detroit Steel."

"The Army's moving into Liberty Park," the Outcast said. "I can feel the minds of their tank drivers. They're going over the rubble of the gate. And a lot of men are following. The Wall's not turning enough of them back."

Modular Man turned to Bloat. "Surrender," he said. "Now. While you can still cut a deal, possibly get an amnesty for some of your people."

"I don't believe I'm hearing this shit," Pulse said. "I should burn your fucking tin head off." The android turned to him.

"You're our most powerful ace," he said. "You couldn't stop him. Every time you hit him, you just made him more powerful. *Snotman absorbs energy!* Then he fires it back. I barely escaped him in the past."

"But you defeated him," the Outcast said. "How?"

"It wasn't me. It was a joker named Gravemold who was able to suck the energy out of him. And Gravemold isn't here, is he?"

A wry smile twitched at the Outcast's lips. "No. He *was* here, but he wasn't on our side. And his name wasn't Gravemold, he was—"

There was an explosion from the direction of the Jersey Gate. The Outcast's head swiveled up. "We've got to stop him."

"Surrender."

"There's got to be a way. *Think.*"

Modular Man did so. It was, after all, an order.

"Order your people to stop firing," he said. "All you're doing is feeding him energy."

The Outcast gave the order. Kafka relayed it to the troops.

"I'm in Detroit Steel's head," the Outcast said. "I'm right behind Snotman. They're jogging up the bridge. Maybe a third of the way across. They have a young woman with them, lagging behind. Her name is Danny, but I can't read her. All the Dannys are too strong for me."

Modular Man decided to ignore this enigmatic remark. "Have you still got enough energy to control matter inside the Wall?"

"Some. Yes."

"Dematerialize part of the causeway ahead of them. That may slow them down."

The Outcast closed his eyes, raised his staff, bit his lip with the effort. The amethyst glowed feebly.

He opened his eyes. "Done," he said. "What now?"

"That was it," Modular Man said. "That was my idea."

The Outcast shrugged. "Well. At least you bought us some time till we think of something else."

"I should consult my creator. Perhaps he'll know what to do."

Perhaps, the android thought, he'd know it was time to leave.

There was always a hope.

The corridor ended in another arched doorway. This one had Bloat's head carved in the center of its lintel. Ray regarded the door suspiciously, but couldn't detect any trapdoors in the ceiling or floor. No obvious ones, anyway. He stepped toward the doorway and stopped when the carved Bloat-head spoke.

"You've been warned," it said in a voice too high-pitched to be stern. "Please. If you go back now you won't be hurt."

"Tell it to Black Shadow," Ray snarled, but he had to admit that they'd been let off pretty light so far. This crazy underground maze could be a killing field. Instead, it seemed to be stocked with weirdos playing games. He took a deep breath and entered the chamber beyond the doorway, looked around, and stopped.

It was a goddamn underground fairyland. The chamber was lit by some kind of natural phosphorescence in half a dozen muted pastel shades of pink and green. It was at least fifty feet tall and more than twice as long. Its walls were multicolored flowstone. Huge stalactites bigger around than Ray could reach flowed down from the ceiling. The ones in the center of the chamber met their opposite numbers, equally impressive stalagmites, in solid masses of living rock. Interspersed around the giants hanging from the ceiling were hundreds of smaller stalactites, little rock icicles dangling like frozen rain on Christmas day. Bats wheeled around the formations near the ceiling, casting darting, silent shadows that were difficult to distinguish from the animals themselves.

Ray's powerful flashlight cut through the shadows as he cast its beam carefully about the columnar rock formations sprouting from floor and ceiling. As far as he could tell there were no traps, nor were any of Bloat's minions lurking in ambush. He turned back toward the party and waved them forward.

"It's beautiful," Danny said.

"Yes," Battle replied, unimpressed. "It's odd, though." He reached out and touched a ribbon of flowstone. "These rock formations appear natural, but they would have needed thousands of years to form. These caverns haven't even been here for months."

"Bloat's power—" Ray began, and interrupted himself with a wordless shout.

He hurtled toward Danny, leapt, and swung out with his arm above her head. Flesh hit stone, and he absorbed the pain and minor bruising without even changing expression as he batted away the small stalactite so that it fell harmlessly to the floor. If he hadn't blocked it, it would have hit Danny right on the head.

"That would have speared me for sure," she said.

Ray felt himself smiling at her, then he whirled at Nemo's startled cry. The Monster was pointing at the stalactite that Ray had knocked aside. For a moment it blurred as it lay there on the ground; then it shifted shape, changing into a naked, nasty-looking gray creature that seemed to be all teeth and claws.

Everyone watched, startled, as the creature leapt to its feet, snarled, and threw itself at Puckett. It fastened itself on Puckett's leg and took a big bite.

The dead ace never changed expression. He just reached down and pulled the thing off his leg. It smoked from the acid he exuded from his palms as he twisted its ugly little head right off.

"What the hell—" Battle said, then another stalactite fell from the ceiling and landed right by him. Within seconds it too turned into a twisted, gray gargoyle with slavering fangs and a nasty disposition. It leapt at Battle, who jumped backward, shouting for Puckett.

The ace was slow to react. The gargoyle would have had Battle if the agent hadn't dodged behind a thick stalagmite. Danny put her shotgun to her hip and let loose a three-round blast and the gargoyle disappeared in a splatter of bloodless gray flesh.

"Look out!" Boyd called.

Ray glanced upward. It was raining the goddamn things. Stalactites were falling from the ceiling like icicles knocked off a roof edge by a bored kid. And when they hit the ground they all turned into the gray little creatures whose only purpose in life seemed to be to bite.

"Let's get the hell out of here!" Ray shouted, and they all began to run.

Ray took a glancing blow to his shoulder that scoured off a patch of flesh. Puckett took a direct hit to the head, but it didn't seem to bother him any. One of the advantages, Ray thought, of being dead. Battle and Danny also took a couple of glancing blows, but their Kevlar armor protected them from any serious damage.

The gargoyles the stalactites turned into, however, were something else indeed.

Within moments there were two score of the things, nipping and biting at their heels. Nemo, trying to run, tripped and fell, and half a dozen of the things swarmed him. Ray dived in, kicking and punching at the little bastards as fast as he could. Fortunately, they broke easily. Unfortunately, they could bite like pitbulls, and as Ray found out when one fastened onto his right calf, their slobber burned like acid.

"Shit!" He pulled Nemo to his feet. "You okay?"

The Monster was bitten about the left arm and right thigh, but he nodded. Ray turned to face more of their tiny assailants, snarling, and drew the Ingram machine pistol he had holstered at his hip. He let go a long burst that cut the little creatures down like a scythe through a wheat field. Danny joined them, her automatic shotgun sweeping a clear swath through them, and they put themselves back to back, with Nemo towering above them in the middle.

Ray risked a glance at Boyd. She—or he—had been remarkably untouched so far. He wondered if being the center of the mind shield was protecting her from the little bastards.

"Make for the other side of the chamber," Ray shouted above the blasting, echoing roars of gunfire. He—or she—nodded, and started off. Battle and Puckett had also gone back to back, Battle beating off the waves of attacking gargoyles with bursts from his assault rifle, Puckett using his hands to mangle them, his acid to burn them.

It seemed like hours but couldn't have been more than a few minutes before they fought their way to the door at the end of the chamber and collapsed outside the room where the beasts were unwilling, or unable, to follow.

"All right!" Ray shouted. He was still jazzed from the fight and the adrenaline running through his system. He stopped and shook his fist at the group of slavering gargoyles crowded around the doorway, unable to pass through it. They immediately turned back to stone. "Ugly little bastards," Ray sniffed.

Battle was breathing heavily. "Let's tend our wounds," he said, shrugging out of his pack and rummaging through it for his first-aid kit. He paused to snarl, "That fat freak bastard is going to pay for this."

"Pay?" Danny said.

"Pay the ultimate price." Battle glared at her, glared at everyone. "He's dead, stinking meat, and he doesn't even know it."

"I thought we were supposed to capture him," Danny said.

"And then do what with him?" Battle sneered. "Haul him off to jail? His fat carcass is too big for any cell. Plus he's much too powerful to keep under lock and key. Look around yourself." Battle gestured at the caverns. "How could we imprison a mind capable of doing all this?" He shook his head. "No. The freak has to die."

As if to emphasize his point he rammed a fresh magazine into his assault rifle and stared at the team as if daring anyone to contradict him.

"All this ridiculous fighting isn't as interesting as watching Bloat *do* things," Travnicek said. "I'm damned near getting bored." He was reclining on the fantastic winged-dragon couch that Bloat had provided for his bunker room.

Modular Man didn't want to know. "Snotman is getting close," he said.

"*Snotman!*" Travnicek sprang up from the couch, waved his arms, the cilia at the ends of his hands waving. The android was surprised by the vehemence of Travnicek's reaction.

"He's broken in at the Jersey Gate. He's destroyed everything in his path, and I don't think he can be stopped. Bloat's too tired to do anything. Perhaps it's time to leave."

"Run from that little fuck? Never!" Agitated, Travnicek jumped up onto the ceiling and began pacing back and forth.

"Sir. I can't stop him."

"You know what that bastard did. He helped Typhoid Croyd try to assassinate me!"

"But you didn't die." Modular Man spoke rapidly. "You *evolved . . .*" Carefully. "To this higher form."

"No thanks to him," Travnicek said. He seemed disinclined to follow Modular Man's desperate logic and insincere flattery. He jabbed an arm at Modular Man, and the cilia writhed into a pointing-finger shape. "Dispose of Snotman. That's an order."

The android knew he was dead.

"How?" he said. "He's immune to any form of attack I can launch."

"Use your imagination."

"I don't *have* an imagination."

"Hah. You got *that* right, toaster." Travnicek paused. "He eats energy, right? So don't give him any."

"How do I fight him without—"

Travnicek, still on the ceiling, leaned closer to the android. His voice was harsh. "Are you a shooter or a shootee, toaster? A winner or loser? That's what you gotta decide." He waved a hand. "Now go do your job."

Modular Man turned about and left through the hatch, and Travnicek dogged it shut behind him.

He tried to think about running away. His programming wouldn't let the thoughts progress very far.

He flew out of the tower, then began heading toward the Jersey Gate.

He swung wide of the causeway for the present, and swept over the gate, moving quickly so that no one would get off a shot. The gatehouse was rubble, with armored vehicles roaring as they climbed over the pile of stone and brick. The two fighting vehicles captured by the jokers were smoldering wrecks. The smell of burning flesh mingled with the smell of hot metal and rose into the sky over the gate.

Shootees lay scattered under the rubble, sprawled in little clumps through Liberty Park and under the treads of the vehicles. Soldier shootees lay outside in the street.

Modular Man, floating high in the fog, soared along the causeway. The military, sensibly, had declined to follow Snotman up the long, narrow causeway, designed as a death trap for advancing troops.

Still keeping high in the fog, Modular Man moved along until he came to the fifty-foot gap in the causeway that Bloat had created. Snotman, Detroit Steel, and Danny Shepherd were standing uncertainly at the end of it.

Go home, the android mentally urged. Go back and get a boat and let me think.

Instead Detroit Steel turned toward Snotman and began hitting him. Strong piston-powered punches, hammer blows, vicious upper-cuts, all rained on Snotman's unaffected body. The young man remained motionless, not reacting in any way, absorbing energy.

The android tried to think of what to do. Rush down, push Snotman into the water?

Useless. He wouldn't be pushed: he'd just suck the energy off the shove and shoot it back at him.

Snotman gave a signal, and Detroit Steel stopped hitting. Snotman bent and, as effortlessly as if he were picking up an inflated punching bag, lifted Detroit Steel from the ground.

The android stared.

Snotman held Detroit Steel over his head as if the armored giant were a medicine ball.

And threw him.

Detroit Steel arrowed through the fog like the heaviest, clumsiest flying ace in history. He landed with a clang in the middle of the road-way ten feet beyond the gap.

Detroit Steel had been providing Snotman's energy. The two were now apart.

Modular Man took instant advantage.

He dove on Detroit Steel, both weapons firing, before the giant could rise to his feet. A blizzard of sparks flew from Detroit Steel's armor as bullets and the maser struck home. The android kept his attention on Snotman and calculated the ace's response—when the timing seemed right Modular Man added lateral power and commenced evasive maneuvers. Bolts of energy sizzled close to him.

The android arced up into the fog, swept around to a new quarter, descended on Detroit Steel again. The giant had risen to one knee. Bullets flailed the roadway around him, precise bursts of microwave energy scorched the reflective armor. Snotman fired another blast, failed to hit his fast-moving target.

Snotman was powerful, but he was firing by eye, without any advanced targeting systems.

Shooter or shootee, the android thought.

He rose up, rolled, came again. His fire hammered Detroit Steel to the ground. Some part of the giant exploded in a burst of vaporized hydraulic fluid.

Snotman didn't bother to fire; instead he trotted back a distance down the causeway, sprinted to the gap, and flung himself across.

His aim wasn't as good this time: he dropped too fast and slammed into a bridge abutment beneath the broken causeway. He dug fingers into the stonework, the gray rock crumbling away under his energy-charged fingers, then began hauling himself up to the causeway.

Danny Shepherd was left behind, on the wrong side of the gap.

During that time the android continued a rain of fire on Detroit Steel. Danny tried a few shots with her rifle, but Modular Man easily evaded them.

When Snotman's head appeared above the edge of the broken causeway, Modular Man rose into the air and disappeared.

He hadn't hurt Snotman at all. Even *trying* to hurt him would be a bad idea.

The last time they had met, Modular Man fought him with the exact same tactics, ignoring Snotman as much as possible and concentrating his attack on Croyd. But at that time Mr. Gravemold had been available to fight Snotman, and with a power that was effective against Snotman's ability to absorb and convert energy.

Somehow Modular Man was going to have to come up with an equivalent of Mr. Gravemold. He was going to have to stop Snotman nonviolently.

He pictured joker commandos rushing Snotman and smothering him in a pile of mattresses. The picture did not convince.

Smothering wasn't a bad idea, though.

Especially when you considered that the alternative was to become a shootee.

◆

The Turtle came hurtling up out of the fog, and almost ran into the flying elephant.

The green steel curve of his shell broke the surface of Bloat's pea soup like a submarine breaking surface, and Elephant Girl was careening down at him, gray ears flapping wildly. She loomed up like an oncoming bus in his forward screens, and Tom had to bank the shell hard to avoid the collision. Up on top, he heard Danny yelp, but the safety net held her securely in place. The elephant vanished into the fog below him.

The demons were hot on Radha's tail.

There must have twenty of them. Tom didn't have the time to count. A dozen armored mermen rode on giant carp, the tips of their swordfish lances red with blood. Other monstrosities out of Bosch flew with them: a toad with long clawed legs, a cat-demon, a thing half dinosaur and half unicorn, a naked featherless bird. They cried out to each other in high, thin, inhuman voices.

They're not real, Tom told himself. *They're not human.* It made all the difference.

He thought of a hand, reached out, grabbed the foremost merman, and *squeezed.* The creature seemed to implode. Scales, fish guts, and black ichor oozed between Tom's imaginary fingers. Green fire flared, and suddenly the thing was gone, as if it had never been. He grabbed another.

Danny was firing. Tom heard the steady chatter of her M-16, saw the head of the cat-demon explode. But there were too damn many of the things, closing in from all sides now. Tom felt panic stirring in his guts.

Then Elephant Girl burst up out of the sea of fog, right among the demons.

A lance was embedded in her throat, and blood ran sluggishly from a dozen deep slashes in her thick gray skin. The wounds just seemed to make her mad. On her back, Corporal Danny blazed away freely with a side arm.

Radha crashed through the charging mermen. A toss of her head sent a tusk right through the featherless bird. Her charge unseated two fish-knights. As they fell, she lifted her trunk and trumpeted her rage.

The toad-man leapt off his carp onto the elephant's head, but no sooner did he land than Radha had him with her trunk. She flung him down into the fog, and Tom heard his high, shrill scream for long seconds after he was lost to sight.

After that, he was too busy with his own demons to pay attention. They came to him from all sides, but inside his shell he was untouchable. He crushed them with his teke, knocked them off their fish, ripped them in half. It was the Swarm War all over again. Their lances shattered harmlessly against his armor; their necks snapped like twigs between his invisible fingers.

It was over in seconds. All of a sudden they were alone in the morning sky, the fog churning restlessly beneath them. He hovered, breathing hard. His hands were shaking. Elephant Girl circled the shell, huge ears flapping slowly. Corporal Danny was bent over, holding her shoulder, but Tom couldn't see a wound. He glanced at the overhead screen, at his own Danny.

Her face was drawn and tight, one hand grasping her shoulder. Blood trickled out between her fingers. She forced a pained smile. "Lanced by a fish," she said. "How humiliating."

"I'm taking you back," Tom announced. "Tell Radha to follow us in."

Danny nodded, biting her lip against the pain.

Elephant Girl came around, heading north.

"Leaving so soon?" a woman's voice shouted down from above them. "The party's just started."

Startled, Tom pushed his chair around in a hard circle, scanning screens, looking for a new enemy.

She was directly overhead, blue and white against the sky, her cape rippling with the wind. Relief swept over him. He turned his speakers up, zoomed in. "MISTRAL," he called out.

She smiled. "Guess again," she called lightly.

The wind hit the shell like a giant's fist.

Ray took a deep breath at the threshold of the next chamber and paused, more in annoyance than anything else. He was getting tired of this shit. He waited, listening, and from faintly inside the room he heard odd little noises, the tinkle of metal scraping across metal, like he had never heard before.

Fuck it, he thought, and went in.

He glanced at the stalactites hanging from the ceiling, but they seemed inclined to stay in place. He moved forward, using the columnar masses of stalagmites surging up from the floor as cover. Tongues of flame were dancing in a cleared area in the center of the room, casting shifting patterns of shadow upon the rock formations and the men sitting in a circle around the campfire.

The sounds of metal tinkling against metal came from their chainmail armor and the clashing of their curved, scab-barded swords.

Why the hell, Ray thought, did Bloat arm his guards with medieval shit? These men should have real weapons.

And then one of them stood and turned toward Ray and the ace saw their faces for the first time, and he realized that they weren't men.

They were short, but also rather top-heavy through the chest and shoulders with a weird, stooped-over posture. Their limbs were muscular and gnarly and their faces all looked like they'd just come from an ugly convention. All had the same design worked into the front of their jerkins, a big, lidless, reddish eye.

One of them saw Ray and approached slowly with an awkward rolling gait that reminded Ray a little of Crypt Kicker. Ray watched, unconcernedly, as the thing got closer. After all, it only had a sword while he had a holstered Ingram. If he needed anything more than his hands.

The thing had no expression as it approached. It stopped half a dozen feet from Ray and asked in passably good English, "Do you have the medallion?"

"Medallion?"

"The keeper of the bridge," the thing explained patiently. "Did he give to you the medallion of safe passage?"

Ray suddenly remembered the big golden thing the old guy at the bridge had worn over his T-shirt. The medallion of safe passage. Shit.

"No," Ray said. "He had to take a little trip."

"Then die," the creature said without emotion, drawing his sword.

"Screw you," Ray replied. There was no sense messing around with these assholes. He drew the Ingram before the poor fuck had a chance to take a step forward and unzipped him with a short burst that punched through the chain mail covering his chest like a can opener going through the lid of a beer can.

The thing was thrown backward by the impact of the slugs. For a moment he just lay there, and then he was gone. He rotted before Ray's eyes, decades of decomposition passing in seconds. For a brief, mercifully short moment there was the unbearable odor of putrid flesh, then that was gone too, and there was just a skeleton in a shot-up suit of armor that promptly stood up on its bony feet and came clanking at Ray, sword raised high.

"Christ," Ray said as the skeleton swung its sword.

Ray blocked the stroke and smashed the skeleton's sword arm. Arm and sword both clattered to the ground. By then the other guards were all around Ray and he had no time to watch the arm flop around on the floor like a fish out of water, swinging the sword wildly and blindly as it tried to inch closer to Ray.

There were a few desperate seconds. Ray was outnumbered seventeen to one, but not all of the guards could get at him at once and he was a lot quicker and stronger than any of the medieval dicks trying to bash him.

He took a sword cut across the ribs, but by that time he'd put three of his attackers on the ground. Then came the welcoming sound of gunfire at his back and he knew that the rest of the team had joined the attack.

The pig-faced guards were blown apart by the explosive bursts of Danny's automatic shotgun and the continuous stream of bullets from Battle's assault rifle.

Crypt Kicker waded into the assault at Ray's side and part of Ray watched and analyzed the dead ace's style. There was no science or art to his attack. He just tore the guards apart with his bare hands, twisting off heads and limbs like a sadistic child let loose on a bunch of helpless Barbie dolls.

These guards also rotted into animated skeletons moments after death, and the skeletons continued to attack.

A few of them had bows. From the corner of his eye Ray saw Nemo take an arrow in the shoulder. But the wound just seemed to piss him off. He roared wordlessly and marched stiff-legged into the guards, dismembering them with the same brute strength and lack of technique exhibited by Crypt Kicker.

It was over in moments. Nemo's bruised shoulder and Ray's sliced ribs were the team's only real wounds. Crypt Kicker had been cut several times by the guard's scimitars, but his wounds seemed to bother him even less than Ray's did.

Another advantage, Ray thought, of being dead.

He heard Danny cry out behind him. When he turned, she had dropped to one knee. She was holding one shoulder, her face tight with pain.

Ray went to her. "What happened? They get you?"

"Not me," she muttered. She took away her fingers. There was no blood. "One of my . . . sisters. Lanced by a fish."

"How do—" Ray began, then asked, "Is she all right?"

"Just a flesh wound." She moved a shoulder hesitantly, then got back to her feet. "I'll be fine."

Clutching skeletal fingers were still clawing at his ankle. Ray brought his heel down hard, heard the bones crunch and snap as he ground them underfoot. "What the hell were these things?"

"Don't you know?" Danny asked. Everyone looked at her.

"No," Ray said.

"Don't you guys ever read?" Ray looked at her bewilderedly. Truth was, he didn't. But he couldn't see what that had to do with anything. "They're orcs. You know, from Tolkien."

"Tolkien?" Ray asked.

Danny gave an exasperated sigh. "J.R.R. Tolkien. *Lord of the Rings.* They're even wearing the insignia of Sauron's Eye."

"Oh, yeah," Ray said. He suddenly remembered a coed he'd dated back when he was in college. He hadn't done much for those four years besides drink beer, play football, and screw cheerleaders, but there was this particular girl who was always trying to get him to read some silly-ass shit about rabbits or habits or something. Maybe he should have read the damn books. She was great in bed but she'd left him for some pussy English Lit major who, she said, was more romantic and cared for her as a person and really, really loved Tolkien, especially the habits, or whatever the hell they were.

Battle brushed annoyedly at some phalanges that were trying to slither up his pants leg. "Whatever they were," he said, "they're dead now."

"Look, we gotta get him up." The Outcast shook Croyd's body once again. Nothing happened. Croyd—looking like Andre the Giant in blue spiked armor—slumbered on. His feet were sticking several inches out from the bed; the spikes had torn holes in the sheet covering him. Several of the spikes terminated in puckered, fleshy mouths—perfect, the Outcast thought—for spitting poison or searing acid or something. This body was a war machine, he was certain of it. Unfortunately at the moment it was a sleeping war machine.

The penguin was skating around the Sleeper's bed. "We could always just throw him at them," it said.

Kafka stepped forward with a glistening hypodermic. "Epinephrine," he said. "Adrenaline. And other stuff. It's an upper cocktail." He jabbed the needle at Croyd's bicep; the needle broke off with a metallic *ting* and went spinning away. Kafka rummaged through the medical kit, muttering, and pulled out a much larger and thicker syringe.

Outside, through the fog, they could hear the continuing assault. The voices of the Rox hammered at the Outcast. The Outcast sent another wave of demons at the Jersey Gate troops; he rebuilt a fallen wall; he sent a messenger knight to Shroud telling him to send reinforcements to the north. He tried to pay attention to a dozen different sites at once. The effort was draining. He could barely see what was happening here in front of him.

Kafka managed to wedge the needle between two scales of Croyd's new skin and sunk the plunger home. They waited.

Croyd began to snore. The penguin giggled.

"Hey, Mr. Wizard! If you're through playing doctor, we could really use some help out here."

Modular Man sailed through the open window. He looked like he'd dodged a close hit—a long black scorch mark ran down one leg. "Where's Pulse?" he asked.

"In the infirmary," Bloat said. "With a glucose feed."

"Then I need you to make another gap in the causeway," Modular Man said. "Ahead of Snotman and Detroit Steel."

The Outcast glared down at the sleeping Croyd. He sighed. Then he tapped the end of his staff on the stone-flagged floor. The glow from the amethyst was very faint, but he could feel it happen. "Done," he said. "Concentrating your attack on Detroit Steel was a good move, by the way. You wounded him, did you know? The right leg and arm of the suit aren't working very well for him, and he's bleeding inside the suit. He's wondering whether they should retreat. Maybe a little more damage—"

"He's not the problem," Modular Man said. "Snotman is. We've got to work out a way to beat him without violence, without directing any energy at him."

"Hey, give His Largeness a break," the penguin said, skating around Modular Man's ankles. "He's a little buried in his work right now."

Modular Man seemed to consider that. "That'll do," he said. "I'll need plastic explosives, a manual, and detonators. And you'll need to evacuate the main gatehouse, because you're going to lose it."

The Turtle lurched sideways. Mistral's wind howled around the shell like a gale out of hell. He heard Danny say, *"Oh, shit!"* Her rifle went sailing end over end past his cameras as the wind ripped it out of her hands. She grabbed the shell with both hands. *"Help!"* she screamed. *"The netting . . ."*

Tom could hear it ripping loose.

He tilted the shell to shield Danny against the fury of the wind. Mistral was floating serenely above him, smiling like the queen of the hop. Tom tried to summon his teke, a cannonball, a fist, anything to knock the wind witch senseless, but it was impossible to concentrate. The gale was pushing him back and down; he had to shove back hard just to stay in the same place. Sweat trickled down his forehead.

Then the sound of an elephant's angry trumpeting cut through the roar of the wind. He saw the charge on his overhead screen as Elephant Girl came flapping up at Mistral.

Three tons of flying elephant does tend to get your attention. Mistral turned her attention on Radha, and suddenly the winds were gone. With nothing to push against, the Turtle bolted upward like a shot from a cannon. Danny shrieked as more of the safety net tore free.

Mistral grew larger on his screens. He reached out with a teleki-netic hand, wrapped phantom fingers tight around her. *I got her now,* Tom thought. Elephant Girl was closing too.

Mistral made a short, sharp gesture at Radha.

The hurricane smashed into the elephant full force. Three tons of solid gray flesh, and the winds slammed her aside like a Ping-Pong ball. Corporal Danny was swept off Radha's back. She flew past, her shout lost in the storm. Tom reached for her with his teke, Mistral forgotten. Then the elephant crashed into the shell, and Tom lost it.

The shell went end over end, a Frisbee in a hurricane. The safety harness dug into Tom's chest. Everything inside the cabin that wasn't tied down was flying through the air. Something bounced off the top of his head. Tom blinked, dazed. They were falling, plummeting like a iron parachute, still tumbling.

All he could think was, *I'm going to die.* The fog swallowed them again, his screens all going to gray. He was too dizzy to care. Every muscle in his body went tight with fear as he imagined the water coming up to smash them. Then he heard Danny screaming.

Somehow Tom made himself close his eyes, take a deep breath, and *push.* The shell jerked to a sudden stop, hung wobbling in the air.

The world around them was an ocean of yellow-gray. There was no ground, no sky. *"Danny,"* he whispered breathlessly.

"Still here," she said. He found her then, clinging tight to the safety netting. Two corners had torn away.

"Your sister . . ." he said, remembering.

". . . okay . . . chute's open . . ." Her voice was ragged. Tom glimpsed motion in the fog overhead. His fingers tightened on the armrests as he tried to ready himself for Mistral, for more demons, for whatever the fuck was coming at him.

Elephant Girl came gliding out of the mists, searching. She blew a short note on her trunk when she saw them. Tom thought it sounded relieved. Radha was in bad shape. Her wounds wept blood. One eye had swollen shut, and the right side of her head was a massive bruise. Tom didn't know how she'd managed to stay conscious, but it was a damn good thing she had.

"RADHA," he said through his speakers. "I"M GOING TO MOVE DANNY OVER TO YOU. HEAD FOR THE JOKERTOWN CLINIC."

"What about you?" Danny said.

"I'VE GOT A SCORE TO SETTLE WITH MISTRAL," Tom said.

"She'll kill you," Danny said. Radha trumpeted agreement.

"I CAN TAKE HER," Tom insisted. "SOMEBODY'S GOT TO DO IT."

"No," Danny said. "We did our job. Leave it be for now."

Tom frowned. "What do you mean, we did our job?"

Danny hesitated a moment. "They never expected us to win, Turtle. We were only a diversion. And it worked. The covert team is inside the Rox, undetected."

"The *covert* team?" He was confused. Then, when he realized what she was saying, the anger took over. "Son of a fucking *bitch!*" he swore.

"Turtle, please. My shoulder hurts. Take me back. I don't want Mistral to kill you." She patted the top of his shell. "You don't have any extra bodies either, I bet."

Tom's head was throbbing. He felt inutterably weary, betrayed, heartsick. All of a sudden, he found he just didn't care anymore. "YOU WIN," he told them. "WE GO BACK."

The shell slid through the fog, toward the northeast and safety. The elephant flapped wearily beside him. No one spoke, all the way back.

◆

A quick flyover showed that Snotman and Detroit Steel were still stopped at the second gap. Snotman had propped the armored man against the bridge rail, and the giant was kicking him over and over again.

Still charging him up. At least it was taking longer.

Jokers were still evacuating the main gate. The android flew through it, absorbing the details of its architecture.

All the energy of the explosions would have to be directed outward. Fortunately there were plenty of sandbags lying around that had been used to help shore up the fortifications, and the android had memorized the explosive manual on the first read-through. Modular Man set charges against the main structural members of the gatehouse, then piled sandbags around them to absorb any energy directed inward.

Snotman and Detroit Steel appeared before he was quite finished, coming down the roadway to the crossroads where the four bridges to the Rox came together. Detroit Steel was being carried on the ace's back, and the giant punched Snotman over and over with his working arm, feeding him energy. The two hesitated on the far side of the drawbridge, Snotman obviously hoping someone would start shooting at him. No one did.

What's keeping him going? Modular Man wondered. Any sensible person would have quit by now, alone in enemy territory with no support and a wounded man. Was Snotman's hatred that strong? Or was he thinking at all?

Maybe he just thought he was invincible.

Modular Man thought he might just have to concede that point.

Detroit Steel punched again and again. Modular Man strung wires.

Snotman held out a hand, pointed. A burst of energy blew away one of the two chains holding up the drawbridge.

Good, Modular Man thought. Keep using that energy.

Another shot hit the other chain, but the hard steel held. More punches and a third shot were required before the drawbridge boomed down.

The portcullis was blown away with a series of shots that put a man-sized hole in it. Modular Man flew back into the outer bailey from the gatehouse roof, trailing wire behind him. Anxiety flickered through him as he peered anxiously at the gatehouse tunnel.

The silhouette of Snotman, carrying Detroit Steel, appeared in the tunnel, and Modular Man pushed the detonator.

The walls of the gatehouse blew outward, and through the gouting flame and dust and flying rubble, the android could see the roof and upper stories falling downward.

He withdrew to the roof of the gatehouse leading to the middle bailey. The cloud of dust rolled over him.

When it cleared he'd know whether he was a shooter or a shootee.

What he hoped he'd done was to envelop Snotman in tons of mattresses—stone mattresses. If the idea worked, Snotman would have absorbed, from the rock falling on him, less energy than he would need to dig himself out.

The dust slowly settled. A few Bosch creatures flew tentatively overhead. The revealed gatehouse was a sloped pile of rubble sitting between scarred walls.

Nothing moved.

Modular Man waited until he was certain that Snotman and Detroit Steel were well and truly buried, then he flew out over the causeway again until he found Danny Shepherd.

She was watching while some army engineers were trying to drop bridging equipment over the first gap in the causeway. Nervous marines crouched over their weapons in the roadway behind.

Modular Man dropped from the sky, snatched up the young woman, and lurched up into the sky. She kicked and yelled. Marines stared, pointed weapons, disappeared into the mist below.

"Stop fighting," the android said. "I'm here to tell you something."

Danny struggled for another few seconds, then gave up. "Okay," she said.

"Snotman and Detroit Steel failed," he said. "You need to tell Zappa to evacuate his people from the perimeter and the causeway."

"Bullshit."

"If they don't leave," Modular Man lied, "Governor Bloat is going to turn all their weapons and armor into very large monsters. Then he'll unleash another wave of hell creatures and everyone will die."

Danny thought about that. Wind blew her blond hair around her face.

"I'm not really on their side," Modular Man said. "I'm being compelled to do this."

"No one's going to believe that."

"If I were on their side, you'd be dead. And all those soldiers on the causeway."

He spiraled downward until Liberty Park stretched below them. He dropped Danny onto the scorched green grass and took off before anyone could respond.

Below him, the shootees lay unmoving.

The Outcast—no, the entire Rox, the whole massed chorus of head-voices—thought that it was over. The Turtle had retreated from the Manhattan Gate; Elephant Girl had moved off into the fog away from the Rox; Modular Man had won the battle of the Jersey Gate, burying Detroit Steel and Snotman and leaving behind scores of dead both from the Rox and the nats. Teddy had fought too, directing the battalions of the demons; trying to keep them between the jokers and the nats; throwing his mind-creatures in suicidal attacks at the strength of the assault; listening to the head-voices of his people and responding, trying his best to be in twenty places at once.

The retreat had happened suddenly, the order relayed through someone—someone plural? the mindvoices weren't clear on that point—called Danny. All the attacking forces had all moved back into the shroud of fog, away from the wounded and broken ramparts of the Wall and out of the Outcast's hearing.

"Oh, thank God," Kafka said. His body shivered with a faint rattling. His walkie-talkie sputtered static-ridden words. "Governor, they're gone. Everywhere. They've left."

"Maybe . . ." Teddy whispered to Kafka wearily. From his vantage point in Croyd's room, he surveyed the broken buildings around them, the tumbling walls of brick and the shattered timber supports. Only the great crystalline ramparts of the castle were still standing, untouched—he had repaired them even as the glass had crumpled under the impact of the barrage. Around the Rox, jokers and jumpers alike were coming from shelter. In the foggy landscape below him, there was a mass exodus outward from the caverns. "I'm going out to see," he told Kafka and the penguin. "Keep trying to wake him up."

Teddy slammed the end of the staff on the ground and willed himself to be at the Jersey Gate, but the expected transition was strange. The insistent, angry voices of the dreamtime shouted at him, and the fragile connections of power were hard to hold on to. He tried to pull in the energy, but his mind was exhausted. For a moment his vision cleared and he found himself looking down at the Great Hall of the castle, bound down with the immense weight of Bloat. Big Bird, one of the joker guards, noticed him immediately.

"Governor," she said, her feathered face contorted with concern. Plaster dust shaken from the roof by the impact of bombs coated her high shoulders and a three-fingered, clawed hand was clenching and unclenching the grip of her AK-47 nervously. There were dead jokers here, five of them that he could see, still lying on the tiles of the Great Hall. The sight made Teddy ill; bloatblack spilled out in response.

The burden was almost too much. It would have been easy to remain in Bloat's body. Teddy struggled, trying to find the power within him to leave Bloat once again. The voices of the dreamtime yammered and howled, angry at his continuing intrusion.

Wyungare gave you our offer. Leave us alone.

You will die, powerful fool. You will die and you will take us down with you. You don't know what you're doing.

"Shut up!" Bloat shouted back.

"Governor?" Big Bird said.

Bloat tried to smile at the joker. "Nothing. It's nothing. Just some ghosts in my head."

Teddy closed his eyes, searching for the dreams, searching for the path to the dreamtime's power and finding them. *There, the channels are there, running through Bloat and away* . . . Teddy followed the path back, back, until he could feel the wind of the dreamtime tousling his hair. Bright forms of energy were spiraling in front of him, and they blocked the path, damming the flow. "Get away," Teddy told them.

"You throw your weapons at us," they cried. "You send us your demons; you create chaos, you drain our power. We can't allow this."

"You can't stop it."

One of the forms came closer; he recognized the leering face of Viracocha as the shaman or godling or whatever he was snorted. "You delude yourself. You're weary. The power will burn you and scar you forever if you continue."

"Tired or not, *you're* not strong enough to stop me," Teddy said. "Wyungare told me that." He pursed his lips, blowing against the wind from his dream, and the energy forms screamed and cried as they fell away. The path was open once more. He could feel the energy, brilliant and invigorating, and he took it into himself, wrapping himself once more in the body of the Outcast.

The Outcast materialized himself on the ramparts of the Jersey Gate. The demons clustered around their master like bats wheeling about a cave mouth; the jokers looked at him expectantly. The damage here was far worse than on Ellis itself. His Wall had been breached, the massive gates facing the city had been torn from their hinges by the brute force of Snotman and Detroit Steel. Most of the gun emplacements were gone, the stones where they had been blackened and broken, and what Teddy saw there sickened him. Death was not pretty—even the swirling, diffuse view through the fog couldn't soften it. There was a smell too: a sickly, sweet odor that made his stomach turn over. He brought a wind to take it away from the Rox, streamers of low gray clouds riding the gale-outward.

The wounded were the worst because he could do nothing for them. The damage to the Wall he could fix—the Wall was only an image taken from his mind and made real with Bloat's gift. But the jokers were real. Though he tried, he couldn't close the wounds, knit the bones, or graft new skin over the burns. They moaned, they screamed, they clutched themselves. Their pain and terror brought tears to Teddy's eyes. *Your fault. This is your fault* . . . He couldn't tell where the words came from, but they clamored in his head. Teddy blinked away the tears, not caring that any of the others saw his weakness. He walked along the rim of the Wall, and with each of the worst of the wounded, he stole a bit of the power and sent them back to the island, to the emergency clinic that Kafka had hurriedly set up.

It was all he could do.

"You'll be fine," he told them, though he was sure most of them would die.

He came to the ruins of the main gatehouse. Modular Man was still there, watching the rubble carefully. Shroud came up from the joker brigade with the android. "Governor," he said. "It was a little bit of hell here. The demons helped, but there were a lot of nats, and the aces . . . Modular Man . . ."

"I know."

"Hope you have a good insurance policy," Modular Man said.

"We're okay." Teddy said it loudly, so that all of them could hear. "You hear me? We're okay. We still have our big guns: Modular Man here, Dylan, Pulse's body, most of the jumpers. We're still trying to wake up Croyd . . ." Teddy found that he was getting tired of the litany himself.

"*Is it over?*" Shroud asked. "Are you sure, Governor?"

Teddy listened to the head-voices, sorting out the jokers and jumpers and trying to find anyone who didn't belong. It was easy to close his eyes. Very, very easy. There *were* two intruding voices in the chorus of the Rox. Two voices: both in agony, both rambling and confused. Below.

"They're still alive," he said.

"Won't be for long, I'll bet," Shroud answered. "Can't be much air down in that mess."

The Outcast listened again. Detroit Steel—no, Mike was his name—was dying as Teddy listened, suffocating to death in his broken suit of armor. Snotman was pinned down, furious, with only enough energy to keep the enormous weight of concrete and stone from crushing him, and that ebbing with each moment. Shroud was right. They would die. Slowly. Horribly.

While he listened.

"Get them out," he said to Modular Man.

"Hey, wait a minute, Governor," Shroud protested, pulling at the Outcast's cloak. "We just lost a lot of our people taking out these two bastards. And you want to dig 'em up again?" Around him, other jokers shouted agreement. "Let the fuckers die," they said. "They're getting what they deserve. Bury the mothers."

Mikey . . . got get out 'cause the kid can't take care of himself . . . he needs me . . . God don't let me die like this all alone . . .

"Dig them up," Teddy said again.

"Governor, are you crazy?"

The Outcast whirled around to face Shroud, and the joker drew back at the fury on Teddy's face. "We *won*," he told the jokers gathered around him. "We won and this time we're going to ask for everything we need and we won't settle for less. We're going to shove this defeat down their throats. We're going to make them pay for every joker who lost a life, for every drop of blood. I promise you that." He paused. "But we gotta have some compassion. We gotta have some humanity. I won't have *anyone* die like this, not when it doesn't have to happen."

He heard the thought, heard it from several of them in a dozen variations. *The governor's gone soft. He's scared and he's lost his edge.* Teddy even wondered if they were right. Maybe he *should* let them die. Maybe it made more sense. It just didn't feel right. He didn't want to have to hear their dying thoughts, didn't know if he could bear the guilt. *The governor's gone soft . . .*

But none of the jokers said the thought aloud.

"Governor, there *is* a certain problem with Snotman . . ." Modular Man interjected.

"I know that. You think I'm stupid?" Teddy took a deep breath, calming himself. "Get Detroit Steel out first. He's not a problem—without the suit he's just a guy. Then start on Snotman. Take your time and be careful when you dig him up. I've been listening to him. He's exhausted now and doesn't have much strength left. Don't touch him: uncover the feet and bind them, then the arms. Tie him up; don't let anyone hit him or shoot him or harm him in any way. Don't, for God's sake, drop him. Just take him to the Iron Keep and throw—no, gently place—him in a cell by the others. Just keep him bound and alone so he can't run against the walls or have someone else hit him."

The Outcast looked at all of them, the sullen joker faces. "Dig them up," he said again. "I want you all to help."

He waited, wondering what he'd do if they refused. Obedient as he had to be, Modular Man had already gone to the mounded wreckage and begun levering away slabs of concrete. Slowly, Shroud turned and went to help the android, the others following.

Teddy, exhausted, felt his body dissolve.

The dungeon was damp and cold, and the blackness had a weight of its own. The bodysnatcher carried a torch to light his way down the narrow, twisting steps.

The girl was slumped against the wall in the back of her cell. There was straw in her hair. She lifted her head slowly, blinking at the light of the torch. After so much darkness, it must have been hard to bear. Her tears had left tracks through the dirt on her face. She stared up at the bodysnatcher with eyes gone numb and dead. Then somehow she recognized him. "Pulse?" Her voice was hoarse and raw. She got unsteadily to her feet, leaning on the wall. "Pulse, help me, please . . ." She moved toward the bars.

"You should take better care of that meat," the bodysnatcher told her. "Molly will be wanting it back. She's sentimental like that."

The girl in Molly Bolt's body shrank back, suddenly afraid. "Oh, God," she said. "You too."

"Your daddy's dead," the bodysnatcher said. "Molly did him real nice. Smashed him like a fat blue bug. You should have been there. But then, you *were,* weren't you?"

The girl just looked at him for a long moment, as if she couldn't understand what he was saying. Then she started to scream. The bodysnatcher smiled and walked away.

Way down at the far end of the dungeon, he felt eyes watching as he passed. The bodysnatcher stopped and peered into the last cell, where a slender, half-naked black man sat cross-legged on the floor. "Your turn is coming," he promised.

"Excellent," Wyungare replied. "I thought room service had forgotten about me. There's been no shortage of roaches, but they're a poor substitute for witchitty grubs."

"That's straw you're sitting on," the bodysnatcher told him. "What do you suppose would happen if I tossed the torch onto that nice dry straw?"

"You would stumble in the darkness on your way out, and be forced to grope your way up the stairs," Wyungare pointed out.

His calm pissed the bodysnatcher off no end. "You'd *burn* to death, you stupid nigger!"

Wyungare shrugged. "That too," he admitted.

The bodysnatcher was thinking about going to his lightform and burning a hole through the abo's face when he heard a deep rumble far above, and the dungeon shuddered under his feet. He almost dropped the torch. "What was that?" he said, startled.

"The beginning of the end," Wyungare told him.

The second explosion was much louder. An instant later, the shock wave shook the Rox like a bowl of stone Jell-O. The bodysnatcher lost his footing, stumbled to one knee.

The bodysnatcher left the Aborigine there to die in the darkness, and sprinted for the light. He ran up the steps. By the time he reached the surface, he was breathing hard.

The afternoon was dark as midnight. Screams, shouts, and moans of pain echoed through the fog. Acrid smoke burned his eyes. Someone was whistling, a high shrill sound like a teakettle starting to boil. The towers of the Rox were outlined dimly against the flickering reddish light of some huge fire on the far side of the island. The whistling grew louder, became a scream that filled the world. He saw the tall shadow of the jumpers' tower turn to light. Then it was gone, while the night rained stone and fire.

Battle turned to Danny. "How's the frontal assault progressing?"

She stared into space, rubbing her injured shoulder and listening to private voices whispering in her ears. "Not so good. They've been beaten back for now."

Battle snorted. "Wimps," he said. "Let's go."

As Battle strode off Danny grabbed Ray by the arm and surreptitiously held him back. "Doesn't this underground playground strike you as odd?" she asked him.

Ray shrugged. "Bloat's crazy."

"Yeah, maybe. But he's not irrational. He's been doing a good job at holding off the frontal assault. Also"—she gestured around herself—"someone who was really insane couldn't have built all this. It's too well designed."

They started after the others. "I see what you mean," Ray said. "But so what?"

"All these traps," she said. "All these obstacles he's put in our path. Sure, some were pretty dangerous, but none were out and out deadly. It's all like some big game with him."

"Game," Ray repeated. That word struck a chord, but just why he couldn't say. "Game . . ." he said thoughtfully, then he stopped, staring.

Tacked to a stalagmite near the end of the chamber was a T-shirt similar in design to the one the old bridge-keeper had been wearing. Only this one bore the legend BLOAT FLOATS around the smiling Bloathead silk-screened on it.

"Hey," Ray called out, "wait a minute, everyone."

The others hadn't seen the T-shirt. They'd gone past it, almost reaching the door set in the chamber's wall. They stopped, turned, and looked at Ray as he shouted.

"Look at this," Ray said, gesturing at the shirt.

As he did, the Bloat-image winked at him. "Bloat floats," the image said. "Do you?"

There was a grinding hum of machinery set in motion, and the floor of the chamber started to move and tilt. Ray grabbed a stalagmite and then grabbed Danny's waist as she slipped past him, pulling her to him.

Battle let out a wild yell. Puckett grabbed his boss by the arm and grabbed Boyd around the waist and waited stoically until he slid toward another stalagmite that he managed to hook a foot around.

Ray smelled salt water as the floor continued to rumble and tilt. "It's a water trap," he shouted, "opening into the bay!"

Nemo bellowed in fear and flung himself flat, desperately reaching for a stalagmite, but his clawing fingers missed by inches. Ray tensed, thinking about leaping after him, but Danny said softly, "There's nothing you can do."

They all watched, horrified, as Nemo, roaring and fighting for nonexistent purchase on the slippery chamber floor, slid inexorably toward the span of open water.

As he hit the water Ray shouted, "Swim for the other side."

Nemo bobbed up and down, arms waving frantically over his head. *"I can't swim!"* he shouted in an agonized voice, and then he was gone, the water closing sullenly over his head.

"Christ," Ray muttered.

There was a moment's silence; then the water split apart and something big and long heaved itself onto the level area of floor on the opposite side of the water trap. It was a fourteen-foot-long alligator, with a blue plastic hospital bracelet around its right front foreleg. Ray forgot the horror of the moment in sheer astonishment as it disappeared down the corridor on the trap's opposite side.

Ray stared after it, hardly aware of the slim, hard-muscled body he held tightly against his own.

"Third time lucky," Danny said to him. One of her slim, strong hands snaked up around his neck and pulled his face down to hers. Their lips touched; then she pulled away.

"Dead end, goddamn it," Battle roared. "Goddamn dead end.

There's no way across this damn moat. Ray! Throw us a line and haul us the hell out of here! We'll have to retrace our steps and hope the other corridor leads to that fat fuck's throne room. Damn!"

Ray reached for his pack and the rope coiled in it, all the while staring at Danny. Once again, she had that internalized expression on her face, but Ray could think only of her sudden kiss, and the promise of more to come.

SATURDAY AFTERNOON

September 22, 1990

HE WAITED INSIDE HIS shell on the roof of the Jokertown Clinic, as he had waited a thousand times before.

Most of his screens were turned to commercial stations. WOR was broadcasting a Dodger road game. They were losing to the Seals out in San Francisco, 8–0 in the second. WPIX had *Wheel of Fortune*. But the networks were all news, and all the news was bad. What had von Hagendaas called it? The most powerful ace task force ever assembled . . . and the Rox had flushed them away like toilet paper.

Mistral, jumped. Pulse, jumped. Cyclone, believed dead. Detroit Steel and Snotman, buried under tons of rubble, believed dead. Elephant Girl, wounded, maybe mortally. And the Great and Powerful Turtle . . .

Tom laughed bitterly. The sound echoed dully in the close confines of the shell. His head was pounding, and one side of his face was stiff with dried blood where he'd smashed it during his tumble. Some heroes they'd turned out to be.

The military had resumed its shelling of the Rox. On CNN, Peter Arnett was broadcasting from the *New Jersey*, out in the Atlantic beyond Cape May. The decks were frantic with activity as the great battlewagon prepared to open up with its sixteen-inch guns. The open mouths of the huge turret guns loomed behind Arnett, vast as caves. Tom was looking at them, and feeling sorry for the poor doomed jokers on the Rox, when Danny Shepherd finally returned. Finn was with her, the little palomino-pony centaur who had been running the clinic since Tachyon left.

Danny's shoulder had been cleaned and bandaged; "LEGION," Tom said in a flat, stiff voice.

She ignored the ice in his tone. "I'm going to live," she announced cheerfully. "Lucky it wasn't my pitching arm."

Tom spoke to Finn. "WHAT ABOUT RADHA?"

The centaur fiddled with his stethoscope. "She's resting comfortably," he said. "We've sent to the zoo for a specialist. She'll have to stay an elephant for a while. Those wounds would be mortal in a human." The joker doctor shuffled his hooves. "Our nutritionist is having kittens. Know anyplace we can get a deal on hay?"

Tom had no answer for him. The silence hung in the air.

"My, ah, sister's okay," Danny said. "The winds pushed me clear of the Wall, thank God. Another me went out with the Coast Guard cutter, so they had no trouble picking me up, even in the fog. I'm back on Governor's Island now."

"GOOD FOR YOU," Tom told her.

"Speaking of which," said Finn, "we've had a visit from your army friends. A major. He's upset that you folks came here. It seems they have a military hospital set up on Governor's Island. All the wounded were supposed to be taken there. He wants to transfer Miss O'Reilly."

That was gasoline on Tom's smoldering fires. "TELL THE MAJOR TO FUCK OFF," he suggested. He wasn't about to trust a bunch of army doctors when the Jokertown Clinic had been dealing with the unique medical problems of aces and jokers for decades.

"I did," Finn said. "More politely, of course."

Danny cleared her throat. "Von Herzenhagen phoned. He wants us back at Ebbets A.S.A.P."

Tom zoomed in on her face. She was so pretty. And right now he just wanted to grab her and shake her. "COVERT TEAM NEED ANOTHER DIVERSION? TELL HIM I DECLINE. ONE SUICIDE MISSION PER DAY, THAT'S MY LIMIT."

This time the anger in his voice was unmistakable. Danny chewed on her lower lip thoughtfully, then turned to Finn. "Dr. Finn, would you mind? Turtle and I need to talk."

Finn didn't mind; there were always patients to attend to. After he had trotted back inside, Danny turned and looked straight into a camera. "What's going on?" she asked.

Tom lowered the volume on his speakers, then found he had nothing to say to her.

"I don't deserve this," Danny said. "Friends don't—"

Tom interrupted. "Friends don't lie to each other. You knew about this covert team bullshit all along."

She didn't deny it. "I'm the link. I had to know. One of me is with them. They're down in the catacombs right now. Black Shadow's been hurt, and Popinjay really isn't—"

Tom didn't give a fuck about any of that. "You *knew* we were only a diversion, and you didn't say a fucking word."

This time Danny flared right back at him. "I had *orders*! I'm in the goddamn army; one of me is anyway; they can shoot you if you disobey a direct order."

"I'm glad you're a good little soldier," Tom said. "But do me a favor, don't talk to me about friendship."

"What the hell would *you* have done?"

"I would have told my friends the truth," Tom snapped back. "You think we would have played it the same way if we had known we were just a fucking *diversion?*"

"If you would have known, Bloat would have known the minute you passed the Wall," Danny argued. "That would have compromised the whole—"

"*Compromised?*" Tom said. "You even talk like them. Well, fine. You kept your little secret, and we all went in there like it meant something. Nothing got compromised but our lives. Cyclone probably died thinking he was doing something real."

"He *was*. And he knew the job was dangerous when he took it. We *all* did."

"I killed God knows how many people at the gate," Tom said flatly. "For nothing. For a diversion. And you let me."

Her face filled his big screen. She was so pretty; it broke his heart. Tom could see tears in her eyes as she struggled for words. "I don't . . . I didn't mean . . ."

He snapped shut his shoulder harness, pushed off. The shell drifted clear of the roof. Danny looked up at him, stricken. "Turtle . . . don't . . . where are you going?"

His shadow darkened her features, turned her eyes into deep black pools. Her ponytail was moving in the wind. He tried to answer, and the words caught in his throat. He pushed himself away from her with an effort, out over the street, across the rooftops of Jokertown. But long after the clinic was out of sight, he could feel the weight of her eyes.

◆

"These MREs really suck," Danny said, sticking a fork disgustedly in a congealed mass of chicken á la king.

"I know," Ray said. He shucked off his backpack and rummaged in it for a moment, finally coming up with a foil-wrapped package. "That's why I usually carry my own rations. Try one of these."

He handed it to Danny, who unwrapped it, sniffed, and smiled. "Pastrami on rye," she said. "I shouldn't. It's not exactly on my diet."

"You don't look like you have to worry much about your diet."

"Of course I do." She flexed a bicep. The muscles stood out like clearly defined metal cable wrapped in their veins and arteries. "The Ms. Tri-State contest is in two weeks. I've got to keep up the definition."

"You're plenty defined," Ray said with as much gallantry as he could muster. "Besides, you can worry about that in two weeks. For now you have to eat to keep your strength up."

"I suppose you're right," Danny said.

"I have some health food too." Ray took an apple out of his pack, cut it in half with a nasty-looking dagger he took from an ankle sheath, and handed a piece to Danny.

"Thanks," she said, and the ground suddenly shook like a giant had rolled over in his sleep.

"Earthquake!" Ray shouted, doing a little dance to keep his balance as the floor shifted under him.

Battle, leaning against a stalagmite a few feet away, slipped, fell, and rolled around like a man with pants full of ants.

"It's not a quake," Danny said. She managed to brace herself in the angle between the chamber's wall and floor. "They're shelling Ellis from the battleship *New Jersey*. Brace yourselves! Here comes another shell!"

Battle wiped blood off his face and felt his nose gingerly where it'd been smashed against the floor. "Finish your rations and let's get going. We can't lollygag all day. We have a mission to accomplish. Corporal Shepherd can let us know when another shell is approaching so we can brace ourselves in time."

Ray sketched an ironic salute and helped Shepherd to her feet. "You have another sister on the *New Jersey*?"

She nodded.

"How many of you are there?"

"Seven," she said.

Seven, Ray thought. The mind boggles.

"Hold on," Danny warned.

Okay, Ray thought, and grabbed her around the waist and anchored himself to a nearby stalagmite. She didn't seem to mind.

Wyungare was brought abruptly back to the Tya world, the earth, by the sound of agitated voices. He entered the consciousness of being confined in the rude stone cell with a recognition of the harsh, familiar voice of Kafka.

The jailer smashed his keyring against the bars of the woman's cell a few meters away. "Hey!" he said. "No pets, lady. House policy." He looked closer into the shadows. "Okay, kitty, we wondered where you disappeared to." He selected a key and started to insert it in the lock. "Time to hit that big sandbox in the sky."

The black cat hissed like a steam boiler hitting critical and swiped out with his right forepaw. The curved, needle-sharp claws flashed. Plated hide or not, Kafka jerked back. "All right," he said. "Chill out. You like it here? Fine. I've got better things to do than argue."

With his other hand, he held a chain looped through two prisoners' manacles. The new arrivals were two men. Kafka pulled them along toward the cells beyond Wyungare's own place of confinement. The bigger prisoner moved slowly. Bruises were evident on his brawny arms. The other man was bound hand and foot, carried along by two jokers.

"Welcome," the Aborigine said to them. "The name is Wyungare."

All three in the hall stared back at him. "Mike," said the big prisoner, aiming a thumb at his own chest. He grinned a little crookedly. He ran the fingers of his free hand through his close-cropped blond hair. "You maybe heard of me as Detroit Steel. Right now I feel a little underdressed."

Wyungare smiled back. The other prisoner, another European but built shorter and more compactly, nodded slightly. "This here's good old Snotman," said Kafka.

The brown-haired man's teeth drew back in a snarl. "It's *Reflector*," he said. "Goddamn it, Orkin-bait, you can at least call me by my right name."

"Your right name's for shit, dipstick," said Kafka. He swung open a cell door. The tarnished steel shrieked. He keyed Detroit Steel's cuffs and motioned the big man inside. Kafka put Reflector in the adjacent cell.

The brown-haired man abruptly smacked his head hard against one of the doorframe posts. Again. A third time.

Kafka shook his head in disgust. "Don't bother," he said to the man called Reflector. "Your skull'll give out long before you're recharged."

"Enough," said Kafka. "I gotta get back up topside. All of you just thank your lucky stars you're not outside in the line of fire. This is maybe the safest place on the Rox."

"Swell," said Detroit Steel, "we'll try and be properly grateful for the hospitality."

The woman prisoner began to weep, keeping her sobs low and strangled in her throat.

"What's with her?" asked Snotman.

"Problems with her old man," said Kafka. The woman's weeping escalated to a virtual wail. Wyungare looked from her to Kafka and then back to the woman. "Don't you recognize Mistral?" said the jailer. "I admit, she's had a real bad day."

"Haven't we all?" said Wyungare.

Kafka shrugged, smiled after his fashion, and left. At the door at the end of the hall, he turned and called back, "No fraternizing, you four. This ain't no day camp." He left, locking the door after him.

After what seemed a suitably decorous time to Wyungare, not to mention safe, he said to his fellows, "Let's continue with introductions. Consider it an inventorying of resources."

They all heard the sob from Mistral's cell. They also heard the black cat's loud purr as he tucked himself against the woman's crouched body.

"Ain't no resource left there," said Detroit Steel, voice sounding more concerned than his words suggested.

"Don't be too sure," said Wyungare. "Look a little deeper."

The old man stood on a rolling, endless prairie. Grazing buffalo covered the hills just behind him like a black, restless blanket. The smell of them was strong on the breeze, as dark as the creatures themselves and as earthy. The ancient one held his hands out—of the fingers, only the first two on his right hand were whole. There was at least one joint missing on each of the others, the flesh puckered and scarred around ancient wounds. Ancient, that is, except one: the second joint of the man's little finger was a fresh cut, the joint amputated only minutes ago. The coagulating blood was still bright and wet, and a leather thong was strung tightly around the base of the finger as a tourniquet.

"I am One Blue Bead," the old man said, and though he spoke in his own language, Teddy could understand it.

"Look, I really can't stay here," Teddy said. "I gotta go. I gotta go right now. They're bombing my Rox."

One Blue Bead smiled, gap-toothed. "Time doesn't matter here. You should know that. Because you don't, I name you Eyes Looking Backward."

"Name me Sally. I don't really fucking care. Just let me out of this fairyland." Teddy concentrated on the Rox; as he did so, the landscape wavered around him. As if through a stage shim, he thought he glimpsed the ramparts of the Wall and the tumbled-down Manhattan Gate behind the prairie and hills.

No. The Rox was gone again. A compelling weariness hit Teddy, like he'd just done a set of pull-ups. His body sagged. *Just wait a minute, then try it again.*

One Blue Bead just continued to smile. "You are as impetuous and as ignorant as they have said. And as powerful. But I offered a finger joint to Wakan-Tanka to bring you here. My flesh holds you, at least for now."

"You're killing people then. The shelling—"

"Time does not move here as it does in your shadow world. To them, you will be gone but an instant." The man smiled again.

"The last one who brought me here tried to kill me."

"Viracocha. I know. I have spoken with him about that, as I've spoken to Wyungare. I might try to kill you also, later. But not now."

"What, then?"

Furrows deepened around the eyes and mouth, deep sun-baked canyons. "I wanted to see you. I wanted to see the face of the one who hurts *my* people. I wanted to see if it was the face of an enemy."

One Blue Bead reached out with a mutilated hand, stretching it toward Teddy's face. Teddy froze, enduring the callused touch on his cheeks, blinking as the hand strayed near his eyes. One Blue Bead's cobwebbed eyes stared, his breath smelled of herbs and fire and decay. At last the man drew back.

"You are just a fat little boy," One Blue Bead said. "Not a shaman. Wyungare is wasting his time with you."

"I'm a fucking joker, asshole. Or don't you have jokers here in fantasyland?"

"We have nothing here that doesn't wish to be here," One Blue Bead replied.

"*I'm* here."

The sarcasm seemed wasted on the shaman. "True. And you sent the screaming birds of shining stone, the ones whose wings were flame and who plucked the children from the huts and ate them before the eyes of their mothers."

"Excuse me?"

"In your world they may have looked much different, but you opened the way for them." One Blue Bead shook his head. "Boy, don't you know or care what you do here? Look at the herd." One Blue Bead gestured at the distant buffalo. "A short time ago they would have hidden the hills entirely. They have sickened because the power of their souls are being stolen from them. The Eagle spirit flew here, but now he hides in his high nest because he is weary. Even the trickster Coyote stays in his lair."

"Look, don't you understand? I'm just using what the wild card gave me."

"Using is not understanding. Listen: in the tales of my people, the first humans were poor and naked and knew very little. So the Old Man who had made them came and showed them which roots and berries they could eat and which they could use for medicine. He showed them how to make hunting weapons and how to kill and slaughter the buffalo, how to make fire to cook the flesh. He also told them that if they wished to have the power of magic, they must sleep. Old Man whispered that a spirit would come to them in their dreams, in the form of an animal. He said that they must do whatever that animal tells them to do. That is how the first people got into the world, boy, through the power of their dreams. Tell me, Eyes Looking Backward, do you listen to your dreams?"

"I don't listen to skating penguins with stupid hats, and I don't listen to dreams. I *make* them."

One Blue Bead scowled at the defiance. The gesture seemed to dissolve the hold that One Blue Bead had on Teddy. He felt a renewal of the link to Bloat and pulled at the delicate connections. The power filled him and he brought it forth. The prairie faded, the buffalo became the stones of Bloat's Wall and the clouds the fog of the Rox.

One Blue Bead remained, standing on the stones at the summit of the Wall. Teddy could see jokers all around them, frozen into stances of fright and horror. Shroud was there, pointing at the Outcast and the old Indian with his mouth open in soundless surprise. "You fail the test," One Blue Bead said. "Again. How many chances do you think we can give you?"

"And I was always such a good student too," Teddy told him.

The shaman's face fell into expressionless folds. He spread his truncated, bloody hand, and the world jolted back into motion around the Outcast. Gargoyle sirens were wailing: like a hundred coyotes baying, like the film Teddy had seen of the Howler trumpeting down the walls of the Cloisters. Teddy could sense Bodysnatcher flashing by overhead, his mindvoice far too fast and high for Teddy to understand any of the words, and then Pulse's body was past the Wall and silent, heading out over the bay. A wind parted the fog for a moment: Modular Man, flying outward himself.

"—ernor!" Shroud shouted. "What's going on?"

"A lot of dying," Teddy grated out. He could still smell the prairie and the ripeness of the buffalo. The power emanating from the body of Bloat was like a stream in a drought, a bare trickle. "Let me listen, would you?"

I am so tired . . . I don't know how much I've got left . . .

Something shrieked overhead, tearing the fog. There was a brilliant explosion behind them: tracers of white and acetylene blue. The sound followed a second later, a concussive wave that staggered the Outcast's body. In Teddy's head, voices screamed in terror and pain. More banshee wails followed: the Wall shook from the multiple impacts, the thunder of the shells was deafening, and a grotesque yellow glare illuminated the fog, fading to a persistent orange.

Governor!

I just want to leave want to leave go HOME . . .

Another shell; this one Teddy saw clearly in a rift in the fog, and he lifted his staff. Energy leapt from the crystal to the sky; the shell canted sharply right and plunged into the gray nothingness beyond the Wall. Waves crashed into the base of the stones a few seconds later. "Damn you!" Teddy shouted, and his rage was echoed in the mindvoices of the Rox. "Damn you all! Can't you leave us alone?"

He had very little left. Already the Outcast was beginning to fade. He was going back to Bloat and then he'd be able to do nothing. Nothing at all. The shells would come and destroy the Rox. Already the Wall was fading from his sight.

"Damn you!" he said again, and he spoke in the voice of Bloat.

Joker guards looked at him in mingled sympathy and fright. Outside the transparent bulwarks of the castle, the fog was tinged with the hues of hell.

"Stop it! You're killing us!" Bloat wailed.

As if in response, a series of long, distant, rumbling bass reverberations trembled the Rox from far out beyond the Wall.

Modular Man ghosted just above the waves with Mistral/Molly at his side. He knew he was going to be taking on an entire naval task force and he wished Mistral could both fly faster and make a less conspicuous target.

His radar caught another salvo in flight. Nine shells, he counted, a full broadside from the *New Jersey,* instead of the ranging shots fired earlier. They'd found the range.

That didn't necessarily mean that every shot would hit, but on the other hand the Rox wasn't exactly an agile, hard-to-miss target, either.

Each shell weighed over a ton. Nothing in the Rox's architecture could withstand them.

He calculated speeds, ranges, flight times. The huge rounds were taking almost a minute to fly from the gun barrel to the target, which meant the *New Jersey* was near the limits of its range, twenty miles or so out. That was a long distance to fly, but it also meant fewer salvos.

"How do we beat a battleship?" Mistral said.

"We don't."

She gave him a look from goggle-covered eyes. "So what are we doing here?"

"Why aren't the shells falling into Jersey City?"

"I dunno. You tell me."

"Somebody's spotting them. Someone's watching them fall and reporting back to the *New Jersey.*"

"But they can't see anything through the fog."

"Right. So the spotting is being done by radar. I know the services have radar sets that are good enough to spot individual shells falling. And apparently the radar spoofers placed around the Rox aren't working well enough. There's someone sitting at the radar sets communicating to the battleship by radio."

"Okay."

"What we do is wreck the *New Jersey*'s radio antennae. They'll have at least a couple microwave antennae for satellite linkage and a whole battery of antennae for radio communication. We don't know which they're using, so we'll have to destroy them all."

"With my winds? Piece of cake."

"I hope so."

The fog parted, twisted into streamers by Mistral's winds, and the ocean opened before them. Lights winked on the horizon, and seconds later came the boom of distant thunder.

Another salvo wailed overhead.

Outcast wavered, his image distorting as if someone were trying to pull a paper cutout apart. He blipped out like the dot on a television monitor when the power is cut.

There was the sound of anvils being struck together. The airburst rained acid down upon the trees in the swampland. Wyungare sought shelter as the droplets hissed and burned their way through the verdant foliage around him.

And then something new, something that dwarfed everything that had gone before, picked Wyungare up like a child grasping an unresisting doll.

It sounded like the sharp crack of thunder rushing on the tail of the lightning striking the plateau of Uluru.

It felt like the ravenous grasp of Wurrawilberoo, the desert whirlwind devil.

Slammed out of his concentration, Wyungare abruptly felt like one of the Keen Keengs, the flying men descended from giants. Except that he was not a giant himself and the stone blocks splintering and clashing around him were as big as he. He was falling.

The cell had come apart, the floor was no more, and his body caromed off hard surfaces. Wyungare heard yells, curses, a scream.

Instinctively he twisted in the air and ducked to avoid a piece of castle that would have smashed his skull like a maira, a paddy-melon. Wyungare allowed his eyes to see what he could of his surroundings more slowly, and so his body could react.

Actually he could see very little. For a sudden and brief moment, a high-explosive flare lit his plunge. Then he fell not quite so far into the crashing, splintering darkness as he had expected. *Perhaps*, his own inner voice guessed, *as little as one level*. Regardless, the fall felt like the plunge from the top of Uluru.

His lungs filled with airborne chaff from the straw that had lined the floor of the cells. He gagged.

Stone, he thought. My landing place will be on granite and my body will break in a thousand ways.

But that did not happen.

His face suddenly whipped through spray and he plunged headfirst into cold water. It was salty ocean water; he knew that as he struggled back to the surface, spitting and blowing like a wounded seal.

Concussive waves battered his ears. Artillery? he wondered. Or carpet bombing. An arc-light operation, he speculated. Debris splashed into the water around him. He could not see anything. This was a case of having to trust to luck. Blind luck.

Then the area lit up with a baleful crimson glow. Some sort of chemical fire cripped down a stone escarpment about a hundred meters away. It looked almost like lava leaking out of a volcanic crater.

Wyungare squinted. He could see the woman prisoner—Mistral—struggling to stay afloat. She was holding on to the fur of the black cat with one hand. The large feline, in turn, was paddling for the shore.

"Wait!" Wyungare called. The chemical fire flickered and went out. The Aborigine started swimming for the place he'd seen Mistral and the cat.

The light flared up again. No woman. No cat. But Wyungare did find a rock he could use to haul himself out of the cold water. On shore, he scanned the heap of jumbled stone wreckage until he found a deeper shadow than the rest, the opening to a passageway.

Wherever it led was fine, so long as that direction was up.

The Turtle took the long way home.

The Rox was between him and his junkyard, hidden beneath a roiling carpet of fog. Tom gave it a wide berth. He veered well to the east, then turned due south over Brooklyn, staying on the fringes of the fog, figuring he'd cross at the Narrows, zip across Staten Island, and come into Bayonne from the south.

The chopper caught him near the old Brooklyn Navy Yard.

Tom had turned off his radio and his external mikes; he didn't want to hear it, whatever it was. The chopper cut across his flight path, missing him by no more than ten feet.

Idiots, Tom thought furiously. It was one of those little two-man bubble-canopy jobs. At first he thought it was some asshole news crew after an interview. Then he saw Danny, waving at him frantically.

It was a different Danny: the young sex star. Even in fatigues, she managed to look hot. She'd tucked her pants into thigh-high lace-up boots that made her legs look even longer. His Danny had seen where he was going, so they'd scrambled a chopper from Governor's Island to intercept.

He turned on the speakers. "I DON'T WANT TO TALK TO YOU. TO ANY OF YOU. STOP FOLLOWING ME." There was no way he could go home with the goddamn chopper on his tail.

The copter came around again. Danny was waving. She looked . . . frantic. She was screaming something at him. Reluctantly, he reached out, flicked his microphones back on.

Even then it was hard to make out what she was saying over the roar of the rotors. Something about New Jersey . . .

"WHAT?" he boomed. "I CAN'T HEAR YOU."

The copter veered closer. Danny cupped one hand around her mouth and screamed at him. ". . . Jersey . . . *under attack* . . ."

"NEW JERSEY IS UNDER ATTACK?"

Danny shouted something else, but the wind whipped her words away. For a moment Tom didn't get it. Then it all fell into place. "THE *BATTLESHIP,*" he blurted.

Danny's nod was frantic.

The battleship *New Jersey* was off Sandy Hook, miles and miles beyond Bloat's farthest reach. If it was under attack . . .

". . . *only one left* . . ." Danny shouted.

The only one left. The last ace in the government's deck. The rest were dead, wounded captured, trashed.

"I QUIT, REMEMBER?"

He couldn't hear her reply.

Frustrated, Danny turned away for a second, said something to her pilot. The chopper lifted suddenly. Tom had to resist the urge to duck as it came in low over the shell, hovered.

He heard a soft *thump* as Danny vaulted down onto the top of his shell. Before he could protest, the chopper had peeled away. Danny clung to the torn netting.

"WHAT THE HELL DO YOU THINK YOU'RE DOING?" he roared.

By then the chopper was well on its way back to Governor's Island, the sound of its rotors receding. "Turtle, please," Danny pleaded. "Mistral . . . Modular Man . . . they're tearing the ship apart. You have to stop them."

"WITH YOU ON MY BACK? YOU WANT TO GET KILLED?"

"No," Danny said, and for the first time Tom heard real fear in her voice. "Turtle, please . . . *I'm on that ship.*"

The *New Jersey* loomed ahead, a steel wall rising from the gray sea. It was three football fields long and its awesome, purposeful architecture made Bloat's sprawling castle look like something from a child's playset.

Gusts tugged at Modular Man as Mistral built a whirlwind overhead. Thus far they'd avoided being seen by the dozen or so ships visible in the task force, but that luck couldn't last.

The windstorm took on shape, purpose. Modular Man sped on ahead, glancing over the superstructure with its array of antennae. There was scarcely a sailor to be seen: nearly everyone had taken shelter beneath the ship's armor. The android fired a burst of microwave energy at one of the satellite antennae, hoping to overload it.

The whirlwind touched the surface of the water and a buzz-saw snarl filled the air.

The three triple turrets fired. A blast of hot gases slammed against the android's body. One-ton shells howled as they shattered the air.

Modular Man fired at another microwave antenna. The shot seemed pointless and ineffectual.

The funnel cloud, mounting, screamed in off the sea. A burst of lightning filled the air with ozone.

The whirlwind engulfed the ship's bridge and the towering array of antennae above it. Glass imploded; pieces of metal blew high as if from an explosion. One of the ship's radars spun away. A panicked sailor ran for the nearest hatch. Antennae were wrenched into pretzel shapes.

The *New Jersey* continued on course, its way unimpeded. The funnel cloud walked up and down the superstructure, concentrating on the radio and radar towers, then began to disperse.

Modular Man counted radio antennae. He could find none in working order.

He turned, sped away toward Mistral. Sirens wailed from the surrounding ships.

"It's over," the android said."We've done our job."

Fire winked from the battleship's side. Antiaircraft rounds cracked overhead. Modular Man put on speed, jinked left and right. Mistral danced near the wavetops as her winds whipped up a screen of concealing spray.

Modular Man put on a burst of speed and left the battleship far behind. He turned and hovered, watched as Mistral jittered away from the bullets and shells that were reaching for her.

The *New Jersey* blew up.

What surprised Modular Man was that it happened in complete silence. There was a blast of flame that threw the stem turret far into the sky, tumbling, gun barrels waving, and then the irruption of boiling smoke and debris that shot into the air, high above the battleship's highest towers . . .

All in silence.

The stern section tilted up and sank in a gush of watery foam, all in less than four seconds. The forward part continued on its course, its momentum too massive to be stopped simply by the event of its own destruction. As it glided forward the bow gradually canted upward until the knifelike cutwater rose into the air. The wake slowly diminished.

The forward part of the ship slowed and just hung there, not quite sinking. Hatches opened and crewmen boiled out.

Mistral/Molly turned, headed for the battleship again. Another whirlwind appeared in the air above the stricken vessel.

Apparently she was going to try to finish it off.

Modular Man remembered submunitions falling on Sandy Hook, the screams of the missile battery troops as they died.

It was all so useless. He had no wish to support Mistral in this ridiculous act of slaughter.

Dual-purpose shells began reaching for him. He put on speed for the Rox.

As he looked back he saw something flash brightly among the running crew of the *New Jersey*. People screamed and fell and died.

Pulse.

Wyungare heard the roar of an angry—or hungry—alligator. He ran down the stone passage, depending on vague shadows in the darkness to warn him against smashing his head against some low overhang.

He rounded a tight elbow in the corridor and stopped behind cover. In the large, flare-lit chamber beyond, he took in the whole picture of it.

In his alligator incarnation, Jack Robicheaux had cornered Wyungare's prisoner comrades. The two men and the woman were backed into a jagged elbow of tumbled stone. Detroit Steel was in front of the other two, his hands outstretched, palm first, toward the reptile. "Get outta here," said the big man. "I've trolled for bigger than you in Lake Michigan."

The alligator took another step forward, jaws opening and closing like enormous steel scissors.

"Beat it," said Detroit Steel.

The sensation Wyungare could pick up from Jack's mind was one of primal hunger. The alligator hadn't eaten in quite some time. The gator version of Jack possessed no patience. Wyungare glanced on beyond the reptile. They saw the dark shape that suggested a tunnel entrance. It was worth a shot.

Go! Wyungare thought at the gator. Food, you'll get food at the other end of that passage. He hated to lie, but this was a time of extreme measures. The reptile grumbled. *Go!* he thought again. *Good food!* He realized he didn't need to sell the concept of food—merely establish the possibility to the alligator's satisfaction.

The alligator abruptly turned and struck for the passageway. He moved faster than Wyungare had believed possible. The reptilian hiss dwindled and died in the passage.

Wyungare trotted to where the other prisoners waited. He realized that Mistral's appearance hadn't accurately reflected the woman's degree of injury. As Mistral drew in her breath and winced, Wyungare discovered that he could feel at least two major breaks in her lower arm. Maybe more, he thought. This is just the top of the iceberg. He said nothing aloud.

Nothing.

"I think she's hurt pretty bad," Detroit Steel volunteered.

Wyungare nodded.

"We can carry her," said Reflector, "if you can guide us out of here."

Wyungare weighed the possibilities. He stared at the passage into which Jack had waddled in alligator form. It looked to be the only way out.

The towers of the Verrazano Bridge were vague shapes in the mist as the Turtle moved through the Narrows. This far south, the fog was starting to thin out. He didn't like that one bit. Down by Sandy Hook, he'd have no concealment.

"Hurry!" Danny urged from atop the shell.

"LISTEN," Tom said, "I'M GOING TO DROP YOU OFF ON THE

BRIDGE. ONE OF YOUR SISTERS CAN SEND A CHOPPER TO PICK
YOU UP."

"There's no time," she told him.

"YES THERE IS. THAT'S A *BATTLESHIP*. EIGHTEEN-INCH GUNS.
SAME KIND OF ARMOR PLATE I'VE GOT. THOUSANDS OF ARMED
MEN, CRUISE MISSILES, MACHINE GUNS, RADAR. IT SURVIVED
WORLD WAR II, IT CAN SURVIVE MODMAN AND MISTRAL."

"You need me," Danny said. "I know where I am. I can take you to
me. You'll never find me without me."

"I'M DROPPING YOU OFF. YOU'RE TOO EXPOSED UP THERE."

"Then let me inside."

The shell moved over the suspension cables, settled toward the
wide span of the roadway. There was no traffic visible anywhere. "I
DON'T LET PEOPLE INSIDE." He looked up at her on close-up. Her
face had gone white. "WHAT'S WRONG? WHAT'S HAPPENED?"

She could barely speak. "The ship . . . my God . . . *they blew up the
ship!*" She bit back a scream.

The Turtle hovered ten feet over the bridge, unmoving, as Tom hesitated. A battleship, he thought. They blew up a fucking *battleship!* All
around him, the fog was being torn into ribbons by rising winds. A
storm to the south . . . Mistral . . .

Tom took a deep breath and punched a combination into his control panel. There was a *hiss* of escaping air as the hatch unsealed. "IN-
SIDE," he said "AND CLOSE THE DOOR BEHIND YOU."

Bloat's underground playground was quiet as Ray and the others made
their way back through it. The traps had already been sprung, the
guards disposed of, and Bloat now had other things to occupy his
mind. Still, every now and then everyone had to grab the nearest wall
while the ground jumped and they shook like pork chops in the bottom of a Shake 'n Bake bag.

Maybe the big guns on the *New Jersey* had slowed down while
the army was trying a second assault. Good thing too, because soon
they'd reach the stone arch over the lava river and that sucker didn't

have a guardrail. Ray wasn't afraid of heights but he had no desire to be halfway across that narrow ribbon of rock when another one of those bombs hit and started everything bouncing and shaking—

There was a scream from the group behind him. It was Danny voicing a wail of fear and denial that echoed weirdly in the confined corridor.

"What is it?" Ray asked.

Danny was staring inward, a look of disbelief on her face. "The *New Jersey,*" she said in a choked whisper. "They blew it up."

"Shit," Ray said, and even Battle looked perturbed.

"Is your sister all right?" Ray asked.

"She's on part of the ship still above water," Danny said. "The Turtle is on his way—"

Ray wondered what would happen to Danny if one of her so-called sisters died. But for once he had the sense to keep his mouth shut.

Every screen was full of death.

"God," Danny whispered from the floor beside him.

The whole stern section of the *New Jersey* was gone. What was left of her had started to settle. Smoke and steam rose hissing from the twisted steel amidships as the seawater poured in.

Tom kept his eyes on the screens, but it was hard to focus. He could feel Danny pressed up against his leg. There wasn't much room inside the shell. He was acutely, awkwardly aware of her, the warmth of her skin against him, the smell of her shampoo. Only last month, he had let Dr. Tachyon inside the shell. Tachyon had been stuck in a pregnant female body at the time, courtesy of the jumpers and his grandson Blaise, and he spent most of his time alternately shouting orders and recoiling hysterically every time Tom brushed against him. Her. That had been pretty weird, but she had still been Tach, and Tom had known Tach for a long, long time. It was different with Danny. She was almost a stranger. Not to mention being a woman. A real woman. All the way through.

A dozen small tornadoes danced around the *New Jersey,* howling, smashing into her armored sides like slamdancers. Tom scanned his screens, searching for Mistral. She was easy to spot. She floated a hundred feet above the wreck, her huge white cape filled with wind, all her attention on the New Jersey as she choreographed her slamdance for cyclones and waterspouts. "There's the wind bitch," Tom said. "So where's the fucking android?"

Charred bodies floated on the whitecaps, bobbing up and down. A few sailors were still struggling in the water, trying to swim, vanishing as huge waves broke over their heads and pulled them down. The rest of the Task Force was fighting its way toward the sinking battleship. The steady chatter of machine guns and the pounding of antiaircraft fire mingled with the banshee roar of Mistral's winds.

"Do something," Danny urged. "You have to help them."

Tom felt sick and helpless. His insides had gone weak with fear. There was nothing he could do for the men who were dead or dying. Once, several lifetimes ago, the Turtle had actually lifted the New Jersey with his teke. He'd got it clear out of the water, and held it up for almost thirty seconds with the power of his mind. Maybe he could keep her afloat for a little while. But not while she was under attack. That was suicide.

"We got to know what the fuck we're up against," he said. "Where's Modular Man? Who blew up the fucking ship?"

His shell was hovering hundreds of feet above the battle. The New Jersey had looked like a toy in a bathtub before he'd zoomed in on it. There was no fog here, almost twenty miles from the Rox. Tom had put the afternoon sun behind him, a trick he remembered from the comics he'd read as a kid. Jetboy always came at them from out of the sun.

"There," Danny said, pointing. "That light."

Tom saw it too. A glowing red streak darting back and forth across the deck of the sinking ship, too fast to follow. "Pulse," he said grimly. "Shit." There was nothing he could do against Pulse, and Mistral had already kicked his ass once today. "I don't like these odds," he told Danny.

"The ship can't take much more of this battering," Danny said. "They can't even use the lifeboats. The storm will smash them. *Do something!*"

Suddenly the bright light flashed off to the north. It was gone in the blink of an eye. It took a moment for it to sink in. "He left," Tom said. He sounded like a kid on Christmas morning. "Pulse left."

Danny was way ahead of him. *"Modman!"* she cried. "There!"

Tom glimpsed something in his peripheral vision, turned, saw him. Modular Man. Weaving in and out among bursting shells.

There was no time. The antiaircraft fire was keeping him busy, but Modman had to know the Turtle was there. Hiding in the sun didn't mean jack shit to the android's radar.

Tom zoomed in, reached down, and *grabbed.*

Midway between a zig and a zag, Modular Man jerked to a sudden full stop and hung helplessly in midair.

The shell dropped toward him. Tom kept one nervous eye on Mistral. She was well below, winds howling around her. Three miniature tornadoes were rushing toward the *New Jersey.* Mistral still hadn't seen him.

Modular Man had managed to wrench himself around in the Turtle's telekinetic grasp. The android was hellacious strong. Sweat was popping out on Tom's brow as he fought to hold him. "I don't want to fight you," Modular Man shouted up.

"GOOD," the Turtle replied. "CAN YOU SAY, *I SURRENDER?* I KNEW YOU COULD . . ."

The android must not have watched *Mr. Rogers.* He just looked vaguely puzzled. "My programming does not permit me to surrender, except to preserve my creator's life."

"He told me before, none of this is his idea," Danny said. "He's being compelled."

"It was Pulse," Modman said. "He must have ignited the ship's magazine. I don't want to hurt anyone."

"TELL THAT TO THOSE SONS OF BITCHES IN THE WATER."

Modular Man seemed to *thrum* as he fired on all cylinders, trying to break free. He didn't move a foot. The guns mounted on his shoulders swung around on the shell. He had a machine gun on his right shoulder and some kind of high-tech laser or maser or taser cannon on his left.

"GIVE UP," Turtle said. "I'LL REPROGRAM YOU."

"I cannot permit my programming to be altered," Modular Man said. The taser swept across the shell in a smooth traverse; hidden videocams fried like popcorn in a microwave. The machine gun was right behind it. Tom heard bullets whining off his armor plate. Three of his screens went dark, then a fourth, a fifth . . .

"BAD IDEA," Tom said. He bent the barrel of the machine gun back on itself, then ripped off the taser and sent it spinning. Sparks arced from the hole in Modman's shoulder. "LAST CHANCE."

Modular Man had nothing to say. Danny was shouting something in his ear. Tom barely heard her. He wrapped invisible hands around the android's ankles. "MAKE A WISH," he said to Danny. She clutched at his arm, frantic. Finally he looked over, just in time to catch a glimpse of blue and white on the screen behind her.

Then the tornado turned his shell into a tiddledywink.

Up was down, down was up, and everything was spinning. Tom's harness held him in place, but Danny was slammed up against the ceiling, then down, then up again. She tumbled across Tom's lap and crashed into the big main screen. The picture tube exploded. Flying glass filled the cabin. Danny cried out. Somehow Tom managed to grab her arm as she went by. He pulled her down against him, hard, and held her tight as the shell went end over end.

It seemed like an eternity before he finally got control again. The shell jerked to a sudden stop. It trembled in the air. Tom had lost all sense of where the fuck he was. Danny was in his arms, groaning. "My leg . . . *shit* . . . I think I broke my leg."

There was no time to worry about that now. More than half of his screens were out. He looked at the others, quickly. Modman was a distant speck, trailing smoke as he fled. He must have held on, wrenched something loose when the wind hit him . . . and Mistral . . . he looked from screen to screen, frantic . . . there she was, coming after him . . . riding the wind . . . her cape rippling like the sails of a clipper ship . . . *smiling* . . .

All of a sudden, Tom wasn't afraid.

All of a sudden, he was angry.

He thought of a bubble.

Mistral's cape deflated like a leaky balloon. It wasn't until she began to fall that she realized something had gone wrong. She looked behind her, below her, not quite understanding what was happening.

The shell fell toward her like a dive-bomber.

"Yes!" Danny said.

Mistral tumbled helplessly. Her cloak was a limp rag now, useless as a torn parachute. Far below, her tornadoes began to dissipate. Tom turned his bubble into shrink-wrap, a telekinetic second skin that gripped her as tightly as her costume. The sea rose up to smash her.

Ten feet above the water, Tom jerked her to a sudden stop. Mistral glared at him. A wind came from nowhere and brushed against his armor. But it was attenuated, feeble.

"NOT THIS TIME," Tom told her.

Mistral's mouth opened wordlessly. She was gasping, struggling for breath. His teke was shutting off all her air.

He turned her upside down, gave her a good look at the bodies floating in the water below her. One of the men was still struggling feebly, clinging to the corpse of a buddy. He didn't seem to know how to swim.

"JUMP," he told her.

Feebly, she tried to shake her head.

"OKAY. THEN DIE." He tightened his grip. His teke closed around her like a vise, squeezing the breath out of her.

Danny had gone pale. "Jesus, are you really going to kill her?" she asked nervously.

Tom didn't know the answer.

Mistral's pretty face was turning blue. It matched her costume. Tom squeezed harder. She was fighting his teke with everything she had.

And then she wasn't fighting him at all.

Tom released her as soon as she went limp, caught her gently as she began to fall, lifted her atop his shell. He could see her chest moving weakly.

He felt Danny grab his arm. "Look," she said. Down in the water, the man who'd been hugging the corpse suddenly kicked free and swam for shore. His strokes were strong and sure. For a moment Tom considered pushing him under.

"The ship," Danny said urgently. "I can feel the deck tilting under me. It's going down!"

Tom sighed. The Turtle lifted slowly into the air and moved toward the foundering *New Jersey* to do whatever he could do. Below him, the swimmer raced toward shore.

The scream startled the hell out of Ray, because it came from behind. He whirled to see the other team members clustered around Danny. She'd managed to cut short her agonized shout, but she was writhing on the tunnel floor, clutching her leg in obvious torment.

Ray ran back to the group, pushing past Battle and Boyd, and knelt by her head. Her mouth was clamped shut and beads of sweat stood out on her forehead. She wasn't bleeding, but she sure as hell was in pain.

"What happened?" Ray asked.

"I don't know," Boyd responded excitedly. "She was walking in front of me all right, then she suddenly screamed, fell, and grabbed her leg."

"It's . . . o . . . kay," Danny ground out between clenched lips. "I can deal . . . with it. It's not . . . my . . . pain."

"Whose is it?" Ray asked.

"Sister's . . . broken leg."

"You feel *everything* your sisters feel?"

Danny nodded. "Once . . . I fell out of a tree . . . I was eight, nine, playing hooky . . . broke my arm. The other me was at school, only her arm broke too, all by itself."

"Christ," Ray said. That was frightening. "You mean every time one of your sisters gets hurt . . ."

"Not every time," Danny said. "Sometimes . . . mostly not, but if we're real close, or if the pain is real bad, or real sudden, and I can't try and dissociate . . . distance myself . . . most times, I *feel* the injury, but that's all." Her fingers massaged her twisted leg. "Nothing feels broken this time. I think I'm okay."

"Which is it, Corporal?" Battle wanted to know. "We can't wait forever while you decide whether or not your leg is broken."

"Give her a minute," Ray snapped.

"I'm okay." She took a deep breath. "I can go on. It's under control."

Ray gave her a hand up. "Lean on me," he said, "if you have to."

She flashed him a smile. "Okay, tough guy."

Travnicek inspected the torn hip joint, the alloy socket with its bright edges of torn metal, the burn, melted, and torn contractile plastic with its fine web of conducting wires.

Down in flames, Modular Man thought. Like a World War I fighter ace.

The android had managed to stop the shorting with some swift rerouting of his inner electronics. The medical staff, a few overworked jokers, only a few with medical training, could think of nothing to do other than supply him with a crutch.

"I thought you were learning how to be a winner, Apple Mac," Travnicek said. "A shooter. You disappoint the shit out of me." The screams of a wounded patient echoed from the stone walls of the infirmary. One of the few jokers with medical training ran to the patient's aid.

At least there were plenty of drugs down here to keep the patients quiet. The android had never seen so many drugs in his life.

"Burying Snotman was clever of you," Travnicek went on, "but I expected better when you dealt with that flying terrapin."

"Can you repair me?"

"Hah! Of course." Travnicek waved a hand; cilia sang through the air. "When I get around to it. After this little adventure is over."

Modular Man's heart sank. Travnicek was lying, and they both knew it.

"I don't know how long I can go on fighting this way," the android said. "Perhaps we should evacuate."

Travnicek paused, held up a hand. Something pulsed under his blue, hairless scalp. His sensory organs unfolded.

"Tub-of-Lard is *doing* something," he said. "Gotta go, toaster."

He sprang away, jumping up to run on the wall when someone got in his way. Modular Man rose from the infirmary bed—there wasn't anything they could do for him here—and tentatively put his weight on his remaining foot. He rewove his programming to compensate for his altered balance and took a careful hop.

He could move faster by walking on his hands, he realized. And faster still just by levitating and flying under the power of his flux generators.

The screaming patient—disemboweled by shrapnel, the android now saw—fell silent as his joker nurse pumped him full of rapture.

The android glanced up, saw Patchwork. She still wore her camouflage uniform and helmet, but had left her pack and firearms behind.

"They told me you were wounded," she said.

He looked into her anxious gold-flecked eyes. "I lost a leg."

She stepped back, looked at him. She was breathing hard; it seemed as if she'd run all the way from the Iron Tower.

"How bad is it?" she said. "You're not suffering the way a human would."

"Take my word for it," Modular Man said. "I'm not a happy individual."

"Your . . . creator?" She waved an arm in the direction of the absent Travnicek. "He's not concerned?"

"He seems determined to fight to the last Bloat."

Patchwork looked at him soberly. "And to the last android?"

"Since Bloat seems determined to put me between himself and danger, that would seem very likely."

"Isn't he—Travni—"

"Travnicek."

"Yes. Isn't he concerned about how to get off the Rox? Or does he think we're going to win?"

"He's not thinking about what happens next. I think he's intoxicated by Bloat."

"*That's* a new reaction to the governor."

The disemboweled patient began to moan. He sounded as if he were working his way up to orgasm.

"When I was first created, I wanted to try everything," Modular

Man said. "Every drink, every dessert, every experience. Sort of like Travnicek is doing now."

"You tried every woman, from what I hear."

"That too. But I didn't put others in danger."

The disemboweled patient screamed in ecstasy. Patchwork's face screwed itself into an expression of distaste. "Can we leave? I don't think they're helping you here, and this place isn't doing me any good, either."

She reached out, took his hand to help him balance.

He found himself not wanting to tell her he could levitate.

He left the crutch behind, leaning against his bed.

"Aren't you supposed to be in the Iron Tower?" Modular Man asked.

"Things are pretty chaotic," Patchwork said. "The governor's rebuilding the fortifications and had better things to do than to see if everyone's at their station. Nobody told my own squad to expect me, so they're not missing me. Last I looked, Bloat's officers were rounding up people to reoccupy the Jersey Gate and Liberty Park. Considering what happened to the last batch, they'll probably have to drive them over the causeway with whips."

Patchwork and Modular Man had found refuge in a room off one of the tunnels under the Rox. It was one of those odd places where Bloat's imagination had failed: the walls were scabbed and fused, and the room was used for storing supplies, mostly huge blue-plastic-wrapped bales of drugs. There were also boxes of ammunition and grenades, the latter labeled WP, for white phosphorus.

Modular Man and Patchwork sat side-by-side on a package of rapture worth about two million dollars on the street. He hadn't as yet let go of her hand. The android touched the bale with his free hand, drew fingers down the gritty plastic. "So the stories about the Rox being full of drug dealers are true," he said. "I thought they might be exaggerations."

"*All* the stories about the Rox are true," Patchwork said. "We're quite a little enterprise here."

"Tell me the story again about how you're all a bunch of noble idealists fighting for your freedom."

"Some of the jokers *are* idealists. And some of them hurt so bad they need drugs just to get through the day."

"In quantities like this? Joker idealism seems rather pliable."

She gave a little laugh. "Well. I was just in it for the red Ferrari, myself. After I kicked the big H, other drugs never had much of an attraction."

"You were a heroin addict?"

"Back when I was twelve, yeah. My father got me onto the stuff."

"Your father was an addict?"

"No. He just thought the junk would make me easier to control."

Modular Man looked at her for a moment in thoughtful silence. Her cheeks flushed slightly and she turned away.

"You're so much older than I am," he said. "I'm something less than five years old, and—"

She laughed. "You're going to ask *me* for wisdom? I got talked into going onto the Rox, and I never even figured out that once I got here there was nowhere to drive the Ferrari. Which I never got anyway."

"I don't want to die," Modular Man said.

Patchwork looked at him, startled. Her gold-flecked eyes were wide. She swallowed hard. "I don't want to die, either."

"I was dead once and I didn't like it."

She opened her mouth, then closed it "Can't top that," she said.

"Hundreds of people have been killed here. Sacrificed for Bloat or for the other side. Some of them volunteered, in one sense or another— the soldiers, people like Cyclone, most of your people."

"You didn't volunteer."

"Nor did Pulse. I've worked alongside Pulse before—he's a good man. Married, children, worked for the city. He didn't want to be a hero, but if he was called he did a job. Now he's a slave, like me. A psychopathic killer is living in his body, and who knows where his mind is?"

She bit her lip. "How can we get out?"

"Who is to say who lives and dies? People like Bloat? People like the lunatic that's inside Pulse?"

"*Dying?* I'm talking about escape."

"What do you do when you don't want the governor to listen to your thoughts?"

Patchwork looked startled. "I told you. I think dirty thoughts. It embarrasses him."

"A lot of people seem attracted to dirty thoughts. How do you know Bloat isn't a secret voyeur? What else do you do?"

"I could think about reciting the Pledge of Allegiance or something. Just let the back of my mind float while I work hard on doing something else, something unimportant. Concentrate on the task at hand."

He turned to her, took her other hand. "Try it."

"Um." She thought for a moment, then began to sing in a tuneless contralto. "Mine eyes have seen the glory of the coming of the Lord."

"I have to obey my creator. I have to look after his welfare. I don't have any choice in that."

"He's trampling out the thing, the whatever where the grapes of wrath are stored."

He tightened his grip on her hands. "I'm *terribly concerned* about him. About what might happen to him when I'm not there to protect him."

Patchwork knit her brows, trying to remember the lyrics. "He has loosed the fateful lightning of his terrible swift sword. His truth goes marching on."

"If the bombardments get bad, he goes into his tower and bolts the door. That's a fairly safe place."

"Glory, glory hallelujah. Glory, glory hallelujah. His truth goes marching on."

"But there's one thing that *really concerns* me. One weakness."

"I don't remember the fucking lyrics. Oh, shit." She took a breath, started again. "Glory, glory hallelujah."

"There are air shafts in the tower that lead up to the outside. They're too small for a shell to go down, of course—"

"Glory, glory hallelujah. His truth goes marching on."

"But a small explosive—a grenade, say, like those over in the corner, or a series of grenades. They could be rolled down the shafts and result in terrible danger to my creator."

"Glory hallelujah. Hallelujah, hallelujah."

"Of course I would be bound to prevent anyone from endangering my creator that way."

"I can't remember." She thought for a moment, then shifted tracks. "To be or not to be. That is the fucking question."

"And of course whoever did such a thing would be risking a great deal from shellfire, because Dr. Travnicek is only in his tower when the shellfire is too much for the defenders to handle."

"Whether it's nobler in the mind to suffer the slings and arrows of outrageous fortune. Or by opposing . . ."

"But still I'm *very concerned*. Perhaps you'll be good enough to help me." He looked intently into Patchwork's eyes. "You'll help *take care* of my creator, won't you?"

"By opposing," she repeated, "end them." Holding his eyes, she nodded.

"I'm very relieved," he said.

"I don't know the rest of the speech."

"Don't think."

"I'll try."

"Concentrate on the task at hand."

He kissed her.

The kiss went on for a long while.

"You kiss just like a human," she said.

"Thank you. I've had no complaints."

She smiled up at him. "What *else* do you do like a human?"

"We could find out."

He wondered for a moment whether he had just made himself another Bloat, another tyrant deciding who lived and died. If he was manipulating Patchwork in ways that were not acceptable, just because he wanted to live.

In a way, he comforted himself, he was doing what Travnicek wanted.

He was becoming a shooter.

Wyungare, the black cat, and the three erstwhile prisoners found the alligator on the beach. It was as though Jack had been waiting for the others to find their way out of the tumbled maze that huge sections of the castle had become. He had apparently found something to eat; something torn to pieces by high explosive. Whatever it was, it had worn some sort of uniform.

And there was the alligator hissing on the sand. Evidently Jack didn't want to share his meal.

Wyungare realized what needed to be done now. "The three of you are leaving," he said "It will be the adventure of a lifetime." He motioned toward Jack.

The bigger, older man, Detroit Steel, said, "You gotta be kidding."

Reflector said, "I'm staying, man. I got some scores to even. Asses to kick. Mikey Detroit, here, can take care of the girl. Shouldn't take much doing; she's so far into shock, she might as well be in a coma."

"Chill," said Detroit Steel. "So what are you gonna do, Snotty? Just abandon her?"

"Maybe for a little while. Hell, *you* can stay with her. All right? Me, I need to go kill some of the dickheads that put us here and then kept us. And don't call me Snotty."

"I'd suggest you get off the island," said Wyungare. "*All* of you. I mean that."

"I'm going to stay," said Reflector obdurately. "No question about it."

"If you wish to be heroic," said Wyungare, "the best thing you could do would be to save this woman's life. She is going to die without care."

"Isn't the same thing," said Reflector.

The Aborigine shook his head. "Yes, it is." He put all the personal power he could muster into those syllables. And when the psychic smoke had cleared, the prisoners sat astraddle Jack, resembling an ill-matched bobsled team. As large and buoyant as the gator was, he now rode fairly low in the water. The black cat took his accustomed spot on top of Jack's head and meowed back at Wyungare.

Wyungare waved and the alligator majestically moved out into the bay, and struck out for the Manhattan shore.

The sky continued to fill with deadly fireworks.

Wyungare prayed they would make it.

"This whole setup is so strange," Danny said to Ray as they traced their way back through Bloat's caverns. "I mean, here we are wandering through these tunnels, running into orcs from Tolkien, scenes from Monty Python movies. Sure, things have been dangerous, but why haven't we met with any really deadly traps? So far it's been like some adolescent fantasy game."

"Game," Ray repeated. That was the second time she'd compared their situation to a game. It set Ray's mind working again, and he stopped, snapped his fingers, and said, "That's it! Christ, you're right!"

"What are you talking about?" Battle called from the rear.

Ray stopped, turned, and said to him. "This whole thing is a dungeon—you know, like a kid's role-playing game."

Battle frowned. "What do you know about those degenerate fantasy games?"

Ray thought back to when the Secret Service had raided the game company out on Long Island, Jack Stevenson Games. He'd read the piles of crap they'd confiscated, looking for something that could be considered remotely illegal and therefore justification for the raid.

"More than I want to," Ray muttered. "But Danny's right. We've gone through real role-playing stuff. I mean, just about the only thing the fucker's missed so far is a treasure trove guarded by a dragon."

"I don't get it," Danny said. "Why wouldn't Bloat just put something down here that could flat out kill us?"

"Because," Ray said slowly, "that's not how a dungeon-master operates. This is still a game to him. He can't just kill the players out of hand . . . that's not much fun, after all."

"Bloat," Battle said through clenched teeth, "is a dangerous, twisted, terrorist, demented genetic freak. Who knows—"

"So am I," Danny said quietly.

"What?"

"A genetic freak." She looked steadily at Battle.

"Me too," said Blockhead. "Even if I'm dead." He jerked a thumb at Ray and Crypt Kicker. "These guys are too. And I think we've had just enough of your insults. I'd watch my tongue if I were you. You're definitely outnumbered here."

Battle looked at him, the vein in the side of his forehead throbbing. "Be careful, you insubordinate bastard—" he began.

"Hey," Blockhead said blandly, "what are you going to do? Shoot me?"

Battle sputtered wordlessly while Ray and Danny both failed to hide grins. Battle finally looked at the expressionless Crypt Kicker and barked out, "Come along!"

"I don't think this situation is exactly what we've been led to believe," Danny said to the others.

"I never liked the bastard," Blockhead muttered. "Well, that's fine for you," he added cryptically, though neither Ray nor Danny had said anything.

Ray looked at both of them "There's something weird going on. I can feel it. But Battle's in charge."

"So what?" Danny said in a low voice. "He's a shifty bastard. I suggest we just keep our eyes and ears open. That's all."

Ray shifted uncomfortably. He was the type who just followed orders and kicked ass. The nature of the orders had never bothered him. But Battle was such a shitbag . . .

"Jesus Christ!"

The shout came from around a bend in the corridor. There was an edge in Battle's voice, a hint of panic that Ray had never heard before. The three looked at each other and started to run, Ray in the lead, Danny following, and Cameo/Blockhead bringing up the rear. They skidded around the turn in the corridor and came to a stumbling stop to see Battle pressed behind Crypt Kicker, who was taking everything with his usual deadpan aplomb.

"What is it?" Ray asked.

"I think," Battle said, pointing over Puckett's shoulder, "I found the goddamn dragon."

Ray suddenly became aware of a sound floating down the corridor like the *chuf-chuf-chuffle* of an asthmatic steam engine. There was the smell of smoky, burned things. He peered around Puckett and there it was. Battle had found it, all right.

A goddamn dragon sitting curled around its goddamn treasure trove.

The first bomb shook the Rox, and Patchwork shuddered in Modular Man's arms.

"It's starting," he said.

"Yes."

"I should check on Dr. Travnicek. Make sure he's under cover and safe."

Another bomb crashed home, this one closer. After the thud came the sound of stonework falling.

Patchwork's face was pale.

"The Turtle destroyed my weapons," the android said. "I will ask Bloat's permission to leave the Rox and return with others."

Patchwork gave a faint grin. "Glory, glory hallelujah."

"Be careful."

"Don't worry. I'll take care of things while you're gone."

There was no special emphasis in her words, none but the sudden rain of bombs and rockets that were hammering Bloat's glass-and-stonework fantasy.

He kissed her again and flew away, out of the fused room, down the twisting corridors, out into the foggy courtyard. His radar imaging was full of arcing aircraft, falling explosives, wildly cartwheeling Bosch creatures. It was clear the military was after vengeance for the *New Jersey*.

Modular Man went in search of Bloat. The governor was himself, not the Outcast, and as more concussions battered the air, the strain showed both on his face and in his temper.

"The Turtle took my weapons," Modular Man said. "There's nothing I can do until I replace them."

"*You can go down and—*"

"I have other weapons waiting at Dr. Travnicek's apartment. May I go get them?"

The governor narrowed his eyes and thought. "I can hold off those assholes for a while," he said. "Get your weapons and hurry."

The android took off, out one of the castle's shattered windows. Below, in the shadow of one of the arches leading down to the tunnel system, he saw a sylphlike figure crouching.

He slowed, waited till an explosion lit the fog, and waved.

Her hand hesitantly rose in response. There was a grenade in it.

It is good, he ordered himself to think, that she has armed herself and will be able to defend herself and Dr. Travnicek if necessary.

He flew on, back to Manhattan.

"Hello. Having a pleasant journey through Bloat's scenic caverns?"

The damn thing talked too. Well, why not? Everything else in this place was screwy. Why not a talking dragon?

"Sure," Ray said. He shoved past Puckett, surreptitiously pulling Danny along with him. If this fucker was a firebreather, and the little puffs of smoke coming from his nostrils seemed to indicate that he was, Ray didn't want them bunched together in the cave mouth where one breath could barbecue them all.

"What are you doing down here?" Danny asked.

"Guarding my treasure, of course," the thing said.

Ray's hopes suddenly rose. The dragon seemed intelligent and reasonable. Maybe they could bullshit their way past it.

"And keeping strangers off Bloat's back," it added.

Well, shit, Ray thought.

"We're just passing through," Danny said, following Ray as he slowly edged around the room. "We don't want to bother you."

"How about Bloat?" the dragon asked mildly.

"Bloat," Battle said slowly, edging forward, "dies!"

He swung up his assault rifle and triggered a long burst. The dragon roared. It stood, ruffling its wings and exhaling enough steam to turn the chamber into a sauna. Battle's bullets seemed to have little impact on its tough, leathery hide as ricochets whined around the chamber like angry bees.

"The stomach!" Ray shouted. The creature's abdomen seemed unarmored. "Aim for its stomach!"

Danny took his advice. She stepped forward and brought her shotgun up and emptied a whole ammo cartridge in something less than five seconds. The flechette rounds penetrated the beast's skin, but not too deeply. They just seemed to anger it.

Danny swore and went down to one knee, rummaging in her pack for another ammo cartridge as the dragon bellowed in pain and rage.

"Get down!" Ray shouted as the beast reared up on its hind legs and drew its head back as if it were going to spit at them. Ray hit the ground, curled, and covered up. A blast of hot air like a wind blowing from hell steamed over him. Fortunately it lasted only a few moments. He looked up to see Danny also rolled in a protective ball. The dragon was shifting its attention to Battle and Crypt Kicker.

Battle fired his automatic rifle, screaming a stream of nonsensical obscenities. Crypt Kicker lumbered forward in his clumsy, stiff-legged way and began to pummel the dragon's exposed belly.

"No," Ray shouted, "don't hit the goddamned thing. You can't hurt it like that."

Ray was right. The dragon was built like a tank, only it was bigger and stronger. It flicked out a forepaw and caught Crypt Kicker in the chest with enough force to kill a normal person. Since Puckett was already dead, he just bounced back after he slammed against the wall.

Then the dragon turned his attention to Battle and Cameo/Blockhead, who still stood behind Battle at the room's entrance. Danny found the cartridge she was searching for and rammed it home as the dragon drew its head back for another blast.

Battle saw death staring him in the eyes. He screamed and dropped his rifle as Danny aimed and the dragon shot two searing tongues of fire as if it had flamethrowers mounted in each nostril. Crypt Kicker staggered forward, arms widespread, palms dripping streams of toxic chemicals just as Danny emptied the cartridge filled with armor-piercing rounds on full automatic.

The fire hit Crypt Kicker's chemicals and the ace and the animal were enveloped by an explosive fireball that blew Puckett off his feet. The armor-piercing rounds hit the creature's soft belly, punching through to the flesh and organs underneath. Blood and meat sprayed all over the chamber. The fireball died out precipitously as the dragon suddenly ceased to flame.

Ray stood up slowly. "Holy Christ," he said.

The air was foul with the stench of burnt chemicals and smoldering flesh. The dragon, lying on its back among the gleaming piles of its treasure trove, had a completely ruptured abdomen. The wound had been cauterized by the fire, but the shotgun rounds and the fire itself had eaten away so much of its internal structure that there was no way the thing could be alive.

Puckett was still smoldering. His uniform had been burned off and most of his skin was blackened. Ray could see why he'd always worn his hood. Most of the right side of his face had been blown away. It didn't look like a new injury. It was what had probably killed him years ago. He was a truly ugly son of a bitch and he smelled even worse than usual. He just laid there like a T-bone that'd been left on the barbecue for far too long.

"Can we do anything to help him?" Danny asked.

Ray shook his head. "I don't know."

"Well you can sure as hell help me," Battle said. He struggled to a sitting position as Ray and Danny approached. He didn't look too bad, though his eyebrows and mustache were singed. He put his hand to his upper lip, and bits of burned hair flaked away. "That rat bastard," Battle mumbled. "That son of a bitch Bloat is going to pay."

"How about Blockhead?" Danny asked. "Where is he?"

"Brian is gone," a voice said.

It was Cameo, coming out from behind the cover of a large stalagmite that rose from the floor just inside the dragon's lair.

"What do you mean?" Battle demanded.

Cameo held up her hand. "The ring slipped off my finger when we dove to cover."

"Where the hell is it?" Battle demanded.

Cameo shook her head. "I'm not sure. I think it flew toward Crypt Kicker and the Dragon."

"Let's look for it—" Ray began, but Battle cut him off with a curt shake of his head.

"It's too late," he said. "Bloat must know we're here. The only thing we can do now is keep moving, keep Bloat off-stride and confused."

"What about Puckett?" Ray asked, looked down at the unmoving ace. "Is he really dead?"

Battle approached his erstwhile bodyguard and nudged him with his toe. Puckett didn't respond.

"Who knows?" Battle said after a moment "He can take a lot of damage, but that goddamned dragon really fried him. Maybe he can regenerate."

"We'll take him with us—" Danny began, but Battle cut her off too.

"No way," he said curtly. "The only way we'll get out of this alive is to move fast. We can't be lugging a body with us. Besides"—he nudged Crypt Kicker again like a prospective buyer checking the tires on a used Buick—"he's probably dead."

"How—" Danny began angrily, but Ray took her arm and stopped her.

"I don't think there's anything we can do for him," Ray said. "If he regenerates it'll be because of his ace, not because of anything we can do. But we'll come back for him. If we can. I promise that."

Danny nodded after a moment, and Cameo did too.

"Well, at last," Battle said sarcastically. "Shall we move on, or should we just sit here and wait for Bloat's minions to come get us?"

"Minions," a choked voice said. Everyone started and looked up at the dragon. It had one eye half open. "Minions. That's a good one. You'd better all watch your asses from now on. The penguin knows you're here, and it's pissed."

"Penguin?" Ray asked.

But the dragon's eye closed and it said no more.

The owl battered insistently against the moonlit window of Teddy's bedroom as he watched from his bed. A thud, a rustling of angry wings, the round, tufted face glaring in at him, and the talons stretched out like grasping hands. It screeched in frustration, backed away, and launched itself at the window once more. Glass rattled in the wood frame.

"Daddy!" Teddy yelled. "Mommy! There's an owl!"

A muffled answer came from the bedroom across the hall. "Listen to your dreams, son." His uncle Alan's voice.

"Where's my daddy?"

"Listen to them . . ."

Teddy watched with the covers pulled up to his chin as the owl swooped out and then back once more. This time the glass bowed and shattered, and the creature fluttered into his bedroom, heading straight for him . . .

Whooooo?

With the query, an image came to Bloat: a squad of military types, the caverns, a recognizable patchwork face.

Jesus, no, don't shoot—

Silence.

"Hey, fat boy, sounds like company down below." The penguin was skating placidly in front of him—and he was Bloat.

"Shut up," he told the penguin wearily. Listening . . . another voice . . .

Carnifex? Can't be . . .

Silence again. "Kafka!" Bloat hollered, his adolescent wail breaking in mid-syllable.

"Calling for Daddy?" the penguin asked.

"Quiet!" Bloatblack pattered onto the floor; an icy dread settled somewhere deep in his vast body. He had visions of a tactical nuke, some sort of chemical weapon or something else just as nasty, set off below Ellis . . . *Omigod, this is what they've been after all along.*

Kafka came skittering into the hall. Dylan, Bodysnatcher, Shroud, and Travnicek followed the joker. They all glanced at the penguin, who favored them with an elegant bow and doffing of its funnel hat. "Governor?" Kafka asked.

"We have intruders in the caverns," Bloat told him. "Five of them in one group, maybe more. At least one of them's an ace—Carnifex."

"Where in the caverns?" Bodysnatcher asked eagerly. He seemed to like Pulse's body now; he visibly trembled with the thought of more destruction.

"The dragon's lair," Bloat admitted. "I don't know how long they've been here. Kafka, they have to be here for a reason. The outside attacks could have been just a huge diversion, so that I—we—wouldn't be looking underneath the Rox."

Outside the walls of the castle, the fog was only a thin ghost of itself—another indication of his exhaustion. Through the mist, he thought he saw an owl swoop low over the island. "Send a squad of jokers down after them. I'll send demons, but I don't know if they'll be enough."

"And you're just too damn tired to do it yourself, right, fat boy?" the penguin interjected. It spread its flippers wide at Bloat's glare. "Hey, just an observation, Your Rotundity. Y'know, you're losing your sense of humor."

Bloat ignored the penguin. "Tell them to be careful. I don't want anyone from the Rox hurt."

Travnicek's flowered, viny torso swiveled toward Bloat. "Send the toaster, then."

"I sent him to Manhattan," Bloat admitted. "For fresh weapons."

Travnicek laughed. "More fool you, slug boy."

"I'll go," Zelda said.

Bloat shook his head. "As much as I'd like to, I need you up here in case they start shelling again . . ." He stopped. Teddy (or was he Bloat? The Outcast? He was confused) had caught the thought from Dylan, even though the man didn't speak.

Herne could do it . . .

"Herne—" Bloat echoed. Softly.

"Y'know, Your Corpulence, I don't want to mention this while you're making all these quick, incisive policy decisions and all, but a whole shitload of innocent people died the last time Herne rode off, and he didn't get the one guy he was after." The penguin opened its wide mouth to grin at Dylan. "Just an observation."

Bloat said nothing. He closed his eyes.

"So far you're the only one who's taking mostly defensive moves," the penguin continued. "Seems like all the rest of these people do things like blow up destroyers and take down national landmarks. Y'know—the spectacular stuff with nice pyrotechnics. I'll bet the nats in the caves have stuff for all kinds of pretty fireworks. What happens if they decide to nuke the Gabriel Hounds?"

When there was still no reply, the penguin skated to a dead stop below the tiny head and shoulders of Bloat, standing atop the moraine of bloatblack. "Hello? Anyone home?"

"Leave me alone." Teddy's voice. A cracking, adolescent rasp.

"I'd love to, but you conjured me up and now I'm part of you. I'm made, and once you make a thing, you can't unmake it easily. It's a burden I have to bear."

Bloat sighed.

"No," Bloat said, looking at the jokers below him. "Not the Hunt."

"Wait, I think sending the Hunt's a good idea, Governor," Kafka said. "It'll be dark soon. We'll send Herne after these creeps."

Dylan shrugged, and the Manchesterian voice in his head echoed the cultured British accent that came from his mouth. "The hounds will find them, no matter where they are."

"Send him, Governor," Bodysnatcher said. "Give him a chance after the *last* fiasco. I hate to agree with the roach, but that sounds like the best plan."

"No." Bloat sighed. *So many jokers dead because of all this. Because of me . . .* "I'll do it myself."

"Oh, that's a *great* idea," Bodysnatcher howled. "You're a worse fuck-up than Herne. You had us dig out Detroit Steel and Snotman when the mothers were buried and out of it. Now the Iron Keep's a shell and they're gone; Mistral too. Another great decision."

"Shut up," Bloat said. "I know all that. You can send the Hunt if you haven't heard from me by sundown. Until then, wait. I'll deal with it. I can take care of them."

He hoped he was right.

Somewhere over Staten Island, surrounded by fog, Tom realized he was never going to make it back to Manhattan.

Two more screens had gone dead. The air in the cabin was still and hot. Circuits overheating somewhere in the walls. Any moment now, he could have a full-fledged fire on his hands. He was flying half-blind as it was, and his headache was a chain saw in his skull. He'd never felt this bad before.

And Danny was in worse shape. Once the adrenaline rush had worn off, the pain from her broken leg had hit hard. The aspirin Tom gave her wasn't nearly enough. She was hanging on gamely, but he could see her fighting not to scream.

She had to get medical help, but the Jokertown Clinic was a long way off. Bayonne was much closer. He altered course. "I'm taking you to Bayonne Hospital," he told her as he veered across Port Richmond.

Danny forced a grin through the pain. "Von Herzenhagen will be pissed again."

"Fuck him," Tom said. "Is your sister still at Zappa's headquarters? The pregnant one?"

She nodded. "I'm still there."

"Good. Tell them I quit."

"Again?"

"This time for keeps," Tom said. "The shell's a wreck. It's going to take me weeks to repair all the damage."

"You're not in such great shape yourself. When we get to the hospital, you'd better have them take a look at you too."

"I'm fine," Tom said. "A little headache, that's all."

Danny reached up, touched his face, just above his mouth. Her finger came away red with blood. "You're bleeding."

"The glass," Tom said. "When you crashed through the TV. I must have been cut." He'd never even felt it.

"That's not it," Danny said. "You're bleeding heavily from both nostrils."

He glimpsed the green, choppy waters of the Kill Van Kull below them on one of the screens that was still functional. "We're almost there," he told her.

"Let them take some X-rays," Danny urged.

"For what? A fucking nosebleed? Leave me alone, okay?"

Danny smiled, touched his hair. "Never," she said softly.

Tom stared down at her. "Excuse me?"

"You have a real name, Mr. Turtle Sir?" Danny asked.

"Tom," he told her. He forced himself to look away from her, back at his screens. He was twice as old as she was, for chrissakes. They'd reached Bayonne. He sailed silently over Brady's dock and the First Street projects where he had grown up.

"Where do you live?" Danny asked.

Tom looked at her again. "I can't tell you that."

"Why not?"

He glanced at his screens just as another one went black. "Fuck, fuck, *fuck*," he said. His head was pounding. He looked back at Danny. "It doesn't matter where I live. You're in no condition to be making social calls."

"So?" she said lightly. "My . . . sister . . . is already on the way from New York. Where do you live, Tom?"

Tom looked at her for a long, long time.

Then he told her.

Bloat let himself sink into dreams.

For a moment Bloat drifted like an obscene Macy's Parade balloon just above the waves in the middle of some sunlit, choppy bay. The unspoiled shoreline was covered by trees. The whole scene had a nagging sense of familiarity to it, but he couldn't quite place what prompted the feeling. A woman clad in a multihued sari was walking across the water toward him, her feet not quite touching the tops of the waves. "Abomination!" she hissed, and raised her hands as if to strike.

Teddy fell. The Bloat-body hit the water in a world-class belly flop. He gulped briny foam and the coldness made him gasp even through the tonnage of Bloat. His tiny, useless arms flailed desperately toward the woman, but she watched his floundering with utter dispassion. "Die," she told him. "Die and let it end."

"No!" Teddy howled.

Bloat did *not* float. Teddy was sinking down in frigid darkness, pulled down by the anchor of Bloat's mass. He closed his mouth desperately, his lungs burning as he searched for the mind-threads of power, as he tried to shake off the weariness and bring back the Outcast.

He couldn't hold his breath any longer. Reflex forced the inhalation. Teddy waited for salty water to flood his lungs.

He gasped air instead.

He was holding his staff. A guttering torch in a wall sconce illuminated earthen and limestone walls. A corridor stretched ahead of him.

"Rough transition, fat boy," commented the penguin, skating in from a side corridor. "But then I can swim."

"Where?" Teddy managed to grate out. He sagged down, kneeling on the ground in exhaustion. The Outcast's cloak rippled around him; there were muscular thighs under the brown leggings he wore. The Outcast.

"We're under the Rox, maybe a hundred yards or so out from the shore. And our sneaky little friends are just down that way." The penguin pointed to the corridor from which it'd come. "They don't look real happy, either."

There were whisperings in Teddy's head, new voices that he'd never before heard in the chorus. "Four of them," Teddy said. "Billy Ray, someone called Battle, Cameo. There's someone else there, a woman. I hear Carnifex thinking about her but I can't hear her . . ."

"Just one big happy family, huh?"

"They're not happy," Teddy said. "They don't even like each other much. And they're here to kill me."

Teddy got to his feet with the staff's help. The caverns were cool; that helped too. He could feel the tenuous connection to Bloat up in the castle, which meant that the drowning dream had been just that—another dream, a nightmare.

Something scuttled past the crossing: it looked like a dog with a baboon's face, and it was nothing that Teddy remembered putting here. The creature gave a barking hyenalike laugh and fled. "This place is getting very strange," the penguin commented. "Or stranger than usual, I guess. Just what is it you're planning to do, Great White Bloat?"

"I don't know." That was only the truth. "See if I can convince them to go back, I guess. Or take care of them myself. Whatever I have to do."

"Excellent," the penguin said, skating backward around him. "It's always good to go into these things with a definite plan of action. All the bases covered, all those nasty little contingencies plotted out—"

"Shut up."

The penguin went silent. The obedience almost startled him out of the Outcast.

He could hear them audibly now, moving down the side corridor toward the intersection. Teddy rapped his staff against the stones; the amethyst glowed once and he willed his body to go transparent. This was nothing he'd ever done before—he wasn't sure that it would work.

It did, with mixed results. He found that the world went slowly dark as his eyes faded. Teddy cursed—or tried to—no sounds emerged from the nonexistent mouth. He brought his eyes back into corporeality and could see again. The penguin was talking but he could hear nothing, nor could he speak when he tried to speak. Teddy sighed and brought back his entire head.

". . . coming toward us," the penguin whispered.

"Come on out," Teddy said loudly. He tried to walk—that didn't work either. He materialized the Outcast entirely and moved toward the intersection. "This is Governor Bloat," he called. "I can hear you. I know your names: Billy Ray, Battle—you want me to go on?" Teddy thought about mermen; a half dozen of them, mounted on gigantic hovering fishes. They materialized in the middle of the intersection, their lances at ready. He put another half dozen of the fantasy warriors down the corridor directly in back of the startled group. They didn't quite look as solid as usual. Teddy frowned and decided he couldn't worry about that now.

You aren't Bloat, a voice thought defiantly from somewhere in the blackness of the corridor.

"I *am.* Did you think that I'd stay in that body if I had a choice?"

I hate this fucking place hate it . . .

Battle you asshole listen to him . . .

"My guardians in the caverns have asked you to go back," Teddy said to the unseen intruders. "I really don't want to kill anyone if I don't have to. But if you insist on going on, I don't have any choice anymore. I'll send the Hunt."

Teddy heard the confusion his words sowed in the group; Billy Ray's thoughts were especially torn. Only the man's intense loyalty toward authority figures held him. Battle was adamant, though, and his mindvoice was that of a fanatic.

Attrite the lousy bastards just get rid of them all . . .

Teddy could almost see them, vague shapes huddled against the rock wall twenty-five yards or so away. They'd doused the torches in the corridor, Teddy let his staff fade back into existence and trickled power through it, imagining the torches lit and guttering—they ignited with an audible *whuff.* "Fuck," Billy Ray said, trying to press back against the cavern wall as the guttering light revealed them. Battle was more belligerent; he brought up his semi-automatic and sprayed Teddy's end of the corridor.

Teddy had known that Battle was going to fire, of course. He brought power to his staff and thickened the air in front of him. Slugs whined past him and tore gory holes in the mermen and their mounts, but the bullets that would have done the same to Teddy hit gellid resistance. They slowed massively and quickly, falling like stricken bumblebees to the earth.

"I hate this goddamn place," Battle said.

"Then leave it," Teddy said. The crystal atop his staff blazed as he restored the mermen Battle had destroyed and bid them forward. They glided down the corridor in a wash of fishy odor and bristling spears. The intruders backed cautiously, then stopped because of the mermen behind. "Oops," Teddy said. "Sorry," and dismissed them. He herded Battle's group with the advancing mermen: one step back, another.

"The fish-folk are looking kinda poorly, if I do say so," the penguin commented at his side.

It was true; they were translucent. Teddy could see the cavern walls through them. Battle had noticed it also. He stopped, glaring at the nearest merman and spreading his chest like a baboon in heat. He flinched as the lance's tip touched him, gritting his teeth—*c'mon you bastard nightmare do your worst*—and then actually smiled as the lance penetrated and came out the other side. As Teddy gaped, the merman continued its advance, walking right through Battle.

"Shit," Battle said. "They're just ghosts." There was an ugly metallic ratcheting as he brought up his weapon again. Behind him, the others had followed suit.

Teddy slammed the end of the staff against the earth, pulling at the dregs of power in Bloat. There was less than he expected. The mermen dissolved into nothingness as he brought the power to bear on the intruders. "Go back!" he husked out through clenched jaws. "I order it! Drop your weapons!"

He held them in the bonds of his mind, but that was all. Their wills struggled against his. Cameo turned first, then Danny. Sweat was breaking out on the Outcast's forehead, dripping into his eyes. Teddy blinked, shaking his head and concentrating, letting the power run from dreamtime to Bloat to him.

Battle took a step backward, the muzzle of his weapon dropping. For a second Teddy thought he'd won. He *ached*. The Outcast's body was shaking as if from tremendous physical effort, but they had all turned now except Billy Ray. Teddy pushed at him, grunting.

Like any such exertion, Teddy could only push for so long. Everything gave way suddenly. In that moment he lost his connection with Bloat and his hold on Ray and the others. Gasping, Teddy knew he was going to die, knew it even as Ray's finger curled around the trigger.

The penguin leapt between them as the weapon chattered death. Downy feathers exploded like a bursting pillow. The bird's carcass slammed into Teddy and nearly knocked him over. Billy Ray was staring, as startled by the suicidal move as Teddy was. For a moment the tableau held as Teddy knelt down to the penguin.

"This is twice now," the penguin gasped. Blood was drooling from the corners of its beak, the black-and-white fur was spotted with red, the skates torn from its flippers by the violence of the slugs, the abdomen a ragged moist cavity. "Fat boy, how many more times will someone have to do this before you get the idea?" It giggled, a sound very much like Bloat, and then gurgled wetly in its throat.

It died.

Teddy stared at the penguin, aghast. He couldn't move, couldn't do anything. The hold he had on the intruders fell apart. He heard Battle's order before the man spoke.

Kill him, you idiots! What are you waiting for?

Teddy had no power left at all to stop them. He let the Outcast dissolve as he fell into dreamtime. Automatic weapons fire gouged the wall behind where he'd been standing.

The Outcast swayed as though he were about to fall. Wyungare put an arm around the man's shoulders, steadying him. There was pain in his eyes, pain in his face. His body radiated anguish and exhaustion.

"Up there," said the Outcast, attempting to point. "It's all like that out there now." He looked like he wanted to cry, but couldn't quite spare the energy for tears. "We're all dying up there."

The gentle southern skies looked like they were shot through with blood and pus and smoke. In the middle distance, Wyungare and the Outcast could hear a sound like the wind blowing hard enough to bend adult trees to the ground.

"I've got to tell you something before it's too late," said the Outcast. "I think probably I fucked up and it may be too late to fix things."

Wyungare squinted. He'd *thought* there was something different about the hero's face. The Outcast looked much the same as he always had, except that the smooth, distended, baby-fat surface was gone. The Outcast no longer looked quite so much like a hyperannuated boy. His features were more like a man's features. Not just any man's—someone who had embarked on a journey through hell. There were new lines deepening around mouth and eyes.

"Wyungare?"

Wyungare blinked. "Go ahead, my friend."

"I'm scared shitless. All those people trusted me, and they're going down like the action figure soldiers I used to trash when I was a"— The Outcast swallowed on a dry-throat cough—"when I was a kid." He looked like he almost smiled. "A *younger* kid." His eyes were bleak and pained. "Thing is, it's not a game. Not like computers or video.

Joker heads get taken off by shrapnel, their brains *stay* smeared over the wall."

"It's a hard lesson," said Wyungare. "There are many who will never deal with it. They will simply run, whether inside their head or in the world."

"There's no reason you have to do this. After the *New Jersey's* shells destroyed your cell, you could have split. No one would have wondered."

The wind roared closer. It sounded out of control, a primal force that would know no restraints.

"I am trying to help a brother," said Wyungare.

"I'll remember that."

The Aborigine set his hand lightly on the Outcast's shoulder. "Then here is something else to remember." He looked into the man's aging eyes. "Someone needs help."

"*I* need help," said the Outcast.

Wyungare smiled.

They stood outside the cabin in which they had watched the boy Jack being raped. The house was even more ramshackle than before, as though it had started to decay and no one living there had the heart to attempt repair. A boy walked slowly out the front door and looked around. He did not appear to see either Wyungare or the Outcast. Or if he did, he didn't react. It was Jack. He held a faded, worn, soft-sided suitcase that looked like it was finished in some hideous carpet design. His hand grasped a handle made from several loops of cotton clothesline.

Then, as though the suitcase were too heavy to hold, as though it were an anvil grasped in his hand, Jack set it down. He fell to his knees beside it and stared into . . . nothingness. There was no focus in his eyes.

He made a keening sound like an animal crying.

The Outcast and Wyungare exchanged looks.

"What . . ." the Outcast started to say. He swallowed. "What can I do?" His voice trembled.

Wyungare turned back to Jack. "You know the weight he bears. You saw."

The Outcast hesitated, as though still waiting for direction. Wyungare gazed back at him. He very nearly could, the Aborigine thought, hear the neurons popping and sizzling in the man/boy's brain.

Then the Outcast crossed the clearing to where the boy still crouched beside the faded carpetbag. At first hesitant, then surer, he strode until he reached Jack.

For just a moment he looked back beseechingly at Wyungare. Then the Outcast sank to his own knees beside the boy. He put his arm around the boy's shoulders and began to speak.

Wyungare could overhear it.

"Listen . . . friend, I, I've sort of been through some of this too, you know?" At first the words stumbled. But Jack looked back at his older companion and his eyes widened as though a less tangible, more articulate message was coming through. You are not alone, said the Outcast. I understand something of what you feel. Talk to me. Maybe I can help. "I know," said the Outcast. "I'll help you if I can. I want to."

The boy slowly tilted his face to meet the Outcast's eyes.

You are not alone. That was the communication that crossed each direction.

This is courage, thought Wyungare, and then he glanced up at the tops of the trees, past them toward the onrushing storm.

"I care," said the Outcast. At first tentative, then sure; the two men, one very young, the other barely older, embraced. Strength, reassurance, healing power, all flowed first in a trickle, then a rushing river.

Now you are a hero. The Outcast could never articulate that for himself. But the Aborigine shaman could do it for him.

Wyungare felt as though he were an observer at an exorcism. Ghosts of smoke and shadows swirled up. And dust. Then all fled.

It took a few seconds to shake off the memory of the dreamtime.

The Outcast blinked, disoriented and exhausted. As always, he quickly scanned the minds of the Rox, checking the familiar minds as a sailor might check the stars. Kafka, Croyd (still sleeping), Travnicek, Bodysnatcher, Molly . . .

"Governor?" Kafka asked. "Glad you're back. I—"

"Shhh . . ." Teddy said.

. . . *'Twas brillig and the slithy toves did gyre and gimble in the wabe* . . .

The passage was an anomaly in the matrix of the Rox. Patchwork was throwing up words like a fog, clouding the interior thoughts.

. . . *All mimsy were the borogoves, and the momes raths outgrabe* . . .

Behind the screening words, Teddy could sense anger and determination. And a name.

"Travnicek," he said.

"Governor?"

"Gotta go, Kafka. Hold down the fort."

The Outcast called on his power and moved. It was much, much harder than it should have been.

"Interesting," Travnicek said. "I could feel it, just a second before you showed up. A shifting in the energy fields, a blurring . . ." Travnicek, his neck lei erect and quivering. Teddy's surroundings were coming into focus now. He was in Travnicek's tower, in the room buried under tons of reinforced concrete and battle armor. It seemed a very dim and uninviting place. Travnicek was observing him like a bug under a microscope. All the flowers of the growth around his head were facing his direction.

In the middle of Travnicek's speech, there had been a faint *plonk* from the opening to the air shaft. Travnicek hadn't noticed it. Behind the art-deco grillwork, Teddy could see an eye empty of its socket, like a hard-boiled egg with a brown yolk.

"Something very unusual happens when you do things, slug," Travnicek was saying. "I think that if I could figure it out—" A second, much louder noise came from the shaft. This time Travnicek turned. They both saw the hand, clutching a large grenade. The pin had been pulled; the fingers held the triggering lever in place, but only barely.

. . . *Shit! The governor's there* . . .

Travnicek screeched and leapt backward several feet, putting himself behind the Outcast. "Get *rid* of it, slug! Put battle armor over the vent, smash it, I don't care!"

"I'm listening to her. She's not going to let go. Not yet."

. . . can't kill Bloat shit shit shit . . .

The Outcast grimaced and gathered the shreds of power around him. He concentrated. Harsh purple light flared in the amethyst of his staff. He blinked. When he opened his eyes again, Patchwork—minus eye and hand—was standing before him. Teddy almost staggered from the effort of bringing her here. He had almost nothing left.

"Beware the Jabberwock," he said, and giggled despite his weariness. "Patchwork has been a *very* bad girl."

"He won't let Modular Man go," Patchwork said. She talked hurriedly, rushing the words as if she could make them more convincing with speed. "You weren't supposed to be here, damn it. I was going to—"

"—kill Travnicek," Teddy finished for her.

"—talk to him," she answered. "Really. I just want him to say the right words. I want him to tell Modular Man that he doesn't have to obey anymore, that he can follow his own mind. And if he won't say them, I'll make him."

"Or kill him. With your vorpal grenade."

"Or kill him," she conceded. "Yes. I figured it would come to that."

"The tin heap's mine," Travnicek spat. "By the way, Governor Slug, how is it that you missed this little assassination attempt?" Travnicek moved to the opposite side of the room, keeping the Outcast between himself and the grenade.

"I've been busy," Teddy said. "I can't listen to everyone all the time. I'm only human." That seemed funny too, but no one but him looked amused.

"Governor," Patchwork pleaded. "Modular Man is a person, as much as you or me. He thinks, he feels. He hates what Travnicek's doing to him." She turned to the man. "He's told you that. He loathes you. He'd kill you himself if he could." Back to Teddy. "He's made Modular Man into a slave, forced him to do things he doesn't want to do. All I want is for him to let Modular Man go. Set him free."

"Hallelujah!" Travnicek mocked. "So I'm Simon Legree. Well, Little Nell, Uncle Tom's a *machine*. I bet you don't let your car decide which way it wants to go. You don't let your stereo play what it wants, do you. And he can't kill me. He can't even *think* that. He's a fucking tin can. Tin cans don't have feelings. I didn't *give* him feelings."

"Maybe he's learned them on his own," Patchwork answered. "Maybe you built him better than you thought. He's more than you know or want to believe. I—I—" . . . *love* . . . Teddy heard the thought. "—care for him. He's a friend and he's done a lot for me. I owe him this."

"You might as well have feelings for a vibrator," Travnicek scoffed. He kept the Outcast between him and the grenade. "Because that's all he is. A big, shiny vibrator. You just like it because you can talk to him afterward."

"I'm not talking about sex," Patchwork said. "If you were even halfway smart, you'd know the difference. Governor, please . . . How can you let him do this? I thought the Rox was all about freedom, about being able to make our own decisions. How can you call the Rox a homeland when you allow this kind of thing to continue? Isn't this exactly what you're fighting against? Isn't it? Damn it, Governor—" Patchwork stopped, breathless. "I'm so lousy with words. I can't tell you how I feel or what I know. If you hadn't been here . . ."

"I'll make it easy for you," Travnicek said. "This is now Toaster Liberation Day. He doesn't interest me anymore. I'd rather watch the slug here, and I'm safe where I am. You want the toaster, you got him. How's that for easy? Now, Governor Slug, why don't you take Grenade Lady here and pop her someplace safe."

"You'll do it?" Patchwork breathed. Her fingers tightened around the grenade's lever. "You'll really do it?"

"Yes, I'll really, really do it," Travnicek answered in a mocking, high voice. "Now take your little playtoy and go."

"Then tell Modular Man now, while I'm here."

"I can't. The slug here sent him on a mission."

"Then how can I trust you? How do I know you'll do it?"

Travnicek gestured at Teddy. "The governor can read my mind. He can tell you exactly what I'm thinking. Since you don't seem to want to blow him into little slugpieces, I assume you trust him."

Both Patchwork and Travnicek turned toward Teddy. "Governor?" Patchwork asked desperately.

The Outcast blinked, his mouth open.

The truth, slug? The truth is that the toaster's programming is hard-wired and I couldn't change that even if I wanted to—and I don't want to. The truth is that frankly Grenade Lady here is too dangerous to live and I'm going to enjoy telling the tin heap to take care of her just as soon as he gets back. That's the truth. And I don't mind telling you. You know why? Because you can't let the toaster go. Do that and you've lost the one weapon that's worked for you in this fight. Let the toaster go and who knows whose side he'll come down on. He knows everything about this place now. You want him bringing back a tactical nuke? You want him taking you out with a well-placed laser burst? I control him, and I've given him to you. I didn't hear you complain about using him. You're a putz, a wimp, the Great White Weenie. I heard what you did with Detroit Steel and Snotman. That was stupid and now you're going to do something smart. You're going to lie. You're going to talk nicely to Grenade Lady and get rid of her until the toaster's back. Go on, slug, tell her that nice Dr. Travnicek will let the poor old toaster have its freedom.

"Go, on," Travnicek said aloud. "Tell her, Governor Slug."

"Patchwork—" Teddy began. Stopped. He was looking at Patchwork, at the defeated sorrow in her face. He listened to her dejected thoughts and rummaged through the images of Modular Man she held. His head whirled with other images and thoughts; Jack in his bayou swamp; his cousin Rob and Uncle Alan; the penguin flinging itself in front of him not once but twice.

"Fat boy, how many more times will someone have to do this before you get the idea?"

"You'd really do it?" Teddy asked, and read the answer in her mind even as he spoke the question. "It isn't just a bluff. You'd really sacrifice yourself to give Modular Man his freedom."

"Hey, slug—" Travnicek said.

Jack, in the dreamtime. Rob, crying under the covers. *There's nothin' you can do, Teddy. Nothin'. Just leave me alone.*

"He lied," Teddy told Patchwork. Travnicek's alien face looked in horror at the Outcast. "He can't and won't let Modular Man go. I'm sorry."

"So am I," Patchwork said. She nodded and tried to keep her next thought from him. Teddy heard it anyway. He tried to send Patchwork one place and her hand another. The amethyst gleamed and faded, but she was still there.

The lever of the grenade hit the floor with a distinct chime.

"Go!" Patchwork shouted at Teddy.

He went. The echo of a twinned scream followed him.

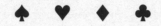

SATURDAY NIGHT

September 22, 1990

ON THE HEELS OF a strong north wind, through a storm of fire, carrying his new weapon wrapped in a tarpaulin, Modular Man returned to the Rox. Forgetting about shoot-and-scoot tactics, Zappa had finally unleashed a continuous barrage from his full arsenal, and though a lot was inaccurate, enough was hitting the target to continually outline the Rox in a glow of fire. Broken turrets yawned to the murky sky alongside shattered domes. Weapons lay abandoned on the ramparts. Smoke rose from the burning.

The last hour of the Rox had come.

The android timed the falling shells, waited for a lull, and dropped into Travnicek's tower. As he flew over the inner bailey he saw that craters of various sizes had shattered the symmetry of the stone flags. The smell of high explosive hung in a noxious cloud. There were dead people, and parts of people, scattered in the rubble.

Modular Man dropped down the long tube of the tower. At the bottom he found Travnicek's door still sealed. He knocked, received no response.

He put a hand to the door. It was hot to the touch.

He took the tarp off his weapon and aimed it at the door.

The gun's official designation was XM-214, but was better known as a Six-Pack. It was a six-barreled Gatling gun developed for the military, a little over two feet long and capable of firing 4000 rounds per minute. Modular Man had stolen it, along with most of his other conventional weaponry, from a military arsenal.

He couldn't mount it normally because the Turtle had seriously wrenched his shoulder mounts, but he'd lightened the weapon by removing the power pack and run a cable through the torn shoulder to his own generators. He set it for the lower rate of fire—a mere 400 rpm—stood so as to minimize the chance of ricochet, and aimed the weapon at the door.

He had to know. He had to know officially. Otherwise he'd just have to obey the last set of orders, defending the Rox till there was nothing left.

The barrels spun too fast for the eye to follow. The weapon was very loud in the closed space. The Six-Pack tore ragged chunks out of the door. Gas and smoke boiled out. The android reached through the door, spun the wheel from the inside, and opened it.

A cruise missile dropped dozens of cluster bombs somewhere on the Rox, the rolling boom going on forever, the light so bright it flashed through the semitransparent tower shaft and cast weird, flickering shadows on the dense, swirling smoke.

Travnicek was lying dead on his smoldering carpet in a sprawl of extended, flaccid neck organs and torn cilia. Modular Man bent by the body, turned it over, touched the neck, and sought a pulse. He couldn't find one.

Modular Man stood up on his single leg. He paused a moment to see if anything would happen, if there was some hardwired circuit he didn't know about telling him what he'd have to do next.

Nothing.

He was free.

He wondered what kind of moral universe he'd just entered. Probably, he thought, the same one Travnicek had lived in all along.

Somehow, though, he'd gotten away with it. That's what seemed to be going on here, people getting away with things. The jumpers had got away with an appalling amount of carnage, so much the military had to be called in to suppress them, and Bloat had got away with an immense amount so far, and whoever was in Pulse was probably still getting away with it, with killing thousands in what seemed to be a personal war against all.

There was a huge explosion and the Rox seemed to jump six inches to the left.

Time to get himself and Patchwork out of here.

Modular Man bent to wrap his weapon in the tarp again.

Something on the floor caught his attention.

Patchwork's brown-gold-flecked eye, gazing blankly from a mass of rubble.

The young Aborigine walked along the beach toward the besieged castle. He glanced out across the water at the topless towers of Manhattan. There seemed a respite in the fighting. Could there be a truce?

Something whistled low and fast across the bay. As it neared the Rox, it simply blinked out of sight. There was a small clap of thunder as air filled the void where the cruise missile had been. Air displacement made the end of the smoke trail suddenly all ragged.

Wyungare smiled, but not happily. No truce.

Certainly there had not been for the past two hours since Wyungare had packed the motley convoy of Jack the Gator, Bagabond's old black cat, the bruised Detroit Steel, an exhausted Reflector, and a nearly comatose Mistral back across the dangerous waters of the lower bay toward safety.

Wyungare had then spent nearly an hour hunkered on a canted slab of broken concrete, staring at the war-torn skies, but not truly seeing them. He was inside, down in the lower world, talking with the guardian warreen, the spirit of Wyungare's companion beast. He had not reacted to or even noticed when debris from the increasing number of shells and ground-based missiles had sliced the air around him. There were priorities, and now it was more important to gather strength and resolve for the trial the man guessed he would be faced with soon.

The warreen had bid him farewell and good fortune with both affection and weariness. It was, Wyungare knew, not at all a good-bye.

In his second hour after escaping from the collapsed dungeon, Wyungare felt the fine engines of his muscles and bones beginning to function in harmony again as he wandered the tattered beaches of the Rox. Occasionally he found injured survivors he could help. For some he stanched the bleeding with bits of multicolored wire as tourniquets. He found ragged bushes, the leaves of which reminded him of mallee scrub. He made rudely blended poultices. He taught one woman to press the point on her torn artery that would keep her from bleeding to death for now. He tried to give her the courage to stay patiently in place—and alive—until aid might arrive.

Another man, he realized, was too close to death and in too much pain. Wyungare gave him release as quickly and mercifully as he could. He used his hands.

After that, Wyungare knew it was time to face that which he had discussed with the warreen. He walked upright and deliberately along the margin of raw sand toward the castle.

What looked like three cruise missiles came in low across the water from three different directions. The scream filled the skies and Wyungare's hearing. Two of the blunt torpedo shapes flickered out of existence at the last possible moment before detonation. The third slammed squarely into the golden dome.

The explosion lifted Wyungare off his feet and hurled him back along the sand. Shards of castle flipped lazily end over end, then started spiking the packed sand like the knives of little boys playing mumblety-peg. The Aborigine lay dazed for a few moments, and saw a ton chunk of masonry bury itself a few meters from his feet. The ground coughed in pain and then was still.

He heard a few desultory splashes as the last of the sky-born debris plunged into the water.

Wyungare shook his head, sat up, then levered himself to his feet. Bloat's refuge had been in bad shape before; now it looked like a sandcastle kicked to wreckage by a tribe of feral children.

Could there be anyone left alive inside?

Wyungare concentrated. Yes. Some of the life within the destroyed complex was agonized, but it was still vital.

He would go inside and find Bloat.

There were echoes of a scream and then the sound of an explosion. Somewhere in that reverberation, Bloat heard Bodysnatcher and Kafka arguing. "You can't disturb the governor!" Kafka shrieked. "He's sleeping. He needs to rest."

"Fuck that, roach!" Bodysnatcher shouted back. "He hasn't got *time* to rest. None of us have any time left."

Bloat's eyelids seemed to have the weight of manhole sewer lids, but he forced them open. "Shut up, both of you," he managed to grate out.

Kafka whirled around stiffly, craning his roach-head back to look up at Bloat. "Governor, I—"

That was all he got out. In that second, Bloat heard the alarm from one of the remaining radar units—far, far too late. In an instant that seemed to last a year, Kafka stood there, his mouth open, the shell-like body bowed backward. Pulse—Bodysnatcher—stood behind him with hands on hips. His joker guards were arrayed before him like a shield, their weapons at ready and trained on Bodysnatcher. The Great Hall glittered around him, glistening in the dark from a thousand lamps.

And it all shattered.

The image of his face graven on the ceiling collapsed in a ruin of steel, glass, and plaster. Something dark and sinister streaked overhead, tearing through walls and into the room behind him. The world exploded. Fire rained back into the Great Hall, the concussion tore at the building with violent sound, and suddenly he could hear nothing but the thundering and see only the fire and the falling stone and brick and steel and glass and even *his* immense bulk was lifted up and thrown sideways and he—mercifully, he thought—lost himself again.

He had pretty much decided that she wasn't coming when the dogs began to bark.

Tom went out to the porch to wait for her. He'd left the gate open and put the dogs on chains. As he watched her headlights come down

Hook Road through the fog and turn into the junkyard, he asked himself for the hundredth time just what the fuck he thought he was doing. He still didn't have an answer. He never told anyone his name. He never brought anyone to the junkyard. But this was a night for firsts.

She parked right in front of the shack. It was his Danny who got out of the car. The first one he'd met. But somewhere along the way, she'd combed out her hair and traded her blue jeans for a dress. She looked around at the junkyard, gave him a lopsided grin. "This isn't the way it is in your comic book."

"Tell me about it," Tom forced himself to say. His mouth was dry. "Come on in."

Danny took something out of the car. It looked like a baseball bat, wrapped in canvas. She carried it up to the house.

"What's that?" Tom asked as she stepped into the shack. He felt incredibly awkward. His house was a mess, a rundown fifty-year-old shack in a junkyard. Why the hell had he let her come?

"The Coast Guard fished it out of the drink," she said. "They thought it was part of a body." She put the packet down on the table, opened it.

Inside was Modular Man's leg.

"You must have pulled it off just when Mistral hit us."

Except for the torn wires and burnt circuitry dangling from the upper thigh, it looked almost human. Tom stared at it with revulsion for a moment. Then he began to laugh. "Oh, great," he said. "Just what I needed." He gestured toward his television, where the head of the first Modular Man stared sightlessly across the room. "Pretty soon I'll have enough parts to build my own."

"Speaking of heads," Danny said, "how is yours?"

"Better," Tom said. He'd taken a long shower, changed into fresh clothes, and swallowed a couple of heavy-duty painkillers Dr. Tachyon had prescribed for him years ago. The headache was still there, but not like before.

"You should have let them x-ray you," she said.

"I only reveal my secret identity to one person a day," Tom said. "It's a little rule I have." He changed the subject. "How is your sister doing?"

"Fine. Sleeping. They anaesthetized her to set the leg. Just as well.

The pain was bleeding through to the rest of us pretty bad. Now we don't feel a thing."

It had been so long since he had entertained a visitor, Tom had almost forgotten how. "I'm not much of a host," he said, suddenly awkward. "You want a drink, or something?"

"No," Danny said. She stepped close, looked up at him. "I want a kiss."

Tom stood frozen. He didn't know what to say. What to do. "Danny," he finally managed. "I don't think . . ."

"Don't think," she told him. "Don't talk." Her hand went around his head, and pulled his face down to hers. "Just feel," she whispered, as their lips touched.

♥

Ray held up his hand. What was left of the team stopped behind him. He glanced back. It was just him and Battle, Danny and Cameo. Him and a nat, an ace who could talk with her so-called sisters and an ace who could channel the dead if she had anything of theirs to channel through. He wished that Battle would give her Black Eagle's jacket like he'd promised, but then wondered if that was just another of Battle's lies. He wondered if the agent even had the jacket.

All and all they were a ragged, sorry-ass bunch. The rest of the muscle was gone. It was up to Ray to see them through.

But, Ray wondered, through what? Battle was still hot to kill Bloat, but assassination was never Ray's style. Still, what could you do with the fat bastard?

The corridor through which the Outcast—was that really Bloat? Ray wondered—had disappeared suddenly opened up into a large chamber that was dimly lit by the internal phosphorescence of its walls. Ray hesitated on the threshold. It was bigger than any of the other rooms they'd come across so far and it was relatively open with few rock formations to provide cover.

There was something about it that made Ray uneasy. He moved into the room slowly, motioning the others to follow at a cautious distance. He was well into the chamber before he noticed the figure at its far end, still and gigantic, looking like a statue in a park in hell.

It was a big man sitting on a big horse. Only the man's legs were shaped like those of a stag and he had eyes that glowed green and a rack of antlers that would do any stag proud. The horse, too, had eyes that glowed. Ray recognized them right away. He had run into them both yesterday morning on New York Bay.

"I'll be a son of a bitch," Ray murmured, and grinned his lopsided grin. Here was something clear-cut, something he didn't have to worry about. Here was serious ass begging to be kicked and Ray knew he was just the one to do the kicking. Grinning, he stepped forward as the big joker on the big horse raised a battered gold horn to his lips and blew upon it. The notes echoed eerily inside the cavern, bouncing and rebounding off the rock walls, striking Ray's ears and stopping him with an involuntary shiver.

A crackle of green lightning pulsed through the air, playing counterpoint to the joker's tune and suddenly there was a spear in his free hand. Ray didn't like that, but he liked the horn's other effect even less.

It called dogs, goddamn ghost dogs slipping through the cavern ceiling, running on air like it was ground. As they neared the cavern's floor their ghostly bodies became more solid. At first Ray could see through them, but once their paws touched the floor they were as real-looking as any pack of white dogs with bloodred ears who were four feet tall at the shoulder and had green fire burning in their eyes and dripping from their tongues could be. There was a shitload of them.

The joker took the horn from his lips and smiled savagely, his dogs howling in a whirling pack at his feet. He pointed his spear at Ray and the others and spurred his night-black stallion. As he charged the pack howled like a chorus of the damned.

"Shit!" Ray said to himself. He turned and sprinted back to the others.

"What the hell is that?" Battle shouted.

"Goddamn Twisted Fist ace," Ray panted. "Start shooting before the fuckers get all over us!"

It was good advice.

The hounds were faster than the stallion. They outstripped the horse and its rider, giving tongue to cries of ferocious blood lust that sparked an answering surge in Ray's veins. He ripped his Ingram out of its holster and triggered a long burst that plowed into the front-running dogs like burning hail.

The others all fired after Ray's initial burst, all except Cameo, who was now wearing an incongruous-looking fedora that she'd taken from her pack. She had apparently summoned another ace, one who was swearing Catholic oaths while hurling balls of electricity at the charging hounds.

The carnage among the hounds was terrific, but they had neither fear nor blood. When they were hit hard enough they were blown to bits, but they neither bled nor cried out in pain. They dissolved into phosphorescent green mist. Half the pack was destroyed as it charged across the open cavern, but there were still maybe forty hounds left. Some were maimed and limping, but all were crying ferociously as they struck the team.

Ray suddenly found himself the center of a snarling pack of mad dogs. There were so many of them that they snapped at each other in a frenzy to get at Ray.

"All right you motherfuckers, come and get it, come on, come on," Ray snarled, not even knowing what he was saying. His expression was a locked, frozen grin as he fought like he'd never fought in his life, whirling and striking with hands and feet, growling back at the hounds, snapping limbs and breaking necks, dodging slashing fangs, ignoring the half-dozen wounds he received in the first half-dozen seconds of combat.

Four bodies lay at his feet, then dissolved, making room for more to attack. Part of his mind told Ray that he wasn't going to make it, that he was going to be gutted again like when Mackie Messer opened him up on national television and he tripped in his own intestines as he tried to fight the psychopathic ace. But the other part of his mind didn't care because this was what he lived for and it didn't matter that his foes were goddamn ghost dogs or aces, as long as they were tough, as long as they were good.

He killed two more of the hounds and then a big brute fastened his teeth in Ray's left forearm, biting through flesh and muscle. Ray bit back a cry of pain as it shifted its grip, trying to get the arm back far enough in its jaws so that it could crush Ray's forearm like a candy cane, and then Ray heard the scream.

It was terrible, high-pitched and wailing, full of pain and fear. It stopped even the hound for a second as it lolled its eyes in the direction of the scream and looked, as Ray did, to see Danny Shepherd go down under a wave of the dogs.

Ray screamed in return. He grabbed the dog's lower jaw and ripped it off. He flung the jaw away and grabbed the hound by its front legs. He surged to his feet, swinging the thing like a flail, instantaneously creating an open space around him.

He glanced around wildly. Battle had his back to the wall and was firing as quickly as he could at the circle of dogs closing in on him. Cameo, or whoever she now was, was holding the hounds at bay with balls of crackling electricity that were more deadly than bullets. But Danny was down and one of the brutes worrying at her pulled her back and lifted his muzzle to howl at the ceiling, his jaws running red with Danny's blood.

The Fist ace, finally close enough to participate in the brawl, lifted his arm to fling his spear and Ray realized that he was the target.

He threw the hound at three others who were springing on him just as the ace loosed his spear, and grinning like a madman, he snatched the weapon out of the air. It felt good and solid in his hands.

Staring straight ahead, he cut through the pack of hounds ripping at him, the spear slicing through them like a sword through smoke. Ray locked eyes with the ace as he charged and saw more astonishment in his foe's expression than anything else. One of the hounds rose up in front of his master and leapt at Ray, but Ray caught it on his spear and skewered it. It worked its way down the shaft and snapped its jaws inches from Ray's face, but Ray kept charging.

He felt another shock run through his arms. When the dead hound dissolved Ray saw that he'd speared the stallion in the side and the force of his charge had run the shaft through its rib cage and knocked it off its feet.

Its rider had slipped off, falling on the other side of the stallion's body. Ray leapt over the horse before it dissolved and landed on the Fist ace, snarling and pummeling his face and body with hammer blows that were too fast to see.

The ace was much stronger than Ray. He grabbed Ray around the waist and flung him away. Ray twisted in midair like a cat and landed on his feet. His opponent lowered his head and charged.

Ray put out his hands and grabbed the ace's antlers, but his huge foe had built up too much momentum to be stopped. Ray screamed as half a dozen points penetrated his side. The ace tossed his head, lifting Ray off the ground and flinging him against the cavern wall.

Ray slammed against the rock, feeling his spine vibrate as if he'd been hit by a car. Blood spewed out from the deep wounds in his side.

"Motherfucker," Ray ground out. He clamped an elbow against the wound and the ace charged him again.

This time Ray sidestepped. He lashed out with his leg as the ace passed him, tripping the Fist who fell heavily to the floor. Ray was all over him in a second. The ace twisted under him and got to his hands and knees, Ray clinging to his back.

"Fuck you, you fucking animal bastard!" Ray screamed. He grabbed the rack sprouting from the right side of the ace's head. He heaved, twisting with all his strength, and the antler snapped.

The ace cried out in distress and pain. Ray hammered him twice in the kidneys, linked an arm around his throat, and yanked, flattening him to the ground. Ray shoved the tip of the antler against his foe's neck hard enough to draw blood.

"Call off the dogs!" Ray screamed, spraying spittle. "Call off the fucking dogs or I'll cut your fucking throat!" He yanked on the ace's neck for emphasis.

"I can't," the ace gasped.

"Do it!" Ray screamed, jabbing the antler deeper into the flesh of his neck.

And suddenly the hounds were gone.

"So," Danny asked him afterward, "you like this model?"

"I like this model just fine," Tom said. His hand moved down the smooth skin of her back. "My favorite."

"Hah," Danny said. She rolled over, straddled him. "Liar!" She was all bare skin and energy. "You like her better, admit it."

"Who?" Tom said, confused.

"Me," Danny said. "The me in the hospital. Admit it."

"Why would I like her better?" Tom said.

"I *designed* her for men to like. She's got all the features. That gorgeous hair. Longer legs. Bigger breasts."

"I like your breasts just fine," Tom said. He touched one of them, watched her nipple harden. This Danny had a tomboy's body, all girlish energy and taut athleticism.

"That feels good," Danny said. "Don't stop." He didn't. "Most men like them bigger than this," she said. She examined her chest critically. "This isn't bad, but hers are better. My ass is tighter. But she's tighter in other places."

He was getting confused. "Are you *jealous*?"

Danny laughed, shook her head. "You men are all so *weird*," she told him. "How could I be jealous of myself?"

Tom was getting hard again. Danny noticed. She reached back with her hand, fondled him, then rose a little off the bed and slipped him back inside her with a small gasp of pleasure.

"This isn't happening to me," Tom said.

"Sure it is," Danny said. She bent forward, kissed him, rocked back and forth gently. He felt her breasts brushing lightly against his chest as she moved.

Tom was just beginning to lose himself in her when suddenly she stopped. He felt her body stiffen.

"What's wrong?" he asked.

At first she didn't seem to hear him. Her eyes were far away. She trembled, and climbed off him without a word.

"Danny, what is it?" Tom asked, sitting up in bed. "Did I do something wrong?"

That got through to her. She gave him a quick glance. "Not you," she said. She stood in the center of the room, naked, trembling, turning as if she were looking for something only she could see. "The dogs," she said in a scared voice. "Oh, shit."

Tom was out of bed in an instant, moving toward her. Danny backed away, but she didn't seem to see him. Her hands came up in front of her face. "No!" she shouted.

Something picked her up and flung her backward. She smashed up back against the bookshelves on the wall. The shelves collapsed; books fell like hail, bouncing off her. She never felt them. Her eyes were wide with terror. She screamed.

Tom ran to her, tried to cradle her in his arms. She fought him with hysterical strength, still screaming, clawing at him. "Danny, *stop*," he said. "It's me, it's Tom, what's wrong? *Danny!*" She wasn't hearing him, she wasn't seeing him. She raked him with her nails, broke free, spun around, fighting desperately against the empty air.

Her calf ripped open in a flower of blood. Danny let out a shriek that knifed right through Tom's soul. He watched in helpless horror as a wet gash opened beneath her chin, weeping blood. He pulled her to him, grabbed the sheet, tried to stanch the flow of blood.

When a chunk of her right forearm blossomed red and pulled itself loose from her flesh, fighting like a living thing, that was when *Tom* began to scream.

Ray released his hold on his foe's throat, but in a final bit of anger and blood lust, he grabbed him by the hair and bounced his face off the floor. The ace cried out in pain and Ray leapt to his feet, looking back to where the others had been trying to hold off the hounds.

Battle had his back against the wall. His eyes were wild, his face covered with sweat, and he was pulling the trigger of his empty assault rifle again and again, aiming at nothing.

Cameo was slumped against the floor, the fedora perched crookedly on her head. She looked up when she felt Ray's eyes on her and waved. She was all right.

And Danny. Ray took two steps toward her, then stopped, groaning. Miraculously, her face had been untouched, but that was about the only part of her unbloodied. Her throat had been ripped out, her right arm was gone. Her Kevlar armor had given the hounds pause, but only momentarily. She looked worse than he had after his meeting with Mackie Messer, but Danny couldn't put herself back together again. He turned away and let out a mixed scream of pain and anger, whirling on the big ace who was kneeling slumped forward, one hand to his face, wiping away the blood that was streaming from his broken nose. He looked up at Ray. His eyes were no longer glowing. "I called them off," he said sullenly, "but was only able to do it because they'd been blooded."

"You shit bastard," Ray said. He hurled himself at the ace, but somebody grabbed him around the waist and tried to pull him back.

"Back off, Ray." It was Battle. "Don't you see? He's our ticket to Bloat's throne room. Don't kill him now!"

Ray stopped, suddenly icily calm. He reached down and took Battle's wrist, and twisted it, peeling his arm away from his waist.

"Oww!" Battle said, going down to one knee.

"Get off me, asshole," Ray ground out. "Don't ever touch me again."

"Okay, okay," Battle said. "Just let me go."

Ray tossed him aside and turned to look at the Fist ace, who was staring at him sullenly. Just as quickly as it had hit him, the blood lust left. He tried to get it back, but somehow couldn't. "Bloat didn't kill Danny, this bastard did."

Battle stood, rubbing his wrist. "I'm willing to overlook this breach of discipline this once—" he began, but Ray cut him off.

"Shut the fuck up," Ray said. He took a deep breath. "All right. You're right. This hairy bastard is our ticket to Bloat's throne room."

Battle's eyes gleamed. "Yes, of course. I knew you'd understand."

Ray stared at him without saying anything. But he was thinking, *And there we'll settle things once and for all, one way or the other.*

One way or the other.

◆

Now that he looked at the bodies and bits of bodies, Modular Man recognized a number of parts other than Patchwork's eye. A jaw, part of the scalp with its brown hair still attached, a slim hand with its thin, knobby wrist . . .

Modular Man took the hand. It didn't seem cold, but neither did it respond to his touch.

A shell landed in the courtyard. The Rox trembled. The android unwrapped his gun again, detached the power cable, threw the tarpaulin out onto the ground, and began to throw parts into the tarp.

He wasn't entirely certain whose parts they all were. He'd sort them out later.

More shells landed as he worked. Glasswork shattered, stones fell. Then there was a shriek overhead and a huge flame exploded through the sky toward Jersey, a fire seemed to suck the air from Travnicek's tower. Shattered stonework was blasted from the ramparts.

Fuel-air bomb, the android thought. It had fallen a hundred yards short, otherwise it would have killed everyone.

Strange lights, bright fractal images, seemed to hang in the air. Part of Travnicek's tower, the wall between it and the Crystal Keep, melted like a river. Bloat was inside, among a litter of corpses. The Statue of Liberty's torch had fallen across him, and he was asleep or unconscious.

A whole host of Bosch creatures—pigs with butterfly wings, a witch on a broomstick, amid them Christ with a halo—materialized in midair, all singing the Yale fight song. *"Boola boola boola boo!"* they hooted, then passed through a door that hadn't been there a moment before. The door slammed behind them.

There was a shout, and Shroud, coughing in the smoke, staggered to the hole in the keep. "Help!" he yelled. "We've got to rescue the governor!"

The android looked at him. "I don't work for you anymore," he said.

He threw some last parts on his pile and bundled the tarpaulin.

Carefully, so as not to spill anything, he rose into the sky.

Someone was screaming, a pitiful wailing like that of a lost child. *It's okay,* he said to the voice. *It'll be okay.* He opened his eyes to see who the child was.

It was him.

Bloat's throat was sore, and the keening sorrow echoing in the silent Great Hall was his own voice. Around him, the Crystal Castle was a shambles. He had been thrown from his platform, his immense body ripping free of many of Kafka's inlet pipes. Raw sewage spilled over huge open wounds. Liberty's torch had been sheared from its supports; the massive sculpture had fallen on top of him, slicing into the slug-white body. Bloat could feel its weight on him. Most of the roof was down, the girders and supports and broken glass littering him like confetti. A monstrous hole had been torn in the back wall.

He had crushed his phalanx of guards. They were underneath him, suffocated and dead, but the same accident of fate that had killed them had saved Kafka and Pulse: Bloat's body had shielded them from the worst of the blast. Kafka was stirring, spinning like a roach on its back in the detritus of the hall. Pulse was brushing bright glass from his/her clothing and wiping away a spray of blood from a cut on the forehead.

Most strange of all, Wyungare was in the Great Hall, staring up at Teddy's head as if he'd been expecting Bloat to awake at any moment. Teddy was beyond surprise; seeing Wyungare here, now, made him feel nothing. Bloat was shivering, his entire body trembling slightly. No one else seemed to notice, but Teddy could feel it, like a fever chill.

Outside, the fog lingered, but through ragged tendrils, he could see the bombed-out buildings left from the brutal shelling. Only a few listless mermen were stationed around the room. Their fish-mounts drooped so that their fins touched the floor, their scales were without luster and tattered. His jokers were dead or had fled.

Kafka managed to right himself. "Guards!" Bloat's chamberlain barked, but Bloat waved a hand—that was more effort than he expected—the gesture more a flap than an imperious command.

"They're dead," he said. His mouth tasted of dust.

Kafka gaped. Zelda stared with her usual antipathy, though she kept her true thoughts hidden behind a carefully constructed wall of images. Teddy closed his eyes for a few moments, ignoring Zelda's hostility and Kafka's concern. He sorted through the mindvoices of

the Rox to find Battle and Billy Ray. He heard incoherent bits of panicked thoughts and mixed images of glowing-eyed dogs, fierce war-
horses, and Herne. The Hunt was on them. That fight had begun.

"They're going to die," he said. A gout of blood suddenly gushed from
his mouth, surprising him with its violence. Bright scarlet splashed on
his chest and over the mound of his body. "So am I, I think," he said
wonderingly. Then, to Wyungare: "Did you know that the penguin . . ."
he began and couldn't finish.

"I know."

"I brought it back once before. I'll do it again, once I've rested. If I
live. God, it hurts. It hurts a lot."

"I know." The Aborigine took a few steps forward through the rubble. "Teddy, they're not going to let you rest," he said softly. "They're
not going to give you time to get better. Not now." He seemed to be
listening to voices in his own head, voices Teddy couldn't hear. "I
came to give you a last chance."

Teddy snickered halfheartedly. "I thought I had to order before
midnight tonight. You know: offer void where prohibited." The torch
was getting heavier and he couldn't laugh. The smell of bloatblack was
worse than he'd ever experienced, and the wounds in his gargantuan
flanks burned as if napalm had been set in them.

The weariness hit him again; the trembling in his body becoming
stronger. The body of Bloat shuddered, rattling the few pipes that still
pierced him until they sounded like a bad thunder sound effect. The
pores of his grotesque body puckered and vomited streams of bloatblack, though the waste wasn't black this time but thin, greenish, and
diarrhetic. *I really don't feel well.*

". . . already going to hit you again," Wyungare was saying.

"And I'll send them to the dreamtime. Again," Teddy insisted,
though he knew it was bravado. A bluff. He had no strength left. He
heard the resignation and despair that Wyungare's words brought to
Kafka, Pulse, and the other jokers. They were as drained as he was.

The shaking of Bloat's body increased, small wavelets rippling
under the skin. Bloat's pores spat out a mucuslike, thick liquid, and
the trembling became an uncontrolled spasm that tore the rest of the
pipes loose from his body. More untreated sewage gushed over Bloat

and the raw wounds and poured onto the floor. Teddy howled at the searing pain.

Pulse laughed.

"Governor!" Kafka shouted, panicked. "We have to shut off these lines! The torch . . . I need some help—"

Wyungare watched, his gaze finding Teddy as he whimpered. "You see?" he said softly.

The pain was worse than Teddy could have imagined. He gasped for breath, the words coming out in shrill bursts. Bloat was shuddering like a great white maggot on God's grill. "I'm tired of all of it. Call your shamans together. Make me a fucking nat so they'll leave me alone."

Wyungare frowned. "If you do that, you must know that everything here that you have made will disappear. Everything. All that you've created will dissolve back into the dreamtime."

"Fuck the Rox," Teddy said defiantly. *God it burns, it burns. I'm going to die, the Bloat-body is going to tear itself apart and I'll die with it* . . . Kafka had fled into the next room; Teddy could hear him trying to shut off the intake valves. "What the hell has being a joker ever gotten me but pain and problems? Let someone else worry about it from now on. I don't want to be a joker. I hate it."

Teddy thought he saw disappointment in Wyungare's walnut eyes, in the folds of his coffee-dark face. But the man nodded. "All right," he said simply. "That's your choice, then."

Wyungare sank down to the floor, sitting cross-legged in front of Bloat. He began a low chanting rhythm, slapping his hands against his thighs in counterpoint to the words.

Even in the welter of anger and irritation, confusion and turmoil around him, Teddy should still have picked up on it sooner. But Bodysnatcher had been spilling out a steady stream of vitriol from the beginning, and in his own pain he simply didn't notice that the thoughts had changed from fantasy to intent. He caught the threat an instant too late.

. . . kill the ugly traitorous worm . . .

Bloat couldn't move. There was nothing left of his power to stop her.

♣

He was going to sell them out!

The bodysnatcher listened from the balcony. The maggot mountain was as weak as all the rest. The nigger had talked him right out of whatever guts he'd started with. Who the hell had let the nigger out of his cell, anyway? He should have killed him when he had the chance; now it was too late.

"Fuck the Rox," Bloat was saying, in his high little-boy's voice. Then he screamed as another pipe ripped loose from his flesh. He was whimpering like a baby as he said, "What the hell has being a joker ever gotten me but pain and problems? Let someone else worry about it from now on. I don't want to be a joker. I hate it."

The bodysnatcher never heard the rest of it. His rage was a blinding red scream inside him. The nigger hunkered down in a squat and started some kind of chant. Bloat was buying it. He was giving up. The bodysnatcher thought of Prime and David and Blaise and K.C. and Molly, and then of Blueboy and the rest, the ones who died when the tower collapsed. It was Bloat's fault, he realized. The slug had stopped a thousand other shells, but not *that* one, oh, no, *that* one he'd let through. Just like he'd let Juggler and the others walk off to die, like he'd stood by and watched while the freaking Oddity snapped David's neck. He'd known. The maggot *always* knew. And he let it happen anyway. Bloat *wanted* the jumpers dead, he'd wanted it all along.

And now he wanted to run away and hide.

I'll kill the traitorous ugly worm NOW, the bodysnatcher thought. He went to his lightform.

All around him, time stopped. The world seem to catch its breath and stand trembling. Everything stretched and yawned away from him. The mountain that was Bloat receded into infinity. The room was bathed in a blue gloom. The chanting, the screaming, the gurgle of bloatblack, the distant sounds of battle; all gone. Silence reigned.

On the floor, the stupid nigger squatted with one hand raised over his thigh, like a statue carved from ebony.

The bodysnatcher had all the time in the world.

He was an arrow of light, a burning lancet. He slid through the air with glacial slowness, floating toward the immensity that was Bloat. Tons and tons of smelly white jelly, his heart and lungs buried God knows where inside. But the governor's head was still almost normal. That was where he'd start, the bodysnatcher decided. The eyes first. Then the ears. And only then the brain. He would make it last.

Then Wyungare got to his feet and floated up through the blue gloom in front of Bloat. "Is it my turn now?" he asked.

Coherent light . . . slowed. Halted. It was impossible.

"My turn?" said the black man again. Wyungare smiled. He interposed his body between the bodysnatcher and Bloat. The lightform hung incredibly suspended in the blue spectral twilight.

A physical impossibility.

"Improbable, yes," said Wyungare aloud, grinning hugely, teeth shining in the gloom. "Impossible, no." He received the electromagnetic translations of words, converted them to speech forms.

You will die now, nigger-man.

"So?" Wyungare shrugged. His hands moved slowly through the air, as though performing the most delicate motions of an elaborate dance. "Dying is not the point of all this. Life is. Healing is."

The lightform seemed to convulse in the suddenly thick air, pulsed as though struggling to move, then slowly accelerated toward Wyungare and the immense being behind him.

Burn, you asshole.

Wyungare took away his hands, baring his breast, exposing his heart. "Need a target, my bodysnatching friend?"

The lightform somehow picked up velocity in this energy halfworld.

The fury: *I'll barbecue you, you miserable jigaboo!*

Wyungare laughed. "Is it so important to you that my color's not to your liking? That I'm what, in a better mood, you'd call black?

"Then try *this!*"

Absolute crimson preceded the lightform. Blue trailed out behind. And Wyungare became black. Literally. Physically. Spectrally.

Black as space without stars. Black as the ace of spades. Black as . . . nothing.

And the lightform entered his heart.

The fury of energy ravened for food, sought fuel to burn, fed on itself, began . . . with horror . . . to be absorbed.

I cannot hold multitudes, thought Wyungare, and I cannot contain all of this.

There are limits.

He absorbed what he could.

And the rest he let flare out harmlessly in every direction except toward the child. The young man. The being he recognized was newly mature. That being he protected.

There was a need.

Wyungare wished he could see himself.

And was glad he could not.

His last image in this world, in this time, in this body, was Cordelia.

His final feeling was love.

And then the energy simultaneously was absorbed, and consumed him.

The Fist ace said his name was Herne. He proved to be a reliable, if sullen, guide. "It's right through there," Herne said sulkily after leading what was left of the team through a number of Bloat's underground chambers. "Not that it's likely to do you much good. The governor knows you're here."

"He hasn't stopped us so far," Battle muttered. He took off his backpack and pulled a package from it. He tore away the wrapping paper, revealing a folded black leather jacket.

Son of a bitch, Ray thought, he really did have Black Eagle's jacket.

"Our ace in the hole," Battle said triumphantly. "Put this on after we enter the throne room," he told Cameo. "Bloat will never suspect the presence of another ace. This will give us the edge we need."

Cameo looked at it doubtfully. "What are we going to do when we find Bloat?"

Battle stared at her. "What we have to do."

"I'm not going to kill him," she said. "I don't kill. Period."

Battle smiled. Ray didn't like the look of it. "We'll see. In the meantime just think of all the extra protection this jacket will give you. It might make the difference of coming out of this dead or alive."

Cameo nodded doubtfully.

Battle looked at Ray. "You're a good soldier," he said meaningfully. "You know what we have to do."

"Let's stop talking and just do it," Ray said. He pushed through the doorway and into Bloat's audience chamber.

They were on a little balcony that overlooked the chamber from a height of about ten feet. The first thing that struck Ray was the god-awful smell emanating from the monstrous white slug that was Bloat. It was one of the most hideous sights that Ray had ever seen. But there was something more, a sense in the room, an air that something had just gone terribly wrong.

The bombardment had not been in vain. A direct hit had shattered the throne room's crystalline dome. Pieces of the dome lay over the floor and Bloat both. There were gaping holes in what was left of the dome through which the stars looked down on a scene of carnage and confusion.

Bloat's joker guards lay dead on the floor like abandoned dolls. Bloat himself was dripping smelly, viscous ichor from a dozen small wounds. He seemed to be in shock as he stared at the loincloth-clad body of a black man who lay dead on the floor in front of him.

"Something big just went down," Battle said. "They're all in a muddle." He shoved the jacket at Cameo. "Now's the time to strike."

She took the jacket after a moment's hesitation and put it on. Battle smiled gleefully, Ray frowned, and Herne watched dumb-founded as Cameo's face suddenly went slack. It remained unfocused for a long moment, then she screamed as if terrified out of her wits as her face twisted into an expression of pure, sadistic hate. Before, when she was Blockhead, you could still see Cameo underneath. Now all traces of Cameo were submerged, as if she'd fled to the deep-est corner of her psyche to escape whoever it was who'd taken charge of her body.

"Cut it up!" Battle screamed, pointing at Bloat. "Kill it and I'll let you keep the body you're wearing!"

"Christ!" Ray whispered.

Cameo's shoulder drooped, as if her back were bearing an unendurable burden.

"Listen to me," Battle said slowly and distinctly. "Kill that mountain of fat over there and you can keep the body you're in. You can live again."

Confusion was replaced by a look of animal cunning as the rider of Cameo's body stared at Battle. She nodded, drool spilling from her twisted mouth. She approached Herne, who stood between her and the stairway that led to the throne room's floor, and she began to whistle a familiar tune as her hands started to vibrate.

"Get back!" Ray screamed at Herne. "It's not Black Eagle. It's Mackie Messer!"

Herne stumbled backward, trying to get away from the reincarnation of the psychopathic ace with the buzz-saw hands.

"You bastard!" Ray screamed, unsure himself whether he was addressing the lying shit Battle or the twisted ace advancing on Herne. He hesitated only a moment, then he moved. He leapt, lashed out with his foot, and caught Cameo's body on the hip. He pulled the blow at the last moment, realizing that he was facing a double dilemma. Mackie Messer, who had once unzipped him from crotch to sternum, was in Cameo's body. Normally, as he understood it, Cameo could control the psyches she channeled. But Messer was a twisted psychopath filled with such murderous rage that he must have momentarily overpowered her and gotten complete control. Maybe she'd be able to force her way back into the driver's seat, maybe not. But in the meantime Mackie had her body and Ray had to stop him without injuring it. Last time they'd met he'd hammered the shit out of the little Nazi, and still lost. This time he had to take him out without damaging him.

Ray knew he had to stop Messer. Ray wasn't a deep thinker. He was a fighter, a living weapon who gloried in combat. But Battle had crossed the line by calling the evil little psychopath back to life. It was up to Ray to stop them both.

Messer tumbled with Ray's kick, falling down the short flight of stairs that led to the chamber's floor. For a moment Ray thought that the fall might have stunned Messer, that Cameo could regain control, but they had no such luck.

Messer looked at him with Cameo's beautiful eyes. "I know you," he told Ray. "You hurt me once." And he was back on his feet, his hands a buzzing blur.

Ray leapt down the stairs, landing on the chamber floor facing Messer. Messer stared at him as drool ran down Cameo's fine-boned jawline. "But I hurt you even more," he said, turned, and ran straight at Bloat.

Bloat finally seemed to rouse himself from his deep stupor. He screamed wordlessly, but that only served to incite Messer the more. He called for his bodyguards, but they were all dead or fled. He was alone.

Ray sprinted after Messer, but the hunchbacked ace had too much of a head start. He reached Bloat and sank his right arm to the elbow in Bloat's sluglike side. He slashed, slicing a three-foot-long gash in the pulpy white flesh. Buckets of foul-smelling ichor pumped out of the wound. Bloat screamed. Ray gagged, but continued the pursuit.

Messer whirled and slashed at Ray, who turned with the grace of a ballet dancer, barely avoiding the blurred hand. Ray switched direction again and came in low, swiping at Messer's legs. Messer scuttled backward like an angry crab, waving his arms in Ray's face. Ray feinted a lunge. Messer buzzed him and Ray pulled back, circling.

"Let Messer kill the fat freak!" Battle shouted.

Without looking, Ray shot Battle the finger. He tried to sweep in low and knock Messer off his feet, but the ace was too fast. He chopped at Ray's neck. Ray dropped back, barely in time, as Messer's hand caressed his cheek that suddenly became covered by a sheet of blood.

Christ, Ray thought. How can I beat Messer without hurting Cameo? And then he had it. He didn't have to beat Messer at all. He just had to beat the jacket.

He reached down for the knife sheathed at his ankle, drew it and pointed it at Messer.

The ace tittered. "A knife? A knife against Mackie Messer?"

"Let's dance, motherfucker," Ray mumbled, his tongue probing the gaping wound in the side of his face.

He feinted a lunge. Messer chopped down with a blurred left arm. Ray went in over Messer's arm and sliced the back of the jacket from the neck to the waist. Messer righted himself and took a sideswipe at Ray that missed.

They were still in close quarters. Ray punched Messer in the gut and the air rushed from Cameo's lungs in an explosive gasp. But Messer still swung reflexively at Ray as he arched backward, and buzzed through the agent's jaw and cheek. Blood blossomed from Ray's face, saturating the front of his fighting suit. Ray growled inarticulately as Messer collapsed, holding his stomach with both arms. Cameo's body wasn't used to such abuse and it sagged with the pain of Ray's blow.

Ray lunged forward again with the knife, slashing at the back of the jacket. It snagged momentarily, then cut through the leather. The jacket separated into two pieces and Messer suddenly seemed to realize what Ray was doing.

He screamed as Ray grabbed both halves of the jacket. Messer twisted and connected again, slicing through Ray's rib cage, but Ray was already winding up and he was pissed and he suddenly didn't care if it was Cameo's body or not.

He whirled Messer by the jacket's arms, hurling him into the chamber's stone wall. Messer slammed into it with stunning force, bounced, and came back right into Ray's arms. Cameo's eyes were glazed as Ray ripped the jacket off her body and in a frenzy of strength tore it to bits before he threw it to the floor.

Her eyes fluttered for a moment and when she opened them again they were Cameo's eyes, unaffected by the sadistic violence of Mackie Messer.

"You're bleeding," she said to Ray.

He looked down at his side. "Yeah," he said. "I do that a lot."

"Where's the ambulance?" Tom wanted to know. His voice was edged with hysteria. "I called for an *ambulance*. We need to get her to a hospital, she needs help, a doctor, *something—*"

"Take it easy, mister," the older cop said. He was a beefy man with a crooked nose and a mop of black hair. He pulled Tom aside while his partner went to check out the bedroom. "The parameds are on their way. Probably took a wrong turn in the fog. Nobody lives down this end of Hook Road."

"She needs *help*!" Tom said. He was shocked at how shrill and crazy he sounded. He turned away, started to run his fingers through his hair, stopped when he saw the blood on his hands. What a sight he must be. He'd pulled on a pair of pants, but he was still bare-chested, still bloody where he'd cradled Danny, talking to her until he heard the sirens. No wonder the cops had looked at him funny.

"You told the dispatcher your name was Tom Tudbury," the cop was saying. "Our records show that Mr. Tudbury died three years ago. Suppose you tell me who you really are, and what the hell you're doing out here."

"That doesn't *matter*," Tom said. "Just *help* her, okay? Where the fuck is that ambulance?"

The cop was about to say something else when his partner emerged from the bedroom. He was a fair-haired kid with freckles. He looked green. "You'd better take a look, Al," was all he said.

Al went to look. His rookie partner stood by the bedroom door, staring at Tom. There was a strange light in his eyes. "What?" Tom said. "Don't look at me that way."

"You son of a bitch," the kid said coldly. "You fucking butcher. Why'd you do it?"

Al reemerged with a grim look on his face. "Call it in," he told his partner. "And get the coroner out here."

"No," Tom said. "She needs a doctor. She's not dead, she can't be dead, you don't understand, she's an *ace*, she has . . . she has powers . . . powers and . . ."

The two cops exchanged a look.

Tom couldn't take it anymore. "*NO!*" he screamed.

The older cop was removing a set of handcuffs from his belt. "You have the right to remain silent," he told Tom. "If you do not remain silent, anything you say can be used against you in a court of law."

Tom held his hands up in front of him, backed away, shaking his head. "You don't understand," he said. "It wasn't me. It was

Bloat. Those bastards out on the Rox. The dogs. She said *dogs* . . . the Hunt . . . her sister was with the covert team . . . they're all the same person, don't you see?"

"You have the right to an attorney," the cop continued as he started toward Tom, cuffs in hand. He grabbed him hard, spun him around, shoved him against the table. "If you can't afford an attorney, one will be appointed for you," he said as he pulled Tom's left arm behind his back, cuffed him, reached for the right.

Modular Man's leg was on the table.

He reacted without thinking, grabbing the leg by the ankle, wrenching free with a strength he didn't know he had, spinning, swinging. There was a sharp *crack* as the leg smashed across the policeman's temple. He staggered. Tom shoved him to the floor, jumped over him.

The kid cop had his gun clear of the holster. He swung it up, aimed it with both hands. *"Freeze!"* he yelled.

Tom froze. Then the kid blew clear off his feet, right back through the window. Glass exploded all around him. He landed on the porch. Tom ran right past him. The dogs were barking as he plunged into the labyrinth of the junkyard. After a moment he heard running footsteps, then curses. The fog was his ally. A warning shot echoed through the night. Then the sounds receded.

He was panting hard by the time he reached the shell.

"Traitor!" Battle cried.

Ray looked up to the balcony to see him pointing his rifle down at them.

"Twisted genes will always show," Battle intoned.

"Fuck you and your genes," Ray mumbled wearily.

"I guess I'll just have to take care of this by myself," Battle said, smiling gleefully and aiming his assault rifle at an again-comatose Bloat.

"I think not," a new voice said, immediately capturing everyone's attention. It was the Outcast. He was hurt and bleeding and obviously dead tired, yet he managed to stand without help. "Put down your weapon," he told Battle.

Battle pouted as Herne snatched his rifle and turned it on the agent.

"No!" the Outcast cried. "The killing's over." He looked down at the dead black man. "Everything's over. He was our last chance. He could have saved everyone without more violence, without more death."

"What happened?" Ray asked.

"He was killed by one of the jumpers."

"What exactly the hell are you talking about?"

"He could have connected us with the shamans," the Outcast told Ray, "powerful men and women who could have taken us to a place where we wouldn't have to fight, where we wouldn't have to be killed."

Ray was suddenly deathly tired. "That sounds good to me."

The Outcast sighed, then winced and tucked his elbow tight against a bleeding wound in his side. "It won't happen now."

"Because this guy is dead," Ray said.

"That's right."

Ray looked at Cameo. "Maybe we can help you."

Upriver, the fog finally grew thin.

He detoured around the Rox, its battlements still cloaked in mist. He could feel its presence even if he couldn't see it. He knew they were there. Bloat and his demons. The jumper bastards who had taken Pulse and Mistral and used them to kill and kill and kill. The antlered hunter and his terrible hounds. All of them were down there, with Danny.

He wondered what she'd been like, that seventh Danny, the one he never knew.

North of the Rox, flying high above the fog, he angled out over the Hudson, and headed north.

He saw the towers of Manhattan dimly through moving curtains of mist, scattered lights burning forlorn and frightened in the night. The fog had shrouded the whole island now. How far would it spread? Did Bloat's power *have* a limit? Could he cover the whole city? The state? The world?

The George Washington Bridge was a steel shadow in the foggy night. Even here, no traffic moved. New York was a ghost town.

He pushed on. Now the Bronx was on his right as he floated up the Hudson, and finally the fog was thinning out. The gray curtains turned to a drifting gauze and then to pale white wisps and then to nothing. The night was crisp and clear, with a moon above and the river rolling blackly beneath him.

Danny's blood had dried on his arms and chest. When he scratched, it fell away in brown flakes.

There was no air in the shell. Most of his screens were dead now. He could smell the circuits overheating. It didn't matter. None of it mattered. He could see well enough to fly.

He was far past thinking.

The Bronx was behind him now. He moved up through Westchester. The New Jersey Palisades loomed up ahead of him. When he was a kid, Dom DiAngelis took him there with Joey, to the old amusement park. He still remembered the jingle. *Palisades amusement park, swings all day and after dark.* Gone now, like so much else.

North he went, and north, following the course of the Hudson, staring into the dead screen in front of him, hardly moving. The shell was full of ghosts. His parents. Dom DiAngelis. Joey and Gina. Barbara Casko, who'd loved him once. Dr. Tachyon. Jetboy. Thomas Tudbury. They were all looking at him. Whispering to him. But he was past hearing.

Somewhere up where the Palisades rose high and white in the moonlight, he slowed, then came to a stop.

All his microphones were off. There was no sound in the shell but his own ragged breathing. But he could still hear her screaming.

He turned away from the dead screen.

The river rolled below him, black as death. The Hudson. It could have been the Styx. As if it mattered. He watched it for a long time.

Then he thought of a wall.

◆

He was and he wasn't.

That was the state of how he discerned himself.

After all, he had never been dead before. At least not that he recalled.

He contemplated all this while he drifted . . . somewhere. This was not the upper world, nor the lower world. It was not the earth. It was not the dreamtime.

He felt no temperature, yet no discomfort.

He could detect no direction home, yet felt certain he was moving. But from where, and to where, he had no idea.

It could have been millennia.

But after a certain amount of time (or non-time) had elapsed, he heard/saw/felt a voice. More than one.

Wyungare. It was more a statement than a question.

"I'm here."

We would speak with you.

"Then you've found me." The voice(s) were naggingly familiar. He had dealt with them long before.

We must know certain things of you.

"Then be direct. I'm dead, you know. Pomposity is lost on me."

He felt a reaction very much like amusement. *We shall be direct, then. About the boy, the one called Bloat. We have to make our own decisions.*

"So what do you want from me?"

You taught him. Tell us of his lesson.

"It's not as though I've a grade sheet," said Wyungare. "No report card. I'm not granting or denying him passage to another form."

We know that, Wyungare. The sensation of exasperation. *Tell us.*

Then a new, individual voice. One with what Wyungare recalled spoke with a West Texas twang. *Never mind those high-minded sidewinders, man. You and me, we've got one hellacious more set of lives in common than them.*

Wyungare would have smiled, had he lips. "Buddy?"

None other, pardner. Mighty sorry you won't be seeing me at the Texarcana Club this go-round.

"Me too." And then he remembered Cordelia. And tried *not* to remember Cordelia. That would come later.

About the Bloat kid, said Buddy.

"All right, why didn't you say so?" said Wyungare. He gathered his thoughts, concentrated, molded a tight-beam image, and launched it like a bottle into the ocean from a desert island. No, more like a sounding rocket blasting into the mesosphere.

The young boy walks away from the place that was his home. It was not a happy place, but it was the only home he had known. And now he's on his way. Gone. Trudging toward the forbidding trees that begin to forest the verges of the road.

Over his shoulder, the boy has packed the belongings that are important to him in a wrapped kerchief. The corners are tied and the bundle is impaled by the stick the boy lays back over his shoulder.

As he walks, he realizes just how heavy his belongings are. He glances back and sees that the bundle has grown. It balloons as he watches, expanding into an enormous and untidy mass.

The boy turns back to his course and resolutely forges forward. His burden grows even heavier. Yet the voices inside him, the voices of his old home, remind him that he has to carry it all. Every ounce, every pound, every ton of it.

—until he suddenly realizes that he no longer has to do that. There is no purpose served.

He releases his grip on the stick. He looses his hold on the burden that has somehow now grown to be larger than what he ever could have imagined he could carry.

It's gone. Left behind him. He cannot believe how easy the final decision was.

As he continues down the road, he glances from side to side at the enveloping trees. They no longer seem as ominous.

The boy whistles. Not to warn away monsters. But in joy.

We see, come the voices. *This was your perception?*

"It is," says Wyungare.

Hey, looks okay by me, says Buddy merrily. *Seriously.*

Some of the voices have faces now. An ancient holy man on a wind-flayed ridge in the Andes. A woman in the Bronx cradling a chicken. A young man tossing knuckle-bones in Riyadh. Many others.

Come on, friends, says Buddy. *Time's a-wastin'. Let's do it.*

And they vote. The decision is quick and anticlimactic.

Wyungare is suddenly aware of his aloneness.

Except for one remaining voice.

Rock on, says Buddy. *You will, my friend.*

And then he's gone too.

What remains of Wyungare is still thinking about something else. The boy shucking his burdens . . . is it Bloat . . . or Jack? Or both?

Billy Ray reached down into the mess on the floor that had been Wyungare. He straightened a moment later, holding a rough-cut opal on a charted leather thong. He handed it to the one called Cameo as if it were a holy relic. Cameo stretched out her hand to take the offering. When she looked up again, her eyes were not her own.

"Hello, Teddy," Cameo said. "It's time to choose." The sudden silence in her head was the silence of Wyungare.

"You really are him?" Teddy asked slowly. "You really are?"

"Yeah, she is," Carnifex said. "So let's get moving."

"Choose," Cameo/Wyungare repeated, frowning in the same way that the Aborigine had frowned. "You still want to be the Outcast, a nat? Then you will be."

"Wait." Teddy licked his blood-flecked lips, groaning under the weight of the torch and the agony of his wounds. The light in the room seemed to be flickering bloodred. Shadows were gathering, like vultures crouching around him. "Wait . . ." he said again, wondering if he could wait or if the deepening darkness would take him.

Teddy glanced around the room, looking at the carnage. *Most of them are here because of you. So many people dead, and they were fighting for you as well as themselves. Wyungare, the penguin, all of them who were killed by soldiers and the shelling . . . For you . . .*

"I'm a fucking lousy hero," he told Cameo/Wyungare. The stench of corruption was overpowering. "I don't want to be the Outcast, don't want to be a nat. That ain't me."

Briefly, Wyungare smiled. "Good," he said.

Cameo/Wyungare began bass chanting. Battle started forward to interrupt, but Carnifex held the man back. At first Teddy felt nothing, but the pain from the open wounds on Bloat's body slowly began to recede and the trembling stopped. He could feel the power swelling deep within the body once more, but the energy was different this time—more diffuse, softer, and yet more powerful than what he had been given before. There was no longer just the connection to Bloat and the dreamtime, but an entire network of bright links, interlacing and flowing, all coming together inside himself. He could hear indistinct voices and a monotone, rhythmic drumming beat that made his blood pulse in time.

He let his consciousness sink into the chant, into the red pulsing, into the flaring, lacy threads.

Teddy looked outward. He had no eyes, no head; he saw in some way he didn't yet understand. It was as if he stood high above the Rox itself and could look out over the entire New York Bay panorama. Through the last haze of the dying fog, he could see something, something far up the Hudson.

The chanting stopped. *Now* . . . said a voice. *Open yourself to us* . . .

He tried. He imagined the Wall falling, collapsing, crumbling into nothingness. He sensed himself falling and he let himself go freely.

D

o

w

n

and then . . .

Entering

♣

He rode five feet above the flood, his shell a green chariot in the moonlight.

Beneath him, the water was a living thing, a black torrent lashed with white, hundreds of feet high, roaring. Even through three layers of plate steel, he could hear its anger.

He had let the water build until it threatened to overflow the Palisades themselves. Then he wrapped his teke around it, pushed his wall up the banks of the river, and forced it even higher. Behind his dam, looming over him like a building about to fall, the river had fought like a living thing, like a monster in chains, like a terrible great beast hungry to be free.

He had let it build until he was trembling from the effort, until he was almost blind from the pain, until he could feel the blood trickling from his nose. He had held it until the last possible moment. Then he had risen, high over the river, high over the Palisades, high over the sword that he had forged.

He looked down at what he had done, and set it free.

Now he rode with it. Faster than he had ever flown before, his head throbbing as he channeled the waters, walling off the shores with his teke, scouring out the riverbed, keeping the torrent on course, aiming the hammer.

The Palisades vanished behind him. The fog sent out its tendrils. The black waters swept them aside. The lights of Manhattan shimmered up ahead. And beyond them, under the rolling mist, square in the mouth of the Hudson:

The Rox.

He pushed ahead of the flood, and turned on his mikes. The roar of the waters filled the world, a thunder out of hell. There was no other sound. There could be no other sound.

And the sound was doom.

A north wind had sprung up and torn Bloat's fog away from Manhattan. The island was remarkably still. Modular Man floated over its brightness, torn between a wish to savor his freedom and a desire to mourn that which was lost. His innocence, not least of all.

Something rolled down the flank of the island.

Foreboding chilled the android's mind. He arched upward to get a better look, saw boiling white water thundering down the bed of the

Hudson, its anger miraculously contained within invisible walls that prevented it from spilling into the city.

The water sounded like a world coming to an end.

And now that he had risen above the tall buildings of the island, Modular Man saw the fleeting radar image of the Turtle leading the angry waters down.

It was the end of the Rox. Nothing was going to survive that impact.

Hovering in air, the android thought for a long moment. He was a shooter. The business of the Rox filled him with little but disgust. The island was full of criminals and killers, all shootees, and had nothing to do with him.

Criminals and killers and shootees like Patchwork.

He dropped to the top of one tall building and placed the tarpaulin carefully on the roof.

And then he was off.

The android's top speed was over 500 miles per hour, and the Turtle was slow, tied to the speed of the tumbling river he was bringing to the Rox. Modular Man made it to the island well ahead of him.

The north wind had torn Bloat's fog away. The island was a ruin, all torn walls and fire. There was hardly anyone moving. He flew through the ruins of the golden dome into the governor's throne room. Bloat lay, bleeding and half-crushed, under Liberty's fallen torch. A young woman sat cross-legged on the floor beside a corpse burned beyond recognition. She was chanting.

The rest of them were staring through the walls of shattered crystal, wondering at the sound of the water that was bearing down on them. There were too many to carry. Plans raced through the android's macroatomic mind.

He flew across the room to Bloat. The governor's eyes were closed. He looked asleep, or dead. The huge weight of the torch had cut deep into his flesh.

The android placed himself beneath it, poured power into his generators, and pulled. Saint Elmo's fire glowed off the broken glass surfaces of the beacon. Slowly, it began to move.

The oncoming wave sounded like a thousand Niagaras.

Modular Man looked at the others. "Huddled masses!" he shouted. "Hurry! Get on board."

Billy Ray moved at once. The woman on the floor did not seem to hear. She kept on with her chanting, oblivious. The man with the mustache hesitated, then followed Ray.

The jokers had not moved. "There's no more time," Modular Man called out to them.

Kafka moved closer to Bloat, and shook his head. Herne hesitated, then backed away to stand beside the other joker. He reached out and took the cockroach-man by the hand. Kafka looked up at him, startled.

The wave sounded like a million typhoons.

Modular Man poured power into his flight modules. He was at the outer limits of his strength. Saint Elmo's fire flickered off the shattered walls of the throne room, off the twisted bodies that littered the floor, off Bloat's pale white flesh, off the solemn face of the chanting woman.

Slowly the torch began to lift.

"Wyungare?" Bloat asked. "Hello?"

He wasn't sure where he was or what he was. He seemed to be everywhere within the Rox: within the ruined Great Hall where people were staring at the ugly, twisted thing that was Bloat; watching as jokers tried to pull the wounded from the wreckage of the shelling; stalking the ramparts of the breached Wall.

Teddy's outward vision was troubled. Under the moon's regard, the water around Ellis Island was swirling, flowing strangely away from the Rox and moving upstream toward the Hudson. Teddy could see a glimmering there, a wall of angry water that even as he watched grew larger as it raged toward the Rox. A feeling of dread touched him with the sight.

"Wyungare, we have to hurry."

There was no answer from the joker who held the Aborigine. Cameo was well beyond the Wall. "Wyungare? Viracocha? One Blue Bead?"

No answer.

Instead, he could hear the unison chanting again, the mingled mindvoices of the shamans. The power that they had lent him was changing again. The portals to the outside world closed like small wounds; the energy flow was now inward, concentrating deep within Teddy. It pulsed with the chant, growing smaller but more concentrated. The gift seared and flared and crackled. It was impossible to look upon.

The mass of light begun to whirl and spin. At the center of the vortex was an opening, a darkness through which Teddy could go—the gateway into the dreamtime. The chanting and drumming redoubled in volume and tempo, and Teddy concentrated on the sound himself, letting the Rox resonate with it, throbbing in time with the sonorous words.

The energy gaped wider, the darkness at its center a mouth that must swallow him soon.

Not soon enough.

New York Bay had dropped several feet in depth. Mud flats extended outward from the shores of Ellis and Liberty islands, fish wriggling silver-scaled in the moonlight as the Mother-Wave up the Hudson sucked the bay into itself. Teddy could see the tsunami rising, towering, a frothing Niagara set on end and spilling over itself as it hurtled impossibly down the Hudson's bank. It was going to smash the Rox like a hammer against a wineglass. It would break him into a thousand pieces. The thing, this monster of water, was unstoppable. There was no power in this world or any other that could halt it.

Teddy felt awe, even as he felt terror.

There wasn't enough time. The shamans were still chanting, still widening the gateway. Teddy readied himself to steal away the power of their rite and try to stop this monster of water even though he knew it to be hopeless. He raged at the Turtle's shell.

You won't kill them. I won't let you. You can have me but I won't let you hurt them. He knew that to do so would close the opening gateway for himself, but he didn't care. *My fault. It's my fault for waiting so long.*

He almost didn't notice that the chanting had stopped.

"Now!" whispered Wyungare/Cameo desperately.

As the wave thundered and pounded over the flats, a nightmare bending to devour the Rox, Teddy took the swelling energy and willed himself to

He was a half mile ahead of his tsunami by the time he reached the foot of Manhattan. The bay opened out around him. He moved across the waters with the thunder coming hard behind him.

The outer curtain wall of the Rox loomed up out of the fog and flashed by beneath him in the blink of an eye. If there was another wall above it, it never touched him. He was beyond fear, beyond doubt, beyond loathing.

Through torn wisps of fog, dimly, he saw the Rox.

Fallen battlements. Shattered walls. Onion domes half blown away by artillery. Towers that ended in jagged stubs. The castle lay spread out below him like a box of broken toys. The fog seemed thinner now. He could see it clearly.

The thunder was louder, a deafening roar behind him.

Faintly, a mile to the south, he could see Lady Liberty and the south curtain wall. Beyond that was Jersey City, Bayonne, Staten Island, with their millions of innocents.

He pictured another wall on top of the one Bloat had built. A wall of steel as clear as glass. Immovable. Impregnable. An anvil for his hammer. He painted it until it burned in his mind's eye, until it was as real as he was.

When he looked down, the fog was gone. The castle stood naked and clear below him, as a moving cliff of black swept down from the north. The sound of the water was too loud to hear now. For a brief second, Tom thought he saw Liberty's torch, burnt and twisted, lifting slowly from inside the keep. The towers of the Rox seemed to shimmer and fade, and he glimpsed Ellis Island as it had been, another ghost come out to play in the moonlight.

Then howling darkness descended and Tom thought, *This is what armageddon sounds like*, as the waters exploded around him.

SUNDAY

September 23, 1990

CHARLES DUTTON WAS WOKEN at six o'clock Sunday morning by a phone call from the night watchman at the Famous Bowery Wild Card Dime Museum. Something was blocking the entrance. Dutton, the owner of the museum, hurried over to the Bowery.

The Dime Museum owned three of the Turtle's old shells, obsolete models that were now part of its permanent exhibit. Dutton walked carefully around the great steel hulk on his sidewalk, and finally crawled inside the open hatch. The shell was empty. He took note of the broken screens, the blackened instrument panels, the smell of burnt insulation. Then he crawled back out. "I believe we have a new exhibit," he told the watchman.

♣

Ray woke up in the Jokertown Clinic to see that the doctor taking his pulse was a woman. She was tall and good-looking even though she had only one eye.

"Say," Ray said, "what time do you get off work?"

Cody Havero looked down at him as he lay in bed swathed in bandages. "Half past never."

"I can wait," Ray replied.

She grunted something noncommittal, then released his wrist. "You have a visitor."

"Oh, yeah?"

"Yeah. A distasteful man named Battle."

"Him." Ray clenched his jaw and immediately regretted it. It was still healing, still sore. He hoped it would come out better-looking this time. "Yeah. I'd like to talk to him."

Havero nodded and left Ray's private room. Battle came in as soon as she was gone.

"What do you want?" Ray asked.

"To discuss your outrageous conduct," Battle said, glowering.

"Outrageous my ass," Ray said. "You keep your mouth shut, I keep my mouth shut, and we're both heroes. You open your trap and I'll be forced to swear to some of the things I saw you do. And I know a lot of reporters who'd just die and go to heaven if they had a chance at that story."

Battle shut his mouth with an audible snap.

"And you know," Ray said thoughtfully. "I like working with you, George. I really do. I think I'll take you up on your offer and join your Task Force."

Battle sputtered. "Why you, you—"

Ray looked at him with eyes as merciless as Mackie Messer's. "It'll be a real pleasure working with you, George, looking over your shoulder as you make your little plans and run your little schemes. A real goddamn pleasure."

Battle shut his mouth and nodded stiffly. "We can discuss this later."

"You bet," Ray said. He felt happy, almost content. At last he'd found a really worthy foe.

"Fine," Battle said, through gritted teeth.

"You know, George," Ray said, "I think this is the beginning of a beautiful friendship."

And he smiled, though his face hurt like hell. Battle, despite the warmth of the hospital room, shivered.

There was still 65,000 dollars in neatly sorted bills on the kitchen table. Patchwork—Modular Woman—was lying in pieces on a plastic dropcloth in Travnicek's bedroom. Modular Man was trying to reassemble her.

He had run into some difficulties. Which eye was which? He couldn't tell the left from right. There were other similar problems with some of the digits; and during the night he had to break into a medical school library and steal some books on anatomy so as to figure out where some of the internal organs went.

And whatever he did, there were still a good many bits missing.

They'll grow back, she had said, *but that takes weeks. Months, sometimes.*

The television chattered at him as he worked. Someone who might be dead, the Turtle, or both was being sought in connection with a murder in Jersey. Zappa had scheduled a press conference for later in the day. He was expected to declare a victory. The battleship *New Jersey*, or the listing first half of it, was being carefully towed to a breaker's yard. Dan Quayle was giving an antidrug speech in Iowa and was unavailable for comment, and George Bush had gone fishing in Maine.

Not much had been made of Modular Man's rescue of a few people from the Rox. He was still being sought as a traitor and outlaw.

The android figured that Canada was sounding better and better. From there he might be able to cut a deal with someone in the government, or alternatively emigrate to Buenos Aires.

But first things first. He needed to put Patchwork back together.

Sorting out the real Patchwork from Travnicek's remains presented a problem. Some parts rather obviously belonged to a joker, however, and others turned cold and began to decay and were obviously useless whether they belonged to her or not.

Patchwork's parts cooled slightly, but not to air temperature. And if he fitted them together properly, they stayed together.

At the moment he was puzzling over a bagpipelike organ that he had identified from the medical textbook as a "ventriculus." The name made it sound as if it belonged somewhere in the heart area.

He put the organ down and reached for a dictionary. "Ventriculus," he discovered, meant "stomach."

He picked the stomach up again. Which end was up?

It was almost enough—almost—to make him wish he had Travnicek back to guide him.

How appalling had it been, he wondered, to arrange for Travnicek's death? And, because he couldn't do it himself, to coax Patchwork into doing the deed?

He had wanted to live. At some point he had decided, like Bloat, that some lives were worth more than others; that his existence was worth more than his creator's.

And now, because he had wanted to live so desperately, he was going to have to live with the consequences of that decision.

And Patchwork would have to deal with it as well, if her life didn't fade as he was reassembling her.

It was possible for a murderer to redeem himself, according to society's rules. There were traditional ways of dealing with those who were guilty of crime. Imprisonment or execution was high on the list. But sometimes the criminal was allowed to redeem himself through service to others.

Another traditional road to redemption was through love. Modular Man thought he might give that one a try.

But first things first. He had to work out which end of Patchwork's stomach went up.

Perhaps he should try attaching it to something.

The intestines were a mess he hadn't dealt with yet, but he'd found a muscular tube that might well be an esophagus. He went to where that was on the pile and picked it up. He matched torn ends together and found that they fused.

Well. One mystery solved. On to the next.

This was obviously going to take some time.

But Modular Man had all the patience required.

Her name was Ariel, but for the last decade she had been called Slash, since she contracted the wild card and moved to Jokertown. Now she sat on a dock along the East River. Dirty, moonlit wavelets slapped the pilings, hiding the faint sound of clashing steel as she moved. Moonlight sparked on a hedge of blades, a bristling snarl of edged steel that lined her body. She was naked; no clothing could last long on her. It didn't matter that anyone could see the flesh between the knife-blade ridges of her body. She was safe. She was always safe.

Always. Whether she wanted to be or not.

Iaido had been her passion—the art of sword-drawing. She had spent years studying, years of sweat with a hakama swirling around her legs and a sai thrust between the belt at her left side. The lure of the blade had taken her from Cincinnati to New York in pursuit of a sensei, then to Japan, then back to New York yet again. Her life had begun to expand in a grand, delightful fashion: landing a big contract as a programmer, studying under a wonderful sensei; finding Dennis and realizing for the first time that there were other types of loves too.

And New York had gifted her with the wild card.

Dennis had fled in terror. The contract had been voided. Her sensei told her that she was a distraction to his other students. She had been made a mockery of herself. Because she had been made into what she loved, she had been made unlovable. Untouchable. The isolation and hatred had grown year by year until—now—she didn't think she could stand it anymore.

Slash sat waiting, throwing mocking, sharp light back at the city's brilliance, not quite sure what or why she was waiting but knowing that she must.

Light glimmered just under the surface of the murky waves—a faint drifting wash of phosphorescence. Just below Slash, water suddenly bulged and ran as something large and rounded rose from underneath. Slash threw herself back, blades clashing. The apparition surfaced: a sphere of gelatinous, semitransparent flesh with wriggling cilia covering its surface and a vaguely human face set atop it. Points of soft, multicolored light dotted the body; gills fluttered near the head. A Hefty trash bag was snagged on its side; as Slash watched, the green plastic slipped loose and splashed back into the river.

There seemed to be something—someone inside the creature. As Slash watched from underneath one of the dock lamps, a woman pushed her way through the belly of the creature and hauled herself up onto the dock. She was—maybe—twenty; blond hair and dark

eyes that seemed to have seen too much, judging by the circles underneath them. The woman glanced at Slash, then at the city. She sighed.
"Charon," she said. "Thanks for the ride."

"It's what I do."

"Yes. I guess it is." The woman's gaze found Slash. To her credit,
she shuddered very little. "Looks like you have a fare waiting," she
said. She nodded to Slash, touched the choker around her neck as if
to make sure that the antique cameo there wasn't lost, then frowned
at the city. She began to walk away from the water toward the lights
without another word. Slash watched her leave.

"Hey!"

Slash turned. "You called?" Charon said. "Get in—it's almost light."

"You came for me?"

"Among other things. I heard you calling. Took me a little longer
than usual to get here. Let's *move*."

"Move where? The Rox is gone. The Turtle smashed it to pieces last
night. I saw it from Battery Park. Bloat's dead."

"Just get in if you're going," Charon insisted.

"But going *where*?" Slash asked again.

"Trust me," Charon said. "Or go back to Jokertown. It's your choice."

Slash glanced back at the city. Manhattan was bright against an
ultramarine sky. The skyscrapers themselves were dark, invisible towers. Only the lights gave them substance, like a stage backdrop built of
paint and boards and strands of glaring bulbs.

The last week had been hell in Jokertown. Slash had tried to get
to the Rox twice; each time she'd been turned back by the police and
National Guard units. She didn't know why she'd wanted to be there
or why it might be different from Jokertown or why she thought she
might be less lonely there—from what she'd heard, she had a better
than even chance of dying on the Rox. Somehow, that didn't seem
to matter. It hurt to stay in J-town; it hurt to listen to the explosions
rumbling between the skyscrapers as they strafed and shelled the Rox;
it hurt to listen to the anger and hatred that boiled from every radio
and television report about the assault.

It hurt just to be.

Slash was certain that bad, bad times were coming for all jokers.

There'd been too much death and too much pain, and the blame had to be placed somewhere. She suspected she knew where that blame was going to rest.

"Just push through my side," Charon said behind the joker. He seemed to laugh. "I'm sure *you* won't have any trouble. Once you're in, we'll go."

Slash turned from the city. She went to Charon, arms outstretched. She plunged her hands—followed almost immediately by the points of several blades—into the yielding cold flesh between the vaulted ribs, felt the sides cling and then part under the pressure. She stepped into Charon's slime-walled belly and sat there. Through the womb of Charon, New York still gleamed, blurred and haloed now. Very distant.

"We're off, then," Charon said.

Cilia thrashed. Gas vented from orifices around the body, bubbling in the dark water. Charon slowly sank below the surface of the East River, the city lights swirling in the current as it disappeared.

On the muddy, trash-filled riverbed, Charon began its long walk home.

♥

Croyd awakened.

Stretched, snorted, and rolled over. And found himself face-to-face with a fish. Now that he thought about it the air had smelled a little funny. The Sleeper experimentally drew another breath. Watched the exhalations, carrying water and carbon dioxide, erupt from the tiny puckered mouths on the ends of his blue spikes.

"Christ, a joker again." That was the intent. What emerged was a series of bubbling sounds.

Visibility was lousy. The Sleeper picked a direction and struck out. Fetched up facefirst in goo. It smelled even worse than the water. Reversing direction he stroked doggedly upward until his head broke the water. The skyline of Manhattan greeted him.

He dog-paddled in a slow circle to get his bearings. Unfortunately there weren't many bearings to be got. Ellis Island was gone. Liberty Island was gone. Liberty herself was gone.

"Jesus, must have been some party. . . . Wonder if I slept through Wild Card Day again?" Croyd mused aloud.

Stunned, angry, grieving, all those things at once, weary and heart-sick, Cordelia let the government man usher her into the small room. She blinked in the dim light, tried to focus through the sudden sheen of tears.

A woman sat behind a simple wooden table. She was young, seem-ingly fragile, face finely sculpted. Her long, wavy, blond hair cascaded around her shoulders. Slightly shadowed, her dark eyes glanced up at Cordelia.

"Yes?" the woman behind the table said. To Cordelia, the voice sounded a little spacey. "You've need of my services?"

"You already know that," said the government man tightly. "We've made arrangements. This is Cordelia Chaisson."

"You *were* mentioned," said the woman to Cordelia. She fingered the cameo at her throat, let her delicate thumb and index finger brush across the black ribbon choker. "Please sit down."

Cordelia sat in the austere darkwood chair in front of the desk. The government man stood at her shoulder.

He placed his hand on Cordelia's shoulder. "This is Miss Allworth."

"Cameo," said Miss Allworth. "We'll leave it at that."

Cordelia nodded slightly. "What . . . can you do? I mean, for me?"

"Maybe nothing," said Cameo. She looked drawn, suddenly years older than her first impression. She turned to the government man. "Give me the opal. His opal."

"Wyungare," said Cordelia. "His name was Wyungare." She wanted, *how* she wanted, to break down and sob. She drew together her strength and did not. For now.

The government man shook something out of a small cloth sack and showed it to Cordelia. It was a rough-cut opal suspended from a leather thong. The leather was seared. Cordelia could smell it.

"I gave him that," she said. She took the piece from the govern-ment man's hand and clutched it momentarily in her fingers.

Cameo extended her own hand, palm up, and let Cordelia drop the opal pendant into it.

"What do I do?" said Cordelia in almost a whisper.

Cameo apparently misunderstood. "Nothing," she said. "I'll do everything that needs to be done." Her fingers closed on the opal and thong. Her fist tightened in what seemed almost a small convulsion.

Her eyes, huge already, seemed to dilate even farther. But there was no focus there. It was, Cordelia thought, like looking into a birthing hurricane—immense power, but no clear form.

Cameo's head jerked back once as if from a blow. Her chair rocked and creaked. Then she looked directly at Cordelia and her features seemed subtly to shift, her face taking on a squarer shape.

"G'day, young missy." Cameo's voice had deepened, broadened, was accented now with the Outback inflections Cordelia knew so well.

"Wyungare?" Cordelia almost breathed the word. She unconsciously started to get up. The government man's fingers tightened on her shoulders.

"Take it easy," he said. "Make the time give you what you want. There's no telling how long this will last."

Cameo's lips turned in a smile. "None other," she said in Wyungare's voice.

"You're, you're—" Cordelia started to say, couldn't.

"Dead?" said Wyungare's voice. The smile took on a gentleness. "We never say dead in my business, but"—a shrug—"I'm afraid I'm close enough for your purposes. My stay on this plane for this time is done."

"Please," said Cordelia. "I need you here."

Cameo cocked her head the way Wyungare would have cocked his. "You *want* me here. You'll discover you don't need me."

"That's cruel!" She tried to bite back the words but couldn't.

"I'm sorry, Cordie," said Wyungare's voice. "I truly am, my sweet, my love. I should not be so glib, and I *certainly* shouldn't be what you keep defining as a wiseass. It's just that I've been through a lot lately."

"I know," said Cordelia, staring at the man looking back at her from Cameo's body. "They've told me some of it. Enough of it."

"Did they tell you about Jack?"

Cordelia shook her head.

"Your uncle helped me enormously with aiding the young master in turn."

"Bloat," interjected the government man.

"Bloat," agreed the Aborigine's voice. "But everyone knows that tale, or at least will soon enough."

"Uncle Jack," said Cordelia, feeling a sudden foreshadowing, daring her first hope in a long, long time, and what was the equivalent of foreshadowing, except outlined in light? Was it like the sun coming out of eclipse? "What about him?"

"He is safe. Even safer than you had hoped."

"Where is he?"

"He is here in Manhattan," said Wyungare's voice. "And so is my cousin, the black cat. When he sees his mate again, he will have such stories to tell."

Cordelia looked stunned. "Mon Dieu," whispered Cordelia. "This is all—"

"Strange? Just wait." Wyungare's voice took on a deeper intensity. Cameo leaned forward across the table. "Your uncle will live."

"Live?"

"You don't have to repeat, my love, though when you do, the sound of your voice thrills me." Cameo smiled. Her pale face was flushed now. "Get assistance from the Jokertown Clinic. When Cody and Finn and the rest of their crew—and yes, even Dr. Bob Mengele—have reclaimed their reptilian patient, they will find that none of the AIDS virus remains alive in Jack's body. The alligator form was too alien and hostile an environment for even those hardy viral organisms. The next step will be to reverse Dr. Bob's procedure and bring your uncle back to human form."

"Can it be done?" said Cordelia.

Cameo's head nodded. "More easily than you would think. The patient will cooperate. Your uncle has regained his humanity within. He is ready to be a man again."

"I can't believe it," the young woman whispered.

Cameo's body suddenly spasmed. "Cordy, I'm going to have to say ta for now."

"*No!*" Cordelia shook off the government man's hand as she jumped to her feet. "You can't go."

"It isn't really my choice," said her lover's voice. "Just remember something, love." Cameo's body walked around the table and confronted Cordelia. The government man gaped.

"Stay," said Cordelia. "Somehow . . . stay. Please."

"Listen to me," said Wyungare's voice. His/Cameo's fingers lay gently on Cordelia's shoulders. "I cannot tell you that I will ever return; nor can I say that you will come to me. Not in your lifetime, not in this place. But believe this: I will always be with you."

"I love you," said Cordelia fiercely, staring at the other's eyes.

"And I, you," said Wyungare.

Cordelia wrapped her arms around the other. Their lips found one another's. They held each other tightly. The gasp from behind them was the government man's.

The two paid no heed.

A young black man was alone in the family room at the Jokertown Clinic, his face between his hands. He looked up when Tom entered. He was wearing a charcoal-gray Armani suit and a blank, hopeless expression. "Do I know you?" he asked.

"I was . . . a friend of hers," Tom said. "Tom."

The black man got up from his chair. He was slender, soft-spoken, good-looking. "Thanks for coming," he said. "I'm Rick." Tom must have looked blank. "Her husband," Rick added. Then he finally noticed the gold band on his finger, and remembered the one the pregnant Danny wore on hers.

It made him feel strange. An intruder. "How is she?"

"Still in a coma," Rick said wearily. "She lost the baby." His voice broke. He turned away so Tom would not see the tears.

"They won't let me into ICU," Tom explained. "They say I'm not family."

Rick nodded slowly, made himself turn back. "I don't know if she hears me, but . . . I'll tell her you were here."

"I'd like that," Tom said. They shook hands.

He walked past the ICU one last time as he left the waiting room, knowing she was in there. Two of her. The Danny he'd rescued from the *New Jersey* and the one who had stayed behind at headquarters, the pregnant one, Rick's wife. They were the lucky ones. They'd had help right there when it happened. The others—two, at least—had died as his Danny had died.

There was one sister he wasn't sure of; the one he'd left at Bayonne Hospital, the one who had shared his shell and asked him his name. He hoped she'd made it, but there was no way he could go back to Bayonne to find out. They'd be looking for him now.

He walked down the hospital steps, past the worn stone lions that Tachyon always liked to pat, hands shoved deep in his pockets, wondering where he *could* go. There didn't seem to be a lot of choices.

The whistle took him by surprise. "Hey, stranger! Want to sign my cast?"

He turned around slowly, not daring to believe.

Danny was standing by the curb, leaning on a pair of metal crutches, smiling at him. The cast covered her foot and the lower part of her leg. Her long blond hair moved in the wind.

"*Danny* . . ." His voice was a whisper.

"I knew you'd show up, sooner or later."

"But how . . . ?"

"They doped me up pretty good, enough to put me out right through the night. I was out of the loop." She smiled grimly. "Lucky me, huh?"

"Then you don't . . . you didn't . . ."

She was way ahead of him, as always. "Whatever happened down under the Rox, I don't remember it." She glanced back up at the hospital. "I *will*, if the rest of me wakes up. I'll remember what they remember. Thirdhand, but . . ." She grimaced. "I'm not looking forward to it."

"*Will* they wake up?"

"Your guess is as good as mine." Maybe it was supposed to sound jocular. It sounded scared. There was a long silence. "What about you?" she asked softly.

"It's over," Tom said bleakly. "The junkyard's gone, the shell, everything. I'm broke, I'm homeless, and I've been dead three years. The police are looking for me. Last night I killed God knows how many people. I keep trying to tell myself it wasn't me, but . . ." He sighed. "God help me."

"Where are you going now? What are you going to do?"

Tom spread his hands helplessly.

Danny took one and held it. "I have an apartment in Los Angeles. It's not much, but . . ."

He didn't know what to say. "I . . . Danny, you don't know how much that means to me, but . . ."

"The right answer was, *when does the plane leave?*" Danny said with a rueful twist of her mouth. "What's wrong? Did we have a lousy time last night?"

"No," Tom said. "You don't remember that either?"

She shook her head. "You'll have to tell me about it sometime." She squeezed his hand.

Tom felt acutely uncomfortable. He took his hand back, turned away. "This isn't right."

"Why?" Danny asked. "On account of Rick?"

"Partly," Tom admitted.

"I love Rick," Danny said. "But he loves *her.* He's only married to one of me. That's the way he wanted it. He always got twitchy when I talked about my . . . sisters. It was all a little too strange for him."

"I know how he feels," Tom admitted. "Last night . . . I was falling in love with her, Danny. She died in my arms. Now I'm supposed to go off with you, a day later? I don't know, it's . . . it's like I'm being unfaithful to her. I *can't.*"

Danny gave a bemused shake of her head. "That's sweet. So how come it makes me want to cry?" He could see the tears in her eyes. She bit her lip as she fought to hold them back. "Oh, you men are all so *weird,*" she said with frustration.

Tom looked at her sharply. "*She* said that too."

"What a coincidence," Danny snapped angrily. "So who *is* General Tso anyway, and why are we eating his chicken?" She turned away from him. "Excuse me. I need to go comfort Rick. He'll think I'm a poor substitute too, but what the fuck." She shoved off on her crutches and pushed past him.

Tom turned and watched her hobble off. She was almost to the steps when he called out. "Danny . . ."

She turned back to him. The wind was blowing her hair in a fine cascade across her face. Tom gazed at her for a long time before he spoke. She looked younger than she was, and more vulnerable. She looked afraid. He knew how she felt.

"What time does that plane leave?" he asked.

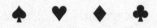

Closing Credits

STARRING	created and written by
Bloat, a.k.a. The Outcast	Stephen Leigh
Modular Man	Walter Jon Williams
Billy (Carnifex) Ray	John Jos. Miller
The Great and Powerful Turtle	George R. R. Martin
Wyungare	Edward Bryant
	and
The bodysnatcher	created by Walton Simons
	written by George R. R. Martin

co-starring	created by
Danielle (Legion) Shepherd	George R. R. Martin
Maxim Travnicek	Walter Jon Williams
Jack (Sewer Jack) Robicheaux	Edward Bryant
Dylan (Herne) Hardesty	Kevin Andrew Murphy
George G. Battle	John Jos. Miller
Phillip Baron von Herzenhagen	Walter Jon Williams
Molly Bolt	Chris Claremont
Ellen (Cameo) Allworth	Kevin Andrew Murphy
Patchwork	Walter Jon Williams

featuring	created by
Radha (Elephant Girl) O'Reilly	Parris

Mike (Detroit Steel) Tsakos	George R. R. Martin
The Reflector (Snotman)	Walter Jon Williams
Mr. Nobody	Walton Simons
Kafka	Lewis Shiner
Black Shadow	Walter Jon Williams
Bobby Joe (Crypt Kicker) Puckett	Royce Wideman
Vernon Henry (Cyclone) Carlysle	Steve Perrin
Helene Mistral (Mistral) Carlysle	Steve Perrin
Cordelia Chaisson	Leanne C. Harper & Edward Bryant
Gregg Hartmann	Stephen Leigh
General Frank Zappa, Jr.	Walter Jon Williams
Cyrus (Pulse) Randall	Walter Jon Williams

with	created by
Quasiman	Arthur Byron Cover
Father Squid	John Jos. Miller
Tienyu	William F. Wu
Dr. Bradley Finn	Melinda M. Snodgrass
Dr. Cody Havero	Chris Claremont
Dr. Bob Mengele	Edward Bryant
Mackie Messer	Victor W. Milan
Charles Dutton	Walton Simons
Croyd (the Sleeper) Crenson	Roger Zelazny

About the Editor

GEORGE R. R. MARTIN is the author of the international bestselling A Song of Ice and Fire series, which is the basis for the award-winning HBO series *Game of Thrones*. Martin has won the Hugo, Nebula, Bram Stoker, and World Fantasy Awards for his numerous novels and short stories.

georgerrmartin.com
Twitter: @GRRMSpeaking

About the Assistant Editor

MELINDA M. SNODGRASS studied opera in Austria, graduated from the University of New Mexico with a degree in history, and went on to law school. She has worked on staff on numerous shows in Hollywood, including *Star Trek: The Next Generation*. In addition to being coeditor of Wild Cards, she is also the executive producer of the Wild Cards TV show in development.

melindasnodgrass.com
Twitter: @MMSnodgrass